D1521659

Railroaded!

By Whitfield Grant

A Novel By

Whitfield Grant

Denver-Austin & **Company**
Publishers

Denver, Colorado

Denver-Austin & Company
Wheat Ridge, Colorado 80033

Printed in Canada
10 9 8 7 6 5 4 3 2 1

ISBN No. 0-9761181-0-6

This book is dedicated to an old friend, Theo. Despite the fact that I don't see him very much, his friendship will always be very special to me.

It is also dedicated to all men who provide positive role models in a world replete with negative influence. Keep up the hard work, and the world we live in will become a better place for our children.

Acknowledgments

After years of effort, **Railroaded!** has finally made the leap from manuscript to finished book.

I would like to thank all of those both here and abroad who took the time to read the manuscript and provide positive feedback. Without your commentary and constructive criticism, **Railroaded!** would not be what it is today. My most heartfelt thanks to you all.

And then there is Ruth Ann Bearden, my editor. Her tireless efforts were essential in the production of this finished work.

Without the stories of professional football espoused by Theo Bell that typically had me rolling on the floor in laughter long into the night, but oftentimes caused me to feel the pain and sadness of a failed marriage because of his profession, the back drop for the story would have not been the same.

A special thanks to Angelique Electra. It was on long walks and anger over the madness of the O.J. Trial, that **Railroaded!** was conceived.

And to you, the reader, I hope you have as much fun reading **Railroaded!** as I had during the creative process.

Enjoy!

Whitfield Grant

Railroaded!

Prologue

July 1964

Anthony Williams ran up to his older cousin and begged him to leave Patricia alone. She was a very pretty fifteen-year-old white girl. "Please, Jed! Just leave her alone. Look how everyone's starin' at you. Please just leave her alone and come on home." Jed had his arm around Patricia. It didn't matter that she had a crush on the tall, handsome Jed, who had just turned sixteen. It didn't matter that he was a bright high school student admired by teachers and friends. It didn't matter that he was articulate. All that mattered was a nigger was laying his hands on a white girl.

"Don't you worry, Tony. There's nothing wrong. Patricia and I are just fine. Now you run along home. I'll see you for supper." Anthony stopped and stared as the interracial couple boldly maintained their embrace and walked through the streets of Dothan, Alabama.

Later that night in the early dog days of summer, Anthony Williams awoke to see a number of flickering, yet rather bright lights through his open bedroom window. He threw back the single sheet that covered him and sat up. He slipped into his overalls that hung on a post at the end of his bed, stepped into his sandals and walked over to the open window. The lights seemed to be not so far away from his home. In fact, they seemed to be coming from near the place where the trees gave way to a large meadow and swimming pond. He climbed out his bedroom window so as not to disturb the rest of the family, especially his parents. He walked sleepily through the pine trees in the direction of the lights.

As the lights got brighter from his getting closer, he became more alert and approached with greater caution. Tony could see

Railroaded!

that the light was caused by flames from torches held high against a night-darkened sky. He could hear the whimpers and groans of a man in distress. He settled in behind a clump of tall weeds and grass and watched in horror as his cousin Jed was whipped by the Ku Klux Klan. Anthony had admonished his cousin about such careless behavior, but Jed laughed it off as nonsense. For his public display of affection toward a white girl, he was being beaten to near lifelessness.

As Anthony continued to watch, tears started streaming down his face. He was completely helpless, also frozen in fear. Anthony continued to watch in horror as one of the white-robed men led a horse out of the trees to stand quietly next to where Jed was tied and forced to endure the ravages of man's hatred and ignorance. In a state of semiconsciousness, Jed was cut loose from the tree and thrown on the horse by two of the robed men, much like a bloodied side of meat from a slaughtered cow. Another Klansman threw a rope over a high branch of the tall oak tree where Anthony and his sister would swing on a tire suspended by a twenty-foot rope. The horse walked slowly to the tree and stopped. A looped rope was placed around Jed's neck and drawn tight. Jed's almost limp body was pulled upward by the neck until he sat upright on the horse. His hands were tied behind his back with a thick rope.

After one of the Klansmen made sure the rope was securely tied to another nearby tree and there was no slack, the horse was slapped hard on his haunches and ran like the wind. Jed's body dangled from the tree and convulsed under the pressure of having his life stripped away. The knot held tight, crushing his windpipe. After a moment, he hung there lifelessly, having been lynched by civilized men hiding under the guise of the Ku Klux Klan hoods and robes.

As the body slowly turned, Anthony recognized the victim and let out a primordial scream of fear. One of the white-robed devils snatched off a hood to get a better bead on the direction of the scream. Anthony saw the face, fell backwards, got to his feet and started running. He ran faster than ever before in his life. The Klansmen did not pursue the observer. They all could tell from the shrill scream that it was a kid. "Better that you remember this forever, nigger! You don't never mess with no white woman!

Never!" screamed the white-robed devil that had removed its hood. The face and words of hatred stamped an indelible imprint on his mind that would last forever. Anthony heard but didn't look back. Instead, he ran . . . and ran . . . and ran.

May 25, 1980

After a long, cold and wet spring, the sun finally returned to Long Island. It came back with a vengeance. At 11:00 a.m., it was already 89 degrees and expected to reach a high of 97. It didn't help that it was also humid from the rain that had pummeled the area for three previous days. Despite the fact that there was a slight breeze from the south, it did nothing to cool the impact of the increasing heat. There were no clouds in the sky, so the rays of the sun rained down on the crowd that gathered for the graduation ceremonies of Hofstra University School of Law. Despite seating for 2,000, there were no empty seats. This mass of bodies, regardless of being outdoors, added to the natural heat generation of the sun.

Each sitting in a long black robe and "Christopher Columbus"-styled hat, the 270 law school graduates were being cooked in the heat and their own sweat. A number of the graduates had prepared for the sweltering heat. Errol Forrest, Jr. was one of them. He had made sure his gown was long enough to expose only the tops of his black shoes. Underneath, he was wearing swimming trunks. His short-sleeved shirt was buttoned at the neck to accommodate a silk tie. For pictures after the ceremony, he would dash into the law school and change clothes. A new gabardine suit, a graduation gift from his mother, was hanging in his locker. He wasn't about to destroy it sitting in the sun while being basted like a Thanksgiving turkey.

Errol Forrest, Jr. sat there in the sun and figured that he would easily lose five pounds in perspiration. He was six-one and weighed about one hundred eighty-five pounds of mostly finely toned muscle. His oval face maintained perfectly trimmed eyebrows and a moustache. His suntanned copper-colored skin accentuated his handsome appearance. His wavy dark brown, almost black hair, had a brilliant streak of gray starting at the left center of his forehead that continued back at a forty-five-degree angle for about three inches. Most of his classmates used to pick on Errol and say that the pressures of law school had caused his hair to turn salt-and-pepper. The truth was that law school, from an academic perspective, had not been particularly difficult. Errol had worked for a law firm while in high school and college and knew ninety percent of the "ropes" before he had started the graduate program. "The cap and gown rental company is going to have a major cleaning bill on their hands," he told his classmate Rusty Frost, seated next to him.

"I came prepared, big guy." Rusty opened a small cooler, which held twelve ice-cold aluminum cans. He pulled out two and handed one to Errol. "Have a beer!" Errol smiled as he popped open the can of Budweiser®.

"Got a spare one? I've got a friend sitting a few rows back who's got to be dying in this heat."

"Sure, but only if you promise to get me his autograph. I'm a Broncomaniac like you, remember?"

"You never let me forget, Rusty man!"

Errol's best friend, Adrian Christopher, was one of the best wide receivers ever to play the game of football. He had retired from the Denver Broncos when his contract was up at the end of the last season. Errol took the beer, motioned to his friend and tossed it seven rows to where he was seated. Adrian, dressed in a vanilla-cream-colored suit, stretched his lean six-foot four-inch frame and made a perfect grab of the flying can. He weighed in at two hundred twenty pounds without an ounce of fat. He looked like a caramel-colored Greek god and, oftentimes, had been likened to Adonis. His jet-black hair was neatly trimmed and accentuated an otherwise extremely handsome face with finely chiseled features. At times it was said that Errol and Adrian looked like brothers, but they were born on opposite sides of the country.

Adrian acknowledged the refreshment by holding it high over his head to the applause of several onlookers. "I'd say you've got more than a few friends seated back there, Errol. Everybody's talking about who's here on your behalf." Errol looked quizzically at Rusty and responded.

"The only people here are my landlord and her friend who are sitting over there under the umbrella, and Adrian Christopher who just received the beer. My mother's not here. I thought she was in the hospital, but last night I found out from her housekeeper that she was out at the movies. As far as my father is concerned, who knows what's up with him. I told him about the graduation but haven't heard from him since. I can't figure the man out." These acknowledgments stressed Errol so he took another gulp of beer. Actually, he had no clue why his family had abandoned him on this red-letter day marking his educational achievement. Inside he was queasy . . . his heart ached and his stomach was in knots. To further calm his nerves, he took another big gulp of beer and tried to maintain a somewhat positive composure. At least his best friend was there.

"Then you don't know who showed up a little while ago, do you?" asked Rusty.

"Who? Ronald Reagan? Jimmy Carter? The Easter Bunny? Are you going to tell me or do I have to choke it out of you?" asked Errol in a curious but playful manner.

"Why don't you ask your friend, Adrian? But just make sure you get me his autograph." Errol turned around and gave Adrian a look that indicated a question. Adrian just put his hands up and shrugged his shoulders. Errol turned back to Rusty and continued.

"You know what? I don't care who's here. It's hot and I just want to get this over with. Three years of law school was easier to handle than this heat." Errol took another gulp of his beer as the Dean started the ceremony. He adjusted his Foster Grant sunglasses and squinted at the podium where the Dean stood.

"Ladies and gentlemen, today is indeed a very special occasion. Today's ceremony acknowledges the fact that another group of men and women have earned a degree that will allow them to engage in the practice of law. Today we are conferring the degree of Juris Doctor on 270 men and women who have completed the educational requirements mandated by the American Bar Association and the State of New York." Everyone applauded, especially the graduates themselves.

"There has been a change in today's program. The speaker who was originally scheduled to deliver the commencement address took

Railroaded!

ill at the last minute. Therefore, he has been replaced by two gentlemen, one of whom will make a short presentation to you." On cue, two men ascended the stairs of the platform and stood on either side of the Dean. "I would first like to present a man who was a former United States Attorney and is now a formidable advocate with the law firm of Johnson, Owens, Sutter & Moss in Pittsburgh, Pennsylvania. As most of you know, he suffered a near-tragic experience here at Hofstra last summer but came through it with flying colors. I would like to present to you, Mr. Raymond Sutter. He will join me in conferring the degree of Juris Doctor on each graduate." Adrian Christopher whistled loudly in support of this announcement. The audience gave Mr. Sutter a standing ovation. Errol sat in his seat in literal shock. What was Raymond Sutter doing here? And who was the second man standing with him? His face was very familiar, but, for the moment, Errol couldn't recall his name. It must have been the heat, beer and surprise at seeing a face that brought back memories he was trying to bury. He wished he had his regular glasses with him because his sunglasses were not prescription.

"Now, ladies and gentlemen, the commencement address will be delivered by the District Attorney for Allegheny County, Pennsylvania, Mr. Lewis Dobson. Mr. Dobson won re-election to the post last November. He is with us today to give you a very special message. Mr. Dobson." The Dean sat down after shaking hands with the burly prosecutor. Errol's jaw dropped in shock. He couldn't believe what was unfolding in front of him. He turned to Adrian and gave him a look of *"what is he doing here?"* Errol sat back down and, all at once, experienced a flood of memories.

Chapter 1

1964 to 1969

The traumatic experience of their son caused the A.D. Williams family to move to Compton, California in November 1964. Despite being farmers, they were making the move to the big city in hopes of making a better life for themselves and their three children. In California, they believed that Negroes could get a fair chance at a good life, without having to deal with the abject hatred of southern whites. In California, there were no separate facilities for blacks and whites. People were just people. They hoped that in California they could get away from Klan injustice, as well as try to put the horrible memories behind them.

Ethel and A.D. Williams, with their life savings, bought the house vacated by the Forrest family, who just a month before, had moved to Detroit, Michigan. The Williams had never before owned a house with indoor plumbing and running water. To their eldest son, Anthony, life had been transformed into a futuristic paradise. No more fighting water moccasins at night when going to the outhouse. No more pumping water from the old well. No more chopping wood for the incessant fire maintained in the stove and fireplace. Life was good -- no. Life was great!

Anthony "Tony" Williams was a handsome eleven-year-old youngster with a sense of humility that would stay with him for the rest of his days. In fact, his humility sometimes was mistaken for shyness.

He hit it off instantly with Adrian Christopher, who lived just a few doors away on East 150th Street. This was a godsend for Adrian, who was still lamenting the fact that his lifelong best friend, Errol Forrest, Jr. actually had the audacity to move to another state,

Railroaded!

let alone another city. Tony's arrival on the scene helped fill the void left by the departure of Errol.

During the summer of 1966, Tony finally got the chance to meet Errol. The Forrest family came to California on a two-week vacation visit. The three boys got along like old "war buddies" and vowed an allegiance to each other till death.

It was also during that summer that Adrian and Errol discovered Tony's only apparent physical malady. The boy, at age thirteen, had the smallest hands you ever saw and couldn't catch worth a lick. In contrast, he had size 11EE feet. They were huge. Tony advised his two friends that the kids back home used to always call him "Duck," a name that he had always hated. Yet the size of his feet proved to be an extraordinary asset. At the Roy Campanella Park was a public swimming pool where the three boys spent not less than four hours in the water every day. Tony could swim like a fish and at high speed. Adrian and Errol couldn't keep pace despite being adequate swimmers, so they would always lie in wait and ambush their friend.

During his junior high and high school years, Tony tried out for and made the swimming team. He set every conceivable record and would have been a legitimate contender for the 1968 Olympics had it not been for his age. He had made up his mind to tryout for the 1972 games in swimming when a chance occurrence in the spring of 1969 changed his future.

The high school bully, "Daryl the Dog," was physically harassing Tony's older sister, Martha, at the edge of the athletic fields. Adrian and Tony, just emerging from the gym after school athletic practices (Adrian was into football and track; Tony, of course, into swimming), saw Tony's distressed sister. Both dropped everything and took off like rockets to the rescue of the damsel in distress. Adrian was the fastest man on the track squad and had been legitimately timed at 22.0 seconds flat in the 220 yard sprint, running in tennis shoes and without spikes no less. But not anymore. Tony "smoked" Adrian so badly that Adrian pulled up for a moment to see this human streak. Daryl the Dog, on seeing the two human speed demons approaching, took off running. Tony reached his sister in a matter of seconds. Her only words were, "Please get that s.o.b., Duck!" Tony was off again and this time overtook the jerk in less than two hundred yards. He lunged forward and tackled the boy, threatening him with immediate and painful death if he ever laid a hand on his sister again. Adrian finally caught up with his friend and pulled him off the bully, who immediately ran away from the two.

Panting heavily, Adrian, between words, admonished his friend. "You've been holding out on me, Tony. Where did you get that speed? You just 'smoked' my butt and I was at full speed! Got a pair of rockets in those size 13's?"

"Must've been seeing Martha in trouble, A.C.," retorted Tony.

"Right!" said Adrian between gasps. "How fast are you?"

"Martha clocked me once last year in the hundred at 11.0 seconds, but that was in sneakers and I didn't try real hard."

"Are you kidding me? That would just about make you one of the fastest men on the face of the earth! You may be a duck who swims like a fish, but maybe 'Flash' is a more appropriate name for you -- Tony 'the Flash' Williams! Maybe we should get you a red suit like the guy in the comics!" Tony laughed and put his arm around the neck of his best friend and thanked him for helping in the rescue of his sister.

"Bet we scared the mess out of 'Daryl the Puppy'!" Both laughed aloud, but Martha reminded the boys that they weren't supposed to use "bad" words. In the heat of the moment, they had forgotten that they had dropped their books in pursuit of Martha's attacker. Unbeknownst to both, the whole event had been witnessed by the football and track coach, who had walked back onto the field to make sure that all practice equipment had been put away.

●●●●●●

The next day, just as both boys had settled in for a study hall period (which really meant doing what they enjoyed best -- designing buildings), Coach George Jones appeared at the monitor's desk and told the boys they were excused into his custody for the period. He silently marched them to his office and set them down in front of his desk. "Is Martha okay?" asked Coach Jones. Both boys looked at each other in amazement. How did he know what happened yesterday?

Railroaded!

"She's fine, sir, but I'm not sure that Daryl Lewis is," said Tony as he and Adrian slapped hands.

"Okay, okay, gentlemen, I saw the whole event." Both men dipped their heads and slumped a little in their chairs, waiting for the coach to lower the boom.

"Sit up straight, you two, and act like the strong Negro men you are! Always be proud and never cower to authority. Respect it, but never cower to it." A combined "Yes, sir" came from the two boys. The coach reached beside his desk and grabbed two boxes. "Here, Adrian. This is a new pair of spikes; size 10 and a half, right?" Adrian nodded his appreciation in a quizzical sort of way. "And for you, Mr. Williams, I believe a size 13 EE is in order. Right?"

"Yes sir, that should be just fine. But, Coach, I'm on the swimming team, not on the track team."

"Both of you get dressed in event uniforms. I want you on the track in five minutes. Adrian, get a 'uni' for your friend. Now hurry up and get going!" Both Adrian and Tony were a bit dumbfounded by this course of events but decided to play along. In three minutes, both emerged from the locker room. Once on the track, they donned their brand spanking new Converse® Special Edition Track and Field Spikes.

"For a quick warm-up, I want you both to jog around the track and give me two 440's. Then meet me at the starting line for the 220." The boys cruised around the track, not really exerting any energy whatsoever. Ten minutes later, they stood at the starting line for the 220 and listened to the track coach. "Adrian, I know that you can run the 220 in tennis shoes at 22 flat. Now we're going to see what you can do in real spikes. I have an official timer here from the U.S. Amateur Athletic Association at the finish line, so there will be no question as to the validity of this time trial and your speed. You know the starting drill, so get to it."

Adrian crouched down at the starting blocks that had been set in lane one. The starting gun sounded and Adrian was gone. He seemed to run more effortlessly with the spikes. He lunged across the finish line in 20.75 seconds. Coach Jones was stunned but didn't show it. The state high school record was 22.2. The U.S. record was 20.5, and the World Record was 20.00 seconds flat.

"How did I do, sir?" Adrian asked of the official timer.

"You'll have to ask your coach, young man." Adrian trotted across the track and asked the coach the same question. He gave Adrian a stern look and told him that he didn't put everything into it and would have to do it again in five minutes. Tony witnessed everything and paid close attention.

After five minutes, Adrian lined up again and, at the sound of the gun, was off. With gut-wrenching determination, Adrian gave it everything he had and, with clenched teeth, crossed the finish line. Coach Jones was as amazed as the official timer. Adrian, at age fifteen, had finished the time test in 19.95 seconds, a new world record for the 220-yard dash. Coach Jones did not show his pride or enthusiasm for what had just happened. Instead, he turned to Adrian and said, "That's more like it, young man." The coach conferred with the official timer in a rather animated way while Adrian and Tony looked on. "Now it's your turn, Mr. Williams. I know you've never run track events before, but just run like I saw you run after your sister's attacker yesterday, with lots of determination and energy." Tony nodded and went to the starting blocks.

Adrian gave him a fifteen-second instruction on the use of the blocks and winked at his friend. When Tony crouched into the preset position, Adrian bent over and said, "Kick ass, Flash! I know you're faster than I am. Just kick some ass."

Tony gave Adrian a wicked grin and said, "How much?" The gun sounded and Tony duplicated his feat of the previous day. Adrian thought that this man really should have a red suit with a yellow lightning bolt across his chest. He crossed the finish line, but the official timer, upon seeing the results, checked the watch and initially decided that the time was wrong or the watch was broken. Coach Jones ran across the track, also astounded by the time on his watch. The two men both checked their watches and determined that both were indeed in working order. Tony had finished the 220 in 19.75 seconds. Coach Jones and the official timer from the U.S.A.A.A. had just witnessed two new world records being set in the space of ten minutes.

"You are going to have to run the race again, young man. The official timer's watch was not properly set. So this time, I want you to dig deep and run as if your life depended on it. I want you to give it your best shot!"

"How fast do you want me to run, Coach?" asked Tony, while catching his breath.

"What do you mean, son?"

"I mean that was just a practice run, right? Same as you did for Adrian?" Coach Jones was a bit stunned by this admission. "I'll try and run harder this time, Coach." Tony trotted across the track to the starting position. Coach Jones followed with a big smile on his face. He knew that he had the fastest human being on the face of the earth as one of his students.

On reaching the other side of the track, Adrian slapped hands with Tony and said, "I saw you pull up, man." Tony was amazed at Adrian's perception. "Now, why don't you really smoke their behinds?"

"Won't we draw too much attention to ourselves, A.C.?" Tony was not used to any public exposure except at the swimming meets.

"This could be fun. Maybe we could go to the Olympics!" Adrian responded.

"But the Olympics are for world-class athletes. We're just a couple of high school sophomores."

"The Olympics are for the best athletes in the world. Age doesn't matter. If we are the best, then we are the best. Too bad Errol isn't here. I got a letter from him the other day saying he ran a 21.5 in the 220 in tennis shoes. That turkey is even faster than I am. And you are faster than both of us!" The coach broke up the conversation and instructed Tony to set himself in the blocks again. In the crouch position, he thought about what would happen if he won an Olympic gold medal -- the joy it would bring to his parents and to the kids back home in Alabama. The gun sounded.

Tony "the Flash" Williams strained every muscle in his body to their limits. He virtually flew around the track, looking as if his feet weren't touching the ground. He lunged across the finish line with a determination that the coach had never seen. The official timer clicked the button to stop the time, looked at the watch and fainted. Coach Jones was jumping up and down shouting "YES, YES, YES!" Adrian ran across the field to his friend, who had his hands on his knees and mouth wide open, breathing heavily. "You really do have rockets for feet. No one is going to believe what I just saw. I know you had to do it under twenty with ease! Let's ask the coach."

By now the coach had jogged over to the official timer and, after two slaps on the face, he was fully revived. "Mr. Jones, did I just witness that boy break his own world-record time by almost one full second?" asked the timer.

"Let's compare watches." They did and the results were identical. Anthony Williams had run the 220-yard dash in 18.90 seconds.

"Of course, I'll have to notify the U.S. Olympic committee."

"In due course. But let me work with them a while, especially since they're not eligible until 1972, when they'll both be in college. By then, who knows what they'll be able to accomplish?"

"Mr. Jones, would you mind if Mr. Williams and Mr. Christopher ran the hundred meters for us in a timed race?" asked the U.S.A.A.A official.

"It would be my distinct pleasure." Coach Jones walked over to the boys and now was showing some real enthusiasm. "Boys," he said, "I would like you two to run the 100 meters in a race against each other."

"I'm not going to get my butt burned by the 'Flash' here," Adrian retorted.

"The 'Flash,' eh? And who are you, the 'Streak'?" Adrian liked the sound of the "Streak." "Listen, Adrian. I just watched both of you break the world record in the 220. Now I want you two to race against each other, but not for competition. Just do it for pure, unadulterated speed. I want you two to run faster than you've ever run in your whole short lives. I want you to freak out that white man standing over there from the U.S. Amateur Athletic Association. I want you both to kick some major ass." Adrian and Tony looked at each other in amazement at having both broken the world record in the event. Then, as if on cue, each smiled a devilish grin and they slapped hands.

"No sweat!" Tony said.

"Excuse me for saying this, Coach," interjected Adrian, exuding nothing but confidence. "If it's ass you want, then it's ass you'll

Railroaded!

get!" said Adrian in the first time he had ever used somewhat abusive language in front of an adult.

They both crouched at the blocks for the start of this new event. The official timer and Coach Jones were both at the finish line. The coach raised the gun . . .

Before it had even begun, the race was over. Tony finished first, as expected, and Adrian, in second place, was not more than two strides behind. The official timer and Coach Jones were both ecstatic over the results. Adrian Christopher had finished second with a new world-record speed of 9.85 seconds. His friend Anthony Williams had finished and bested him in what was also a new world record time of 9.65 seconds. Little did both boys know that, during these quickly organized time trials, their speeds were better than the Olympic and World Record speeds set in the 100-meter race in Mexico City during the 1968 summer games the year before.

Coach Jones hugged them both and thanked them for their participation in these unscheduled and spontaneous events. "Well, aren't you going to tell us the results?" asked Adrian. Both were anxious to know. Instead, Coach Jones told them both to go get showered and return to class. Once in class, there was an announcement over the school's public address system by Coach Jones.

"Boys and girls, I am pleased to announce something that may have a major impact on our school in the future. Yesterday, by pure chance, I saw something that was frightening and yet mystifying. Today I verified what I saw yesterday. Just a while ago, I, along with an official of the United States Amateur Athletic Association, verified a series of facts. We at Kennedy High School have the honor of having in attendance two of the fastest human beings on the face of this earth. They are Adrian Christopher and Anthony Williams. Aside from the fact that both are honor students in their academic endeavors, we in the administration hope that when the next Olympic trials take place for the 1972 games, they will be in attendance to represent our country and the tradition of excellence in athletics here at Kennedy."

The kids in the study hall class gave the two boys a rousing round of applause. After school, both boys were summoned to the principal's office. Once there, they were greeted by sports reporters from the *Los Angeles Times*. That night, they both lay in bed thinking of what it would be like to wear Olympic Gold.

Chapter 2

1971 to 1975

On graduation from high school in 1971, both boys had already made decisions as to where they would attend college. Tony decided to attend the University of Colorado at Boulder, and Adrian was going to be reunited with his old friend Errol Forrest, Jr., who was now a sophomore at Dartmouth College in Hanover, New Hampshire. Errol's efforts were significant in helping both men get admitted to their respective schools. Errol had tried hard to convince Tony to come to Dartmouth. Tony, however, was stubborn and had his heart set on Colorado. Both had visited Errol in Denver during the summer of 1970, and it was a spiritual love of nature that descended on Tony. Errol had dated the daughter of the University of Colorado Director of Minority Admissions' for a hot minute so he pulled a few "strings" to get his friend the best "academic scholarship" package available, and rightly so, since Tony had worked hard to finish high school with a 3.5 grade point average. He also had a combined 1350 on the Scholastic Aptitude Test. All three men strongly believed that attendance at college was for intellectual enrichment. They would not subject themselves to the whims of sports scholarships; sports participation was merely supplemental to academic achievement.

The University of Colorado was also a good place for Tony since the United States Olympic training grounds were in Colorado Springs, a scant one hundred miles away from the Boulder campus. Tony had fixed his sights on Olympic Gold in 1972.

As luck would have it, fate once again played another hand. Just two nights before the fourth football game of the season for the Colorado Buffaloes, the team's All-American free safety, in a freak accident, fell down a flight of stairs and broke his leg in two places. The coach was distraught because a promising season was going to flit away if he couldn't find a speedy replacement for the defense. As he sat in his armchair lost in thought, his eyes glanced at a newspaper report that Anthony Williams, a freshman from Compton, California, had run a 9.9 hundred in time trials earlier in the week. The coach's eyes sparkled. Maybe there was a chance.

That night, while studying, Tony received an unexpected knock at his door. He got up from his armchair and stretched his six-foot two-inch one hundred ninety pound frame of lean muscle. Dressed only in gold track shorts that were in stark contrast to his milk chocolate-colored skin, he answered the door, angered by the disturbance. He flung open the door ready to pounce on the intruder -- but was totally surprised by the visitor. "Mr. Williams, I'm Jake Hilliard, head coach of the football team."

"Pleasure to meet you, sir. You must be looking for my roommate, Larry. He's out right now." Larry Johnson was the freshman wonder-of-a-running-back, on whom Colorado was pinning its hopes of success in the future. Tony realized that he was dressed only in shorts and actually was a bit embarrassed by his appearance. He had actually expected one of the students who bothered him from time to time to be at the door.

"I didn't come to see Larry. I came to talk to you. Congratulations on that 9.9 time you ran in the hundred yesterday!"

"Wasn't really my best. My concentration was broken just before the race, and I didn't get a good start out of the blocks," Tony responded. Coach Hilliard shook his head. He was both amazed and somewhat mystified by the man who stood before him.

"Listen, Tony. I'm not going to beat around the bush. Have you ever considered playing football?"

"No, sir. I've got small hands and can't catch worth a lick. But I love the game. I always wished that I could catch like my two friends . . ."

"You mean Adrian Christopher and Errol Forrest. I wanted them both, but they chose Ivy League." The coach had done his homework.

"They both wanted me to join them at Dartmouth College, but I wanted to be here, close to the Olympic training facility in the Springs. I hope to make the U.S. Olympic Track Team next year and run in the 100 meters, 200 meters, 400 and 800 meter relays.

Railroaded!

If I'm lucky enough, maybe I'll qualify in a swimming event or two. My stroke is still fairly strong!" Coach Hilliard laughed as he listened to Tony. He was only one of the strongest competitors and the fastest man on the CU swim team.

"You know, you can still play football and not have to worry about catching the pigskin. I bet that you would be one helluva free safety. All you have to do is run down people and knock the ball away from would-be receivers. The only other thing would be to stop running backs from getting past you. This wouldn't interfere with your Olympic training at all. In fact, if you help me out, I'll personally see to it that you get an early tryout with the squad at Colorado Springs." Tony couldn't resist this offer, but he didn't want the football coach to think him too anxious. He could swim, run, and now play in the same sport with his two friends, except on the other side of the line.

"Can I think about it for a day or so?" asked Tony.

"In reality, son, I need you to play on Saturday. Are you game?"

"In reality, then, I'll have to evaluate it with respect to my studies. They come first. Everything else is secondary. What if I give you my answer in the morning?" This response was not what the coach wanted to hear, but he had to respect Tony for his tenacity.

"I'll be in my office at seven sharp. Stop by and I'll buy you breakfast at the faculty lounge."

"That's a deal. I'll be there at seven." The two men shook hands and the coach left. Jake Hilliard would keep his fingers crossed all night. Tony, after the door closed, stood for a moment in shock, ran his fingers through his long curly Afro and grabbed the phone to call Adrian in New Hampshire. As luck would have it, Errol was also there in Adrian's room. Tony recounted what had just happened and waited for the response from his two friends. Errol, despite being an excellent receiver, had opted out of varsity football because of a flare-up of an ankle injury sustained during his high school years. In reality, he preferred skiing and playing dorm-league ice hockey. Adrian, on the other hand, was a world-class wide receiver with outstanding natural talent.

"I'm sure glad that I don't go to a Big Eight school," Adrian told his friend. Tony was a bit perplexed with this response.

"What does that mean?"

"Do you think I want those high-arched, size double E rockets chasing my butt all over the football field?" Tony laughed aloud at this response. "Don't forget who first found out about your world-class, speed Mr. Tony 'the Flash' Williams."

"I don't think you'll ever have to worry about that, A.C. You guys are a million miles away in the backwoods of America. I don't think I can run that far."

"Damn good thing, too," retorted Adrian. Errol was rolling in laughter at the thought of these two squaring up on the football field.

●●●●●●

In the summer of 1972, Tony got his wish. So did Adrian and Errol. They all got tryouts for the United States Olympic Track and Field squad. Tony and Adrian made the team for several track events. Tony also qualified for swimming events. Errol pulled a hamstring and, as a result, didn't make the team. Despite his own blazing speed, non-participation was okay. He preferred to be their business agent after they won their events -- and win they did.

Tony won four gold medals and two silver medals at the summer games. Gold medals were won in the 100 meters for a world-record speed of 9.8 seconds flat (which he later admitted wasn't his personal best), in the 200 meters for an Olympic record, and for being the anchor leg in the 400 and 4 x 400 meter relays in world-record time. He also won silver medals for swimming in the 400 meter freestyle and for the 1,000 meters freestyle. Never before had a man participated in two such strenuous classes of competition and won medals. Tony was a legitimate world-class athlete.

Adrian didn't fare too badly either. He won a gold medal for his participation on the 400 and 4 x 400 meter relay team with Tony. He won a bronze medal behind Tony in the 100 meters and the 200 meters, and a silver medal for the 1,500 meters, which clearly was not his event. The two men returned as Olympic heroes going into their sophomore year at college.

Railroaded!

Tony, however, was the real star because he accomplished a personal goal that was set that day on the track at Kennedy High School. Now he could concentrate entirely on becoming Anthony Williams, world-class architect.

For the rest of his college career, his studies were solid. He loved what he did. His artistic and design ability came naturally. Sometimes it even overwhelmed his professors. Academically, Tony Williams attacked every class he took with a fervor and tenacity rarely seen by his professors. But never was he arrogant or egotistical in the display of his ability or knowledge.

Tony's successes on the collegiate football field were just as amazing. Tony "the Flash" Williams, was the terror of the defensive secondary. Every trick in opposing teams' game books was used to keep him out of a play. When the opposing team did so, it played into the hands of the rest of the defensive squad. The ploys worked perfectly, and with Tony's rocket speed, he could catch any offensive player in the open field.

Spring 1975

For the balance of his three years at Colorado, Anthony Williams excelled at everything he did. Just before graduation in the spring of 1975, he was awarded another athletic honor when he was drafted as a free safety by the world-champion Pittsburgh Steelers. He signed immediately for $500,000 per year on a five-year contract. He also received a signing bonus of $500,000. He was about to graduate with honors from college along with a contract to play big-league NFL football. His was a charmed life indeed. Tony called Adrian to let him know the good news. After a moment of rambling on about the draft, Adrian interjected.

"Damn, Tony! We have a real problem." Adrian's tone was very somber.

"What's wrong? Are you all right . . . is Errol all right? What's going on?" There was a moment of silence from Adrian.

"I got drafted by the Denver Broncos as their first-round draft pick," stated Adrian while laughing his head off. "But I'm going to defer for two years because I just received a notice that I've been picked as a Fulbright Scholar. So, at least I'll have two full years of game films to study before we meet head-to-head on the gridiron."

"The hell with football! Congratulations on the Fulbright! Now that's a real accomplishment! I'm really proud of you." He paused for a moment and then inquired about the other member of their triumvirate. "How's Errol doing in the midst of all this?"

"He's at the library right now. That boy is working his butt off in Classical Archaeology. In fact, he's planning on going to Egypt this fall to do on-site research. That twenty-month suspension the Dean and his mother arranged did the trick. He's more of an academic maniac than you. He's acing everything in sight. The time off from school really did him a lot of good. Anyway, I can't wait till the three of us start working together in the future. We'll set the world on fire!"

"So where do you go for the Fulbright, or are you going any place in particular?"

"Only to Montreal to study at McGill University. They've got a great graduate-level architecture school, so that's where I'm headed. I've got to try and learn as much as you already know. I may have the Fulbright Scholarship, but you're the natural talent in architecture," said Adrian, acknowledging his friend's abilities.

"Compliment accepted, A.C." Tony changed the subject back to football. "How long is your contract with the Broncos?"

"I only got three years, but $800,000 per year and a signing bonus of $250,000. Neh, neh, neh, neh, neh, neh!" Adrian chortled in a nursery rhyme-like voice.

"Adrian, you really are a pain in the ass," Tony bellowed.

"World-class pain in the ass, just like you, and don't you forget it, 'Flash' Williams. By the way, are you going to let Errol handle your contract negotiations?" inquired Adrian.

"Is there anyone else? Besides his knowledge of architecture, Errol's first love is business. How many brothers do you know who passed the bar exam in high school, negotiated NASA contracts at age nineteen, or negotiated a $2.5 billion manufacturing contract at age twenty-one? No other ones that I know. Besides, you know he's a tough cookie and not going to let us throw away any money. He believes in long-term safety and security despite his apparent penchant for taking short-term risks," stated Tony.

Railroaded!

Errol had arranged for the three of them to work together at Martin Marietta as summer associates in 1973. It was during this summer that he was on the NASA contract team for the company, while Adrian and Tony worked in the design group area on the construction of a new steam power plant.

"You know Errol wouldn't lift a finger unless he knew how the tendons and bones worked together. He's the most thorough investigative type I ever met. Nothing ever, ever, ever gets past the watchful eye of Errol Forrest, Jr. Nothing! He's probably the most brilliant of the three of us. To tell you the truth, Tony, sometimes his brilliance is scary. I'm glad he's our best friend." Adrian took a breath and continued. "You know he's planning to go to law school when he finally finishes here next year. He's already looking over a few schools where he can specialize in business. He keeps telling me he has no desire to practice law. He just wants the education and the degree to put in his back pocket for a rainy day. It's really too bad that he chose not to play football. It would have been interesting to see him play as well. He still is a great receiver and could probably get with a team on a walk-on basis."

"Listen, A.C. Errol loves the Broncos more than life itself and wouldn't want to play anywhere else. He can watch you play in Denver. Now he needs to concentrate on finishing Dartmouth and getting into law school. Playing professional sports isn't for Errol. Hell, man, it's not even really for us. We're not the typical dumb athletes who are driven by the slavemaster owners. But I'll do it for a while and enjoy the momentary glory . . . and the money. It's a means to an end. It gives us the capital we need to do something later. Let's both agree at the end of our contracts to quit football and set up our own architectural design firm. Okay, big guy? By then, Errol will have graduated from law school and we'll all be set!"

"That's a great game plan, Tony. All three of us are playing for the same end. Let's get on with it. But, for now, I gotta go. I haven't collected that signing bonus yet and am still a humble student."

"I know, I know," stated Tony.

"I'll tell Errol to give you a call when he gets back. In the meantime, later, asshole," responded Adrian.

"Later 'asshole' to you, 'Streak' Christopher." The salutary 'asshole' was born.

●●●●●●

During his collegiate years, Anthony Williams worked extremely hard. First and foremost, he concentrated on his studies and the development of his first love and chosen career, architectural design. Second was the development of his athletic prowess. The achievement of Olympic fame did not create an arrogant egomaniac. It was only a goal that had been pursued and met. Tony remained the down-to-earth man he always was, never forgetting his humble beginnings in the backwoods of Alabama.

Despite the fact that women continuously threw themselves at him, Tony never developed any long-term love interests except for a tall, pretty girl from Broken Arrow, Oklahoma, a suburb of Oklahoma City. Shelli Anderson had a golden complexion and shoulder-length, reddish-brown hair. She had a very even personality but never backed away from a confrontation. Despite being in the same graduating class, Shelli was one year younger than Tony. She had skipped a grade during elementary school. She was also a bona fide genius who had majored in civil engineering.

Shelli's intelligence attracted Tony more than her good looks. She was always there to support him. She helped him and he, her. They learned from each other. She was totally in love with this man, not for his speed on the playing field or his brilliance in his academic pursuits. She loved him over and above all of his marvelous talents because he was one of the most compassionate and caring men that she had ever met. Unlike other football players who pushed themselves on their women, Tony never made any untoward advances to Shelli (not that she didn't want him to). She was careful not to push their relationship because she didn't want to alienate the man she hoped would one day be her mate for life. Instead, she made herself indispensable as his friend, confidante and supporter.

Shelli remembered when she had met Adrian and Errol, together with Tony, for the first time during the Olympic trials in 1972. She marveled that three handsome black men could be so talented and

Railroaded!

yet not be in competition with each other. She marveled at their innate brilliance and how they actually complemented each other. She was glad that Tony might soon be hers, even though any one of the three would have been a great catch.

●●●●●●

The NFL was no place for accomplished single men with high moral standards. Throngs of women would be throwing themselves at these masterpieces of manhood. Shelli Anderson was informed that Tony would be going to play for the Pittsburgh Steelers in the fall. Summer camp would begin in early July. On May 16th, the fourth anniversary of their meeting after a swim meet, Shelli invited Tony to dinner at her apartment to commemorate the occasion. Tony agreed reluctantly because he said he was studying for a final exam in Advanced Steel Structural Design. He told her he would be over about 8:00 P.M. but couldn't stay very long since it was imperative that he finish his studying. Shelli, knowing not to push when it came to academic issues, agreed.

Tony appeared at Shelli's door at precisely 8:00 P.M. with a single blush-pink rose in hand. It had the desired effect, as she blushed and stood on her toes to kiss her statuesque man on the cheek. She had prepared a table with candlelight and served a large pepperoni pizza with extra cheese from Pizza Hut. This was the same meal they had shared on their first meeting, only at a nearby restaurant. Tony was greatly amused and yet totally impressed with this goddess of a woman. He knew that what he was about to do was indeed the right thing.

At precisely 8:30 P.M., the doorbell rang. Shelli was distraught that someone could be interrupting her anniversary dinner. She stormed to the door to chase away whoever was there. Instead, she received a huge box wrapped in brightly colored paper and a dozen yellow, long-stemmed roses from a deliveryman. The note on the flowers read, *"From Your Secret Admirer."* Tony, acting as if he didn't know anything about it, asked incredulously, "What's all this, Shelli?"

"I have no idea, Honey Lamb. This isn't from you?" Tony shook his head in apparent disgust.

"You might as well open the box so we can find out who the jerk is behind this intrusion." The look on Tony's face was stern and cold.

"Are you sure? I can just throw it away."

"Not on your life, Shelli." She nervously proceeded with the task at hand, having no expectation as to what would be the outcome. Unnoticed, Tony reached into his pants pocket and retrieved a small velvet bag. Shelli worked away while Tony slowly positioned himself. At the bottom of the box was a card in beautiful calligraphy that read, *"WILL YOU MARRY ME, SHELLI?"* She turned to Tony, who was on his knees holding what appeared to be not less than a three-carat, diamond-solitaire engagement ring. In amazement, she watched as he put it on her left ring finger. Then she stood up, for once towering over Tony, and slapped him.

"What kind of game is this? Do you think I'm crazy?" Tony must have guessed all wrong, and his face began to drop. On seeing this change of demeanor, Shelli bent down and threw her arms around Tony and kissed him passionately. "I'll only marry you if you tell me you love me, you silly man." Tony felt immensely relieved and vowed his undying love for this woman. Changing the subject, she asked her almost-fiancé, "But what about the exam you have to take tomorrow?"

"What exam? You mean the Structural Design exam that I 'aced' this morning? Darling, the only remaining final exam I have to take is to see what it's going to be like making love to you for the rest of my life."

"In that case, Mr. Anthony Williams, I would like to introduce you to the future Mrs. Anthony Williams." With those words, she undressed in front of her husband-to-be.

● ● ● ● ● ●

Four weeks later, they were married in a small ceremony attended by the Williams clan, the Forrest Clan, the Christopher clan and Shelli's family. Also in attendance were Tony's high school coach, George Jones; the University of Colorado football

Railroaded!

coach, Jake Hilliard; and Gordon Mound, head coach of the Pittsburgh Steelers. After the reception party, the couple left immediately for their honeymoon on a private jet chartered by the owner of the Pittsburgh Steelers. The first two of three weeks would be spent island hopping through the South Pacific. The last week would be spent at a private beach villa in Costa Rica.

Adrian wondered whether, if he got married quickly, he could get the same kind of deal from the Broncos. Errol, on the other hand, was having problems with a girlfriend of several years. All that mattered was that he was extremely happy that one of his best friends had found a legitimate woman that cared for him as a man and not for what she wanted or could get from the relationship. Both he and Adrian hoped that when their turns came, they could be as lucky as their friend, Tony Williams.

Chapter 3

1979

Four years passed on the five-year contract Tony had with the Pittsburgh Steelers. Because of his success, his salary for the third, fourth and fifth years was increased from $500,000 to $750,000 per year. All of the increases were stashed in a series of high-yield annuities that suited Tony and Shelli just fine. Errol had arranged everything for these high-yield investments for his friend. Adrian also started playing with the Broncos in 1977 and had the enviable luck of being on a Superbowl participant team in his rookie year. Despite the Bronco's loss to the Dallas Cowboys in January 1978, Adrian was a solid performer who was admired by the fans, as well as the head coach.

●●●●●●

At the end of the 1978 football season (January 1979), both Adrian and Tony were selected to play in the Pro Bowl in Honolulu. Shelli was pregnant with their second child, so she opted to stay home and let the boys go play without a chaperone. Besides, she had gone to Honolulu on their honeymoon and really wasn't that impressed with the place. But Maui was different. To her, that was paradise on earth. Shelli made Tony promise that he would never, ever go there without her. Besides, during the Pro Bowl week, there would be no time for side indulgences.

On the Friday night before the game, a lot of the players were involved in drunken orgies with women from every part of the globe. After all, these were the NFL's best and most sought-after hard bodies.

Railroaded!

Adrian and Tony decided to let loose and ended up at a private beach party where the ratio of women to men was four-to-one. While this was paradise for Adrian, who was still one of the most eligible bachelors of the NFL, Tony was satisfied to be a relative wallflower and drink and drink and drink. Egged on by Adrian, Tony drank to excess and got totally plastered. In this way, he didn't have to get involved in the sex play that was rampant among the partygoers.

Tony looked around and saw that Adrian was about to hit the door with a pretty young thing . . . "Goin' to the beach?" he yelled at his friend.

"Yep. Are you all right, Tony?" asked Adrian in return.

"Will be as long as the drinks keep comin', A.C." Tony sat back in a LazyBoy chair and sipped on his Bacardi Cocktail. He raised his glass to his friend and said, "You better hurry up and get married, A.C. I can't do this shit much longer . . . especially playing chaperone for your raggedy ass."

"All right, all right. I'll be back in a while to check on you. Add a few club sodas in between those drinks." Instead of heading off, Adrian asked for a moment's indulgence from the woman at his side. He got a tall glass of water from the bar and took it to his friend. "Here, T-Bone. This is Errol's secret weapon against hangovers. Drink up!" said Adrian. Tony did as ordered. "You're not through yet, mister. Go get another one and do the same thing. Then down two club sodas before taking another sip of alcohol."

"Where's Errol when you need him?" mumbled Tony under his breath.

"He's in New York at law school. Come on, Tony. You're not that drunk." Adrian looked at the young woman who was getting frustrated that he was paying attention to another man and not her. He motioned that he would be there in just a moment. "I promise I'll be back in not more than one hour. Gotta go! And keep downing those waters and club sodas."

"Go ahead, man, and have some fun. I just wish Shelli were here. I'll be fine." The two men slapped hands and Adrian disappeared out the door to the beach with what appeared to be a very attractive woman. "Hope he gets lucky and somebody ties his butt down real soon." Tony sipped on the Bacardi Cocktail and then downed another glass of water. "I don't know if I can take too much more of this madness."

Fifteen minutes later, Clyde Morris came in like a house on fire. The big running back for the Steelers was a known womanizer, despite being married for almost ten years. On issues of fidelity, Tony and Clyde were known to have heated arguments, sometimes approaching a knock-down, drag-out fight. While Tony, happily married, patently refused to engage in extramarital affairs, Clyde depended on them to feed his almost maniacal ego.

"Tony, you've got to help me out. Please man . . . just take one of these women off my hands. You don't have to do anything. I got a big-time Jones coming on and got to get me some trim! Please help me out, man, please! I'll do anything you want!"

"Anything?" asked Tony sarcastically. "That could cost you a small fortune, Mr. Cockhound!"

"Why you gotta be so damn hard on me all the time, T-Bone? Lighten up, you self-righteous son-of-a-bitch," responded a man approaching anger.

"And you want me to help you? Get the fuck outta my face," said Tony while slurring a few words.

"I'm sorry, man. I'm sorry. Everyone else is already paired off. Come on, T-Bone. Give a brother a break." Tony looked up at Clyde, who had his hands together as if praying.

"I hope the 'tang' is worth it, you asshole. Go, get outta here."

"I'll never forget this, man. I owe you big-time!" said a smiling Clyde Morris.

"That you do!" retorted Tony.

"Want to dance?" asked the blonde woman who was dumped on him by Clyde.

"That's about all I'm good for," responded Tony. He stood to dance to a round of Chic's *"Good Times."*

When the song was over, Tony turned to go back to his seat and drink when the young woman grabbed him, kissed him fully on the mouth, then whispered in his ear, "How would you like to fuck this blonde cat and make her purr?" Tony wiped his mouth in distaste and pushed her away, almost violently.

Railroaded!

"*No damn way!*" exclaimed Tony in a loud voice that momentarily stopped all the action at the party and totally embarrassed the young blonde woman. "Go find that fool you came in with. Yeah, Clyde Morris. He's your type!" With all eyes focused on the young blonde, she bolted from the room and disappeared into the night. Tony, a bit shaken and angered by the intrusion, finally returned to his seat. He motioned to the bartender to bring another drink. While he waited, he sat there motionless as if in a trance-like state. "Why would some stupid white girl do something that crazy?" He cringed inside as he thought about the childhood memory of his cousin being lynched. "Where the hell is A.C.? Out doing the same thing that Clyde is . . . chasing women. Shit, what am I doing here?" he asked himself. After several more drinks and the fact that Adrian had not yet returned, Tony decided to try to make his way to his room.

Outside the main party area, Tony was cajoled by a different specter. Half-blind from being almost totally drunk, but not wanting to engage in the frivolous sex play that abounded, he tried to walk to his bungalow but stumbled and fell twice. Not seeing or thinking, he took the hand that was extended to him and stood again. "Thanks a lot."

"Just trying to help," said the soft voice. Tony was led away by a shapely blonde whom he could barely see. He was taken to a private room in the large bungalow next to the main house. As they walked, Tony recognized her as the woman who earlier had flagrantly accosted him after the dance. At this recognition, Tony quickly turned to go back but stumbled. The young woman caught him. "Sorry about earlier. I'll just help you get to a room to crash, and then I'll leave." Tony reluctantly allowed himself to be led to the room, thanked her for the assistance and passed out, fully clothed on the bed in front of him.

Tony awoke the next morning to find the same white woman sleeping beside him -- in the nude! He strained his memory but could not recall any sexual encounter with her. What the hell was she doing there? All he remembered was passing out on the bed fully dressed in his white linen slacks and Hawaiian flower shirt, clothes that were now neatly folded and placed on a steamer trunk at the foot of the bed. Tony panicked. Fear consumed his spirit. He remembered what would happen to black men caught with a white woman when he was a kid. They would be whipped and hanged to death . . . lynched by the Klan. He put his hands to his head and began to shake violently.

Just then, Tony heard a familiar voice. Adrian, despite nursing a major hangover, was looking for his friend. Tony got out of bed and quickly put on his pants and shirt. He grabbed his sandals in hand and ran out the door. He found Adrian and, in a rush of emotion, recounted what he could remember. Adrian went back to the room and surveyed the situation. Returning, he told Tony it was nobody that he knew and that he should just forget about it but call Shelli immediately so there would be no surprises. Despite how distasteful it seemed, he found a phone and called Shelli, recounting the whole series of events. Tony was still an emotional wreck.

"Calm down, Tony. I know that, even plastered, you're not that stupid. You haven't strayed in four years with the NFL and God knows how many women have tried. So don't worry about it. Just play the game and come home, okay? Steven and I miss you. Just come home."

"Okay, baby. I'll be home on Monday. I hope you're not mad at me. You know I love you more than life itself, don't you, baby? I know I got drunk, but I would never do anything like this to you, never." Shelli reassured her husband that everything was all right but hid the fact that she was furious that some half-wit white woman would try to take advantage of her husband when he was drunk. She worked at putting the thoughts out of her mind as the baby she was carrying began kicking inside.

● ● ● ● ● ●

Almost five months passed without event. Right after the birth of a daughter they named Nicole, crazy things started happening. In the mail, Shelli received a blind letter reading *"I really loved how your husband made love to me in Honolulu."* The postmark was Los Angeles. Besides family, they didn't know anybody in Los Angeles. When Tony arrived home from a luncheon appointment, Shelli was standing in the kitchen. She handed the letter to Tony

Railroaded!

and inquired, "What the hell is this?" Tony read the letter and became visibly angry and upset.

"I already told you nothing happened! We've been over this a thousand times!" responded an angry Tony.

"It's not that I don't believe you, but why is this happening? That's what I want to know," stated Shelli very emphatically. "Either you're lying to me or that bitch is playing a deadly game!"

"Look at the letters, darling! Each one has been cut out and pasted separately to the page." The thought that Tony was a target caused even more anger in Shelli.

"Some white fool is stalking you, and she might as well be stalking me! That means we're in trouble and have to be on guard. I don't want to live my life like this . . . always wondering. We don't need the NFL, if that's what it means." Shelli was really infuriated. Instinctively, however, Tony reached over and took his wife in his arms to assuage her anger and welling fears.

"Whatever it takes, darling, I'll make sure we're okay. Nothing ever happened in Hawaii except that I drank too much and got drunk!"

"I know, I know," said Shelli reluctantly. She stepped back for a moment and pointed at Tony. "But if I ever meet that hussy, her eyes will be sooo black they'll never turn blue again!" Shelli let out an exasperated "Ohhhh" and continued with, "Why can't we just be left alone?" Tony did not respond but instead just pulled her close and held her tight. He did not see that Shelli's anger was turning to fear . . . fear of the unknown world of a crazed white woman. Yet there in the arms of her husband, she felt safe. There in the arms of her beloved, she let go of her pent-up emotion and started to cry.

Two weeks later, another letter arrived in an unknown handwriting, also from Los Angeles. Two weeks later, another arrived from Pittsburgh! Someone indeed was stalking Tony and making his life miserable. He and his wife consulted with an attorney, who indicated that unfortunately there wasn't much that could be done until the mystery woman or person appeared.

Training camp was about to begin and Tony needed to concentrate on these activities. This was the last year of his contract, and because of the events surrounding the mysterious interloper, fuel was added to his decision to end his NFL career, as he and his friends had agreed earlier, in order to begin their architectural design firm. Out of the limelight, his family life could achieve normalcy once again, without being hassled by the strains of the NFL.

Errol was firmly planted at Hofstra University School of Law in Hempstead, New York. He would begin his third and final year in August and be finished the next spring. The three could be together again with plenty of capital.

Chapter 4

Training camp began and Shelli continued to get letters from Pittsburgh, now on a weekly basis. There was still no trace of this mystery woman who was straining Tony's whole being.

Four weeks later, the first preseason game took place at home against the Denver Broncos. Tony welcomed the opportunity to see his friend, Adrian. Training camp hadn't gone very well because of the stress of whoever was taunting his family. His mind was not on the game. Adrian, worried about his friend, got permission to fly to Pittsburgh ahead of the team so he could meet with Tony. Tony met Adrian at the airport and seemed to be instantly relieved to see his longtime friend. Adrian inquired about Shelli and the kids. He also told Tony to be strong -- that everything would be okay. There was only one more season to go and they both would be finished with the NFL.

That evening, Tony took Adrian to dinner at a private club where he was going to introduce Adrian to the owner of the Pittsburgh Steelers, Ned Scott. Tony asked if he was ready to meet the old boy and Adrian nodded his acknowledgment. Scott was joined at his private table with his mother and a young blonde woman whose back was turned to Tony and Adrian.

"Ah, Anthony, my boy." Ned reached across the table and shook hands with Tony. He then turned to his friend. "You must be Adrian Christopher. Glad to meet you, son. It's too bad you don't play for us." Ned stood and shook hands with Adrian. "Let me introduce you both to my mother, Elizabeth Cobb, and my youngest daughter, Marianne, who's home for good from school. She's a new UCLA graduate." Adrian instantly recognized the young woman from Hawaii. So did Tony, whose eyes were instantly glazed over in fear that abruptly turned to anger. "Are you all right, Anthony? You've been under a lot of stress lately -- not performing up to your usual, exacting standards." Adrian slapped Tony on the back and he instantly regained his composure.

"Sorry, Mr. Scott. I thought I saw a ghost. Your daughter reminded me . . . looked like someone from my past. Pleasure to meet you, Ms. Scott," Tony said softly. Out of sheer courtesy, he extended his hand.

"Indeed, the pleasure was all mine, Mr. Williams," said Marianne as she squeezed his hand and winked. The anger inside Tony was welling up to explosive proportions. He could have exposed everything on the spot. If the look in his eyes were any indication as to the hatred that he felt for this woman, Marianne would be lucky to remain alive. Adrian could sense his anger and excused himself and Tony. Luckily, dinner was being served at their table.

"So that's the bitch that's been terrorizing you and Shelli. She would have to be Scott's daughter," Adrian muttered to his counterpart across the table. He paused for a moment and then continued. "Maybe I should go tell Scott about his daughter!"

"No way, man! Who's he going to believe? It could backfire on us . . . on me. Just let it go. This shit will be handled some other way," stated Tony, regaining his composure.

"Why don't you resign tonight and get the hell out of Pittsburgh? She's up to no good and will be nothing but trouble for you and Shelli. Hell, man. Why don't we both retire tonight and quit this scene?" Adrian was ranting on, and now Tony had to calm him down.

"Let's just play for the balance of the season as we agreed and get out of the NFL. There's no sense in throwing away more than a million dollars between us. That'll cover at least five years of salary for the three of us in our new firm." Adrian cooled down and agreed with his friend.

"Why don't we forget about dinner and head straight to your house so we can brainstorm with Shelli? She needs to know everything and be in on the planning for the balance of the season. Besides, I could use the rest."

Railroaded!

"I'll go call Shelli and tell her what's happening. We can use her as an excuse for our departure," stated Tony. Tony got up from the table and went to call Shelli. On his return, they both smiled and went over to Mr. Scott and apologized for their hasty and unexpected early departure. Despite the fact that Marianne stood next to her father, neither of the two athletes looked at her.

Marianne Scott knew she was in trouble because these two guys were not the usual air-headed jocks she had relentlessly screwed so many times before. No athlete had ever turned down her sexual requests before or embarrassed her in front of her friends. Tony would serve as an example of what happened to guys who dared to put her down. Ever since that night in Hawaii, Marianne had become obsessed with making Tony's life, as well as that of his pretty wife, nothing less than miserable.

Adrian Christopher had not figured into her plan for the evening of cornering Tony into another compromising situation. Both men were well-documented intellectuals who together would figure out how to resolve the threat she posed. As she put her wine glass to her frosty pink lips, Marianne slyly smiled at the challenge. She was not finished and decided to turn up the heat before they exposed her egregious attempt at homewrecking to her father.

At the Williams residence, the lights burned long into the night. Adrian suggested that Shelli should attend every game, whether at home or away, without fail, retrieve Tony personally after every practice or team meeting, and never let him be seen in public without her on his arm. Adrian had become like a brother and she trusted his judgment implicitly. Tony also agreed with this strategy.

Marianne drove by the Williams house at 2:00 A.M. and noticed that the house was abuzz with activity. This meant that the three were planning their strategy for dealing with her incursion into Tony's life. This activity meant that a battle was being planned. She also had to prepare, as her time was running out. With the lights of her black Corvette turned off, she carefully left Woodfield Hills and headed back to her townhouse to prepare her own game plan.

●●●●●●

During the first NFL preseason game on Thursday night, despite being suited up, Adrian did not play. Tony did play because his training camp had been rather poor. He played through three quarters of the game without incident. In the fourth quarter, the unraveling of Tony's life began.

The Bronco quarterback signaled a routine and unimaginative second-down play. It called for a swing-out pass to the wide receiver on the left side, who would drop back three yards behind the line of scrimmage to receive the football. The running back and tight-end on the left side would provide blocking for advancing the wide receiver, now turned a running back. Tony read the play and called for the strong safety to advance and fill the gap behind the cornerback on the defensive right side. Tony, from his free safety position, would add extra speed in the backfield should there be any failed tackles. The center snapped the ball and Tony started zeroing in on the wide receiver from his position on the defensive left side. In what was only an instant, Tony felt his back explode into pain as if it had been broken in two. He sustained a blind-side, illegal, crack-back block from the second Bronco running back, who had circled around behind him from the offensive right side. Tony went down hard and didn't see the yellow flags that flew into the air. Ned Scott, watching on a closed-circuit television set in his private club, stood up and started ranting like a mad man at the egregious play that had felled his star defensive back. Marianne, sitting with him, only smirked. "I'll be back, Daddy." She kissed her father on the cheek and left the club.

Adrian, from the Broncos' sidelines, ran straight onto the field and hovered over his friend, who was lying on his side, unable to move. In an apparently semiconscious state Tony asked, "Mind if we cut the season a little short, Adrian?" Tony grimaced in pain as the trainers arrived.

"Hold on, Tony. Just hold on." Adrian was beside himself in anger. In the stands, thousands were on their feet, infuriated at the devastation of the illegal block. The fifteen-yard penalty was not sufficient. Without hesitation, a stretcher was delivered onto the field and was used to transport Tony to the locker room for immediate x-rays. Adrian went back to the Bronco's bench and got permission to go to the Steelers' locker room to check on his friend.

Railroaded!

The results of the x-rays were very encouraging. No broken bones were found, but there seemed to be a compressed vertebral disc. There would be no more football for this man. The trainers iced his back for a while and then helped him get into the whirlpool, where he would languish in the warm waters for an hour or so. They would check on the injury tomorrow with the orthopedic specialist and make a determination as to what should be done.

"Adrian, this is the first game of the preseason. Why did that asshole hit me like that?" Tony asked in a groggy state. He had been given an injection of a drug to numb the throbbing pain in the middle of his back. "Look at the films. He was totally out of the play. He came after me intentionally. Find out why -- he's your teammate." The thought of an intentional hit to seriously hurt his friend really angered Adrian.

"I'll be back after the game is over. Be cool, man. Just be cool and keep your mouth shut. Let the painkillers do their magic and rest easy before you get into the whirlpool. I'll get Shelli and fill her in." Shelli was waiting outside the locker room door. Adrian, at Tony's request, told her to go on home and take care of the kids. Her husband would take a cab home after being treated by the team doctors. Shelli reluctantly complied.

Adrian should have gone back to the Broncos' bench. Instead, he went to the coach's booth and asked if he could see a replay of the block that put Tony out of the game. The offensive coordinator acknowledged that the rookie who made the block was so far out of position that, if he didn't know better, it almost looked like an intentional hit. Someone was out to get Tony, but why? Tony played one of the roughest games in the world and always made sure his hits were clean and noninjurious to the receiving party. He preferred speed and finesse to brute force. Adrian was going to find out why.

After the game, Adrian stormed into the Broncos' locker room and confronted the rookie running back. First, Adrian knocked him against the lockers and then punched him squarely in the nose. "What the fuck were you doing . . . trying to kill that man?" Adrian hovered over him and put his finger right in his face. "You've played the game for seven years, high school and college. I was in on your recruitment from UCLA. You never did anything that stupid before, so why now?" Adrian was screaming at the top of his lungs. The rookie, in a fit of anger, lunged at Adrian, who used his agility to duck out of the way. A major fight was about to erupt, when the head coach walked in and broke it up.

"Pack your things, Johnson. There's no place for you on this team as a Denver Bronco." The rookie hung his head as he walked to a payphone in a quiet corner and made a telephone call. He then showered alone, quickly packed, and left the stadium. Outside, a black Corvette waited for him. The passenger's window lowered and a soft voice told him to get in. A gloved hand offered a large envelope to the displaced player. Inside was $350,000 in cash to cover the rookie's first-year earnings. Now he had to disappear for at least one year. The rookie was satisfied. Hanging out with and screwing the daughter of an NFL team owner had finally paid off.

After a short team meeting, Adrian was about to return to the Pittsburgh locker room when it dawned on him that the dismissed rookie was from UCLA. There had to be a connection between Ned Scott's daughter and this mock assassin. Adrian ran out of the facility, but he was already gone. Frustrated, he ran to the Pittsburgh locker room to check on Tony, who was now in the whirlpool. He seemed more alive but was still in a lot of pain. Adrian told him that he would sit there with him until it was time to go home. Tony thanked his friend but told him to go on home with his team. He would be all right. Besides, they had to follow up on their plan. Having a compressed vertebral disc would be a sufficient reason to allow him to accelerate his retirement from the game. He would make the announcement on Monday and forego playing the last year of his contract -- with full pay for being on the disabled list.

Adrian called Shelli and told her that indeed, Tony was going to take a cab home after finishing in the whirlpool and receiving a light topical massage from one of the trainers. It was very late and there would be no need for her to come all the way back into town to pick him up. Adrian bade Shelli goodbye and then called the taxicab company himself. He ordered two cabs, one for him to go to the airport immediately to catch the team flight back to Denver and one to take Tony home. The pickup for Tony was scheduled for 1:00 A.M.

Railroaded!

"You take care of yourself and that beautiful wife of yours. The guy who hit you is no longer on the team. The coach cut him immediately. At least that's some vindication for what happened to you. I also got in a pretty good lick. My hand still hurts a bit, but his nose is no better off for it." Tony laughed a bit and thanked Adrian for his concern and protectiveness. "By the way, that asshole was from UCLA, and I'll bet there is a connection between him and the infamous Ms. Scott."

"So you think this whole affair was deliberate, Adrian?" Tony grimaced in pain as he repositioned himself on the table.

"I do. I think she still has a grudge and used that guy to draw attention away from herself. Your credibility is beyond reproach, so she has to make things look as if she had nothing to do with it, especially in the eyes of her daddy."

"You may have something there, Adrian. But for now, get out of here so you won't miss your flight home. Later, asshole! Call me in the morning, okay?"

"No sweat, asshole. Just make sure you keep your butt in one piece." Adrian patted his friend on the shoulder and waved good-bye to the trainer. He left the training facility to find a waiting taxicab. He made it to the plane as the rest of the members of his team were boarding. As he settled into his seat, a sense of foreboding came over him. He looked at his watch. It was 12:45 A.M., just about time for Tony to go home. Adrian inquired as to whether there was a phone on board the plane. The flight attendant told him that one hadn't yet been installed. Adrian returned to his seat and tried to relax.

The not-so-speedy "Flash" Williams was barely able to walk with crutches and, at precisely 1:00 A.M., left the stadium. After being helped into the limousine, he said "later" to the trainer, who stayed behind to turn out the facility lights.

● ● ● ● ● ●

Ned Scott was watching the game on closed-circuit television at his private club. He was pleased with the report that his prized defensive athlete was going to be okay. Everything being equal, Ned thought that Tony Williams would be able to play the last half of the season . . . especially ready for the play-offs. Ned silently wished that he could put out a contract for the demise of the Broncos rookie who had stripped his team of its greatest defensive threat for at least ten games. As he sipped his Beefeater® Martini, he noticed that his daughter, who had just returned, seemed a bit anxious. It was probably nothing more than the fact that it was late. She probably wanted to get to the after-parties that were post-game standards for wild entertainment. After all, the Steelers had defeated the Broncos 28 - 19 after a major fourth-quarter comeback. Two touchdowns were scored after Tony had been hit. "What expensive-assed motivation!" Ned thought to himself.

Ned was getting very tired now and called a cab. He had already sent the limo to the training facility to take Tony home. He didn't want to entrust Anthony to a cab company and have something else happen. Besides, it was indeed too late for Shelli to drive back into town and pick him up. Marianne, however, had different ideas. "Daddy, could you call the limo driver and have him pick me up here at the club before he takes Mr. Williams home? That way I can go on to some of the victory parties afterward and you don't have to worry about me drinking and driving."   Ned Scott looked at his watch, then looked at his daughter and thought what it would be like to be her age again. He made the call at 1:03 A.M.

Chapter 5

Tony was not surprised to find the owner's limo waiting for him. Ned Scott customarily sent injured players home in his car after home games. The chauffeur dismissed the waiting cab and closed the door after Tony was situated inside. As he pulled out of the lot, the telephone rang in the car. After a brief conversation, the driver informed Tony that they would be making a slight detour to the club and then head directly for his home. He nodded his approval and estimated it would be an hour before he got home. Tony asked the driver to call his wife and inform her as to the estimated arrival time so she would be waiting at the door. He instantly complied. Tony figured he could take a quick nap to forget about the pain radiating though his back. He closed his eyes and drifted off to sleep.

The limo pulled up in front of the club at 1:15 A.M. Waiting inside the vestibule were Mr. Scott and his daughter, Marianne. She kissed her father goodbye and got into the waiting limousine. The door was closed behind her and the black Lincoln drove off into the night, headed for the Anthony Williams home.

Tony was still asleep. Marianne, in full view of the driver, pulled up her dress, took off her panties, and straddled Tony. She held his head in her hands and kissed him passionately. Tony awoke instantly and, in a wide-eyed rage, threw the vixen off him. "What the hell are you doing? Are you crazy? Stay away from me!" He motioned to the driver to stop the car and demanded to be let out.

"But I have my instructions, sir," yelled the driver. "Mr. Scott will be . . ."

"Damn Mr. Scott, and damn this daughter of his. Just let me out!"

"Calm down, Tony, and just remember the good time we had in Hawaii," said Marianne in a seductive manner. "You said you loved screwing me. You said you loved me. So I came home to be with you."

Tony was totally enraged and threatened to kill the driver if he didn't stop the car and let him out. In fear, the driver tried to call his boss, but he wasn't home yet. Finally, yet reluctantly, the driver complied, swinging left and pulling the car over on an empty street next to a phone booth. Tony struggled to get out, not thinking about the pain in his back. Marianne was hanging all over him and also got out of the car. Tony pushed her away, but she persisted until he, in a fit of rage, slapped her, knocking her to the ground. He got to the phone and called Shelli immediately. Tony told his wife that this wild woman had gone off the deep end and to come get him now. Shelli, fully enraged, grabbed the car keys and left the house in her robe, not wanting to waste any time.

Tony told the driver, who had witnessed everything, to collect "the trash" and take it home. Marianne, who had regained her footing, refused to go with the chauffeur. The driver, not wanting to be implicated in anything, instead quickly left the scene. Marianne continued her sexually-driven advances until she noticed that the limousine was out of sight. Then, like an evil sorceress, she backed away for a moment and instantly changed from seductress to viper.

"No one spurns me and gets away with it, you black bastard! Your ass is going to pay for what you did to me -- the embarrassment you caused me in Hawaii!" With these words, she charged Tony, knocking him to the ground and further aggravating his injury. She kicked him twice in the side and once between his shoulder blades. With eyes glaring, she said, "You're going to pay, motherfucker!" She ran down the darkened street and got into a waiting car, which, without lights, disappeared into the night.

Tony, now half-crazed, was on the ground in front of the phone booth, writhing in excruciating pain. Fifteen minutes later, Shelli found him in the same position. She helped him crawl to the car and then supported him while he got into the backseat. They drove straight home without a detour. Shelli tried to call Ned Scott at

Railroaded!

home, but there was no answer. Ned had decided to spend the night with a casual acquaintance.

●●●●●●

During the drive home, Tony recounted everything to Shelli. She cringed at the thought that he had hit the woman to stop her onslaught and that the assault was witnessed by the driver. But it was probably better that he did. If Shelli had been there, she would have done everything short of killing her. At 2:10 A.M., they drove into their garage. Shelli helped Tony limp into the house. They would call their attorney in the morning. Despite the pain medication, sleep was fleeting for Tony. Shelli spent a restless night contemplating her actions.

A thousand miles away and flying at 35,000 feet, Adrian finally relaxed and drifted off to sleep. Not more than five minutes earlier, Shelli and Tony had safely arrived home. The injured gladiator had returned to the safety of his castle.

●●●●●●

Later that morning, Tony's world collapsed even further. He was actually feeling better but could only walk around on crutches. Shelli dubbed him Tony "the Snail" Williams and set him down at the kitchen table for breakfast. As they were finishing, the doorbell rang and Shelli went to answer it. There were four patrol cars parked in front of their home and a throng of uniformed police officers standing at the stairs with hands positioned on their weapons.

"Are you Mrs. Williams?" questioned one officer.

"What is this all about?" Shelli returned the question.

"Is your husband available, ma'am?" retorted the officer.

"For what reason?" Shelli was starting to get angry at the cat-and-mouse routine of the police officer. The officer continued and had to force the words.

"We have a warrant for his arrest -- for the battery and rape of one, Marianne Scott." Shelli, normally the coolheaded one, exploded.

"That little bitch has been stalking my husband for months, and now she thinks she's going to get away with this. Never! Never! Never!" She turned to Tony who was approaching the door in his snail's pace and said, "Go get dressed, honey. That white bitch daughter-of-the-owner has freaked out and has accused you of beating and raping her. She's gone too far this time. We'll get to the bottom of this real damn fast." She turned to the policeman and ordered him to dispatch the cars from the neighborhood. "One car is enough to escort us to the police station." She also told them to make sure that the bitch was available and so was Mr. Scott when they got there. Shelli, already dressed, went into further action. It was time to round up the troops. War had been declared, and she assumed the duties of field general.

First, she called Adrian and told him what happened. Adrian would be on the next flight out. Next, she called their family attorney, Dave Robinson, a junior partner at the law firm of Johnson, Owens, Sutter & Moss, one of the most prestigious law firms in Pittsburgh. Dave Robinson was one of Errol's classmates, who had done everything on a super-fast track at Dartmouth College. He had graduated in three years and then had gone on to complete law school at New York University in three years with a Juris Doctor degree and Master of Laws degree in Taxation. He handled all of their financial affairs, working closely with Errol. Dave Robinson listened intently to Shelli, dropped everything he was doing, and said he would be right over in not more than twenty minutes with a colleague who would handle the criminal matter.

Next, Shelli called her best friend at the local NBC affiliate and setup a press conference for 2:00 P.M. She wasn't about to let the richest family in Pittsburgh get a leg up on her husband and destroy him because of a nymphomaniacal lust on the part of one of its daughters. Next, she called Tony's parents and her parents. Then she called Errol and left a message for him. Last, she called Ned Scott, but the secretary informed her that he was not taking calls in light of the developing events. This action was on the advice of the family's attorneys.

So the battle lines were being drawn. Shelli was prepared. Now she had to keep Tony in line. His childhood fears resurfaced and were so great that he now feared everything. She helped Tony from

Railroaded!

the bathroom to the bedroom to get dressed. She hugged her husband and ordered him to hold himself together. "Don't you dare let this madness get you down. You've got to focus on getting well. In the meantime, our lawyers will take care of everything. We'll get through this mess together and come out unscathed." She helped him sit at the foot of the bed and assisted him in getting dressed. As she put on his socks, she continued to admonish her husband. "No matter what happens, you keep your chin up and trust your inner strength, as well as my resolve and fortitude. This is going to be a test of our collective strength to bring down that goliath bitch who's attacked our peace."

After a few moments, Shelli went back downstairs, where she directed the two impatient police officers to the kitchen. Despite being angered at their presence, Shelli, being the gracious hostess, served them coffee. Moments later, she was back upstairs helping her husband descend the stairs. Dressed in a dark suit and dark paisley tie, Tony slowly made his way to the library, where he sat and chatted with their attorney, Mr. Robinson, and his colleague, senior partner Raymond Sutter, who had just arrived.

Raymond Sutter was the best criminal defense attorney in Pittsburgh. He had recently again achieved notoriety when he successfully defended a bank president against charges of mis-appropriation of funds, embezzlement, and bribery. The entire issue was one of entrapment. The prosecution thought they were going to railroad this prominent businessman into a quick jail term after being set up to take a fall by the FBI that was out on a customary witch hunt. They hadn't counted on the likes of Raymond Sutter, who, after ten years as an assistant U.S. Attorney, knew most of the games played by the FBI. He had tired of government practice and was wooed away by a private law firm which instantly made him a senior partner. This man was unorthodox, cool under fire, and always looking for the edge. His motto was simple and direct, "Don't go for the jugular – cut it!"

The two attorneys listened to everything that had happened. Raymond knew this was not going to be an easy matter to resolve, but eventually it should be cleared up. It all depended on whether old man Scott was going to take the word of his known-to-be scuzzy daughter or listen to the facts of how a totally moral, honest, and intelligent black man had been framed by a white woman for spurning her sexual advances. Everything would be clear after he got a copy of the warrant and complaint from the District Attorney's office. He called his office to organize this request immediately and to have the documentation waiting for him when he and his client arrived at the police station. He instructed Dave Robinson to return to the office and coordinate activities from there. Shelli called him a cab, and fifteen minutes later he was on his way.

Tony finally calmed down and regained his composure. Shelli was actually pleased because she could see that, as he recounted the events in Hawaii and how his wife had received the stalking letters, he was now starting to get angry. It was the anger at the injustice that would carry him through this whole mess. Tony remembered his readings in Sun Tzu's *The Art of War* and decided that it was necessary to take a completely offensive posture and overwhelm the enemy -- overwhelm the enemy with brutal honesty and factual morality.

The officers were getting a little antsy, but Mr. Sutter told them to just cool their jets. This was no ordinary case. Besides, Tony had agreed to go to the station and be booked on the charges, knowing full well that the whole situation was a sick joke. Just then, the phone rang and Shelli answered it. "Hi, Adrian. Where are you?"

"I'm at Stapleton Airport. My flight departs in fifteen minutes. I'll arrive in Pittsburgh at 3:50 P.M. Should I take a cab to wherever, or is someone going to pick me up?" After a moment of inquiry, Mr. Sutter agreed that a car from his firm would pick up Adrian and have information as to where everyone would be. "How's Tony?"

"His anger over this whole mess has blocked the issue of his painful injuries. He's livid at being abused by the witch and ready for a war," answered Shelli.

"Good. We have to keep him in this position so he doesn't focus on his childhood experience with the Klan. Besides, we've got to fight a whole different type of Klan now. Can I talk to him for a moment?" Shelli handed Tony the phone. "Hey, Duck. First, you get hit by a half-crazed rookie, and then you get blind-sided by a sex-crazed bitch. I bet the next time you see a white

woman coming after your butt at full steam, you will DUCK!"
Tony laughed at his friend's remarks. "Anyway, that witch doesn't
know who she's messing with. She's got to fight three of us."

"With you and Errol as my best friends, my enemies are toast.
I appreciate your coming back so quickly, Adrian."

"Listen, I'm sure that rookie has something to do with this
whole affair. On the plane last night I explained the situation to
Coach Stiller, and he said he would put out a *'be-on-the-lookout-
for'* bulletin with all the team offices. When he surfaces, we'll nail
his butt and get to the bottom of this once and for all." Tony
thanked his friend for his support. "By the way, I talked to Errol
a few minutes ago and he should be arriving there late tonight.
He's driving over. He'll just come straight to the house.
Independently, he can do some digging for us if need be.
Remember his nose for details."

"You guys really are great. I couldn't have better friends in the
whole world."

"Hey, just remember that we three swore an allegiance to each
other through thick and thin till death, dude . . . and you ain't
kicking the bucket no time soon. Got to go. Later, asshole!" Tony
acknowledged the salutary "asshole" and hung up the phone. The
fact that his two best friends were coming to his aid increased his
strength. Shelli noticed his change of demeanor and was pleased,
as well as relieved, that the entire burden of sorting through this
sordid affair would not rest entirely on her shoulders.

"It's time to go slay a dragon for the honor of my Lady!" Tony
stood up and ushered everyone out of the house. He did not ride
downtown in the police cruiser.

●●●●●●●●●

The caravan of one police car and two private cars arrived at the
courthouse to find a throng of reporters waiting. Raymond Sutter
got out of his car and quickly intervened. Questions were fired
from every direction as the two policemen escorted Tony into the
Allegheny County Courthouse, which looked more like a dark
fifteenth century prison than a judicial center. Mr. Sutter told the
group that a news conference would be held later and that the whole

matter, which was nothing more than a tragic joke gone awry, would be cleared up in short order.

Inside the main interior courtyard, the affair took another turn for the worse when Tony came face-to-face with Marianne Scott. She was screaming and raving. "There he is! That's the man who did this to me! He said he loved me; instead he beat me and raped me!" Tony, Shelli, and Raymond Sutter were all stunned. Marianne had indeed been beaten. Her face was black and blue; one eye was swollen shut from multiple blows and her lips were broken and swollen. How could this be? Tony had slapped her only once to get her off him. What the hell was going on? In the face of this new development, Tony tried to remain calm but instead exploded. He propped himself on one crutch and pointed the other at his accuser.

"I don't know who beat you or raped you as you claim. But whoever did has played a sick joke on you. And you're trying to use that to get at me. Why don't we tell the reporters the whole story right now? Why don't we expose the truth right now so the world can see what you really are? Why don't we expose your real motives, Ms. Scott?" The fire leapt from Tony's eyes as he repositioned himself on his crutches. The reporters were silent after Tony's outburst. Marianne backed off for just a moment but then, as if on cue, rose to the challenge and screamed hysterically.

"I'll get you! My daddy will get you! He won't let you get away with this!" The act was very convincing to most in the large hall except for Raymond Sutter and his client. Sutter recognized the play-acting and knew that this case had to be fought "fire-with-fire." He pulled Tony and Shelli aside to discuss his strategy.

"I'm willing to bet that this little girl is all show and no go. I'm also willing to bet that if we expose everything we know, every aspect of this case in the press conference, then we can throw enough cold water on her to cause her to change her tune and fess up to what is the real story. This strategy is like trying the case in public before we even get to court. With opponents the likes of the Scott family, we might as well use every cannon we have and take advantage of every preemptive strike we can." Tony and Shelli agreed.

Railroaded!

Anthony Williams was led to a small room next to the prisoner receiving area where he was photographed and fingerprinted. The whole process took not more than ten minutes. He was then placed in a holding chamber along with seven other men. Raymond Sutter, at the same time, had arranged a 2:00 P.M. arraignment before Allegheny County Court Judge Gerald O'Connor. Shelli went to work and changed the news conference to 4:00 P.M. in order to allow sufficient time for the arraignment proceedings.

Chapter 6

In the Allegheny County District Attorney's office, there was a virtual mutiny in process. None of the regular staff prosecutors wanted to touch this case with a ten-foot pole. On the one hand, you had a plaintiff who was a daughter of the richest family in Pennsylvania. On the other hand, you had a defendant who was a national sports hero, super athlete, devoted family man, brilliant scholar and architect, as well as a renowned community activist. To make matters even worse, he was popular enough to run for governor and win!

As was usual in matters of staff defection, the shoe fell on the most junior associate prosecutor, who had just been hired after graduating from the University of Pennsylvania Law School in Philadelphia and passing the bar exam in February on his second attempt. Joseph (Joey) Kearns wore bifocal glasses that gave him a rather "nerdish" appearance. He was a five-foot eight-inch, wiry and wimpish-looking person with no physical presence whatsoever. He had been rather sickly as a child. He hated athletes in general, especially football players. This was his golden opportunity to show his mettle, a chance for David to bring down Goliath. After successfully handling his first trial just two weeks before, an assault and rape case, Joey Kearns gladly accepted the challenge.

He quickly interviewed the victim and decided on an initial strategy. At the arraignment, he would seat the victim next to him in full view of the judge as an intimidation factor. After all, a defendant had the right to face his accuser. He then received a call from Ned Scott.

"I understand that you will be handling the case against Mr. Williams."

"I am, sir. What can I do for you?"

Railroaded!

"Just find out the truth and do it quickly. I can't afford the problems this situation may have upon my team. If he is guilty, hang his butt. But if he's innocent, I want to know now."

"Based upon your daughter's recounting of the facts and crimes committed, it seems that a full-blown prosecution of Mr. Williams is in order. Based on her positive identification of the perpetrator, we can bypass a grand jury hearing for determination as to an indictment. At this point, the facts seem to speak for themselves."

"Then so be it. Hang his ass for what he did to my daughter. Just do it quickly!"

"Are you coming to the arraignment, Mr. Scott?"

"No, Mr. Kearns, I'm not. This whole mess has already turned into a media circus and Williams's wife has called a press conference at 4:00 P.M. God knows what they'll say. With that wild man, Sutter, as their attorney, be careful. He's good, virtually impregnable, and definitely unbuyable."

"I believe the case will stand on its own merits, and you and your family won't have to engage in any illegal or unsavory activity to assist the prosecutor's office." Joey Kearns was angry at Scott's arrogance and slammed down the phone. He was good enough to win this case on his own without anyone's help.

●●●●●●

Judge Gerald O'Connor, at age fifty-two, had been a county court judge for thirteen years. He was the stereotypical depiction of a judge: five-feet nine-inches and very rotund, weighing in at two hundred forty pounds. He wore half-moon glasses for reading but let them always rest on his nose. His hair had gone completely gray. Physically, he was indistinguishable from a typical, middle-American "couch potato." Professionally, he liked to get the hard cases, the ones that required intellectual prowess. He had his sights set on being appointed to the Pennsylvania Supreme Court. Maybe this case would provide the boost he needed. Great care would have to be taken to render perfect judgments so as not to anger the richest family in Pennsylvania or the public, which had a long-standing love affair with the defendant.

At precisely 2:00 P.M., he entered the courtroom to the usual "All rise" from the bailiff. The bailiff further announced the case as "People v. Anthony Williams, Case Number CR79-6539." Judge O'Connor sat down, as did everyone else in the courtroom. He looked up at the prosecution and his attention was instantly diverted to the victim, Marianne Scott. What had happened to this woman? Aw shit, he thought. This really is going to be a mess. He put his head in his hand for a moment and then sat back in his high-backed chair.

"Introduce yourself for the record, young man," said the judge to the young prosecutor whom he did not recognize.

"Joseph Kearns, for the People, Your Honor," returned the prosecutor.

"Let the record show that Joseph Kearns has entered his appearance for the People of Pennsylvania, and that the esteemed Mr. Raymond Sutter is appearing for the defendant, the renowned Mr. Anthony Williams."

"Thank you, Your Honor," said Raymond Sutter standing next to his seated client.

"Mr. Kearns, this is an arraignment hearing and nothing more. Please ask the victim to leave now. I will not be distracted by your attempt to influence my judgment." Joey felt a sense of success because, in the acknowledgment of Marianne as a victim, the ball was already rolling in his favor. Joey put his hand on Marianne's shoulder so that she did not move just yet.

"Thank you again, Your Honor." Raymond Sutter was furious at the grandstand attempt of this upstart prosecutor. Seeking to take away any initiative from the prosecution, Mr. Sutter continued. "Your Honor, my client wishes to enter a plea of not guilty to both counts and also seeks to be released on his personal recognizance. Our firm will guarantee his presence at all hearings of whatever nature."

"Objection, Your Honor." Joey Kearns was now very angry. "The People would like bail set at $1,000,000 and will not accept the guarantee of presence by the esteemed firm of Johnson, Owens, Sutter & Moss. The crime committed was a wanton act of terror against the victim. There is substantial physical evidence that points to . . ."

Railroaded!

"This is an arraignment hearing, your Honor, not a pre-trial hearing. The prosecutor is out of order." Raymond Sutter was cutting to the quick.

"Gentlemen, both of you be seated -- now!" The attorneys quickly responded following the judge's instruction. The last thing needed was for things to get out of hand at this stage. Totally unexpectedly, Tony stood up using one of his crutches for support. Judge O'Connor was caught equally by surprise and inquired, "Do you have something to say, young man?"

"I do, Your Honor." This was not planned, but Raymond Sutter, instead of restraining his client, let him proceed. His speaking ability was well documented. Furthermore, Sutter was a bit curious as to what his client was going to say.

"Proceed, Mr. Williams," was the instruction from the bench.

"I am not guilty of the two charges levied against me. Furthermore, I have no knowledge as to why this woman is out to destroy me and my family. Therefore, it's my responsibility, while we mount a vigorous defense, to assist the Prosecution in finding out the truth. Despite the pain I endure from the injury, I will be here at whatever hour for all hearings. I intend to get to the bottom of these allegations and clear my name. If Your Honor feels it is in the best interests of the court to set bail, so be it. Regardless of your ruling, the court will have my undivided attention and cooperation." Raymond Sutter was totally impressed. So was Judge O'Connor. So was Joseph Kearns, recognizing that this defendant was not the usual street scum that appeared through the D.A.'s office. Marianne Scott, however, who had not yet left the courtroom as ordered, was shaking in her seat. She may have really screwed up and totally underestimated her quarry. Joey Kearns felt her tremble as his hand was still on her shoulder.

"Well, Mr. Kearns, since your victim has not left the courtroom as ordered, does she object to the personal recognizance?" Joey Kearns was angry because the momentum had shifted and his ploy was backfiring on him. Not looking at Marianne, he answered.

"The People's request remains the same, Your Honor."

"Very well, the defendant is released on his personal recognizance as guaranteed by the firm of Mr. Sutter. Furthermore, it is in the best interest of the entire community to get this trial going as soon as possible. Based on the nature of the complaint and the facts outlined therein, I will set this case on a fast track. Pre-trial hearings will be held in three weeks on Tuesday, August 21st at 9:00 A.M. The trial will begin two weeks later on Tuesday, the fourth of September, after the Labor Day weekend. Apparently there will not be much discovery needed. Am I correct in this assumption, gentlemen?" Both attorneys nodded their assent. "Fine, then. Mr. Kearns, you may be new to this court, but don't you ever pull a circus stunt like this again."

"I apologize, Your Honor," he said reluctantly, hanging his head.

"Mr. Williams, I hope your back heals in short order from that illegal hit. You're faced with a whole new set of stresses that will demand your best health and full attention."

"Thank you, Your Honor," said Tony.

"This hearing is adjourned." The judge stood and left the bench for the sanctuary of his chambers. Joey Kearns winced at the judge's closing remark to the defendant. Judge O'Connor must be a Steeler fan. He closed his file and left with the victim.

Raymond Sutter turned to his client and shook his hand. Shelli walked up and hugged Tony. They both listened to Raymond's immediate recommendation. "I think we should prepare for the press conference that starts at 4:00 P.M. Let's go to the cafeteria, get a quick snack, and talk it over."

"Good idea, Mr. Sutter. Besides, I need to take a pain pill. My back is killing me." Shelli wanted to put her arm around her husband, "the Snail," but could only watch and walk by his side as they slowly made their way to the cafeteria.

"You know, Anthony, we can always cancel the press conference and reschedule it for later," said Raymond expressing concern for how his client was feeling.

"First, call me Tony, okay?" Raymond smiled and nodded his approval. "Second, we have to stay one leg up on the woman. I get the feeling that the judge is not impressed with this whole matter."

"I got the same impression. He was probably selected for this case because he is one of the most thorough men sitting on the bench in Pittsburgh. I believe we couldn't have a better judge. He

Railroaded!

takes no bullshit from anyone. You remember the case last year of the banker who was set up by the FBI but was finally acquitted of all charges?"

"I remember that case, Tony," Shelli said. "It turned out to be a clear case of the federal government trying to set up a man who legally and regularly bucked the system." Tony acknowledged his recollection of the case.

"Judge O'Connor presided and I was the defense attorney. The judge is one of the best I have ever seen except for the likes of Thurgood Marshall or Hugo Black on the Supreme Court or 'Hang'em High' Cyril Johnston on the U.S. District Court in New York. I once presented a case before him and wasn't fully prepared. He threw me in jail for five days to think about how important it was to be fully prepared as a U.S. Attorney on prosecutorial matters. Since then, I've never lost a case as a prosecutor or defense attorney. Proper planning always prevents piss-poor performance. At least that's what everyone says and I believe it. So, let's plan our strategy for the news conference." Tony and Shelli were impressed with their counselor. They felt that they were in good hands. Tony thought of Errol at Hofstra Law School and knew that his friend would one day be a mirror image of this brilliant and eloquent man.

●●●●●●

The time had come for the press conference. It was going to be held on the steps of the courthouse. Adrian Christopher had arrived on schedule from Denver and was picked up at the airport by Dave Robinson. Loren P. Johnson, the most senior of the partners and founder of Johnson, Owens, Sutter & Moss, was also present and would make a brief opening statement. All in all, this was an impressive show of support for Tony. Collectively, they had decided to present the whole case to the public and take their chances on an unusual frontal-assault strategy. Raymond Sutter was certain that he would be reprimanded by Judge O'Connor but felt that was irrelevant when it came to the destruction of his client's integrity, family, and physical health. And so the die was cast.

Some distance away, Marianne Scott watched from the solace of her sprawling townhouse as the press conference got underway. She was extremely curious as to what was going to be said by this group. The rookie, who had been a long-standing sexual encounter at UCLA, was safely out of the way and, for the moment, very happy with his cash windfall. She believed in her own mind that she had successfully engineered the demise of one of professional football's greatest athletes, the single man who had the audacity not to take advantage of her body. "Hell hath no fury like a woman scorned who's the daughter of the richest man in Pennsylvania," she said to the television set as Loren Johnson stepped up to the podium.

"Ladies and gentlemen of the media, my name is Loren Johnson, senior partner with the law firm of Johnson, Owens, Sutter & Moss. Our firm has been retained to defend one of Pittsburgh's most renowned citizens and forward-thinking community activists. He also happens to be the fastest man in the National Football League and in the world, for that matter. It appears that he has been the target of a very sick joke that has resulted in criminal charges being levied against him. Because of these charges, we have assigned Mr. Raymond Sutter of our firm to defend our client. Mr. Sutter will provide the details." Loren Johnson stepped aside as Raymond Sutter replaced him.

"The star free safety for the Pittsburgh Steelers, Mr. Anthony Williams, has been charged with first-degree battery and with rape." The crowd was basically silent except for the noise from camera motor-drives as photographers took hundreds of pictures. "The problem is that the complainant is none other than Marianne Scott, daughter of the owner of the Pittsburgh Steelers!" Raymond knew that sanctions were imminent because disclosure of the victim's name was supposed to be withheld. However, he felt comfortable in doing so after her scene in the foyer of the courthouse earlier in the day. That would be his defense. She had disclosed her identity, and therefore it was public information. "Our client denies the allegations. Furthermore, it all seems more than a bit incredible especially when just last night at 10:25 P.M., we all witnessed his being carried semiconscious from the playing field on a stretcher after being the recipient of a massive and illegal

Railroaded!

crack-back block from one of the opposing team's players. It appears that Ms. Scott has been intimidating the family of Mr. Williams for several months by sending 'poison pen' letters to his wife, Shelli, in an egregious attempt to wreck their family. Mr. Williams, having done nothing at all to Ms. Scott, decided to handle the matter in a different way. He will now provide the details. Mr. Williams." A rousing round of applause was heard when Tony stepped up to the podium. This seemed more like a college pep rally than a press conference. Propped up on one crutch, Tony lifted his hands to calm the audience.

"Last January, I was selected to play in the Pro Bowl in Honolulu. Two days before the game, my best friend and I attended a party at a private residence on one of the beaches there. During the course of the evening, I was approached by an unknown young woman. She asked if I would engage in sexual relations with her. I forcefully pushed her away and told her no. This act caused her a lot of embarrassment. I chose not to fraternize with any women. However, I did have 'one too many' and decided that it was best to crash and sleep it off rather than drive back to the hotel. As it turns out, the same woman, who assured me of no further sexual advances, led me to an unoccupied bedroom where, fully dressed, I passed out on the bed. The next morning, I awoke to find this same woman sleeping next to me. I had no memory of any further encounter with her since I had passed out. A few moments later, my friend, Adrian Christopher, appeared and together we confirmed that nothing had happened, but we couldn't determine the identity of the woman. I called my wife immediately and informed her of this strange occurrence. We three -- Shelli, Adrian, and I -- determined that it was just an aberration and nothing to worry about. In four years of marriage and four years of freely available sex from women known to surround professional football players, I have never once participated in any act that could even remotely be considered as infidelity to my wife. I have too much respect for her, and my love for her is sufficient that I do not need, nor will I ever need or have the desire, to have casual sexual affairs with other women.

"After returning from Hawaii, all was quiet until Shelli started receiving letters from Los Angeles referencing the party in

Honolulu and stating that this mysterious woman was in love with me after I had supposedly pledged undying love for her. We consulted our attorney but determined there wasn't much that could be done until the person surfaced. The letters became more frequent in the past two months, and the postmark changed to here in Pittsburgh. Again we decided that nothing could be done until the woman surfaced. Last Thursday evening, she surfaced at a dinner party at the private club of Mr. Ned Scott. To my surprise and chagrin, the woman turned out to be Ned Scott's daughter, Marianne. Adrian and I both recognized her.

"At this recognition, Adrian and I both decided that since this was the last year of our contracts, we would retire from professional football rather than risk a public confrontation over an ugly private matter. Originally, we were going to call a press conference to announce that decision. Out of pure respect for Mr. Scott and his family, we had no desire to address such unfathomable issues privately or publicly. Maybe because of our naiveté, we thought that everything would just go away with the announcement that we were retiring at the end of this season. Unfortunately, however, things took a turn for the worse. I sustained the hit that I believe may have reduced my ability to play in the defensive backfield for the Steelers. The trainers believe that I will be out for at least ten games. To further confuse matters, we have reason to believe that Ms. Scott may have an involvement with the running back who performed the illegal block. As you know, that running back, a graduate of UCLA like Ms. Scott, was immediately released from the Denver Broncos. Now I've been wrongly accused of beating and raping Ms. Scott.

"Now, let me tell you what really happened. The crack-back block caused a diagnosed compressed vertebral disc. I was in severe pain and barely able to move. After the administration of physical therapy and pain medication, I was able to be mobile enough, with the use of crutches, to barely walk. I expected to go home in a cab which had been ordered by Adrian. However, Mr. Scott sent his limousine to take me home, a customary procedure injured players after home games. The waiting taxicab was dismissed by the limo driver. En route to my home, I was informed by the driver that he was going to make a stop at Mr. Scott's private

Railroaded!

club. I acknowledged his comment, asked him to call my wife and inform her of our estimated arrival time, and then dozed off to sleep. I awakened to find Ms. Scott on top of me in a sexual straddle while attempting to remove my clothing and force herself on me. I threw her off and demanded the limousine driver to stop the car so I could get out. I got out near a phone booth with the intent of calling my wife to come get me. Ms. Scott, however, got out of the limousine and continued to physically harass me. I admit that I slapped her but only once to stop her vicious onslaught. I called my wife, who arrived some twenty minutes later. After the call, Ms. Scott charged me like a woman possessed and knocked me to the ground. While I was lying there, Ms. Scott kicked me in the side and back and continued her noxious verbal assault. I couldn't move. I lay there until Shelli found me. The limousine driver had already left the scene without Ms. Scott. As I lay on the ground, I saw Ms. Scott get into another car, one with no lights on that must have been tailing us.

"I didn't beat Ms. Scott. I didn't rape Ms. Scott. I have no idea why she is doing this other than for my having turned aside her sexual advances in Hawaii last January. The prosecution is responsible for getting at the truth. Then let's find out the truth as to who perpetrated this crime against Ms. Scott. And to you, Mr. Scott, who have been like a surrogate father, I have more respect for your family than to do something like this. If you believe otherwise, then I have misjudged you.

"To the team, let this be a lesson as to what can happen at those after-parties. There may be unscrupulous women waiting to take advantage of you. Just be careful and think about what you are doing.

"My career in professional football may be over. As a matter of fact, I intended to retire at the end of this season. But maybe it's time for me to embark on a new career, one where I can serve the same people who have supported me for the past five years.

"To my wife and friends, and the people of the city of Pittsburgh, I thank you for your continued support."

Tony received a full, one-minute round of applause from the media corps and the 1,000 odd people who had gathered to hear his presentation. Afterward, he was escorted by Adrian and Shelli to a waiting car. Tony's back felt like it was on fire and tied in a thousand knots. He was relieved to sit down and not have to rely on the crutches for support.

After Shelli got in the car, she looked at her husband incredulously and asked, "So now you want to jump from the frying pan into the fire?" Tony tried to speak, but Shelli put up her hand to stop him. "You just wait till we get your butt home. Wait till Adrian and Errol jump on your raggedy behind. Your back isn't the only thing that may need surgery!"

●●●●●●

Across town, Marianne Scott was a nervous wreck. She had really messed with the wrong guy. This man was just as powerful as her dad, though not so monetarily. He was the "Darling of Pittsburgh." She called her grandmother, and in tears said, "Grandma, I need to talk to you. I need some help. Things have gotten out of hand and I don't know what to do."

"Now, now, Marianne. You just calm yourself down and get over here immediately. You can tell me everything and I'll make sure that your father fixes everything. Just leave it to me." Elizabeth Cobb hung up the phone and then turned off the television set. She was infuriated that this incident was being played to the media's insatiable appetite for scandal and lurid details. But, being from the old Southern school of thought, the elder Cobb believed there was no place in society for an "uppity negra." This Williams boy had maligned her granddaughter and the family name; and for that, he would pay.

Chapter 7

The Friday afternoon news conference seemed to have worked its magic. The three network news programs each featured editorials about how this entire event had to be a sick joke -- that Ms. Scott must have been engaged with someone else, a person of unsavory character, and was looking to cover her "inappropriate behavior" by trying to throw the blame elsewhere. In each case, she was chastised for targeting such an upstanding man of the community, whom everyone in the world saw take an "assassination-type blow" on national television. The likelihood of rape by her accused after sustaining such injuries was absolutely non-credible. The Sunday morning editions of the "Pittsburgh Press" and "Post Gazette," aside from an abundance of editorial commentary, even featured a syndicated cartoon caricature of the incident. One featured Tony lying on the ground in full football uniform and being the victim of a collision with Marianne Scott, dressed in a skimpy football uniform with a freight train as a logo.

Ned Scott saw and read it all. Sunday morning was not peaceful. Instead, he was infuriated that he was caught in the middle of the biggest scandal in Pittsburgh history. In his heart, he knew that Anthony was not the type of man who would commit such personal atrocities. Yet his daughter had been beaten. The external bruises and cuts were clear evidence of an attack. He read and reread the reprinted speech that Anthony had given at the press conference. In his heart, he knew that something was wrong, terribly wrong with this whole mess. He had watched the man get almost torn in two by the illegal block, so how could he have done this? It just didn't seem possible. Anthony and Shelli had been over to his home many times and he had always regarded him as the epitome of morality, stature, and class. Nevertheless, this was his daughter, his own flesh and blood. He had to support her no matter what the consequences. Either way, Ned Scott dreaded the outcome and felt a sense of personal loss.

As he sat at the kitchen table with his head in his hands, a different problem arose. "Ned, what are you going to do about this undue attention that the family is getting? And over some nigra football player who has raped and beaten my granddaughter?" Elizabeth Cobb was in high form, totally enraged. "Have you read the newspapers this morning? The news programs on every channel called Marianne everything but a street whore! Dammit, Ned. We can't let the Scott family name get stomped into the mud. We've worked too hard to get where we are. Your great-great grandfather was a major plantation owner in Mississippi. He never had any such problems with nigras then. Your grandfather turned all the slaves loose with that Emancipation Proclamation by Lincoln. Your father sold the land and moved us here to Pennsylvania and bought another smaller farm. You even remember the day when he struck oil in the corn patch. You were with him and came back to the house all covered in black. I thought the old tractor had exploded. The challenge then was to try and keep it secret until he could buy up all the land surrounding the farm. He did, and look where it got us today. The Scott family is the largest land developer in Pennsylvania and owners of the Pittsburgh Steelers. And now you're going to let some high-brow nigra destroy everything we've worked for because he couldn't keep his pecker in his pants?"

"Ma, listen to me." Ned reared back in his chair and caught himself before he flipped it over. "Don't start the old family tree stuff again. Something's not right here, and I just want to find out what in the world it is." Elizabeth Cobb walked over to her son, stood over him and glared while shaking her finger in his face.

"No, you listen to me, Ned Scott! You do whatever it takes to destroy that boy and restore the good name of Marianne and our family."

The anger inside Ned was increasing and he really wanted to tell his mother to get lost. Instead, he hesitated and responded with a weak "yes, ma'am." Seemingly satisfied, Elizabeth Cobb left the breakfast area without having anything to eat, thereby killing a long-

Railroaded!

standing family tradition dating back more than one hundred seventy-five years.

Ned went out to question the chauffeur and have him take him to Marianne's townhouse. Howard was not there. Apparently he had taken Ned's mother somewhere.

●●●●●●

"Where to, Mrs. Cobb?"

"First, just drive me to the stadium. I don't go there much and I'd like to walk around it while its empty. Afterward, you can take me to Marianne's. By the way, you are to pay strict attention to what Marianne tells you and no one else about the events of last Friday night."

"What about Mr. Scott?"

"Of course, you do what he tells you. I'm talking about the incident with that boy the other night. Besides, I hired you thirty-five years ago when it wasn't even fashionable to have a white man as a driver. I hired you because I knew that I could always trust your vision and judgment."

"Thank you, Mrs. Cobb. I understand, and you can count on me to tell it just like I saw it . . . when the time comes." Howard was disappointed that he would have to stretch the truth. But couldn't go against the family. His family was totally dependent on the Scotts for income, housing, schooling for his daughter, everything. He actually hated being caught in the middle between Ned and his mother.

"And by the way, Howard, I want you to take this check to the bank tomorrow and use it to pay off the balance on your BankAmericard. I noticed that it seems to be strikingly close to your limit." She handed Howard a folded check which, out of courtesy, he didn't examine. Instead, he immediately put it in his inside jacket pocket. He knew that his limit was $7,500.00 and his balance was $6,950.00. This would take a little pressure off his family, allowing Saundra, his wife of thirty years, to do some much-needed clothes shopping.

"Thank you very much, Ms. Cobb. Saundra will be very happy also."

"Don't mention it, Howard. You're a fine upstanding man."

Elizabeth Cobb sat back in the rear seat of the stretch Lincoln and knew that Ned would cave in on matters surrounding this Williams boy. As far as she was concerned, he treated this nigra too much like a son instead of the chattel property that he was. Arriving at Three Rivers Stadium, she left Howard in the car and went in just to walk. After walking around for a while, she sat in the stands thinking of her late husband, Charles. She talked aloud, "I know you were sometimes a vicious man, Charles. But I hope that our son doesn't throw away everything we built over some nigra because he and Judy, God rest her soul, never had a son. I don't know what it is about you Scott men. You both always were compassionate toward the 'colored,' but I never could figure out why." She didn't notice the figure who had come in and seated himself six rows behind her.

"Because without them, you wouldn't be sitting here today." Ned had gone to the stadium and noticed the limo out front. "Do you think for an instant that our ancestors could have found enough honest white people to man the plantation in Mississippi? Do you think that Dad could have accomplished what he did here in Pennsylvania without black people? No damned way. You have everything you want in the world because of their helping our family, especially in hard times. And I don't treat my players as slaves either. Sure they can be traded and sold to other teams, but not like it was in the old days. Thank God I don't have the hatred inside that you do. I know that you found out that Dad was having an affair with a black woman who worked at his oil company." Elizabeth Cobb was stunned at this revelation. "I know that you had her fired and sent away, which broke Dad's heart. He had long since lost you to the glitz of high society in Pennsylvania. You were reliving childhood stories of the South while he just wanted life to be simple in the midst of his enormous success. You turned your back on him and then kicked him in the teeth. He became a vicious businessman after you stole his heart." Ned was in a virtual rage. "So, no problem, Mother. We'll do it your way. I am a Scott and I will defend the family name. But if Marianne has turned out to be a common slut, then she will pay dearly for what she has done. But if she's right, then Anthony will feel my wrath like no one else in this world!" He turned and started walking up the steps, but paused for a moment. Turning back from his new vantage point, he said, "And may God have mercy on your hateful soul."

●●●●●●

Across town, things were a bit more lively. The Sunday editorials had cut Marianne to shreds and the Williams family was reveling in the positive press coverage. Tony was still moving around like a snail, but the pain wasn't as intense. Shelli was also a bit more cheerful, feeling that despite whatever the Scott family could or might throw at them, public opinion at least was on the side of her husband.

As she fixed breakfast, Shelli marveled at the comradery of these three men. Sitting at the breakfast table, she realized that they hadn't been together in one place since January 1978 when the Broncos played Pittsburgh in the AFC playoffs. Tony and Adrian had squared off against each other on the field while Errol sat with Shelli and watched from the stands at Mile High Stadium in Denver. Errol had come home for the Christmas holidays after completing his first semester of law school. It turned out to be a perfect reunion.

"I guess the world is finally going to see that Scott wench for what she really is -- a scraggly nymphomaniac who can't live without you know what!" Adrian slapped hands with Tony on that one while everyone else was laughing aloud. Adrian was glad to see the public support of Tony. He knew that without it, his life would be one uphill battle after another.

"Maybe we should ship her to 42nd Street in New York. At least there she could get paid well for her habit," added Tony. All three men again erupted in laughter. Even Shelli was laughing, despite the negative reference.

"You guys are terrible," injected Shelli playfully. "Eat your breakfast before it gets cold." Despite Errol's participation, he seemed rather removed and distant. "Something's bothering you, Errol. You're not usually this quiet unless that outrageous mind of yours is working overtime. I can see the wheels turning." Errol looked at everyone briefly and then spoke.

"I'm glad that the press is so supportive. That's very important indeed. But just to make sure, you're not serious about the political bullshit, right?" Tony raised his hands as if to acknowledge the error.

"Sorry, I went off the edge. No harm, no foul, okay?" asked Tony.

"All right already!" stated Adrian. "Architecture, not politics, agreed?"

"Agreed!" they said simultaneously.

"But back to basics. Why are you so preoccupied, Errol?" asked Shelli.

"Because this Scott woman is extremely dangerous. Maybe even more so than any of us have imagined."

"We all know you are the smartest and most contemplative of us, Errol, but she's just a piece of trash that didn't get what she wanted from Tony." Adrian was trying to make light of the situation.

"Listen, guys. I've chased women all over the country and pissed off some really mean sisters with some of the things I've done. You guys have been in the NFL for two and four years respectively and have had women chasing your raggedy behinds since Day One. Thank God, at least Tony got married and had sense enough not to indulge in extracurricular pursuits." Shelli put up her hands and scored two points for the home team. "But still they tried anyway, right?" Tony and Adrian both nodded in the affirmative. "Shelli, before you met Tony, that low-life junior basketball player at CU damn near broke your heart. Right?" Shelli rolled her eyes after being reminded of a freshman-year experience that she had long since forgotten. Errol continued. "But, in all these cases, did you ever know of a woman who was willing to have herself beaten and risk permanent physical scars to an attractive and unmarred face, just to get back at a man?" Everyone sat back in their chairs. "I think this woman is the most dangerous thing that collectively we could possibly confront. I think that her motives are guided not only by sexual lust, but also by racial hatred. This thing is wrong, very wrong, and we need to be totally prepared for what may be a long and very bitter fight to prove our side of the story." The room was completely silent as they each contemplated Errol's comments. Adrian's smile disappeared. Tony sat back dejectedly at the prospect of a long battle, however Shelli sat up and confronted Errol.

"In other words, Errol, you're saying that it would be easier to face one of those water moccasins that Tony's always told me about rather than to deal with this witch." Shelli was not deflated by Errol's commentary. She knew a war was brewing.

"At least confronting that snake, you've got a good chance of survival. Just stay out of its striking distance. But this woman -- she is relentless. The deeper this mess gets, the harder and more deadly she'll become. She could have easily walked away from the whole mess at dinner that night. Instead, it's probable that she enlisted the aid of that rookie to get you. When that didn't work, and after the scene in the limo, she went and had someone beat her unmercifully. Personally, I think we should forget what the press says and hunker down for a long campaign. I picked up two extra copies of *The Art of War* from the Walden Books at Roosevelt Field Mall before I left Hempstead. I thought we could review it and refresh our memories with respect to strategic thinking, planning, and maneuvering." He reached into a paper bag that he had set beside his chair and pulled out two new copies of the book. He handed one to each of his friends. "Shelli, you can read my copy. You'll have to excuse the notations in the margins."

Shelli loved the way this man thought. So did Tony and Adrian. After breakfast, Adrian stretched out on the family room floor with his copy of the book, and Tony sat back in his favorite Boston rocking chair to read his. Shelli put the kids down for a nap and retired to her bedroom to pray. Errol changed clothes and went out in the backyard. He dove into the swimming pool and swam several laps, all the time thinking of how to defeat this deadliest of opponents.

Chapter 8

Monday morning. Raymond Sutter awoke early at 5:30 A.M. and immediately hit the floor, fully energized. His dark-chocolate complexion was accentuated by a well-proportioned, but not extraordinary, physique. At five-feet eleven-inches and carrying one hundred eighty pounds, he was comfortable -- but worked hard to maintain this condition. His father had been a portly fellow of two hundred fifty pounds, so Raymond vowed early on never to suffer the same fate. His curly hair was mixed with gray which gave him a very distinguished and sophisticated look.

After a quick set of fifty sit-ups and fifty push-ups, he dressed in sweats and went out for a brisk walk that covered a total of 3.2 miles. As he pounded the pavement, he thought that the events of the past weekend had been unnerving. Maybe he had gone a little too far with the press conference. But in his heart and head, he knew it had been the right thing to do. Whatever the consequences, he would accept them. He struggled with the thought that the so-called victim had allowed herself to be brutally beaten, all for not getting a man to screw her? There had to be some other fact that was deeply hidden. Maybe Tony knew something. Maybe he didn't know anything at all and was just in the wrong place at the wrong time. The bottom line was that the Scotts were going to be nothing less than formidable opponents. The wild card, if there was one, was this new prosecutor. Raymond was sure that Joseph Kearns was going to do everything in his power to make a name for himself. He had already heard the scuttle that no one in the DA's office had wanted to touch this case, so the shoe had fallen on the new guy. Raymond smiled because he knew that's the way it used to happen in the U.S. Attorney's office also. He shook his head and finished his walk.

In the sanctuary of his study, he unlocked a file drawer, opened it, and pulled out a telephone. This was a clean line. He called a number into the data processing room at FBI headquarters.

"Sutter, what are you doing up so early?" said the voice on the other end.

"I know you're a workaholic, Jensen. Always have been and always will be. When are you going to find yourself a man?" asked Raymond.

"I did, but he left me for a big-time private practice." Dorothy Jensen was dead serious. She had been in love with Raymond Sutter for almost seven years. She figured that she could wait a little longer because he was worth it. In the madness of D.C., there weren't too many eligible bachelors who were quality stock like Raymond.

"Listen, baby," Raymond started.

"Don't call me 'baby' unless you tell me you love me, okay?" Raymond knew that, though being playful, she was also very serious. He hated to leave her in Washington and wanted to marry her. Truth was that when he moved to Pittsburgh, he had wanted a break for a while. Now he was tired of being alone and really wanted a long-term companion.

"Listen, darling, I need to see you to discuss a few things, like what we're going to do for the rest of our lives. Get my drift?" Dorothy was smiling on the other end of the phone.

"When?"

"As soon as I finish this case, which is scheduled for trial on September 4th."

"Maybe I'll take some vacation time and come and see you in action. You know, I used to do that when you were at Justice." Raymond remembered and loved having her support.

"That's fine. I'd like that a lot. It reminds me of the old days. In the meantime, I need some help that only you can provide. I need everything you can put together for me on two people.

"And they are?"

"Ned Scott and his daughter, Marianne Scott."

"Isn't that the guy who owns the Pittsburgh Steelers? What do you have to do with him?" And then it clicked. "You're defending that football safety, aren't you? I saw something about that on the news yesterday."

"The whole thing's a mess. Once you get your info together, give me a call only on this line, and I'll fly right down."

"In that case, I'll be ready to see you next Saturday. Bye for now, lover." Dorothy Jensen hung up and Raymond knew she was serious about having a complete file by close of business on Friday. She had helped him numerous times in the past and was diligent in her investigations, thorough and fast -- very fast. Raymond replaced the handset, closed the file drawer, and locked it. Immediately, he went to shower and dress. He was out of his Mt. Lebanon condo by 7:00 A.M. and would be at the office by not later than 7:40 A.M., assuming normal traffic.

As he drove to the office, he started picking a team to assist him. In all the confusion, fees hadn't even been discussed. No matter. That would be handled in due course. He wanted to make sure that Dave Robinson was on the defense team. He was a tenacious little bastard who, in matters of taxation, was formidable. The IRS hated his guts because he usually won most of the cases for his clients. Exposure to criminal law would be good for him, especially since the IRS, from time-to-time, prosecuted criminal matters. He also wanted to make sure that he had Arnold Benton on the team. He completed his undergraduate years at Temple University and after graduation had enrolled in the Pittsburgh Police Academy. After two years on the force, he was promoted to detective. Three years later, he had tired of investigating street crime and applied to law school. He went back to Philadelphia to Villanova, where he finished in a normal course of three years. Benton was now a second-year associate at the firm. He could detail what was "fact" or "fiction." Maybe he still had some inside connections at the department.

Guy Markham, the firm investigator, would round out the main tactical unit. He was a licensed private investigator who knew more tricks than imaginable. He seemed to be a fairly ethical character though and that appealed to Raymond. This was sufficient for now. Tony came with his own support team of Adrian Christopher and

Railroaded!

Errol Forrest. Both seemed to be very sharp and should prove invaluable.

His first stop would be to see Loren Johnson, who always arrived at 7:30 A.M. Much to his surprise, when he got off the elevator at their twenty-first floor offices in the Mellon Bank Building, Loren was sitting in the reception area waiting for him.

"Are you ready to go for the jugular and cut it?" Loren was indeed in a good mood to use Raymond's credo. Raymond laughed aloud and responded.

"I feel like David ready to fight Goliath. But this case is a bit different. We're fighting an invisible monster, and I'm not yet sure what it is."

"Then let me clue you in. 'Hell hath no fury like a woman scorned.' The truth of the matter is that we're fighting a simple-minded little bitch that didn't get the stud she wanted. Unfortunately, she's arrogant enough to think that she can get away with her charades by hiding behind her daddy's money and power."

"But Ned Scott isn't acting like a father who's been enraged and is out to kill the perpetrator of the crime. He's been too quiet, and that can mean any number of things."

"Like maybe he doesn't believe his daughter?" Loren slapped Raymond on the back as together they walked down the hallway to Loren's office. "By the way, Raymond. I know you haven't discussed fees with the Williamses yet. Don't. I haven't worked up a fee structure yet. But the positive publicity for the firm will be more than what we received when you whipped the FBI's ass on the savings and loan case. That brought us the business community. This case will bring us the real community." Raymond continued to listen. Loren was on a roll. Now sitting down at his desk, Loren asked, "So, who do you want on your team?" Raymond recounted his ideas and Loren agreed. "Done! Go kick that broad's ass with my blessing." Raymond got up to leave. "And one more thing, Raymond -- don't go for the jugular and cut it." Loren was shaking a pen at Raymond. "Just put her away, regardless of the cost." Raymond noticed that there was an intense fury in his eyes that typically was absent. For whatever reason, Loren P. Johnson had his heart set on having this Scott woman destroyed.

At 8:30 A.M. in the small conference room, the first powwow began. In attendance were Arnold Benton, Dave Robinson, Gail Young (the paralegal), Guy Markham (the firm's criminal investigator), Loren Johnson and Raymond Sutter. Loren spoke up first.

"Okay, people, we all know why we're here. We are the defensive team for Anthony Williams. He's a good man who has been falsely accused of a terrible crime. We have to prove his innocence and get him acquitted. Only then will we have been successful. Anything less is utter failure. It's one thing to lose a case. That happens. But it's entirely different when a person has been wrongly accused of a criminal act and we fail to uncover the truth. In this case, our client has been wrongly accused of rape and battery. If convicted, he could be subject to up to twenty-five years imprisonment for something he didn't do. If we don't find out who did commit the crime, then we must at least prove that it wasn't our client. The entire support of this firm is at your disposal. Uncover every available clue. Scour the streets of Pittsburgh and get some answers. Somebody out there really knows what happened."

"Marianne Scott knows and she's untouchable," interjected Arnold Benton.

"No, she's not, and maybe we can get her to crack. Turn up whatever heat is necessary. Raymond is the lead counsel, so he's in charge. He's the best there is. His motto is 'Don't go for the jugular -- cut it!' I told him this morning that I wanted this woman destroyed. Why? Because there is no worse example of a person on the face of this earth than one who would cause another's life to be destroyed by lies and false incrimination. Take her down. Take her down hard!" The room was silent. Loren said "thank you" and walked out of the conference room.

Raymond turned and said, "Let's get to it, but first things first. Gail, have your secretary do two things. First, call Anthony Williams and have him here by 11:30 A.M. Second, arrange for lunch to be served in the executive conference room; it will be a working session. As of now we have a few weeks to prepare before the prelims, and I want us to be totally ready, no holes anywhere." Ms. Young got up and left the room to do her appointed tasks.

Railroaded!

"Okay, then, first things first. Anybody got anything on this Kearns fellow?"

"You bet. I know him from law school," stated Arnold Benton. "I had a couple of moot court competitions against the guy. He likes to think of himself as the next great Perry Mason. He's tenacious and unpredictable. He's got a brilliant mind and does his research. Don't let that little man behind the thick glasses fool you. He's one tough cookie. The DA really doesn't know what an asset they have. Oh, and one more thing. He hates football players. His girlfriend of several years, during law school, dumped him for a member of the Philadelphia Eagles."

"That's just great, a negative predisposition on the part of the prosecutor." Raymond was a little perturbed, but this came with the territory. "What about the police report?"

"Right here, boss," said Guy Markham. He slid copies of it to every person in the room. Just then, the conference room phone rang. Ms. Young, who had just returned, answered it.

"Mr. Sutter? It's Judge O'Connor on the line." Raymond knew the fireworks were about to start.

"Put the call through on the speaker. You all might as well hear this." In five seconds, the judge was on the line.

"Mr. Sutter, what was that grandstand event that took place on Saturday afternoon? By right I should have you thrown in jail for at least ten days to cool off that testy mind of yours. If not for the antics of Ms. Scott in the rotunda area, you'd be visited by the sheriff about now."

"I understand, Judge," responded Raymond.

"Let me make one thing perfectly clear. The media has already turned this into a circus. Jury selection is going to be next to impossible. However, because of what you've done, no motions for a change of venue will be granted. You started this mess, so you have to finish it right here!" Judge O'Connor was indeed fired up, but Raymond decided to take the offensive.

"I didn't start this mess, sir. Marianne Scott did. Furthermore, the prosecutor started pulling stunts early in the game, so the defense responded appropriately under the circumstances."

"Don't screw around with me, Raymond. You're too good an attorney and know both sides of the fence. I've already admonished the prosecutor and given him the same lecture. This trial is going to be handled by the book. No more tricks, understood? Whether you know it or not, this trial has sparked national interest. The major networks have already submitted motions to allow cameras in the courtroom. I have denied them all and agreed to the allowance of the usual courtroom artist." Everyone was snickering in the conference room.

"If you keep that prosecutor in line, Judge, then we won't have to resort to upstaging, which does nothing except create animosity." Raymond was trying to be a bit conciliatory.

"I'll do my part, and you do yours. I want this case wrapped up quickly and efficiently. No surprises, okay?" Raymond could sense the frustration in Judge O'Connor's voice. Already his courtroom had been invaded by outsiders. He got the feeling that Judge O'Connor knew this case was a bust. There would be no winners, only losers. "By the way, I want a list of all the people you expect to testify Wednesday. I assume it should be a rather short list."

"Very short, Judge. And we will comply with your orders." Ms. Young pushed the button to cut off the connection. "Well, people, you heard it directly from the horse's mouth. We've got a mess on our hands, so let's kick that prosecutor's butt." Everyone was charged and ready. "Is everyone going to be here at 11:30?"

"Yes, sir, they were expecting our call and will be here and ready to go," responded Gail Young.

"Okay, then, Anthony Williams has been framed. *Round up the usual suspects*, and get your butts in gear. We can reconvene for lunch." Raymond had always liked the line from the movie *Casablanca* spoken by Claude Rains after Humphrey Bogart had shot the German officer.

Chapter 9

"Everything is perfectly clear, Your Honor." Lewis Dobson hung up the phone and checked to see if he still had a rear end. He yelled, "Get Kearns in here right now!" The district attorney did not like getting his butt chewed out by a presiding judge regarding one of his associates, especially the newest guy on the staff. After not more than thirty seconds, Joey Kearns came running into his boss's office.

"You wanted to see me, sir? Should I close the door?"

"Hell, no! Sit your ass down and listen to me, you little twerp. I just got my ass chewed out by Judge O'Connor for that circus stunt you pulled at the arraignment hearing. Where was your mind? On that asshole from the Philadelphia Eagles who stole your girlfriend?" Joey Kearns cringed at this brazen outburst but had to take the heat.

"My thoughts were entirely on winning the case, Mr. Dobson." He decided to lash back to keep from being eaten alive. "Nowhere in the statutes does it say that having the victim at an arraignment hearing is improper, irregular, falls outside the realm of good jurisprudence, or is against court rules of procedure. The defendant has a right to face his accuser. I thought it might make a difference with respect to the issue of bail." As much as Dobson hated to admit it, this upstart was entirely correct. It actually was a good strategy that he wished he had thought of himself. Lewis Dobson walked around to the front of his desk, stood over Kearns, and put his finger in his face. Kearns saw that, at age forty-seven, Mr. Dobson had thick fingers to match his thick hands. He was built like a tank . . . not too tall, not short, but very stocky. Angry and crouched over, he was a potential nightmare waiting to happen.

"Let me make a few things perfectly clear, young man. Anthony Williams is one of the most highly respected men in Pittsburgh. I'm up for election next year and have no desire to have egg spattered all over my face or over this whole department. Is that understood?"

"Perfectly, Mr. Dobson."

"Furthermore, none of your esteemed colleagues wanted to touch this case because it smells of 'frame.' But because it's Ned Scott's daughter, we have to go through this exercise."

"It's not an exercise, sir. I believe that the defendant is guilty and I intend to prove it."

"Oh yeah? I bet you're bucking for assistant DA because you know if you win this case, you will have done the impossible with the unimaginable. Right?" Joey did not respond. "Well, am I right or not?"

"Something like that, sir. I would hope that a promotion might be in order."

"Well, don't you dare even consider screwing up because if you do, I'm out of a job come next election. And I guarantee you that if I'm gone, you'll be editing casebooks for the rest of your insignificant life! Are we clear?"

"Perfectly clear, Mr. Dobson. I will not embarrass you or the department." At that, Dobson walked back around his desk and sat down.

"Now that we understand each other, tell me how you're going to win this case." Outside, a group of the other associates was huddled together listening to the events in the boss's office. "Get your butts back to work!" bellowed Dobson. Everyone immediately scattered. "By the way, Kearns, you can call me 'Lew.' You're on your way to earning my respect. What do you have?" Joey Kearns was pumped. He had been chewed up one side and down the other but had just received a huge vote of confidence.

"In chronological order, we have an eyewitness to the events in Hawaii last winter; we have an eyewitness to the initial battery; and we have a semen sample taken from the victim. I believe the charges are well supported. I should have most of my conclusions ready for your review by the end of the week."

Railroaded!

"Sounds very good, but what about the statement given by the defendant at the press conference? It seems to refute everything that Ms. Scott has stated."

"I'm working on that, sir. Judge O'Connor has asked for a list of witnesses by Wednesday. I don't believe there will be any delay at all. Before I submit the list, I will run everything by you for your clearance." Lewis was impressed. This youngster was being very systematic and clear. He made no assumptions and took no chances. "I'm sure there will be a problem with the medical issues as a result of the injury the defendant sustained prior to the commission of the crime, but I believe I will be able to clearly address that also. I have a friend in Philadelphia who is an orthopedic surgeon. I plan to consult with him for some insight into what happens when one suffers from a collapsed vertebral disc -- what one's limitations are, that sort of thing."

"Very good, Kearns. Get on with it. Here's my home phone number. Anything you need, you call me day or night. Time is irrelevant. I want to be advised of everything. This case is too hot, too much media attention. Understood?"

"Yes, sir. I mean, okay, Lew."

"And by the way . . ." Lew put his hands up to his mouth and increased his voice so everyone else in the office could hear his announcement. "If you win this case, I'll make you an assistant DA to fill the current vacancy."

Joey Kearns was really motivated. He flew out of Lew Dobson's office and down the hall to his cubbyhole-of-an-office to continue his work on what was now being billed as "the case of the century."

● ● ● ● ● ●

Thirty minutes later, Joey Kearns received two unexpected visitors. Raymond Sutter went in to see Lew Dobson, and Joey was called into Lew's office once again. "I'm sure you two have already met, but I don't think you know Mr. Arnold Benton." Joey Kearns shook his hand, almost paralyzed in fear.

"Nice to see you again, Mr. Kearns. Last time we met was at New York University -- the moot court competition. Remember?"

"All too well, I'm afraid." Lew Dobson didn't like the look on his associate's face. Joey Kearns knew Arnold Benton all right. Benton and his moot court partner were the only team to systematically beat U. of Penn's team of Kearns and Madison. If not for Benton and Gallagher, Kearns would have gotten national recognition for his litigation skills and may have gotten better job offers. To make matters worse, this was the same asshole who had introduced his former girlfriend to the Eagles player. Nobody ever said life was fair; he'd just have to hunker down and put aside his distaste for this man. An extremely nice promotion was at stake.

"Well, now that it's established that we all know each other, let's get down to business. The judge has chewed both of us out. The prosecution has agreed there will be no more surprises."

"As has the defense, Lew," Raymond said. "So let's get to the issue of evidence and witnesses, okay? The police report says that the victim was examined by a Dr. Phyllis Martin, and that semen was recovered. Intend to run DNA on it, Lew?"

"Of course, we do. The test is scheduled to be run in a few days. And we expect the defendant to cooperate by providing a specimen for analysis."

"And what if we object based on his medical condition?"

"Then that's something we have to take up with the judge at the preliminary hearing," retorted Lew Dobson. Joey Kearns was puzzled. Why would the defendant object to providing a semen specimen if there was a remote chance that it could clear him? This was a tactic that he had not considered and would have to ponder seriously. It might make his work a bit more difficult.

"Another thing, gentlemen. Will your victim subject herself to a polygraph test?" asked Arnold Benton. "In that way, we can determine what's real and what's not, and, in the process, save everyone a lot of time and trouble."

"Ms. Scott is not on trial here. The defendant is," injected Joey Kearns. "Besides, that might be an issue for trade -- say polygraph for semen." Raymond Sutter had anticipated this response and answered harshly.

"This is no game, young man. We're not here to bargain for evidence. Your responsibility is to find out the truth, whether your 'victim' is lying or not. Only then can you determine if you have a case worth prosecuting. You might consider it for your own satisfaction before you get too deep in the stench that's going to choke this city." Raymond was hot. Lew was not fazed by this outburst but clearly understood the ramifications of Raymond's commentary. "Draw up your motion as our client will not provide a semen specimen." Raymond and Arnold got up to leave. Arnold pointed his finger at Joey Kearns.

"Hope you're better at the real thing than you were in moot court, Joey." Joey cringed inside but responded harshly.

"You better have all your shit together, Arnie. This time your suave style won't save your tight ass from my wrath. I'm going to send you and that football star client of yours straight to hell!" Raymond heard it all and stored it away. He would confront Arnold outside. There might be a chance that Joey Kearns's hatred of Arnold Benton could work in the defense's best interests.

●●●●●●

Outside the courthouse, Raymond asked Arnold a very simple question. "How bad did you beat Joey Kearns?"

"We whipped him and his partner, Julie Madison, on two occasions. The first time was during the regular season. The second time was when we won the National Moot Court Championship. By the way, Julie Madison was Kearns's girlfriend. The guy who stole her was my partner, Lester Gallagher." Raymond stopped, turned, and commented, having made the connection.

"You're telling me that 'Mean Lester Gallagher,' the infamous linebacker, was your moot court partner at Villanova?"

"One and the same. He was twice as big as me. But off the field and in a business suit, his mind was sharp as a tack, not the animal he appeared to be on the football field. He intends to finish out his contract with the Eagles and start his own practice. There's no doubt in my mind that he'll be successful."

"Well, well, well. Now I know why we took you instead of Lester." Arnold was a bit puzzled. "Eagles never fly very well in the polluted air of Steel Town." They both laughed and walked the few short blocks to their office building.

Chapter 10

The executive conference room of Johnson, Owens, Sutter & Moss looked more like a five-star restaurant than a soundproofed area used incessantly to interview clients or conduct meetings. The table was large enough to accommodate sixteen high-backed, leather-covered chairs. Before each chair was a place setting fit for a king. After all, the firm was banking on the fact that winning the case for Anthony Williams would bring a long stream of new clients.

The menu for lunch consisted of a shrimp salad appetizer, mixed green salad, prime rib, lobster, steamed asparagus, steamed zucchini, and, for dessert, cheesecake flown in from Junior's in Brooklyn, New York. Loren Johnson was a Brooklyn native and loved their world-famous cheesecake. So did Errol Forrest. Errol, during his tenure at Hofstra Law School, often dated a second-year classmate who lived in Brooklyn. Together they visited Junior's often because of its proximity to her home.

Everyone was there at 11:15 A.M. and moved into the conference room at exactly 11:30. Anthony was in considerably more pain this morning, witnessed by the fact that he was moving very slowly. He decided against taking a pain-killer so he would be as lucid as possible. He walked in on crutches, with Shelli to his right, Errol to his left, and Adrian directly behind him.

Loren Johnson sat at the head of the table. To his right sat Raymond. Next to Raymond sat Arnold Benton, Guy Markham (the investigator), Ms. Tolliver (a secretary), and Adrian Christopher. Next to Adrian sat the Pittsburgh Steelers trainer, Elton Rogers. To the left of Loren Johnson were seated Anthony and Shelli. Dave Robinson sat next to Shelli Williams. Ms. Young

Railroaded!

sat next to her. Last on that side was Errol Forrest. Errol actually preferred this seating arrangement because he could sit back and observe everyone else.

The small talk of lunch was exactly that, except for one issue. After being seated, Anthony told Shelli to write a check to the firm for the anticipated retainer. Loren Johnson interceded quickly. "You can put that away, Shelli. We won't be requiring a retainer at this time." All of the client party was a bit puzzled. "The firm intends to absorb the partners' fees for this case. The only expenses that will be billable are for the support staff and associates. Their fees will be billed in arrears every month." Anthony and Shelli were still perplexed. At that point, Raymond Sutter took over.

"It's our intention that, after this case is won, we hope to represent you in the ensuing civil action involving a violation of your civil rights -- you know, libel, slander, defamation of character, the whole shebang. We anticipate an initial claim for damages in the range of $25,000,000 to $35,000,000. Assuming the success of this case, the civil trial will proceed smoothly and a jury should be favorably disposed to support one of Pittsburgh's favorite sons." Anthony was smiling. So were Adrian and Errol. Shelli was a bit more reserved.

"The firm would like to handle the civil case on the usual one-third contingency basis," added Loren. Errol sat back and watched as the firm members positioned themselves for this case. "Therefore, if any check should be written, it will be on an after-the-fact, per-billing basis. I would estimate that the total amount should be, say, not more than $25,000 to cover everything for the criminal proceedings. We don't expect the trial to last more than five days and the investigatory costs to be other than nominal." Shelli was pleased with this amount as it meant that it wasn't necessary to dip into the family's long-term investment accounts, which were not easily accessible. This amount could be easily written on a check from one of their cash management accounts at Merrill Lynch, in which they regularly maintained balances of between $85,000 and $90,000.

"I insist that you let us give you a check, Mr. Johnson." Anthony was firm in his statement. "Write the firm a check, Shelli." She wrote a check for the specified amount and handed it to Anthony, who, in turn, handed it to Loren. Loren didn't even look at it and immediately placed it in his jacket pocket. "Thanks, Anthony. I want you to know that the entire resources of this firm are at your disposal. This madness with the Scott woman will be solved in short order. But I think we'd better get to lunch before it gets cold!"

The air of seriousness was replaced with one of frivolity. There was a series of lawyer jokes told. Errol was questioned about his tenure at Hofstra and post-graduation plans. Adrian discussed their collective plans to start an architectural design firm. Raymond stated that he might one day like to run for county court judge, to which Loren replied, not until after he was dead.

Arnold Benton and Adrian hit it off pretty well. Errol, however, was more focused on Guy Markham. He was not a lawyer and continuously surveyed the room, as did Errol. Errol knew this man had some blockbuster information that had not, as of yet, been disclosed to anyone. He was a bit antsy and was waiting for a chance to impart his wealth of knowledge. After lunch, everyone took a break while the caterers cleared the conference room. All that was left were two pitchers of water and, on the credenza, coffee service and soft drinks.

"Mr. Markham, my name is Errol Forrest. I've been friends with Tony and Adrian since 1966. We've been through a lot together."

"I heard that you three were best friends. This is an impressive show of support, Mr. Forrest," responded the investigator.

"Thank you for your support, sir. But, if I may make a comment." Guy Markham nodded his acceptance as he drank a Pepsi. "Somehow I get the feeling that you have found out something that is material to Tony's well-being. You were a bit anxious at lunch -- almost like 'let's get on with this and not waste any time." Guy Markham was quietly impressed with this man. "If there's anything I can do to help you in your investigation, please let me know." Errol scribbled some information on a page from a legal pad and handed him the folded sheet of paper with his address and phone information in Hempstead.

"Thanks. I'll keep it all in mind." He paused for a moment and then continued. "It seems that your friend has quite a following in

Railroaded!

Pittsburgh. Except for one Marianne Scott, I believe that he would do well at the political game. Lots of 'higher ups' are afraid of Anthony Williams. They think he might try to run for political office one day."

"Tony? Governor? Not in a million years. He's too mild-mannered. He's a perfect Clark Kent. But his super abilities end on the football field. After that, he's a recluse who would prefer to be designing buildings."

"Then why has he been engaged in so many community affairs?" asked the investigator.

"Very simple. Tony was dirt poor as a kid in Alabama. He watched his cousin get lynched by the Klan. After we met him, we taught him everything we knew about just being a regular guy and not being afraid of ghosts -- and that was no easy task. His inner fear of being in the private company of a white woman is so great that he would cut his own throat rather than have to deal with such an encounter."

"I see. But why the community efforts?" Guy Markham was insistent with this line of questioning.

"He simply decided to get involved in community organizations that help poor people. It's based on the principle of giving something back to the community . . . something a lot of people don't do. But Tony never let race be an issue and, as a result, he's well-liked by everyone because he helps everyone. Tony isn't a saint, but he's pretty damned close to being one."

"Well, then, first things first. Let's get this Scott business out of the way. Then you and I may have to chat later. While there are some powerful people who don't like your friend, there are also a lot of equally powerful people who do like him and would promote him in the political arena." Errol looked Guy Markham squarely in the eye and responded.

"I'll take that under advisement, Mr. Markham."

"Spoken like the true lawyer you are about to become, Mr. Forrest." They shook hands with an unspoken understanding of the conversation. "Let's have a seat. It seems that we are about to reconvene." Everyone sat in the same seats where they had enjoyed lunch. Once again, Loren spoke first.

"I hope that lunch was suitable for everyone. Now let's get down to business and establish a clear-cut process for destroying the credibility of Marianne Scott." At this point, Raymond interceded.

"I have prepared a statement of the facts that we know." Ms. Tolliver passed out a document to all of the attendees. "Everyone should take a moment to read this summary and we can proceed afterwards." There was silence in the room as everyone read the summary. Tony was uneasy reading the material. He broke concentration for a moment, asking for aspirin or Tylenol to ease the pain in his back. He refused to take a painkiller because it would relax him to the point of sleep. He wanted to remain completely alert despite the discomfort. Ms. Young left the conference room and returned with a bottle of Tylenol from her desk. She was used to the headaches from the stress of the legal profession. She handed Tony three. Tony took the Tylenol and continued to read the document. The facts were clear . . .

Marianne Scott had tried to seduce Anthony Williams in Hawaii. He pushed her aside and, after a night of heavy drinking, crashed fully-dressed, in a bedroom by himself. He awoke to find a nude Marianne Scott, sleeping next to him. Adrian Christopher came to his aid. Neither man, at that time, recognized the Scott woman.

After several months, Shelli Williams started receiving letters from Los Angeles and then Pittsburgh claiming that an as-yet-unknown woman had enjoyed sex with Tony in Hawaii and that Tony had claimed his undying love for this unknown personage.

That on Thursday, July 26th, Adrian Christopher had arrived from Denver, Colorado, about 3:30 P.M. He was playing for the Denver Broncos in the preseason game the next day.

At approximately 7:00 P.M. that same evening, Tony and Adrian met Ned Scott, owner of the Pittsburgh Steelers, for dinner at his private club. Accompanying Mr. Scott was his mother, Elizabeth Cobb, and his daughter, Marianne Scott. Both men recognized Ms. Scott as the same woman whom Tony had spurned in Hawaii. Not wanting to get entangled in a power

Railroaded!

struggle with an NFL team owner over hearsay issues, both men decided that they would continue to play football to fulfill their contracts, only to the end of the current season.

The next day, July 27th, Tony Williams was blind-sided by the Denver Bronco rookie running back, Lucas Johnson. The illegal crack-back block knocked Tony out of the game. He was later diagnosed by Dr. Jonathan Stone, the team orthopedic specialist, as having sustained thoracic disk damage between vertebrae numbers 18 and 19, and 19 and 20. While the damage was not permanent, his playing days were all but over.

Adrian postulated that there must be some connection between the rookie, Lucas Johnson, and Marianne Scott. Lucas Johnson had recently graduated from UCLA, as had Marianne Scott. The rookie was cut immediately by the Broncos head coach. He quickly disappeared.

After receiving treatment for the injury, sufficient to get him through the balance of the weekend, Tony left the training facility at 1:00 A.M., barely walking on crutches. Elton Rogers, the trainer who had worked on Tony after Dr. Stone's examination, stayed behind to close the facility.

The limousine of Ned Scott was waiting to take Tony home even though a cab had been called earlier by Adrian. The chauffeur, Howard Werner, waved off the cab and helped Tony get into the limo. The chauffeur then received a phone call and advised Tony that he was making a quick stop by the club before taking him home. At Tony's request, the chauffeur called Shelli to advise her that he was bringing Tony home and of their estimated arrival time. Tony drifted off to sleep.

A bit later, Tony awakened to find Marianne Scott sitting on top of him with her dress hiked up and wearing no underwear. Tony knocked her off him and yelled for the chauffeur to stop the car. He finally did and Tony got out of the car. Marianne Scott also got out and clung to Tony, at which point he slapped her, knocking her down. The chauffeur witnessed everything, but, for whatever reason, drove off. Tony went to a phone booth not more than fifty feet away and called Shelli to come pick him up. After the limousine disappeared, Ms. Scott charged Tony, knocking him to the ground. He collapsed in pain. Marianne stood over Tony and told him that he would pay for his refusal to accommodate her sexual advances. She also kicked him in the right-side rib cage. He saw Marianne run down the street and get into a waiting car that seemed to appear from nowhere. He couldn't make out the license, who was driving, or even determine what kind of car it was, except that it was dark-colored. Shelli arrived about twenty minutes later, helped Tony into the car, and left for their home near the Wildwood Country Club. They arrived home about 2:15 A.M.

These were the facts. They were incontrovertible. They were clear. Tony was guilty of slapping Marianne Scott. This was not, however, aggravated battery. It was not sexual assault. It was not rape.

"I believe this is a reasonable summary of the facts," asserted Raymond.

"Except for two very big issues," injected Guy Markham. "What time did you pick up Anthony, Mrs. Williams?" There was a look of puzzlement on Shelli's face before she answered.

"It was 1:50 A.M. I remember looking at the car clock when I saw Tony lying on the ground by the phone booth."

"Is there any chance you made a mistake?"

"None, or else we couldn't have been home at 2:15. What's the point?" asked Shelli.

"Just one more question, please." Everyone was a bit curious about this questioning, except Errol. He intuitively knew there was a very good reason for this line of inquiry. "You picked up your husband on the corner of Lockhart and Cedar, at East Park, right?"

"That's correct. The street was very dark except for the light of the phone booth and the distant light of the Allegheny General Hospital at the end of Cedar."

"And that's precisely my point. Ms. Scott claims to have been raped by Mr. Williams there on the corner of Lockhart and Cedar. She could have walked or crawled to the Allegheny General Hospital for treatment, just seven or so blocks away. Police are at the hospital round the clock. Instead, she went to the main police building, which meant that she had to leave the scene of the alleged attack and cross the Allegheny River on the 9th Street Bridge.

Railroaded!

As you know, there's a community of vagrants that live around the 9th Street Bridge. I checked and no one saw a woman matching her description cross the bridge on foot that night."

"Isn't that asking a bit much of the local winos, Guy?" questioned Raymond.

"Not when you consider that I also checked every taxi company's dispatch records and there is no record of anyone being taken from anywhere to the Main Police Station between 1:45 and 5:37 A.M." Arnold Benton started shuffling papers and recovered the copy of the police report.

"It says here that Ms. Scott came into the Main Station at 4:35 A.M. There's no record of how she got there except her statement that she got there on foot." Arnold Benton was quick to follow the investigator's line of reasoning.

"Without anyone seeing her?" asserted Guy. "The people under the bridge may be vagrants, but they are not heartless. They would have helped a woman claiming to have been raped. They have helped distressed people in the past, even those threatening suicide. No, I believe that Ms. Scott left the scene with someone who was following her. She then had intercourse with someone to give the appearance of rape, and finally had that person beat her to justify the battery charges. In view of the fact that the chauffeur saw Anthony hit Ms. Scott, he could be a damaging witness."

"I agree, Guy," added Loren. "To make matters worse, he's very loyal to Ned Scott and could be paid off to skew his testimony."

"Maybe we should demand a polygraph?" added Dave Robinson, who had been sitting back taking in the colloquy.

"Too early, Dave. That would spook the man and show our hand. Better to get him to perjure himself on the witness stand or tear apart his testimony. That will be more damaging for Marianne and positive for our defense."

"If the times are so out of line, doesn't that help to prove our position?" asked Shelli.

"In reality, it's one of our strongest points," answered Raymond. "You picked up Tony at 1:50 A.M. She didn't report the rape until well after four. It doesn't take two hours to get from Lockhart and Cedar to the Main Station, not even during rush hour.

If she did walk, she should have gone to the hospital. That's a pretty seamy area, you know. There wouldn't be too many people wanting to help a white woman over there."

"The principal thing we have to do is to get the records from the telephone company covering the phone booth where Tony called you to come and get him. Once that is verified, it will go a long way toward corroborating Tony's story and establishing that you received a call from him at 1:20 to come and get your husband," added Guy Markham. "And I'm already on top of that request."

"Excellent work as usual, Guy!" Loren Johnson was very enthusiastic over these pronouncements. "What else is there?"

"Only one more thing." Guy hesitated for just a moment and then continued. "There is a local precinct station just three and a half blocks from the alleged scene of the attack. Why did she go to the Main Station when help was so close?" Everyone sat back in virtual silence.

"Maybe she didn't know it was there," responded Dave Robinson.

"She knew about the station, all right. Turns out that when she had just turned eighteen, she was booked one night for driving under the influence. She was taken to the Ohio Street substation. Her daddy, of course, bailed her out."

"Very interesting, Guy," added Raymond. "This whole case is very disturbing."

"Why so?" inquired Loren.

"There are too many disjointed facts that can be used for or against Tony. This woman is not to be taken lightly. She knew exactly what she was doing. The only question is, how far will she go to cover her tracks? To what extent is she going to be able to use her daddy's money and power to convince people of her victimization?" There was a moment of silence. Then Adrian spoke up.

"There has to be a connection between Marianne and Lucas Johnson. I could go out to Los Angeles and do a little digging. The college players will talk because they'll think I'm there for an advance look for the Broncos."

Railroaded!

"But they don't report for another week or so. Besides, you're in the preseason, or did you forget? When are you going to have the time?" asked Tony.

"Just remember, that I wasn't scheduled to play last Friday, nor am I scheduled to play except for a few series during the next two games. I'm sure Coach Stiller will give me some extra time to help you out. The Broncos don't want a black eye behind this incident," responded Adrian.

"Does anybody know where this Lucas Johnson character is right now?" asked Errol. "I think that if we can find him, we'll get the keys to the kingdom."

"I agree with Mr. Forrest," said Guy Markham. "That should be our number one priority."

"Anyway, we have to get our witness list together for the judge and submit it by Wednesday. If anyone thinks of anyone who could be of importance, please let us know." Raymond was interrupted by the ringing of the conference room telephone. Ms. Young answered it. Once again, it was Judge O'Connor. She put the call through.

"Listen, Raymond. I've just received a motion to produce from the prosecution," said the Judge.

"To produce what?"

"This motion reads -- *The People moves the court to order the defendant, Anthony Williams, to produce a semen specimen for laboratory analysis.*" Shelli was stunned, as was Anthony. Raymond lifted his hands to keep everyone calm.

"We vigorously object, Judge. There is no . . ." Judge O'Connor cut him off.

"I expected your objection. Therefore, I will hear arguments from both sides tomorrow morning in open court at 10:00 A.M. sharp. Afterwards, I will render an immediate decision. Is that clear?"

"Perfectly clear, Judge," responded Raymond flatly.

"And no continuance will be allowed. Just be prepared, Raymond."

"Also understood." Raymond hung up the phone and shifted gears. "Mr. Rogers, it's critical that we get Dr. Stone in here immediately. Can you do that?"

"Yes, sir. When do you want him here?"

"Four o'clock would be perfect."

"Okay then. I'll get right on it." He got up and left to go to Three Rivers Stadium.

"In the meantime, Shelli, why don't you take Tony home. There's nothing else he can do here today. Mr. Forrest and Mr. Christopher, you can stay if you like. I'll make sure you get back to Anthony's later." Raymond was angry and trying to hide it. Adrian and Errol got up to help their friend, who was in pain. Shelli got up, thanked everyone, and left to go get the car. The threesome slowly left the room together. After the door to the conference room was shut, Raymond flew off the handle. "I'm going to hang that little bastard by the balls. He doesn't know whom he's messing with." He paused for a moment and then said, "Sorry, ladies."

"Can I do it instead?" questioned Arnold.

"No, but you can write a short brief in support of why the defendant should not be required to provide a semen specimen. You and Dave work on it together. I want a working draft by the time the doctor gets here at four." Both attorneys stood up and left the room. The secretaries also left. Loren, who had been sitting quietly, now asked a question of Guy.

"Just between the three of us, okay?" Raymond and Guy nodded. "Do you still have that connection in the police forensics lab?"

"I don't know anybody over there. But if you're perhaps asking for a sample of something?"

"Wouldn't it be interesting to conduct our own lab analysis without the prosecution knowing it? Of course, it would be off the record," stated Loren.

"Let's just hold this in abeyance until after the motion hearing tomorrow," stated Raymond. "No need to rush things -- but proper planning prevents piss-poor performance."

"What about Anthony?" asked Guy. "Will he cooperate?"

"He didn't do anything, so of course he'll cooperate. Besides, it will absolutely kill Marianne's credibility, not that she has any to start with," said Loren.

Railroaded!

"Hold the fort, gentlemen. I don't know jack shit about this," stated Raymond. "I won't turn down the findings, but I don't know anything about what you're planning. Besides, in the final analysis, I don't need it to win this case."

"We're right with you, Raymond. Guy? Just handle it. In the meantime, I could use another cup of coffee. This is all very exasperating." Loren poured a cup and left the conference room. Guy winked at Raymond and also left the room.

Raymond sat there for a while and wondered how involved Ned Scott was going to get in this whole matter. Was he going to cover for his daughter, or was he going to let her go it alone? To Raymond, this was the only wild card.

●●●●●●

Guy Markham returned to his offices, that were abuzz with activity. His company had grown substantially since being retained as the chief investigative firm for Johnson, Owens, Sutter & Moss. In fact, he had progressed from a two-man shop to a firm with eight staff investigators and thirty-two support employees. He was proud of the accomplishment. His skills had been properly developed during his service in the Navy Seals. Afterward, he contracted his services to wealthy families around the United States. He had settled in Pittsburgh eighteen years ago.

"There's a call on line one for you, Mr. Markham," said the voice on the intercom. Guy picked up the phone and gave his usual greeting.

"This is one of your former employers," said the voice on the other end.

"Well, I'll be damned! I was wondering if I was going to hear from you."

"So, your firm is responsible for the investigation on the Williams case."

"That's right," responded Guy. "What can I do for you?" was the question.

"Just tell me if Anthony Williams is guilty or innocent. No holds barred. Just the facts," answered the party on the other end.

"And if he did do it, then what?" asked Guy of his former employer.

"Then he's a dead man -- in no uncertain terms." Guy was not pleased with this response.

"And if he didn't do it?"

"I don't give a damn, just fix it to look like he did. The courts will take care of everything else. I know you have the capability. Just do it. There's $1,000,000 cash in it for you. Is that enough motivation?"

"I'll let you know."

"Wrong answer, Mr. Markham. But I'll raise the stakes to two and a half to get your undivided attention. Are we in sync now?"

"Of course. Apparently it doesn't matter, but Anthony Williams is innocent and the woman wasn't raped. For whatever reason, she's framed Anthony Williams and you want him to take the fall. Why does he scare you so much?"

"That's not your concern. Just handle the scenario, Mr. Markham." The former employer hung up. Guy slammed down the phone and buried his head in his hands. He actually liked Anthony Williams. And he definitely liked the company he had built. But for $2.5 Million, he could disappear to some far away island and lie on a beach sipping his favorite drink, piña coladas. First, he had to see what the judge's ruling on the prosecution's Motion to Produce was going to be. Then he had to assess the parties. There was only one troubling aspect to this whole case. Everyone was a known quantity except Adrian Christopher and Errol Forrest, Jr. Errol had brains, perception and the inquisitiveness of an eager law student. Adrian had money, brains, and the backing of the Denver Broncos, who didn't want to be embarrassed in a sexually related scandal. In any event, he would wait for a week to ten days before he did anything. He would make his decisions about how to "fix" everything later, after gathering all the facts.

Chapter 11

After what had been a dark and very stormy night with severe thunderstorms producing pea-sized hail, the early morning sun provided a first glimpse at what would be a spectacular Tuesday morning. The air was crystal clear and fresh. There was not even the slightest hint of the pollution from the steel mills that plagued the city. Adrian and Errol were up at 6:00 A.M. and hit the road for a brisk walk, then jog, then run, then cool-down period. They wished that the third member of the triumvirate could have participated, but that was, for now, impossible. Both men were dressed in blue and orange Denver Broncos sweat pants and blue T-shirts. Passers-by must have thought them crazy to wear such heretic clothing in the middle of Steelers country.

"Well, do you have any new thoughts this morning, A.C.?" asked Errol.

"Not right off hand. How about you, Trees?"

"I thought a lot about the events of the past several days. You know this all happened within just five days?" Adrian nodded as they picked up the pace a bit. "Raymond Sutter is a good attorney. Loren Johnson is after the publicity that will bring new business to the firm. The other attorneys are gophers. They will do exactly what they're told to get in the good graces of the bosses. But for whatever reason, I don't trust Guy Markham. Yesterday, he kept asking me about Tony's political aspirations. I told him that Tony helped poor people without regard to color. I told him that Tony was not a political animal. He responded by saying there were people who didn't want to see Tony continue to be so popular. He said there were people who were afraid that Tony might seek election and start a successful political career. I tried to assure him that politics was not in the game-plan despite the press conference announcement."

"Why in the world would anyone worry about that? We plan to open an architectural design practice. If anyone is the political animal, it's you, Trees. You have an opinion on everything, and they're usually well thought out and supported by incontrovertible facts. If anything, the world should be worried about your flabby behind. Come on now . . . pick up the pace! Law school's got you sitting on your butt!"

Errol laughed and sped up. In reality, he was in pretty good shape. He played tennis three times a week, walked three miles a day and rode a bicycle almost everywhere he went in New York. Besides, the New York law school football league would be starting in a few weeks, which was big fun. Hofstra had won the title for the last two years. Errol was the star wide receiver on the team and killer safety. In reality, this fast-paced workout was just what the doctor had ordered to clear his head.

"Listen, Trees, I have an idea. On the QT, you and I should talk to Raymond Sutter about this concern of yours. There's no reason he shouldn't know about every possible issue that affects his client. Besides, politics doesn't blend with anything. On the wrong side, it can get you killed. We should tell Tony and size him up. If he's not interested, then the three of us need only agree to stay out of politics forever. If he is interested in politics, then maybe we need to assess things a bit further. We can't let him get thrown to the wolves. If this investigator is curious about these issues, then there must be some pretty freaked-out white boys in Pennsylvania these days who are worried about their political well-being."

"That brings up an interesting point," Errol added.

"Yeah? What's that?" Adrian was starting to pant a little. So was Errol.

"I wonder to what extent Marianne Scott will play into the hands of the politicos and if they'll try to use this as a mechanism to get rid of a future threat. Get my drift, man?"

"I see. We need to have a little powwow and be extremely watchful for signs of anything unusual." Errol was panting a bit more than Adrian. "Can we just finish this exercise in futility and head back?" Errol said, speaking of their morning jog-run.

"Come on, Trees! I thought you had more staying power than this."

"I do, A.C. Run, run, run . . . just as fast as you can. You can't catch me cause I'm a fast black man!" Errol took off like a rocket and in a short burst, smoked Adrian up the short incline. At the top of the hill, Errol and Adrian both stood with their hands on their knees, panting like whipped dogs. "Let's get back and find out what's on Tony's mind."

"But only if we walk back, Trees, only if we walk. I always hated running up and down hills." Adrian put his arm around Errol's shoulder and they sauntered back to Tony's house.

Back at the house, and after cleaning up, the three men huddled outside by the pool while Shelli fixed breakfast. Tony was disgusted that he couldn't join his friends on their morning run but knew that would come later. He was actually feeling a bit better today after getting a solid twelve hours of sleep. Errol reminded him that the ancient Greeks used to state that "sleep was the doctor for all ills."

When Adrian and Errol advised Tony of their suspicions, he told them in no uncertain terms that he was not a political animal. His philosophy was very simple. "I came from nothing. I grew up in the backwoods of Alabama dirt poor. I got lucky and achieved a little fame and notoriety because of my sports ability. No one has seen me use my brainpower except you guys and Shelli. So, in the meantime, I help poor people. Anyway, when I leave this world, I'll leave it with the same amount that I came into it with -- nothing! I'm an architect. So are you, Adrian. And you, my dear Trees, you're an architect and an anomaly. But someone has to watch out for our collective business interests, so you're the lawyer-businessman. Besides, you're smarter than both of us and have more global experience, which makes you potentially the deadliest of us three. If these assholes knew that, then some heads would really turn." Adrian gave Tony a 'high-five' on Errol being the "mastermind."

"But this isn't about me, Tony. No one knows anything about A.C. and me except that we're your childhood friends. It's about *you,* you, who are in the spotlight. It's *you* who have unknowingly stepped on someone's toes. That investigator was asking those questions for a reason. They didn't come out of left field. Something's not right. There's more to this matter now than just a silly white bitch that didn't get screwed. There are other forces at play that we have to watch, and watch carefully. This case is not just about proving your innocence against the accusations of Marianne. Shit, man, you could do that blindfolded."

Adrian sat back and listened carefully. He knew that Errol was 100 percent correct in his analysis. He started to feel a sense of foreboding but didn't disclose it. Errol hesitated for a moment and then continued. "Look, Tony. This case is going to turn on how much power, whether perceived or real, the politicos think you have. We have to be wise to the game and outsmart the bastards. We have to win this round and take away their home-court advantage."

"But I live here," retorted Tony.

"Brother, for this one, you might as well be back in Dothan getting ready to take on the KKK." Errol was dead serious when he levied this statement. Tony was momentarily stunned by this admonition but quickly recovered. "School doesn't start for me for three more weeks. I can defer my job for now till after school starts and stay here to help you. I hate to admit it, but I'll need a little help with expenses. I'm still a struggling student. You two are the superstars."

"I'll take care of whatever you need, Errol," said Adrian. "Tony's got enough headaches."

"Never, never, never! This is my war," Tony recounted.

"No, it's our war," interrupted Shelli. "I've been listening to your commentary and Errol is right. So whatever it takes, Errol, you're welcome here and don't worry about your living expenses. The three of us will cover them." The men were a bit surprised at this spunky intrusion. "Now it's time for breakfast. Do you want to eat in or out here?"

"Out here is fine, darling," Tony responded. Shelli disappeared back into the house and started the meal transfer to the back patio.

Railroaded!

"You are one lucky sucker, Mr. Anthony Williams. They don't get any better than that. Maybe we should have visited you at CU more often!" Adrian secretly wished he could find someone as nice as Shelli for himself. He turned to Errol and asked, "How's your little one from D.C.? Are you two still planning on getting married in November?" This was news to Tony.

"Married? Are you kidding? What about Sharla Hampton?" She's a world-class chippie that you better hang on to," responded Tony.

"I never could tell this guy anything," responded Adrian. "Besides, Robin is too short for you. I know you think you love her, but you're still pissed off with Sharla. Just fight for her, dude. She'll come around." Sharla had been a classmate of theirs at Dartmouth. She was now Errol's classmate at Hofstra Law School.

"The jury's still out on everything, gentlemen," Errol responded. "Sharla punked me by not having faith in our ability to take care of each other. She gave in to her old man's threats to cut her off. You both know that."

"So what?" Tony responded. "No, I'll tell you what. When I get rid of these crutches, A.C. and I will go over and whip her old man's butt!"

"It's not her old man that I'm concerned with. Besides, we have to win your case first and get you out of here," retorted Errol. At that moment, Shelli returned with breakfast. She kissed Tony on the forehead and sat down.

"Eat up, guys. We have to leave here in one hour. You can strategize on the ride into town."

●●●●●●

The foursome arrived at the courthouse at 9:30 A.M. Tony wanted to make sure that they arrived at the courthouse early enough to talk with Raymond and the defense team to briefly discuss a strategic move to short-circuit the prosecution. The idea was actually Adrian's, and a good one it was.

Raymond walked down the hallway and looked very sharp in his double-breasted navy-blue blazer and gray slacks. As a matter of fact, Arnold Benton and Dave Robinson both wore navy blazers.

Despite the fact that each wore a different color of trousers, one could have almost sworn that this was a law-firm standard uniform. Tony was dressed in a tan sport jacket with no tie and dark brown slacks. Adrian and Errol were each dressed in a black suit. Shelli was smartly dressed in a gray two-piece pantsuit. She had to check in at her office, just for the afternoon.

Raymond approached and shook hands with all four members of the Williams party. "Listen, Raymond. Errol noticed something at your office yesterday that has us a bit concerned." Tony went on to recount the discussion of the political aspect of this case.

"I see," said Raymond. Guy Markham had not yet arrived. In reality, Raymond wasn't expecting him to show. If he did, he would know that something was afoot. "And you would like me to do what?" questioned Raymond.

"We think that, if it's possible, the trial date should be moved up. If you can handle it, we would suggest that you waive the pre-trial conference. You could suggest that time is of the essence, especially since the good name of the Steelers is at stake. That would shake the prosecution in their shoes. It would also tell you whether they're hiding anything."

"And you're ready for this now?" asked Raymond.

"We could start this afternoon, if it were feasible. How much time do you need to plan?"

"Not more than two weeks. As you know, there aren't that many witnesses, and the testimony should be very matter-of-fact. The key is going to be the judge's ruling today. If he rules in our favor, then I will make a motion to move the trial up to the date for which the preliminary hearing was originally scheduled. And I agree -- such a motion will force the prosecution's hand."

"Thanks, Raymond, and good luck in there." Tony shook his hand again and everyone entered the courtroom.

At precisely 10:00 A.M., Judge O'Connor entered the courtroom to the usual "all rise" from the bailiff. The bailiff announced the case as "People v. Anthony Williams, Case Number CR79-6539." Judge O'Connor sat down, as did everyone else. He looked around the courtroom for a moment and wondered how so many people knew about this hearing. After all, he deemed it to be a routine matter. Not so the public. There were reporters from every major television and radio station in Pittsburgh. Marianne Scott was absent and so was her father. He sat back in his high-backed chair and began.

"The Prosecution has filed a motion asking the court to order that the defendant provide a semen specimen for analysis. They argue that, by providing such a specimen, it will save the People time and money in the prosecution of this case. Is that a reasonable summary, Mr. Kearns?"

"Joseph Kearns, for the People, Your Honor," returned the prosecutor.

"By now, the whole world knows who you are, young man. Will you just answer my question?"

"Your commentary was a reasonable summary, Your Honor," said Joey Kearns. Arnold Benton noticed that Joey Kearns was wearing a new gray, pinstriped suit. He had forgotten to remove one of the tags.

"Where is the victim today, Mr. Kearns?" asked the judge.

"Inasmuch as this is a hearing for the production of evidence, I thought it reasonable that she sit this one out, Your Honor. She is still recovering from the assault."

"The defendant is here, Mr. Kearns. Unless I instruct you otherwise, make sure that the victim is here for every hearing. There will be no unfair advantage granted for either side. This is not an admonition, young man. Let's just say that it's my requirement."

"I understand, Your Honor." Joey was relieved. He didn't want to land on the bad side of the judge again.

"Now, Mr. Sutter, I suppose that you are going to follow with the objection you made on the phone yesterday. Correct?" asked Judge O'Connor.

"Absolutely, Judge. As a matter of fact, we would like to call one witness to support our position." Judge O'Connor expected this and leaned forward, resting his arms on the bench.

"Objection!" shouted Joey Kearns.

"I assumed nothing less, Mr. Kearns."

"The Prosecution objects on the ground that this is not an evidentiary hearing."

"Your Honor, we are treating this motion as a quasi order to show cause as to why the defendant should or should not have to produce the specimen requested."

"That's an interesting analogy, Mr. Sutter. I will hold your objection, Mr. Kearns, and rule on it in due course. Proceed, Mr. Sutter."

"The witness we would like to call is Dr. Jonathan Stone, an orthopedic specialist employed by the Pittsburgh Steelers. His testimony will be directed only at the capability of the defendant to provide the requested sample and whether it is medically sound to do so at this time." The judge looked over at Anthony and asked another question.

"Mr. Williams, how's the back today?" Raymond was surprised but told Tony to go ahead and answer.

"It hurts like hell, Your Honor. I'm on a regimen of full-strength pain medication and will be for at least another week. My movements are restricted so that I don't do anything to aggravate the ruptured vertebral discs."

"Very well, Mr. Williams. I think we can dispense with the doctor's testimony. I'll sustain the Prosecution's objection, but only because the defendant has clearly indicated his current state of physical well-being. Further testimony is not required at this time."

"Would you allow us to dismiss Dr. Stone so he can get back to Three Rivers Stadium?" asked Raymond.

"Be my guest, Mr. Sutter." Raymond turned to the gallery and waved to Dr. Stone. He got up and left immediately. "Okay, Mr. Sutter, now what?"

"My colleague, Mr. Arnold Benton, will provide a discussion on the reason why you must deny the motion, Judge." Raymond sat down and Arnold Benton stood. Joey Kearns wondered what these guys were up to. He had hoped that he wouldn't have to deal with this jerk again.

"Arnold Benton, for the defense, Your Honor."

"Proceed, young man," retorted the judge.

"It is a time-honored legal tradition that the burden of proving a case rests with the plaintiff, or prosecution. If you grant the motion that is requested by the prosecution, you will be shifting the burden of proof to the shoulders of the defendant. The prosecution cannot claim that it will be saving the People time and money by having the defendant produce the specimen. In fact, the prosecution has a case based on circumstances only. Shifting the burden by requiring a semen specimen is tantamount to giving them evidence to create a case when no such evidence exists."

"Mr. Benton, what about the fact that there is a semen specimen in police custody at this time that was taken from the victim after the alleged crimes were committed?" asked Judge O'Connor.

"The Prosecution may indeed have a sample in custody, Your Honor. Who it belongs to is something different. Actually, personal origin is totally irrelevant, Your Honor. It's irrelevant because it is only one piece of the puzzle that the Prosecution must put together."

"It's relevant if it originated with the defendant, isn't it, Mr. Benton?" asked the judge.

"Only if the defendant is guilty. He maintains his innocence and has so pled. The defendant is not required under any statutory authority to comply with the Prosecution's motion for production. Nor is there any constitutional precedent that requires the defendant to comply, thereby allowing the Prosecution to shift the burden of proof in a criminal proceeding."

"And I suppose you have a brief to support these arguments?"

"We have, Your Honor. Two copies, one for Your Honor and one for the Prosecutor. We would suggest a fifteen-minute recess to read the brief."

"Good idea. Court is recessed for fifteen minutes. Mr. Kearns, be prepared with any objections when we reconvene."

The judge retired to his chambers. Raymond was impressed with Arnold's presentation. It was short and to the point.

Joey Kearns read the brief and knew that he had been aced out again by his former nemesis. No need to object. The request for the production order was a long shot anyway. The fifteen minutes went by quickly. The judge re-entered the courtroom.

"Mr. Kearns, I'm sure you know that the defense's brief on this issue is very clear and on target. So, you have a choice, young man." Joey Kearns nodded that he understood. Either the judge would rule against him or he could withdraw the motion. The junior prosecutor hesitated for just a few seconds and then spoke.

"Let the record show that the Prosecution withdraws its motion for production of a semen specimen."

"Very well then, Mr. Kearns. The motion is withdrawn. I still expect the witness lists in my hands tomorrow without fail, gentlemen. Is there anything else?" Raymond Sutter stood.

"Judge, the defense would like to waive the preliminary hearings and move the trial date up to Tuesday, August 21st -- if that's acceptable to the Prosecution. We have no necessity to interview the witnesses. We feel that everything should be done in open court. Besides, by starting earlier, the case should be wrapped up so as not to have a negative impact on the Pittsburgh Steelers or the community at large."

"Well, Mr. Kearns, I'm so inclined to advance the date. What about you?"

"May I call my office, Your Honor?"

"Are you working on any other case at this time, Mr. Kearns?"

"No, Your Honor. This is the only one," responded Joey.

"Then make your decision where you stand." Joey thought for a second. He wasn't about to be outdone by the defense again after just having lost a battle of his own initiation.

"Your Honor, the People would suggest starting on Monday, the 20th of August in order to give us five full days that week." Judge O'Connor looked at his calendar and replied.

"Very well, young man. Mr. Sutter, is that acceptable?"

"Very much so, Judge."

"Then I hereby order that the preliminary hearing is waived by mutual agreement of the prosecution and defense, and that the trial will begin at 9:00 A.M. on Monday, August 20th. This hearing is adjourned." Judge O'Connor used his gavel to pound on its base one time. He stood and left for the privacy of his chambers.

Everyone seemed pleased with the success of this strategy, especially Adrian, Tony, and Shelli. Arnold Benton knew that Joey Kearns had only agreed to the advancement of the trial date because he didn't want to look bad after being beaten on his motion request. Raymond didn't care one way or the other. He knew that the quicker the trial got underway, the better off everyone in Pittsburgh would be. Raymond had his work cut out for him. The idea of

Railroaded!

political involvement in an otherwise simple sexual assault case bothered him. He would call Washington later in the evening.

As the lawyers and defendant huddled around the defense table, no one seemed to notice that Guy Markham had slipped in during the proceedings and out at the end, virtually unnoticed -- except by the watchful eye of Errol Forrest, who also sat in a back corner.

Chapter 12

From a distance, Errol followed Guy Markham out of the courthouse and watched as he left the building and made a call from a payphone on the street. This was a curious move since they had just passed two banks of payphones inside the building. The investigator obviously didn't want to be seen in the building making a call from just outside the courtroom. That may have raised questions. Errol retreated back into the inner hallways of the courthouse and found an old-style phone booth to make a call to an old classmate from Dartmouth. An Ivy League education did have its advantages.

During his freshman year, Errol had taught a sophomore who lived on the same floor of his dormitory how to wash and iron his own clothes and become more self-sufficient. Harvey Sloan, from Dublin, Ireland, was somewhat tall at five-feet eleven-inches and perfectly proportioned at one hundred eighty pounds. He had reddish brown hair that Errol remembered to be shoulder-length. He used to be a wild "fraternity rat" who could drink most people under the table.

Upon his graduation from Dartmouth in 1973, Harvey returned to the British Isles where he landed a job in the Special Investigations Department at Interpol. Errol had bailed Harvey out of several "jams" during college and Harvey never forgot it either. They kept in touch and also vowed that they would visit together in Europe one day and tour the local watering holes, that is, when Errol decided to give up being a student. Harvey had taught Errol the fine art of drinking beer. Adrian knew of Harvey Sloan, but not much else. He knew that Harvey and Errol were friends before he arrived at Dartmouth in September 1971.

Railroaded!

"Harvey, you potato-head son-of-a-bitch. How the hell are you?" asked Errol.

"Well, Mr. Trees, the asshole, I presume?" said Harvey. "To what do I owe the pleasure of this call? Are you all right? If so, a Wah-hoo-wah to you, my friend."

"Likewise, Harv." Errol was being very short and Harvey could hear it in his voice.

"Something's wrong, Errol, isn't it?"

"Do you remember my friend, Tony Williams -- the guy Adrian Christopher grew up with in California?"

"You mean your Olympic buddies who made the team when you pulled up lame?" Harvey was trying to keep things on the lighter side. Errol smiled and responded.

"One and the same. Tony has been charged with rape and aggravated assault on the daughter of the owner of the Pittsburgh Steelers. And don't worry; he didn't do it. He's being framed by her, and aside from a woman's scorn, we don't know why."

"Sounds like a simple legal matter to me, Errol. So what do you want me to do? Want me to check someone out, mate?"

"Yeah, but not one of the adversaries. I need you to check out a private investigator named Guy Markham." Errol slowly spelled his last name so there would be no mistake. He also gave him the address of his company. "He's the investigator for the law firm that's representing Tony. Something about this guy is bad news. And I'd like to know any details you can get on this man so we can protect Tony. He's been asking a lot of questions that have nothing to do with this case. It's as if someone else wants Tony to take a fall for this bullshit."

"Curious, my friend, very curious. Where can I reach you, Errol?" Now Harvey was being very businesslike. "There's not too much in this world that can rattle the likes of Errol Forrest, Jr. So, for you to call me, there must be serious problems. Are you sure you're okay?"

"I'm okay. I just don't think that this case is going to be resolved as easily as it should. I'll be staying at Tony's house, but I think it's better if I call you from somewhere other than Tony's home phone."

"Good idea, Errol. Give me forty-eight hours and call me Thursday. That will give me sufficient time to run my traps. By the way, when you finish Hofstra Law School next spring, you should really consider coming to work with me at the 'Pol.' You're one smart and perceptive son-of-a-bitch who can cook his ass off." Errol laughed aloud and quickly thought of when he used to cook meals for a group of guys who were trying to save some money over the cost of eating at Thayer Dining Hall.

"Listen, Harv. I gotta go. This is costing me a fortune from a payphone. Say, how did you know I was graduating from Hofstra next spring?"

"I work for the 'Pol,' you dunderhead. Get your simple ass off the phone and call me not later than 2100 hours GMT on Thursday." Both men hung up. At that moment, Errol turned to see Adrian, Tony, and Shelli standing behind him.

"Is everything okay?" asked Tony.

"Don't know. I'll know more in a few days. It's just about Robin," responded Errol. Adrian could tell that Errol was lying and holding something back that related to Tony -- something crucial. Errol changed the subject and became more positive. "I think we need to congratulate Adrian here on his strategic prowess. Great results in there, don't you think? Your strategy worked just fine." As they walked out, Adrian knew something was terribly wrong. Errol never addressed his friend as "Adrian" when only they were around. Shelli and Tony recognized it also. Errol recognized his error and tried to change his tactics really fast. "Say, Tony. I don't know a thing about this city. Where can we get a good pizza? It's lunchtime and after this morning's workout, Shelli's breakfast is already gone. I'm starved." This statement was acknowledged quickly and Shelli went out to get the car. Tony disappeared to the men's restroom.

"Listen, Trees. Tony and Shelli are gone, so level with me. You know something and it's bothering you," stated Adrian. "And don't feed me that Robin bullshit." Errol was trapped.

"Okay, okay, A.C. I'll know that on Thursday afternoon. I'll have some answers to some very hard questions. Then we can collectively discuss what to do and let you do some more of your strategic maneuvering."

Railroaded!

"Is Tony in some kind of danger?" asked Adrian. Errol hesitated for a minute and sighed.

"I don't know. I just don't know. Watch your back, Adrian. I don't like what's happening here. To make matters worse, I don't have a clue what we're dealing with."

"What should I do?" asked Adrian.

"Can you leave for California tonight to go to UCLA? You have to get something, anything on Lucas Johnson. He was drafted by the Broncos. If Blu Stiller will allow it, use their file as a base. We have to get this guy. If we don't, Tony could be in big trouble."

"First, I'll fly to Denver this afternoon and get what we need from Coach Stiller. Then I'll be off to California. Listen, Trees. Why don't you go with me? You know Los Angeles as well as I. We can work faster together. Besides, it'll give you a chance to stop in and see your mother and father on the way."

"As much as I'd like to see them, we should just keep going. We have until Thursday at 4:00 P.M. to get some answers so we can put this puzzle together. I somehow feel as though Tony's life is in danger, but there's no logical reason for it. Anyway, I don't have any money for short-notice air travel. I'm still a struggling law student. I opted out of football, remember?"

"You made the right choice, my friend. Don't worry about the cost. You know plastic works wonders. So, it's settled then. You and I will fly to Denver this afternoon, pick up the recruiting information on Lucas Johnson, and continue on to L.A. I'll call ahead to arrange everything. Besides, this will give Tony and Shelli some time alone that they could use." Errol liked this plan. Tony came out of the restroom somewhat struggling with his crutches. Adrian told him of their plans. Tony agreed and offered to pay for their expenses. Adrian patently refused. Instead, Tony silently thanked his lucky stars for two such loyal friends.

They put off the pizza idea and drove immediately to Tony's house, which was in the opposite direction of the airport. Shelli called her office and begged for forgiveness. She promised her boss that she would be in to work as soon as she could. For the rest of the day, however, she played chauffeur.

After lunching with Arnold Benton and Dave Robinson, Raymond Sutter went back to his office. There he ran into Guy Markham. "I'm ready to proceed whenever you are," commented the investigator.

"Aren't you going to ask the results of the hearing?" asked Raymond.

"Don't have to. The results are all over the news, both radio and television." Indeed they were. And thank goodness for that public exposure because he would have had no reasonable basis for getting the advance report except from Raymond or Arnold Benton.

"Fine then, I'll let you know when I'm ready, Guy."

"The sooner the better. It takes a little while to get things processed." Guy was trying to press without being noticed. It didn't work on Raymond though, as he recognized the tactic.

"When I'm ready, Mr. Markham, I'll let you know. Besides, there's a simple matter of getting the physician's clearance." This was a statement thrown in just to cut off Markham.

"Understood," said the investigator flatly.

Raymond looked him coldly in the eye, and Guy backed off and walked away. What was this man up to? Maybe Errol Forrest's suspicions were right after all. From inside the sanctity of his office he decided to find out.

"Ms. Young?" Raymond said on his intercom. "I need to speak to Errol Forrest. He's staying at the Williams home. Would you get him on the line for me?" Raymond sat down at his desk and turned in his chair to look at the vista from the twenty-first floor. A few moments later, Ms. Young walked in and informed her boss that Mr. Forrest had gone to the airport to go to Denver and Los Angeles. "Why so fast?" Raymond thought. Maybe they went to do the digging on the rookie who had hit Tony. But they wouldn't have left without telling him, or so he thought. Something wasn't right.

●●●●●●

Joey Kearns walked into the D.A.'s facilities to find Marianne Scott sitting in his boss's office. Lew Dobson motioned him to come in. Although he didn't want to, he complied. "Didn't do so well, did we, Joseph?"

"On the contrary, sir. We both knew that the motion was a complete long shot. Shifting the burden of proof is damned near impossible, especially with an experienced attorney like Raymond Sutter." Joey noticed that Marianne Scott was totally relaxed and not the aggressive victim she had been previously. Before, she seemed to be out for blood. Now she was a tame kitten. "How are your bruises and wounds? Healing well, I presume?" asked the prosecutor.

"Yes, they are. There's not as much pain today," Marianne answered.

"That's good news." Changing the subject, he continued his questions. "What do you think about the results of today's hearing, Ms. Scott?"

"To tell you the truth, I'm very relieved," answered Marianne. Her answer caught both men off-guard to the point that they each did a double take.

"Excuse me?" Joey asked incredulously.

"Why so relieved?" asked Mr. Dobson. Marianne knew that she had slipped, so she answered quickly.

"I mean I'm relieved that the trial date is going to be advanced. This way, the whole mess can be put behind us very quickly. Furthermore, it will have less impact on my daddy's team because everything should be finished before the start of the regular season. Right, gentlemen?"

"Good answer," thought Joey. This woman was truly a little bitch. Maybe there was some truth to what Anthony Williams had said after all. Maybe it was all a frame. Nevertheless, he had a case to prosecute. Specimen or not, he could win this case and make a substantial name for himself in the process. The evidence still pointed in the direction of Anthony Williams, and that was the direction he was going to follow. "Ms. Scott, will you excuse us? We'll call you when we need to talk some more," said Joey flatly. This dismissal worried Marianne. She didn't know if they believed her answer or not. She got up and left Mr. Dobson's office. Joey closed the door behind her. This was not a good sign.

"Listen, boss, I'm having a hard time trying to locate that Lucas Johnson. You know. He's the rookie that hit Anthony Williams. I believe that his testimony will be crucial to our case. We have to find him before the defense does."

"And if we don't and they don't?" asked Lew Dobson.

"Then it's just another chasm we have to cross. But if the defense finds him before we do, anything's possible."

"On what are you basing your thoughts, Joseph?"

"Just a gut reaction to Marianne's response of a moment ago."

"Then pull in your gut and go find that man. Scour the earth. Find that asshole. Shit, my reelection is dependent on finding a dumb black athlete that may have been having an affair with a white woman. This whole mess is getting ugly, very ugly. Before it's over, it will be out of control." Joey sat there taking in what his boss had just said while watching his intensity build. "Don't just sit there, Kearns. Get your ass up and go to work!" Joey said nothing but left Lew Dobson's office immediately.

While sitting at his desk, Joey seemed to be unfocused . . . to be lost in thought. But then he focused on a plaque he was given by his criminal law professor after he was hired at the district attorney's office. The inscription read, "Your highest duty is to seek out and expose the truth!"

● ● ● ● ● ●

Ned Scott sat in the privacy of his anthracite gray BB 512 Ferrari. He started the engine and was about to take a drive when he heard the news on the radio about the results of the hearing. "Shit!" he said aloud. He turned off the engine and sat back in the molded cream leather seat of the Boxer. Now he wouldn't be able to find out whether his daughter was lying or telling the truth. Despite the pain it caused, Ned's gut reaction was that Marianne was doing something wrong. Tony wouldn't hurt a fly, let alone a white woman. Ned knew all about Tony's childhood experience with the Klan. Ned knew about the Klan in intimate detail. Some of his distant relatives were still Klan members in Mississippi.

Ned knew that Marianne loved sports, especially football, hockey, and basketball. In fact, Marianne had a better outside jump shot than most men. She was not the awkward girl who couldn't throw or catch a ball. On the contrary, she was very talented. During her sophomore year, she had played women's basketball at UCLA. In mid-season, she was dismissed from the team for curfew violations -- attending a pregame party. She asked her father to use his influence to reverse the coach's decision. Ned refused, thinking it to be a valuable lesson. In the sports arena, rules are rules.

Ned remembered that Marianne had gone to the Pro-Bowl game last January. He remembered paying for the trip for his daughter and her best friend, Leslie Seymour. This was a pre-graduation trip. Ned also remembered having to bail his daughter out of jail on a charge of drinking under the legal age during her freshman year at UCLA. She had been attending an L.A. Rams victory party. He hoped that this information didn't get out because he had paid dearly to have the case files obliterated from the system. He feared that the implications from this prior experience would prevent discovery of the truth in this present fiasco.

Nevertheless, his resolve was the same. He restarted the engine, revved it a few times and drove off. If his daughter was trying to frame Tony Williams, there would be hell to pay. If Tony Williams had raped his daughter, he was as good as dead.

In another part of the Scott estate, Elizabeth Cobb was fuming. She thought to herself that, if the courts couldn't handle their responsibilities and look out for the best interests of her granddaughter, then she would handle matters herself. Elizabeth picked up the phone and made a call to a small town near Natchez, Mississippi. "Hello, Frank? This is Aunt Lizzy."

"Hi there, Aunt Lizzy," Frank said in a thick drawl. "What's doing with you and the Yankees up yonder? We heard about Marianne."

"That's what I'm calling about. I've got a job for you and your boys. I need some old-style Klan intimidation up here in Pittsburgh!"

Chapter 13

The flight to Denver was only a few minutes less than three hours. Adrian and Errol emerged from the United Airlines Boeing 737 to find Coach Blu Stiller waiting for them. As usual, he started barking orders and admonished Adrian to find Lucas Johnson quickly. This was necessary to help put an end to the madness surrounding the blind-side hit as well as the ridiculous allegations of Marianne Scott.

"If you need any help from the Broncos, just call me, Adrian. We'll be standing by, day or night. Just get it done. By the way, your connecting flight is just down the 'B' Concourse at Gate 21. The flight leaves in twenty-five minutes. When you arrive in Los Angeles, it will be just after 11:00 P.M. I've taken the liberty of booking you both in at the Airport Marriott®. Everything is prepaid. You and Mr. Forrest be careful out there. Also, your spot is secure on the team, so don't worry about the next couple of pre-season games. But sooner or later, you'll need to get some practice in with the quarterback, more for timing than anything else." Adrian rolled his eyes at Coach Stiller in playful defiance as they walked down the concourse. "Here's a file with everything we know about Lucas Johnson." When they arrived at the departure gate, Adrian shook the coach's hand, as did Errol.

"Thank you, Coach. We'll give you a call tomorrow." Adrian and Errol turned and presented their tickets to the gate attendant and walked down the jetway to board the Boeing® 727.

● ● ● ● ● ●

Railroaded!

At 12:15 A.M., Raymond dialed Dot Jensen's private home line. She answered in a bit of a haze. She usually went to bed at 11:00 P.M., watched the news and turned off the TV at 11:35 when the news was over. She would typically get up at 5:15 A.M., leave by 6:00, and be at the office by 6:30 even though she didn't have to report for work until 8:30 A.M. Because of her routinely early arrival, on most days she left the office between 3:30 and 3:45 P.M., thereby avoiding the traffic on the drive home to her house in upper Northwest D.C., overlooking Rock Creek Park.

"Hey there, sleepyhead. Somebody loves you and needs a big favor," said Raymond softly.

"No favors until you come see me," answered Dot in a soft, sexy voice.

"I'm coming down on Friday night as I said, and I'll stay until Sunday. But if you take a little vacation time, we could drive back together. I could use a little moral support behind this case. It's going to turn out to be a mess." Dot sat up in her bed and paid close attention to Raymond. He had never asked her for moral support before. The Williams case must really be troubling him.

"Listen, baby. Whatever you need, you know I'll help you. I'm doing the research you asked for, and as I promised, I'll have everything ready for you by the time you get here. In the meantime, what else do you need?"

"I need to bring Tony Williams down for a semen specimen analysis. If it's done in the FBI lab, then I'll know everything's kosher."

"And do I get to be the medium for production on that hunk of a man?" she asked jokingly.

"Not if you want to live to see Saturday morning, you don't." Raymond was just as funny with his response. "When should we be there?"

"Not later than 3:30. We can access the afternoon shift, and since it's a Friday, there will be less activity and fewer hassles. Is that okay, darling?"

"That's fine. His wife can drive my car back on Saturday morning. We can drive back on Sunday or fly back. Your choice," answered Raymond.

"I'll check on my vacation time tomorrow. By the way, what are you going to do with the results of the tests?" she asked.

"Just save them for a rainy day. I don't think I'll need them to prove Tony's innocence, but I'd rather be safe than sorry. This must be done in strictest confidence. The prosecution was denied a motion to produce a sample, so this is only for our protection."

"Understood, but only as long as I get my very own personal sample from you know who." Raymond smiled and regretted that he had to wait three days to see her.

●●●●●●

Wednesday morning in Los Angeles was cool and foggy. The marine layer was thick and not forecasted to burn off until early afternoon. Adrian and Errol were up at 6:30 A.M. and had breakfast together at 7:00. At 7:30, Adrian rented a car so they would be completely mobile. Besides, later that night, both were going to join Adrian's parents, Raymond and Gloria Christopher, for dinner. At 7:50 A.M., the two drove off down Century Boulevard and got on the 405 northbound for Westwood. Hopefully, they would get some answers. Unfortunately, they got bumper-to-bumper traffic that would last from Slauson to just before Wilshire Boulevard, their exit. The drive took almost one hour, which during the L.A. metro morning rush hour was quite normal.

Upon arriving at the UCLA campus, their first stop was the office of the athletic director, Mr. Harlan Struthers. Adrian and Errol decided to get his blessing before they confronted any coaches or players. Mr. Struthers was surprised to hear that the two men were waiting to see him. He remembered trying to recruit Anthony Williams and Adrian both. He also remembered that Errol Forrest was a world-class speedster himself. He quickly asked the men into his office. After a few moments of explanation and a call to the Denver Broncos head coach, Mr. Struthers agreed to carte blanche support of their investigation. He called his secretary and told her to prepare a memorandum requesting all players and personnel to give these two gentlemen any assistance they required during their short stay. As luck would have it, the varsity football players were scheduled to report after lunch today for the first team meeting and

Railroaded!

light drills. In the meantime, Mr. Struthers suggested a meeting with the head football coach, Mr. Johnson Turner. After signing an autograph, "The one that got away," Adrian and Errol left the athletic director's office and headed to the football coaching facilities on the opposite side of the stadium.

"Why would anyone give their kid two last names?" asked Errol, speaking of Johnson Turner.

"Your guess is as good as mine. Maybe he was a pain in the ass before he was born. Must have kicked his mother to death!" responded Adrian. Both men laughed aloud.

"Maybe that's why he keeps kickin' ass today!" They laughed even harder and continued their stroll. As they crossed the field, they noticed that several of the players were already there doing wind sprints and basic calisthenics. At the sight of Adrian Christopher in a Broncos team shirt and Errol in a shirt and tie, the players started putting on their best performances. They knew this had to be a preliminary scouting trip.

Errol's eyes focused on one player in particular -- a tall young man who appeared to weigh 225 to 235. He was fast and agile. "See that guy, Adrian? The Broncos need serious help on the line. Bet he would make a good tight end if he can catch. That way he can take out a blitzing linebacker and slip in between the line of scrimmage and the secondary."

"Okay, smart guy," Adrian said. "Let's see what you know." Errol chuckled to himself. Maybe this could be fun. Both walked over to the young man. Adrian started by introducing himself. "Hi, my name is Adrian Christopher and I'm here . . ."

"As a scout for the Broncos?" Deke Flannigan was curious and thankful at the same time. "You guys are here a little early, aren't you?"

"Very early. Are you a Bronco fan?" asked Errol.

"My name is Deke Flannigan. I'm a die-hard Broncomaniac despite being from Ft. Worth, Texas. I hate the Cowboys and the Raiders. Supposedly, a couple of Raiders scouts are going to stop by here later today." Deke was very talkative.

"When?" asked Errol. "We don't want to be seen on the same field with those guys."

"About three this afternoon," answered Deke.

"By then, we'll be long gone but will have made enough preliminary contacts," added Adrian.

"Tell us about yourself, Deke," said Errol, acting the part of a scout.

"To answer all your questions, I play tightend, sometimes full back. Depends on the play. Basically I'm a tightend but don't get utilized very much. Not since we got those two outrageous running backs. I'm actually glad we lost Lucas Johnson to graduation. Maybe I'll get some more playing time this season." The mention of Lucas Johnson gave the two men an unanticipated opening for some questions.

"What did you think about Lucas Johnson?" asked Adrian.

"Damn, he was good. You guys drafted him and for a good reason." Deke paused for a moment and scratched his head. "But it just doesn't make sense. Luke was smart. He wasn't just a dumb jock. No one here understands why old Luke fucked up with his blind-side hit on that Pittsburgh player last week."

"Yeah, neither do we. Coach Stiller was so pissed off, he immediately cut him from the team, even before he left the locker room after the game. That kind of action is not taken lightly by the coach," retorted Adrian.

"Well, he didn't really want to play for Denver anyway." This was news to Adrian and Errol.

"How come?" asked Errol. "The Broncos gave him one helluva good package."

"Everybody here fully expected him to go play for the Steelers. You see, I was his roommate for about three months during his junior year, my sophomore year. We didn't get along too well. He was more of a party animal, so I moved out. My major is chemistry, so I have to study a lot."

"But why the Steelers?" Adrian asked further.

"Well, Luke was having this really torrid love affair with this chippie who turned out to be none other than the daughter of the owner of the Pittsburgh Steelers." Adrian was in shock. Errol had guessed it and questioned further.

"Did it ever break off, Deke?"

"Up until graduation, it hadn't. They were still a hot item. It really pissed off the Scott girl's other boyfriend. I don't remember

Railroaded!

his name except that he was the assistant director of player personnel for the Detroit Lions." Both men were ecstatic at this unbelievably lucky break. Adrian encouraged him to keep on talking, so Deke continued as they strolled slowly across the playing field. "Yeah, at graduation in June, people were laughing and saying she was going to have dark chocolate dessert with white icing. She was a real rabbit who particularly liked black athletes, not that some of us couldn't handle that piece. She even used to go to the local pro games and hang out at the after-parties. That used to piss off Luke pretty bad." Deke paused for a minute. "I hate to admit it, but I would have liked to take a tumble with her myself."

"Instead of tainted 'tang,' how would you like a tryout with the Denver Broncos, strictly on the QT?" Adrian asked.

"Are you shitting me, man?"

"Nope. I'll call Coach Stiller and tell him we've spotted a significant tightend prospect. You can catch, can't you?"

"Is the Pope still Catholic, man?" answered Deke Flannigan. "I'm the best there is in college today. It's just that no one knows it yet." Adrian sensed a degree of sincerity in this young man and liked him instantly. Errol was a little more cautious. To him, he was only a source of pertinent information that might bail their best friend out of trouble.

"Well then, we can get the director of player personnel to come and see you and arrange for a tryout now before the season gets underway. See how you like it. I'll make the call today." Errol took Deke's information for two reasons. First, Adrian was a man of his word and would talk to Coach Stiller about this player. Second, they needed the information for purposes of a subpoena. "I'll even clear the tryout with Coach Turner," added Adrian.

After a few more minutes of discussion covering the tight end's athletic statistics, Adrian and Errol both shook Deke Flannigan's hand and continued their walk to the football coaching office. On their arrival, they found Coach Turner standing in the doorway of his office waiting for them.

"Best tightend we ever had here at UCLA, that Deke Flannigan." He invited them in and walked around behind his desk. "What can I do for you, gentlemen? I just received a call from Struthers, who instructed me to help you in any way I can."

Johnson Turner was very direct and not known for loquacious oratory. He was always short and brief.

"Quite honestly, we're trying to get as much information as we can to help Tony Williams," said Errol. Coach Turner changed the subject for a moment.

"Why didn't you stay home, Mr. Christopher? We could have used you here." Coach Turner was serious. He had recruited hard to get Adrian. Errol came to the rescue.

"It's all my fault, Mr. Turner. I convinced Adrian to go to Dartmouth. Education was always more important than sports with the three of us. So I helped make sure that Dartmouth gave Adrian a financial aid package he couldn't refuse."

"Damnedest thing I ever saw. Never had a young black man turn down UCLA for the Ivy League before . . . especially a fine athlete like you. Hell, you guys couldn't even play in post-season bowl games!" said the coach a bit more animated.

"But at least I got a Super Bowl ring," Adrian answered, sporting it with pride. "Even if we were on the losing side." The coach relented while examining the ring on Adrian's finger.

"Back to the subject. What can I do to help?" asked Coach Turner.

"We need to know as much as possible about the relationship between Marianne Scott and Lucas Johnson." Errol was very clear and direct.

"You know about that already. Well, shit." Coach Turner shook his head and sat down in his high-backed desk chair. Adrian and Errol sat also. "Marianne Scott was the scourge of my players until she hooked up with Lucas. Lucas Johnson loved her, and she loved black men -- particularly athletes. College or pro, it didn't matter. To make it worse, she was a good athlete herself. Hell, if she hadn't been on a party binge, she would have been one of the best women basketball players this country's ever seen. She got busted for a curfew violation and kicked off the team in her sophomore year."

"What was she doing when she broke curfew?" asked Adrian.

"She was out at a pre-game party with some of the players from the men's team. The next day, Lucas was in my office crying about Marianne's escapades. I tried to counsel him on the problems that he would face being involved in an interracial relationship. I further tried to counsel him that it was a relationship that would never be allowed by the Scott family."

"Why?" asked Errol.

"Last time I looked, the Scotts were from Mississippi." This was news to both men.

"If that's the case, then why would Marianne chase black men?"

"Maybe because they were verboten in the old days," said Coach Turner. "Who knows?"

"I thought Marianne was born and raised in Pennsylvania," said Adrian.

"She was, young man. Except her mother died when she was only ten or eleven. Her grandmother, a Mrs. Elizabeth Cobb-Scott, raised her. She visited Marianne quite regularly during college. As a matter of fact, she attended all three basketball games before she was dismissed from the team."

"Tony and I met Mrs. Cobb at dinner the night before he got hit. Marianne was there also, and we both recognized her as the woman who had been terrorizing Tony and his wife," interjected Adrian.

"Sounds like something Marianne would do. I always thought her to be a treacherous little snake. I just never understood why she gravitated to black men when it would piss off her father and grandmother. That girl is really screwed up. I actually thought that I had talked Lucas out of his relationship with her and was really pleased when the Broncos drafted him. If he had gone to Pittsburgh, he probably would have wound up dead at an early age." Coach Turner lifted his cap and scratched his head. "Anything else I can tell you?"

"Can we count on you to testify if need be?" asked Adrian.

"Only if it doesn't interfere with my coaching schedule."

"What about a statement taken in front of a court reporter, sort of a deposition?" asked Errol.

"Do you know you're asking me to cut my own throat, young man? You probably don't." He rocked in his chair and thought for a moment. "Ah, what the hell. I'm getting too old for this shit. Just let me know what I have to do. Anthony Williams shouldn't have to take a fall behind that little bitch and her daddy's money."

"We'll be in touch again soon, Coach Turner. If not one of us, then probably Mr. Williams's attorney, a Mr. Raymond Sutter." Errol handed the coach one of Raymond's business cards.

"By the way, you might check into the fact that Marianne got busted for something in her freshman year, but her old man covered it up real good. I doubt that you can find a trace of the detail anywhere." That was indeed intriguing information. Adrian and Errol looked at each other and decided not to pursue a new line of questioning.

"Thank you very much for your time, Coach Turner," said Adrian.

"Likewise," said Errol.

"It will be my pleasure when I see that Deke Flannigan is signed by the Denver Broncos. Let's just say it's my charge for cooperating by walking in a bed of rattlesnakes. Get my drift, Mr. Christopher?"

"And then some, sir. It has been my pleasure to see you again. Good luck with this season." Adrian and Errol left his office. Looking back, Errol noticed that Coach Turner was still sitting back in his seat staring out on the practice field.

Down the hall, Adrian saw a payphone and called his mother. He told her that they would not be attending dinner but would be heading immediately to Denver to have the coaching staff intercede with the Detroit Lions in order to follow-up on the lead provided by Deke Flannigan. Adrian hoped that Lucas Johnson was getting closer to exposure.

When they got back to the car, they decided to have lunch back at the hotel, check out, and then grab the first available flight to Denver or Chicago. Changing planes would be easier there for flights to Pittsburgh. The drive to the Marriott was only twenty minutes as there was no traffic.

At the hotel, Adrian called Coach Stiller and relayed the full stats on Deke Flannigan. He agreed to send the director of player personnel to L.A. to look at the kid. If things were as reported by Adrian, they would fly Deke to Denver immediately for discussions and draft possibilities in the spring. Second, Coach Stiller listened intently to the situation with Lucas Johnson. With Adrian on the line, Blu Stiller called the owner of the Detroit Lions. All three

Railroaded!

men agreed that if Lucas Johnson showed up, he would be held in "protective custody." Adrian forgot to inquire about the assistant director of player personnel for the Lions, being entirely focused on Lucas Johnson. At the end of the conversation, Blu Stiller told Adrian to go back to Pittsburgh, where this information needed to be handled immediately.

After a quick lunch, Adrian and Errol took the hotel shuttle bus to LAX. Luckily, they were able to get a direct flight to Pittsburgh -- one stop with no change of planes. They would arrive after midnight at 12:45 A.M. "We need to call Raymond and tell him what we've learned," said Adrian.

"Not just yet. No one is expecting us until Friday, so let's just disappear into the woodwork until Friday morning and see what develops. We can call Raymond tomorrow." Errol wanted to be very cautious about the dissemination of information until he heard from Harvey Sloan.

"What should we tell Tony?"

"We can tell Shelli what we know, but not Tony. Tony needs to know only that we're on the right track and we may be in a position to uncover the whole story on Marianne. We just need a little more time." Errol was hedging his bets with Adrian.

"Why can't we tell Tony everything we know? What's bugging you, Errol?"

"I'll tell you everything after five o'clock tomorrow. Let's just get some rest and put everything out of our minds for now. We need to be as fresh as possible. I need you to be sharper than you've ever been, Adrian. The shit is about to hit the fan. I just feel it." Adrian did too and that made him more uncomfortable because Errol was holding back, or didn't yet know something that was critically important. "You call Tony, and remember, just tell him that we may be able to break this whole case, nothing more. I'll call Shelli at work tomorrow and fill her in. Tomorrow, we'll know more. I promise you, Adrian. We'll know more."

Adrian called Tony and gave him the information just as Errol suggested. He further told him they were on their way to Oakland, California, where Lucas Johnson was born and raised. Maybe they would be able to find him there. Tony agreed and thanked them for their continued help. Adrian hated to lie to his friend, but for the moment, he shared Errol's sense of caution. They could easily explain later.

The flight to Pittsburgh departed on schedule. For its entirety, the two friends didn't speak. Adrian slept until just moments before the landing in Pittsburgh. Errol stared out the window and fell into a deep sleep. He was awakened from that sleep by the initial bounce of the jet on the runway at the Pittsburgh airport. As the plane taxied to the gate, he noticed that he was soaking in sweat. The dreams he had during the flight were not pleasant. He envisioned that Tony had indeed screwed Marianne Scott and, in the midst of the act, had professed love for her. Tony had engaged in this scurrilous behavior in front of a hangman's tree with a dark shadow suspended from the branches.

Chapter 14

Adrian convinced Errol that they should bring Tony up to speed on what they found out in California. Errol was not thrilled with the tongue-thrashing by his friend, and so against his better judgment, he relented. What harm could it do anyway? The real question was, what kind of information, if any, did Harvey Sloan get on Guy Markham? Errol was anxious to find out and would make sure that he was alone when he had that conversation. It was only 10:00 A.M., so he had to wait for at least four more hours before making the call to his fellow Dartmouth alumnus. He would use the excuse of going to an afternoon movie to get away. Adrian and Tony both enjoyed movies, but Errol was the avid movie-goer/amateur critic. He had, from time to time, written critiques for the "Daily D" at Dartmouth. No one would question his disappearing for a while from the rigors of the local events.

"Listen, A.C. I think I'm going to take a break from everything and go catch an afternoon movie. I'll catch up with you at Tony's house afterwards. I should be there about six or so."

"What are you going to see?" asked Adrian.

"Don't know yet. All I know is my brain is tired and I want to separate myself from reality for a few hours. I can re-engage after that." Adrian understood. His brain was also tired from all of the events. He thought he should go with Errol but sensed that Errol wanted to be alone. Adrian thought it best to let him go on his own, especially since he had given him such a hard time about telling Tony what they had learned about Lucas Johnson.

"Just have a good time and fill us in on the movie afterwards. We'll see you for dinner then. I've already talked to Shelli, and she'll be fixing tacos."

"That's great. Tell her to make sure she has some Salsa Brava on hand," said Errol. "And if you can't buy it here, then have some flown in from Denver!" said Errol laughing aloud. Errol was actually the master taco chef. What he didn't know was that he was going to be pressed into service to fix them for everyone when he got back to Tony's.

●●●●●●

Star Wars had been re-released, so Errol went to see it for the twenty-third time. At 3:30 P.M., the movie was over. He went to a phone booth in the lobby of the theater and made the call to Harvey Sloan. "Yes?" came the answer on the other end.

"It's me, Harv," replied Errol.

"If you are on a pay telephone, just give me the number and hang up. I will redial you in several minutes." Errol recited the number and quickly complied, hanging up the telephone. After thirteen minutes that seemed more like thirteen hours, the phone rang. In eager anticipation, Errol grabbed it.

"Why the subterfuge, Harv? What's happening?" asked Errol.

"I'm covering your ass, mate. Guy Markham is not to be messed with in any manner whatsoever. It's a good thing he's on your side, mate."

"Why so? I believe he's also reporting to someone else, as I told you before," responded Errol.

"Then everything's wrong, and you're in a pickle, Errol." Harvey paused for a moment and added in a very somber tone. "You and your friends could be in very grave danger!" Errol was not exactly surprised by this response, but his curiosity was getting the best of him.

"Just give me the straight facts, Harvey. I'm a big boy and so are my friends. I believe that we can take good care of ourselves." Errol was being a bit arrogant with his friend.

"If the investigator weren't a former assassin for the Navy Seals, I wouldn't give a shit and say you're right." Errol almost dropped the telephone receiver in disbelief. The arrogance was gone. The danger was real. To whom was Guy Markham reporting and why? A myriad of questions raced through Errol's mind. He continued

Railroaded!

to listen to Harvey's report. "As a matter of fact, it's been rumored that he has done a few jobs since he retired from active service, both government and private. While there's no proof, one was supposed to have been done right there in Pittsburgh some nine or ten years ago . . . something about a football player who died in an auto accident. If you have access to a facsimile machine, I can send you the details. But after you read them, you have to promise me to burn the material."

"What the hell is a *facsimile* machine?" asked Errol. Rather than waste time explaining the latest 1979 quick communications technology, Harvey agreed to send the material by a special courier. He gave the instructions for picking up the material. "I understand everything and will follow your instructions to the letter. When can I expect the delivery?"

"Not until Monday or Tuesday. I will call you to confirm the day and time. To tell you the truth, it would be better if you go back to New York. It's much easier for me to arrange for the drop there. I'll call you on Sunday at 2130 hours GMT with full details. In the meantime, you know nothing, absolutely nothing. Tell your friends that you rode into a blind alleyway."

Errol could sense the fact that his friend was extremely concerned about what he had discovered. He also sensed that there must be a link between this information and what was happening, or could happen, to Tony. "Thank you, Harvey, just thank you."

"Keep your head above water, mate. You're going to owe me at least five consecutive nights of drinking and a different girl for each night, Errol Forrest, Jr." This remark broke the somber tone of the conversation and made Errol chuckle. "I'll speak to you on Sunday in New York." Harvey hung up, as did Errol. He left the theater and drove to Tony's house, all the while thinking about Guy Markham and praying that no harm would come to his friend.

●●●●●●

Errol sometimes drove his 1977 Firebird Formula with reckless abandon. This was one of those times. He had purchased the car new in October 1976 while he was working with the Pillsbury Company in Atlanta. Despite the fact that he had a company car,

Errol bought the car for safety, assuming that if anything ever happened to his job at Pillsbury, he wouldn't be without wheels. Mechanically, the car was flawless except for a slight shimmy in the front end; New York City streets were tough on the car's radial-tuned suspension.

He pulled into the driveway of Tony's house and screeched his brakes to come to a stop. Tony had company. Errol didn't recognize the almond-colored Cadillac Seville parked in front of him. Errol sat back in the recaro-styled seat for a moment and, holding onto the steering wheel, closed his eyes and refocused, asking God for clarity of vision and strength to persevere through this whole mess.

As he opened his car door, he was greeted by Anthony's son, Steven. "Hi, Uncle Errol. Everybody's waiting for you to cook tacos for us."

"Are they now, Steven? This is news to me," stated Errol as he turned to get out of the Firebird.

"Please, Uncle Errol? Please? You know you make the best tacos in the whole world." Errol gave Steven a big hug, picked him up, and carried him into the house. Once inside, Errol was greeted with a concerted "please, please, please?" from everyone standing in the living room. What a big conspiracy. Errol set Steven down and resigned himself to being a short-order cook for the waiting throng of friends and associates.

The Cadillac belonged to Loren Johnson, who was visiting along with Raymond Sutter. Errol actually hoped that Adrian hadn't yet discussed the situation in California. He definitely wanted to be part of the disclosure process. While cooking, Shelli informed him that while she, Tony, and Adrian had discussed their findings in detail, the subject had not yet been broached with the two attorneys. As a matter of fact, they had only arrived fifteen to twenty minutes before Errol.

Dinner was rather lively and, at times, raucous. Tony enjoyed the atmosphere of frivolity. So did Shelli, Steven, and Adrian. Errol, despite his participation, was entirely focused on other issues. It was still not yet dark at 8:30 P.M. when dinner was finished. After a round of "good nights," Shelli, Steven, and the baby,

Railroaded!

Nicole, disappeared into the inner reaches of the Williams home for bedtime. The men retired to the back porch and sat outside by the pool. "It appears that my friends found out quite a bit while they were in Los Angeles." Tony opened the remarks before Loren and Raymond. "Adrian and Errol can fill you in, but the bottom line is that Marianne Scott and Lucas Johnson were a hot item in the social strata at UCLA. It has been confirmed by independent sources that, through graduation in late May, they were still together. Adrian, go ahead and recount what you learned." Adrian complied and systematically disclosed everything that had been learned during the trip to the West Coast. Errol was very much impressed with his restatement of the facts.

"If I didn't know better, I'd say there was a lawyer in you somewhere, Adrian." Loren Johnson and Raymond Sutter both took note of Adrian's eloquent style.

"I'm just an architect who wears a superman suit once a week for twenty or so weeks!" responded Adrian. Everyone laughed aloud. Errol thought about it a little further, knowing that his friend would make a damn good attorney.

"Listen, gentlemen," said Raymond. "I've got an idea that I would like to address with you."

"And what's that?" asked Tony.

"I'd like Tony to go with me to Washington to the FBI's central labs. I want to get a semen specimen taken and analyzed, and then the results put into a sealed file. That way, when or if the issue ever comes up, we will be fully prepared for counter-measures. I have a friend inside the Bureau who can arrange everything. Everything will be handled on a safe and secure basis. That way, we'll know there's no chance for contamination." Loren was surprised at this suggestion because he thought that Guy Markham was going to "procure" part of the evidentiary sample held in custody at the main precinct station.

"When are you planning this little caper, Raymond?" asked Loren Johnson.

"For tomorrow . . . Friday, that is, if you're up to it, Tony. We can fly or drive. Personally, I would prefer to drive. That way, there's no record of the trip," responded Raymond. Errol was a little edgy at this suggestion. Something didn't sit right.

"Why is this necessary, Raymond?" inquired Errol.

"Do you have a problem with it, Errol?" asked Raymond, doing what lawyers do best -- answering a question with a question.

"Whether I have a problem with it or not is irrelevant. What is important is our friend is being asked to provide a specimen for analysis after the court said it wasn't necessary. I think it only fair to explain your thinking so we can discuss the strategy in detail. No one here is questioning your ability, sincerity, or connections. If we did, you wouldn't have enjoyed four of my famous tacos!" Loren laughed aloud at his commentary. Raymond Sutter had been upstaged by a third-year law student. Errol Forrest was very, very articulate. Silently, Raymond was amused and intrigued.

"Gentlemen, the prosecution is still going to try getting the evidence introduced into the record. Furthermore, they will probably get an expert witness to testify as to the accuracy of the tests. By having our own test reports, we can refute any such evidence or testimony, and, if appropriate, introduce our results as evidence gathered at the FBI labs. The credibility of the evidence will be incontrovertible."

"Thanks, Raymond. I appreciate the explanation. Makes good sense, Tony. I'd go ahead and do it, if you feel up to it. There can be no harm done." Just as he said the words, a chill ran through Errol for no apparent reason.

"When do we leave, Raymond?" asked Tony.

"Tomorrow morning at 9:30," was the reply. "What do you think, Tony?"

"I'll take a painkiller and then sleep most of the way. Do you mind coming along, Adrian?"

"No problem. I don't mind driving long distances."

"In that case, I'll head back to New York tomorrow and come back for the trial or whenever you need me," interjected Errol, needing an excuse to return home.

"Why don't you come with us, Errol? We'll be back late tomorrow night. You can rest here on Saturday and drive back to New York Saturday afternoon. Besides, it's been a long time since we took a road trip together." Adrian and Errol both laughed, thinking about some of their college road trips to the women's schools in New England.

Railroaded!

"That's a good idea, Tony. Besides, I'd like you three guys to meet a good friend of mine in Washington," added Raymond. Errol agreed. They would rendezvous at 7:30 A.M. for breakfast at a nearby Denny's. Raymond was going to stay in Washington and fly back on Sunday. He would take a cab to the rendezvous point and leave his car in the garage. Since he had clothes in Washington, he needed to take only his briefcase. If anyone was watching him, they would think that he was just taking a cab to work.

"In that case, I guess everything's settled. You gentlemen have a safe trip and call me if you need anything. Thanks for your tacos, Errol. Maybe you should let us figure out how to set up a franchise for you." Loren Johnson shook everyone's hand, bid "good night" to Shelli, who had just returned from the children's bedrooms, and left with Raymond, who followed behind him.

●●●●●●

The trip to Washington went off without a hitch. Errol didn't bother calling a woman he knew who lived there. The trip was pure business. There was no time for socializing, or for Errol or Adrian to chase women. It was conducted more like a search-and-destroy mission -- get in quick, get out quick. After only two hours at the FBI labs on late Friday afternoon, the three men were on the road again, headed back to Pittsburgh. They had accomplished their mission and were satisfied with the handling of the whole matter. Dorothy Jensen had invited them to stay for dinner, but the three refused. It was all the better for Dot, who wanted to spend more quality time alone with her man.

●●●●●●

At 11:30 P.M. that same night, a phone call was made from FBI headquarters in Washington, D.C. to Pittsburgh. "Viper," said the voice on the other end over a secure, dedicated line. " I've got some information that you might find interesting. We had an interesting set of visitors today. I'll send you full details by the usual courier method." The man, code-named after a deadly snake, listened carefully, hung up the phone, then lit a cigarette.

Chapter 15

At 2:05 P.M. on Tuesday, the 7th of August, Errol Forrest walked from his apartment to the Hempstead Station on the Long Island Railroad. He took the train to Jamaica, and there, transferred to another train destined for Penn Station. He ran across the platform and found car number 1602. He sat in the third row from the front as instructed. In the seats in front of him were a woman and child and a disheveled, unkempt man from the islands with heavy dread-locks. At Kew Gardens and Forest Hills, several people got on, none of whom looked unusual. No one seemed to be carrying anything that could be passed along.

Once in Penn Station, Errol, following instructions, walked over to the AMTRAK side, and in the circular lobby area, went to a bank of telephones and called a number. The voice that answered told him that he had not been followed. He should go back to the LIRR side of the station to Nathan's hotdog stand next to the ticket windows, buy a hotdog, and then take the 5:08 express train to Hempstead. Further instructed, he was to sit in the third car, fourth row from the front. Errol took down the instructions and complied.

The 5:08 to Hempstead was running three minutes late, which for rush hour trains was not unusual. When he entered the train car, Errol found the fourth row and immediately sat down. The rush-hour mass of humanity overpowered the air conditioning on the train. It was hotter than hell in the train tunnels. The heat was exacerbated by that generated from so many bodies desperate to get out of Manhattan to their suburban Long Island homes. Just as the train was about to depart Penn Station, the same disheveled island man walked up to Errol and said, "You left this at the hotdog stand, Mr. Trees. Have a nice ride to Hempstead." He thrust a dark

Railroaded!

brown envelope into Errol's hand. On one side was a label that read "Christopher, Forrest & Williams, Inc., Architectural Design Consultants." Errol looked up again, but the island man was gone.

"All aboard!" yelled the conductor. The bell sounded, announcing the closing of the doors. Errol sat back and watched as the train rolled into the tunnel under the East River. He didn't open the package despite the fact that his curiosity was about to get the best of him. Instead, he put the material in his briefcase and held it in his lap the whole way.

On arrival at the Hempstead LIRR station, he decided to walk back to his apartment rather than take a cab. It had been a beautiful day that was turning into a more beautiful evening. When he turned onto Fulton Street, a cab pulled up and the driver inquired, "Need a ride, mate?" Errol recognized the voice instantly and got in without hesitation. "You really should consider signing on with the 'POL' when you graduate from Hofstra Law School next year, my friend." Errol was amazed at the fact that his fellow alumnus was sitting in front of him.

"What are you doing here, Harvey? London's not just around the corner, you know."

"Hell, I needed a break and figured that since you were in over your head, I'd come over and brainstorm with you on how to get your ass out of some really deep shit. I know you're free for the evening, so how about us going to the beach? It's cooler there and we can talk freely." It was almost 90 degrees out. "In the meantime, I'd suggest that you tell me where I can stop and buy us some beers. We've got a tradition to live up to, you know." Errol laughed at the reference to the drinking days at Dartmouth.

"We can stop at the MAB store on Hempstead Avenue and then take the Meadowbrook Parkway to Jones Beach," Errol instructed.

"Lead the way, Errol. After we stop at the liquor store, you can start reading the material. I'll fill you in on the rest of the details afterwards. By the way, how did you like my Jamaican associate? He's a Holy Cross, Class of 1973 vintage."

"No shit?" remarked Errol.

"You even know the bloke. You stole his girlfriend during your freshman year. Remember that little chippie who lived in

Severance Hall at Wellesley College? You know the cute one who was introduced to you by your Denver neighbor?"

"You mean Carla what's-her-name?"

"One and the same, mate. Harry said he couldn't resist the opportunity to see you again face-to-face, knowing full well that you'd never recognize him."

"At least he got her back and doesn't carry a grudge. As I recall, they got married within ten days after she graduated from Wellesley in 1974."

"Been divorced three years now. She's fair game again, if you like."

"Shit, Harvey, I've got enough problems of my own right now."

"Like trying to choose between Robin and Sharla? Or is there someone new this week? You're the one who taught me 'study long and study wrong!'" Errol laughed out loud as they pulled up into the parking lot of MAB Liquor Store.

"And what about you, Mr. Sloan? Any new conquests to speak of?"

"Not me. I'm a confirmed bachelor for life." Harvey was laughing at the question from his friend. Errol knew that Harvey had fallen in love with a girl from Pembroke College who one day just disappeared into thin air. No trace, nothing. It was a big mystery that was never solved by the school or the girl's parents. It was one of the reasons that Harvey had gone to work for Interpol. He always believed that one day he would find out what happened to his Christina. Errol, on the other hand, decided to leave well enough alone.

Some twenty-five minutes later, the two men pulled into one of the parking lots at Jones Beach. Errol had finished reading the material during the drive and just sat there staring into space. He and Harvey walked to the beach and sat down on the hard sand about six feet from where the water advanced after the waves broke on shore. The wind was blowing smartly from the southwest. Harvey took out a book of matches from his pocket and struck one new match to burn each of the twenty pages of material.

"I hope you now understand that you've got a world-class mercenary in your camp. He'll sell you out in a minute, Errol. If you think he's reporting to someone else, chances are that Tony's already been sold down the river. All you and your friends can do is mount a tenacious legal defense during the trial and leave nothing uncovered. You're going to have to completely destroy the credibility of Marianne Scott, and in the process, draw the ire of her father. That, in and of itself, is very dangerous. As you've read, the Scott family is not known for their temerity." After he burned the last page of the material, Harvey looked at his friend and noticed a tear streaming from his left eye.

"We can't win, can we?" asked Errol in a somber tone, still staring out over the Atlantic Ocean, which also seemed to be agitated.

"Sure, you can, but only if you disengage that brain of yours and drink this Miller Lite." Harvey popped open two cans and handed one to Errol. "Wah-hoo-wah to you, my fellow Granite Head." They sat yet for a while and reminisced about their days at Dartmouth.

●●●●●●

Every single day since the charges had been filed, the media had continued its own character assassination of Marianne Scott. Anthony Williams was nowhere referred to as the perpetrator of a heinous crime. Instead, he was glamorized as one of Pittsburgh's finest citizens who had been unjustly accused of a crime that, for all intents and purposes, was virtually impossible for him to commit. Everyone in the whole of NFL football land had seen the hit. Letters were pouring in from all over the United States in support of Anthony Williams. Financial support was even sent by fans to contribute to Anthony's legal defense. The biggest financial support came from the NFL Players Association. During a hastily arranged press conference on Friday afternoon, a representative from the NFL Players Association delivered a check in the amount of $50,000 to Johnson, Owens, Sutter & Moss. The union vowed that, if the legal expenses were to cost a penny more, they would cover any excess costs, regardless of the amount. The union leadership had determined that this case was a good example of things that could befall the players if not careful in the social environment.

At the end of the press conference, Loren Johnson read a statement from the NFL Commissioner. While not openly in support of Anthony, the Commissioner had stated that the whole affair was reprehensible and hoped that the truth would be clearly revealed during the trial. He had further stated that he was glad that the trial would be held and finished during the preseason so that it would not have an impact on regular season play. The trial was still ten days off and already the whole world had lined up against Marianne Scott.

Elizabeth Cobb and her granddaughter sat and watched the Friday evening television news blitzes. The programs implied in their reports that the youngest Scott was a liar and the most dangerous type of harlot imaginable, one that would systematically target a decent and upstanding family man for crimes not committed, and for other reasons as yet unknown.

"What are we going to do, Grandma? The trial starts a week from Monday and I'm scared to death. The press keeps crucifying me." Marianne was completely agitated, especially now that the NFLPA had stepped in to help Anthony. "It's almost like the whole of Pittsburgh has forgotten who we are and what we've done for this city."

"I haven't and your father hasn't, and that's all that matters! The people of Pittsburgh are gullible sheep. Just remember that your father is taking care of everything." Elizabeth Cobb was distracted and angered by all the negative media attention focused on her granddaughter.

"If he is, how come I don't feel like it? How come the media is still persecuting me at every turn? How come I have become the perpetrator instead of the victim?"

"Because you were stupid, Marianne! You should have known better than to pick on one of your daddy's prized stallions." Elizabeth Cobb stood up and started pacing around the large family room. She then began lecturing to Marianne. "In the old days, things would have been simple. The nigra would have been taken out and whipped or lynched. There was no need to waste valuable time on worthless nigras."

Railroaded!

"This isn't Mississippi, Grandma. Despite all the Scott family power, it appears that I may be in a fight for my life!" Marianne was very animated, almost screaming at her grandmother.

"You just calm yourself and remember to respect your elders, young lady. I'll not have you sassing me like some common street urchin. This is your mess that you've created. I'm not the enemy, young lady. Anthony Williams is the enemy. Lucas Johnson is the enemy. He violated you just like your mother was violated. I'm not going to sit by and watch another Scott woman destroyed by the likes of another nigra man. I hope you've learned your lesson and will leave them alone for the rest of your life. They are uncivilized barbarians and should be nothing more than servants to the Scott family." Elizabeth Cobb stood over Marianne and shook her carved wooden cane that she used more for effect than necessity.

"But what about Daddy? It's his fault that Mama's dead. He's the one that killed her. It's like he pulled the trigger himself."

"Damn it, child! So what if he did? Is that any reason for you to destroy your life gallivanting around like a common floozy? Even the thought of your purity being violated under a black body is utterly revolting to me. If I were twenty years younger, I would have killed Lucas Johnson myself. And now you've gone and picked up another nigger from out of the woodpile?" Elizabeth Cobb was infuriated.

"Come on, Grandma. You're getting too worked up! There's no need for you to have a stroke over this. I'm the one in trouble, not you." Marianne stood up and hugged her grandmother. Both women were crying.

"Just remember that you're a Scott and we always take care of our own. I guarantee you, Marianne, that what happened to your mother, will not happen to you."

● ● ● ● ● ●

On Wednesday night before the trial, Tony's three-year-old son went to bed wearing Superman pajamas. Steven, as usual, went soundly to sleep as soon as his head hit the pillow. Well after midnight, he stirred for a moment and twisted his small body around in what seemed to be a different contortive position. After another few moments, he twisted and squirmed again. He pulled his knees up to his chest in a fetal position and adjusted his head on the pillow.

After another few moments he opened his eyes and noticed a bright yellow glow on his mirror. He got out of bed and looked out the window. After staring for just a moment, he ran into his parents' room at the back of the house. "Mommy, Daddy, wake up. Please wake up." Shelli stirred first from a deep sleep.

"What's the matter, baby?" Tony also started to stir.

"Jesus has come to our house, Mommy. He's in the front yard!" said an animated Steven.

"What are you talking about, Steven?" asked Tony.

"I woke up and saw Jesus in the front yard. He's still there!" Tony and Shelli instantly arose and ran into Steven's front bedroom. Looking out their son's bedroom window, Shelli screamed aloud, but she did not hear the primordial scream that came from the depths of her husband's childhood fear.

"You bastards, you bastards! Leave us alone!" In a rage, she tried to call the police, but the phone was dead. The line had obviously been cut. She could only hope that a neighbor would see the conflagration on the front lawn and call the police and fire department. After checking on their daughter, she ran through the house to see if everything was safe and secure. Nowhere was there any apparent damage to the house or sign of break in. She ran back into Steven's room and noticed that Tony had collapsed under the window and was curled up in a ball, babbling like a child.

Shelli tried to comfort her husband, but to no avail. He kept babbling in a childlike voice, "Please don't hurt me. Please don't hurt me." The twelve-foot burning cross had reignited old memories and old fears. The Ku Klux Klan was back -- back in Pittsburgh. This wasn't Alabama or Mississippi. This was Pennsylvania. Now there would be a whole new set of fears. But fear was not guiding Shelli Williams. Instead, white-hot anger ran furiously through her veins.

"Steven, you stay here with Daddy. Everything's going to be all right. Everything's going to be okay." She stroked his curly head and made sure he sat down next to his father. "You have to be like Hercules and look after your father." Steven complied.

Railroaded!

First, she ran into Nicole's bedroom and checked on her. She was sleeping peacefully. Next she ran back into their bedroom and retrieved a Colt 45 automatic. She checked the magazine and made sure it was full. Shelli was a crack shot up to two hundred feet with the sidearm. She proceeded to the kitchen and then into the garage, all the while being cautious not to expose herself to any outside windows. Inside the garage, she got into one of the cars and turned on the electrical system. On the CB radio, she reached the police and informed them of the situation. The police said they would call the fire department, but they didn't arrive for some twenty minutes despite the fact that the station was only a seven-minute drive from the Williams residence. The police did not appear for almost thirty minutes. To Shelli, it seemed as if this whole incident had been planned.

Next, she went back into the kitchen and got their 35mm Canon camera. She ran back upstairs and took several pictures of the blazing cross from a clear, second-story vantage point. She would make sure the press got the film of this egregious event. After taking twelve pictures, she went back to Steven's room.

Tony was a basket case, still balled up in a corner. Shelli got him to take one of his painkillers, which would hopefully get him back into a deep sleep. Tony took the pill and drank the glass of water that Shelli had presented. She helped him stand to walk back to their bedroom. At the bedside, he fell in slow motion, again curling up into a tight ball. Shelli was at least pleased with this small degree of success. Next, she gathered her children together and put them in the bed with their father.

When the police arrived sometime after the fire department, she ventured outside the house in a long robe. The Colt .45 was hidden in her robe pocket. Dealing with the police was no easy task. Instead of being helpful or trying to ascertain if the perpetrators were still in the neighborhood, they seemed reluctant to do anything except let the fire department do its job. Instead of rallying the troops to try to find who had committed this crime, they did nothing more than apologize for the intruders. To Shelli, their apologies were almost antagonistic. Shelli clearly understood the implications of this response. Nothing was going to be done.

After the police left, Shelli did not leave the house fearing a return by potentially lurking Klansmen. She was a prisoner in her own home because the telephone lines were cut. None of these events could be reported to anyone until morning. She sat in the rocking chair in their bedroom with the Colt .45 on her lap.

Shelli Williams was afraid, but not dominated by fear. Instead of outrage, calculated anger now controlled her thoughts. Someone had come into her world and violated the sanctity of her family. She knew the Scotts' fifty-acre rambling estate was only three miles away. The police department for the Wildwood Country Club area was the same for the towns of Elfinwild and Allison Park. She knew the Scotts were powerful enough to buy off the small local police department despite the overwhelmingly favorable media in support of Tony. She knew that the Scotts were originally from the South and had migrated to Pennsylvania from Mississippi. She knew this was a ploy to create massive fear within Tony based on his traumatic childhood experience. She knew this whole event had to have been staged by Ned or Marianne. Despite these apparent truths, Shelli could do nothing but rock and think. She did know one thing, however. The Scotts were not going to destroy her family.

The faint glow of daylight was starting in the east. As she stared out the bedroom window, Shelli stopped rocking and fell asleep. It was almost 5:00 A.M.

Chapter 16

Shelli awoke at 7:30 A.M. and first took a hot shower to prepare herself mentally for the tasks at hand. After getting dressed in jeans and a T-shirt, she started on an offensive pace that would have scared most soldiers. While everyone was still sleeping, she left the house and drove to the Wildwood Country Club clubhouse. Once there, her first call was to the telephone company. The representative to whom she spoke promised to have a repairman available and on her front porch in not more than thirty minutes. Next she called her friend at the television station. She said she would be right out to pick up the film that Shelli had taken of the burning cross. Next, she called Errol, then Adrian, and finally Raymond Sutter. Raymond would be right over, along with Loren Johnson. Adrian couldn't come to Pittsburgh until Sunday. He was scheduled to play in the Saturday night preseason game. Errol would leave immediately and drive to Pittsburgh. At 8:05 A.M., Shelli was back at home.

The telephone repairman arrived first at 8:10. He was thrilled to be doing the work despite the trauma of the surrounding events. He was a big fan of Anthony Williams. He even put in a buried secondary line so that, if the main line was cut again by unscrupulous individuals, the Williams home would still be able to get through to the outside world. Shelli was very appreciative of this extra service and offered a substantial tip. "Not necessary, Mrs. Williams. But if you could have your husband, when he's up to it, send me an autographed picture, me and my kids would be much obliged." Shelli agreed and took the repairman's name and address.

Raymond and Loren arrived next about 8:30 A.M. Accompanying them were three agents from the Pittsburgh office of the FBI. The agents determined, after examining the grounds of the house, that not fewer than eight men had been there during the night. They also found a message painted on the side of the house, in red paint, to symbolize blood: *"The nigger must die!"* After pictures were taken and the FBI agents were finished with their work, Shelli called a local contractor to come to remove the egregious graffiti.

About 9:00 A.M., Tony awoke, put on a T-shirt and slowly walked into the family room. Shelli went over to him and held him tightly. "I had a terrible dream last night, darling. I dreamed the Ku Klux Klan had burned a cross in our front yard and were trying to hang me just because I told Marianne I didn't want her. It scared me to death." Shelli then led her husband slowly to the kitchen where Raymond, Loren, and the special agent in charge of the investigation were standing and chatting. Tony was surprised to see these men standing in his kitchen. He couldn't recall any meetings scheduled for this morning. "Did I miss a meeting, gentlemen? I seem to be a little out of it this morning."

Loren Johnson spoke first. "Tony, this is Special Agent Jason Moore from the FBI office in Pittsburgh. He's here at our request, along with two other agents."

"Request for what?" asked Tony.

"Last night, darling, someone *did* burn a cross in our front yard." Shelli stood beside Tony, who was visibly beginning to shake. "You've got to pull yourself together, Tony. Don't be afraid -- get mad. Get mad that someone came out here and messed with us over this Marianne Scott case. Someone's trying to intimidate you so you won't be at your best for the trial next week." Tony sat down at the kitchen table and put his head in his hands.

"So I wasn't dreaming last night. I wondered why the kids were in the bed with me when I woke up." Tony gathered his wits and then inquired of his wife, "Are you all right, Shelli?"

"I'm fine, and so are the kids. A lot has happened and I've set some things into motion to start counter-measures. We'll discuss that after the FBI is finished. They need to get going."

Railroaded!

"Mr. Williams, I'm sorry that you endured the trauma of last night. We are going to conduct a full-scale investigation into what's going on," said the FBI special agent in charge. "We'll keep you or Mr. Johnson fully informed as to our progress."

"Maybe you should start with the Scott family. They hail from Mississippi. I wouldn't be surprised if Marianne and her father rallied some old relatives to do this. Ned also knows about my childhood experience . . . I watched a cousin of mine get lynched by the Klan when I was ten."

"I think we'll start right there," stated Agent Moore.

"Thank you for your help, Jason. I'll call you later." Loren Johnson shook the man's hand, as did Tony and Raymond.

"Are you going to be okay, Tony?" Raymond asked. Raymond was burning inside with anger. Not because his client had been traumatized by a deliberate, insidious act, but because as a black man himself, he also understood the pain that Tony was enduring and the apparent position of helplessness facing his family.

"What do we do now, Raymond?" asked Tony, who was now more composed. "I don't think I'm going to take this lying down. Before, I just wanted to clear my name and get on with my life. But now, my family has been assaulted. Before I let that happen again, someone will have to kill me first. I want that Scott bitch destroyed, summarily destroyed. And if we have to do in Ned Scott in the process, so be it. This is war!"

Tony was resolute in his statements. Despite the fact that Raymond and Loren were trying to calm him down, Tony was ready to go to the deepest depths of hell to destroy the woman who had terrorized his family. Shelli was pleased but now more afraid than ever. Errol and Adrian would be able to talk sensibly to their best friend. Hopefully, they could calm his building, raging anger. "Sit down, gentlemen. We have a lot to do." Shelli recounted the events to the men and what she had done thus far.

●●●●●●

The Ku Klux Klan was back in Pittsburgh, terrorizing one of its favorite sons. The commentary of the press was pointed, angry, and disgusted. This whole scandal involving Marianne Scott had gone too far. Now, one of the worst embodiments of racism had raised its ugly head in an otherwise tranquil city.

●●●●●●

Elizabeth Cobb, at seventy-three years of age, was in excellent health. The five-foot seven-inch woman, who didn't at all look her age, bounced around the Scott estate like a spry spring chicken. If she couldn't physically touch the boy who had tormented her granddaughter, then she, through her Klan relatives, could wreak havoc on his family. Elizabeth Cobb was extremely pleased.

That Thursday morning was calm until almost eleven. The elder Scott looked out the kitchen window and saw a charcoal-gray Mercedes sedan heading straight for the kitchen, appearing to be out of control. The driver slammed on the brakes of the 6.9 Liter Mercedes and came to a stop not more than fifteen feet from the kitchen wall. Ned Scott got out of his car and damn near broke down the kitchen door. "What the hell have you done now?" Ned was totally enraged. He grabbed his mother from the kitchen chair and started shaking her, almost violently. "You hateful, evil bitch! You damned, hateful, racist bitch! You called those backwoods relatives of yours and told them to come up here, didn't you? Answer me before I kill you where you stand!"

The chauffeur, who saw the Mercedes come to a screeching halt mere feet from the kitchen wall, came around to investigate. He looked through the window and saw Ned manhandling Mrs. Cobb. He ran into the kitchen and intervened. He pulled his employer off his mother. Still smirking while straightening her sundress, she answered coyly, but with a straight face, "Ned, I don't have any idea what on earth you're talking about. I've been here all morning and haven't done anything." Then she turned to the chauffeur and said, "Thank you, Howard, for rescuing me from my son. He's very out of sorts this morning."

Ned momentarily calmed himself and sat at the kitchen table. Howard knew why his boss was angry. He had already seen the very disturbing news. "Get out of here, Howard. I appreciate your concern, but leave now!" Howard took his cue and left the kitchen, headed for the garage.

Railroaded!

"Shall I repark your car, Mr. Scott?" the chauffeur asked, trying to be helpful as he left the room.

"Get the hell out of here! I don't care what you do with the damned car!" Howard turned and didn't look back. Turning back to his mother, Ned Scott continued. "It's all over the news, Mother. Last night, someone burned a cross on the front lawn of the Anthony Williams home. Everyone in our little affluent community is pissed off. They are all scared, white and black alike. The police chief from Allison is nowhere to be found. It seems he doesn't want to be questioned by the press."

"You think I had something to do with a cross burning? Well, I declare. Whatever has come over you? This is Pennsylvania, not Mississippi. It's 1979, not 1879!" Elizabeth Cobb was talking just like a phony Southern belle.

"Didn't you, Mother? I'd stake my life on it. But that's not the best part. The media is implicating us. The FBI already came and questioned me. What the hell is going on around me? I had an unfaithful wife. I've probably got a slut for a daughter, and now, to top it off, I've got a mother who's a world-class racist bitch. What a fucked-up family!"

"Hmpf," she responded in a more normal tone. "Serves that Williams boy right for treating Marianne like so much cow dung."

"I don't believe you. Haven't you heard a word I've said? My family, no, *I* am being blamed for the Ku Klux Klan coincidentally showing up in Pittsburgh just in time for this trial. This has gotten completely out of hand. Marianne's not talking to me. God only knows where her head is. Probably messed up from listening to your evil bantering. You're acting like the Williams family deserves to be terrorized by the Klan. Damn you, Mother!" He stood over her and slapped her. "Damn you to hell!"

Elizabeth Cobb stood up and, in a fluid stroke, retaliated. She slapped her son, exclaiming, "When are you going to grow up and start acting like a Scott?" Ned was totally pissed off with his mother's antics. He stormed out of the kitchen, got in his car, which Howard had properly parked in the traffic circle, and drove off.

Elizabeth Cobb, despite smarting from being slapped by her son, was thrilled with the results. She made a phone call. "Atta boy, Frank. You did real, real good."

"We'll continue to follow your 'structions, Aunt Lizzy. If you need anything else, jus' call me. By the way, me and the boys haven't had this much fun since we were involved in beating the niggers doing the civil rights marches in the middle sixties."

"Well, you just keep up the good work, Frank. I suspect the trial will be over by the 30th. Then you can all go home. If you need any petty cash for expenses, just let me know."

●●●●●●

Ned Scott was so infuriated with his family that he couldn't see straight. Once and for all, he had to know the truth. He couldn't wait for the trial to expose reality. He was in jeopardy of losing his NFL franchise. The implication that the Scott family was involved in the reemergence of the Ku Klux Klan in Pittsburgh was already being discussed in the League headquarters in New York.

He sat in his Mercedes in front of the townhouse complex where Marianne lived. He had been waiting for her for almost forty-five minutes when she drove up in her black Corvette. She parked the car in front of her unit and got out with three shopping bags. She didn't notice her father's car parked across the way. Nor did she notice him get out and advance toward her. Before she opened the door, he was upon her, grabbing her arm. "We've got a lot to discuss, young lady."

"You're hurting me, Daddy!" cried the surprised Marianne, who was caught completely off guard.

"You're not too old for me to whip your behind, if it's in order. And whip it I will, if you lie to me. Get in there." Marianne opened the door and the two Scotts entered. She started crying, but her father was not impressed. "Sit your little ass down. You know you've got a lot of explaining to do." Marianne complied with her father's commands.

"What do you want, Daddy?"

Railroaded!

"I want you to tell me everything that happened . . . every single detail. If you leave one thing out, then I will tear you apart myself. Do you understand, young lady?"

Marianne was terrified, really terrified. She remembered the night that her father had found out about her mother's affair. The yelling and screaming were unbearable. The crying and sobbing were heart-wrenching. She had to be careful, extremely careful. She knew that if she could sway her father, Anthony Williams was as good as dead. If not, she could wind up being a corpse.

Marianne recounted the events in Hawaii, but this time she added a new twist. She produced and handed to her father a single photograph of two people in bed together; Tony was asleep and appeared to be snuggled next to his daughter. As she continued to explain the events that took place in Hawaii, she could see the anger start to build in her father.

"Why should I believe what I see in this photograph when you could have manufactured this picture to suit your needs? Tony Williams says differently and I'm inclined to believe him."

"My girlfriend, Leslie -- you know her -- she's the one who took the picture. She was pretty drunk, too."

"So what about all the people who supposedly witnessed you being spurned by Tony Williams? How do you account for their reports? And if they testify, how are you going to overcome this apparent discrepancy in your story?"

"Everyone was drunk, so how would they really understand what they saw."

Ned considered her response. Tony Williams did admit that he was drunk. His friend Adrian had also admitted he was drunk. Drunkenness meant uncharacteristic behavior. Ned thought to himself that having the public image that he did, Tony would dislike any public display of affection or someone making a "pass" at him, even if inebriated. Marianne continued.

"Anyway, Tony wanted to be secretive and discreet. He got mad because I made a public gesture. But later, we sneaked away to a bedroom together. I had Leslie take the picture so I could send it to his wife as a potential insurance policy, to make sure he told his wife about us. I was getting mad and impatient at all his broken promises."

"Why the harassing letters to his wife?" asked Ned, changing the subject.

"He told me he loved me and wanted to be with me forever. But first he had to fix things with his family." Ned listened and let her continue. "When I first got home from school, I didn't try and reach him because I was still sorting things out with Lucas Johnson." Ned rolled his eyes and grew angry for again being reminded of his daughter's promiscuity and the fact that one of his players had been seriously injured by her former lover. "Lucas wanted to marry me, but I told him that I was in love with Tony. He was at first heartbroken and then angry. I guess he went off the deep end, and that's why he hit Tony the way he did. Lucas was jealous and angry and wanted to get in a parting shot. He thought that if he could seriously injure Tony, he could win me back." Ned couldn't believe what he was hearing.

"And what about the events after the first preseason game? You conned me about going out to some victory parties, didn't you?" asked Ned incredulously.

"I wanted to make up with Tony so I surprised him in the car. Instead, he was mad and told me it was over, that we were through." Marianne's voice started to crack.

"Howard tells me that the two of you were physically engaged but then something happened. Tony demanded to be let out. After he stopped the car and the two of you got out, he saw Tony hit you one time. He then drove off. So what happened then?"

"Tony told Howard to stop the car and then tried to push me out. When he couldn't, he got out and I got out after him, still trying to convince him that we should be together. He hit me hard and I fell to the ground. Then I told Howard to leave."

"And what then?" asked her father.

"When Tony saw there was no one around, he looked at me with a look I never saw before -- a look of hate. Then he said, "if you want me so bad, then I'll give you what you want." He got on top of me and hit me continuously. Then he ripped my dress and, right there on the public street, he raped me."

Marianne approached her father tentatively and took his hand. She looked up at her father with misty eyes and continued, "Daddy, I know I haven't done very many things to make you proud of me. I haven't been the ideal daughter. But do you really think I would go so far as to allow myself to be beaten and raped or try and put a family man in prison because he was dragging his feet on a commitment? How could I deliberately put myself through this public humiliation or jeopardize everything that you've built? Do you really believe that I could do all of this on purpose?" Tears were flowing as Marianne continued her hysteria.

Ned held his daughter by her shoulders and looked deeply into her pale blue eyes. At that moment he began to see his little girl again. He looked at her and realized that she *couldn't have* wreaked such havoc deliberately. Ned was overcome with emotion at the trauma that he perceived his daughter must have experienced. Instead of pursuing the time discrepancy, Ned succumbed to his daughter's sterling performance.

"Calm down, darling." Ned drew his daughter to him and embraced her. "I'm so sorry this happened to you, so very sorry." Ned started to cry. "I'll protect you, baby. No one will ever hurt you again. No one fucks with the Scott family, no one!" After a few moments, both began to calm down from the emotion of the moment. Ned told his daughter that he had some things to do and would call her later.

"Thanks for believing in me, Daddy," said a still emotional Marianne. Ned kissed his daughter and left the townhouse.

He sat silently in his car for just a moment. "How could I have been so wrong about Tony? I wonder how much is real and how much is bullshit?" He looked at the picture that he had confiscated and said, "If you fucked over my daughter, Anthony Williams, you will pay with your life!"

Besides the emotional display and plausible tale of woe, things *still* didn't ring true. Ned was perplexed because something was missing from this whole sordid mess. He would figure it out later. But for now, the primary question was why did Elizabeth call in her Klan relatives? "I wonder," he said as he tapped his fingers on the steering wheel. He started the car and drove away.

After her father had pulled away, Marianne went to the bathroom to wash her face and erase the black lines under her eyes from running mascara. A little Visine removed the red from her eyes. After drying her face thoroughly, she applied fresh make up.

Whitfield Grant

Leaning over the basin to get closer to the mirror for lipstick application, she smiled and said, "Best damned Academy Award performance ever seen. The old man's hooked and I'm 'Scott free'!"

She called her grandmother and restated the course of events that had just transpired. "Excellent, my dear. Well done," stated Elizabeth. "Now things will start to go our way. That Williams boy is finished."

●●●●●●

Ned Scott returned home and apologized to his mother for slapping her. He did not apologize for the inference that she had invoked the presence of the Klan. "I want you to stay out of this whole mess, Mother. I know you like to put your hands in things from time to time, but this one is for the big boys. I understand everything now. I will take care of everything from now on. After all, no one messes with the Scott family and gets away with it."

"Now you're talking, son. That's all I ever wanted to hear," responded Ned's mother, pounding her fist on the kitchen table. Elizabeth Cobb was thrilled at the results of her son's confrontation with Marianne.

Ned left the kitchen and stopped at the powder room to use the facilities. Then he went into his study for a moment before leaving to go back to the office. As soon as he left, Elizabeth made another call to her Southern contingent. "Listen, Frank. I don't think I'll be needing you boys around any more. Thanks for everything."

"No sweat at all, Aunt Lizzy. But we'd like to stay just the same. You never can tell 'bout these things."

"Suit yourself, boys. Enjoy your stay in Pittsburgh. If I find out that everything is really okay, I'll have you boys over for dinner one day next week, okay?"

"Thank you, Aunt Lizzy. We'd be very 'preciative." She hung up the phone and continued to bounce around the house, being of extraordinarily good cheer. All the Scotts were kicking butt in unison, and Anthony Williams would soon be old news.

Chapter 17

As Arnold Benton listened to the news, his upbeat mood changed to one of disgust. For some unknown reason, he had to talk to Joey Kearns right away. He picked up the phone and dialed the opposing counsel on their now celebrated case. "Joseph Kearns here. May I help you?"

"Joey, this is Arnold Benton."

"What the fuck do you want? The whole damned world is going ballistic and I get a call from you of all people." Joey was raving like a lunatic.

"Calm down, Joey. Just calm down. I didn't call you about the case or the trial or any of the KKK bullshit that's all over the news. I thought that you and I could go have lunch and just talk."

"What about, Benton? What could you possibly have to say to me?"

"Listen, man. I just wanted to apologize for what happened in law school and bury the hatchet. You guys were good. Gallagher and I were lucky . . . lucky because you were intimidated by us. We fed on that intimidation, which wasn't particularly fair to you. I just thought you should know and I wanted to apologize." Joey Kearns was silent. "Are you still there?"

Joey was completely taken aback by Benton's friendly overtures. Cynically, he doubted his opponent's sincerity. Being curious, however, he considered that Benton might be useful to him in the future and therefore decided to respond in a friendly manner.

"You can buy me a couple of drinks after work. I'll need them by then." Arnold was relieved. Joey continued. "Besides, Arnold, you're supposed to feed on being able to intimidate your opponents.

You just did a better job than we did. By the way, I'm going to whip your ass in this case."

"May the best man win, Joey! I'll meet you in front of the courthouse at 4:45. We can get drunk and talk about old war stories before we really gear up for war on Monday."

"I'll be there." As both men hung up their telephone handsets, Arnold Benton felt a chill run through the whole of his body. After a moment, he dismissed it as nothing.

● ● ● ● ● ●

Judge Gerald O'Connor was aghast at the new turn of events surrounding this trial. All he needed was to have the greater Pittsburgh community turn on itself over pure racist bullshit. After hearing the news on the radio at 11:00 A.M., he organized a quick conference call with lead counsel on the case and set a meeting for tomorrow, Friday, at 10:30 A.M. With Raymond Sutter and Joseph Kearns on the line, he laid out the basic rules: if there were any displays or accusations of racism, the offending party would be put up on charges and disbarred.

On Friday morning at 8:45, Judge O'Connor arrived at his chambers to prepare for the attorneys' conference, which was scheduled to take place in less than two hours. "Plenty of time," he thought to himself. As he finished a call to a television reporter from Los Angeles, during which he reaffirmed his position that there would be no cameras allowed in his courtroom, he received a Federal Express overnight delivery. He wasn't expecting any deliveries so this was extremely curious. He opened the package and inside found a note and a Gold VISA® Card. He read the note in utter disbelief.

"How do you spell Pennsylvania Supreme Court?
C-O-N-V-I-C-T-I-O-N!
The attached Card is a token of appreciation for your support."

Judge O'Connor looked for an airway bill to see who would have the audacity to send such a package. The shipping document had been removed. He called Federal Express®. Without the air bill, there was no way to trace the package. He sat back in his

Railroaded!

leather chair and thought, all the while staring at the Gold VISA® card sitting on the desk in front of him. He leaned forward, picked up the card and examined it closely. He called the number on the back and inquired as to the card's validity. The customer service operator said it was indeed valid. He inquired further as to the credit limit and was instructed to hold for one moment. Thirty seconds later, she came back on the line and asked for his social security number, date of birth, and mother's maiden name. He responded to all three. "Your credit limit is $1,000,000, sir."

"There must be some mistake," stated the judge in disbelief.

"No mistake, sir. I'm reading the information off the computer monitor," stated the customer service agent.

"So, if I use this card, I have to pay back what I use?" asked the judge, still recovering from the shock.

"One moment please while I connect you with the issuing bank." The agent went off-line for a few moments. The next person to come on the line had a distinctly foreign accent that he could not place.

"May I help you, sir?" she asked in perfect English.

"I received a credit card that I didn't apply for and I do not understand . . ."

"You have properly identified yourself so I can tell you that your credit card is attached to your numbered account here at the Union Bank of Switzerland, Geneva Branch. It is a courtesy we extend to all our preferred customers."

"My numbered account? Who opened the account? I've never been to Switzerland. Anyway, if I use the card, how do I repay?"

"There was an irrevocable deposit in a numbered account to your order in the amount of $1,000,000 US Dollars. You do not have to repay, sir. Your credit card is tied to a specialized debit feature. You can use it until the balance in the account is exhausted. Of course, your account balance will earn interest at the rate of 5.0% per annum, compounded daily. Your account statements are held here at the bank, but balances can be checked anytime. All account information is private and confidential. Only you have access to the account records. Can I be of further assistance, sir?"

"No . . . no, and thank you for your help." Gerald O'Connor hung up the phone and sat back in his chair, hinting at a smile. He had been stung with *Gold Fever.*

●●●●●●

Judge O'Connor sat in his chambers and admonished the counsel from both sides to use their best efforts to maintain the decorum that was expected of officers of the court. He emphatically stated that the events of Wednesday night were not part of these proceedings and should have no bearing on the trial or its outcome. Raymond Sutter disagreed.

"On the contrary, Judge. The issue of the Ku Klux Klan is very germane to our defense. It is proof of one more crazy action by the Scotts. They are willing to go to great lengths to destroy Anthony Williams. It's part of an already established pattern. It goes to the heart of the defendant's state of mind in being able to commit the alleged crimes. If we are not allowed to engage in a line of questioning relative to his experience with the Klan, then you effectively relegate the defendant to a guilty verdict."

"Listen, Raymond. I'm not trying to do any such thing. But haven't you noticed? This town is about to explode over this crap. And you, Joseph, your presentations will have to be crystal clear. No Mickey Mouse circular reasoning -- no circumstantial proof -- just hard facts. Okay?"

"I understand, Your Honor. But if Mr. Sutter wants to address the KKK's relevance to Anthony Williams's state of mind as to the rape and battery charges, let him address the issue in open court at the appropriate time. The prosecution will review it objectively and reserves the right to object at that time. However, the relevance and admissibility of events that postdate the crime are out of the question. To those, we will vigorously and consistently object." Joey Kearns was cool and deliberate.

"Listen, Judge," added Raymond, becoming a bit frantic. "We both know that the Klan action at the Defendant's home was a retaliatory act on the part of the Scott family against our client. We have to be able to address this issue."

Railroaded!

Joey Kearns grew angry at this allegation, stood up and blurted out. "Your Honor, there is no proof to support Mr. Sutter's almost outrageous allegations, nor have the police implicated the Scott family in the incident that occurred Wednesday night. Using the KKK incident against the Scott family is simply the defendant's device to deflect attention from this defendant's egregious crimes! I'm sick and tired of being told how to argue this case. Damn it, the man is guilty. There is substantive evidence, and I intend to prove it, even with one hand tied behind my back!"

"It's not your decision to make, young man," retorted the Judge. "Sit down now!" Raymond was totally puzzled at this response. Holy shit! The prosecution had just agreed to allow the defense the benefit of the doubt to proceed with a crucial piece of testimony, and the judge was pooh-poohing this affirmation even though the prosecutor reserved his future right to object. Gerald O'Connor never made blatant errors like this. This was not the Gerald O'Connor that Raymond knew and respected. This was wrong, all wrong.

"It is the People's decision not to deny, at this time, the Defendant's ability to address the issue of the Klan in their defense." Joey was deliberately calm in his address to Judge O'Connor. "We will review the relevance of that testimony as we will any other proposed testimony. We will not be too premature in our disposition. If I am to prove the Defendant's guilt, I will do so on the merits. I'm not going to beat up on a defendant whose hands are tied so as not to be able to mount a vigorous defense." Lew Dobson could see that Judge O'Connor was getting thoroughly irritated with his young associate. Nevertheless, Lew Dobson was also pleased with his stance. It showed true, unadulterated character on the part of his most junior associate.

"I support Mr. Kearns's position, Your Honor," added the district attorney. Judge O'Connor was feeling a lot of pressure. There was silence for a moment and then . . .

"I rule that the alleged Ku Klux Klan action of Wednesday night against the defendant will not be discussed in any manner whatsoever. Any testimony to that effect shall be stricken from the record and the actionable attorney held in highest contempt by this court. Is that clear, gentlemen?" Raymond slammed his fist on the table and asked the judge a question in a derogatory tone.

"Since when did you start playing prosecutor? That's not your style."

"Contempt of court, Mr. Sutter. You are ordered to pay $500.00 before your opening statement." Loren Johnson was completely outraged and started to attack the judge. Raymond intervened and kept him at bay.

"What about his childhood experience, your Honor?" asked Raymond, trying to keep up the pressure.

"The Defendant's *alleged* childhood experiences with the Klan bear no relevance to the charges. I warn you not to approach this court with this kind of testimony. The entire issue of Ku Klux Klan activities stops right here and now. There will be no testimony regarding that subject matter. That is my order. Now I want everyone out of here. We start at 9:00 A.M. Monday morning for voir dire. Now get out, all of you!" The judge's chambers were cleared in less than fifteen seconds.

Counsel for the defense was flabbergasted at the events that had just transpired. There was no reasonable basis for the judge to turn on the defense before the trial started. Just because the KKK had surfaced in somewhat impeccable timing and was threatening a mass demonstration during the trial, there was no logical or judicial reason to disallow Tony's testimony as to his childhood experiences and what impact they had on his adult life.

Judge O'Connor was sweating bullets. After the last man had left his office, he put his head on his desk. He then sat back and took a series of deep breaths. Gerald O'Connor had been compromised by an unknown party. If he didn't perform, his life could be in danger. If he did, there was a chance that he could get appointed to the Pennsylvania Supreme Court. There was also a chance that he could get framed just as he believed Anthony Williams had been framed. He would burn the Federal Express® package as soon as he left the office. He put the Letterpak and note in his briefcase and locked it. He placed the credit card in his wallet, sat back in his chair, and once again mentally reviewed all the possible persons known to him who could be behind this action. The stench pointed directly to Ned Scott. Scott was known to contribute heavily to political campaigns to get certain "favors." But what if it wasn't Ned Scott? Then who? Who wanted Anthony Williams out of the way so badly that a conviction would thrust him into a position that he desperately wanted? Why would the responsible party throw in an extra million dollars?

The trial was going to begin on Monday. Judge O'Connor got up out of his chair and walked over to the window. He started talking to himself. "Shit, this is completely out of control and I'm going to be the focal point. I can put the credit card in my safe-deposit box at the bank this afternoon on the way home. It can sit for six months. That will allow for everything to blow over."

●●●●●●

At 4:30 P.M. that same afternoon, an unnoticed observer watched as Judge Gerald O'Connor signed in at the vault of his local branch of the Pennsylvania National Bank. The observer was pleased. The hook had been set. Moments later, the observer stopped at a payphone and made two phone calls. The first was for instructions. After receiving his instructions, he made the second call to an unlisted number.

"Hello, Governor, I believe you know who this is."

"Well, hello there. It's been some time since we last chatted. What can I do for you today?"

"I've been instructed to advise you that it's time for you to consider a candidate for the vacant Supreme Court position."

"And who is being recommended?" asked the Governor in a friendly tone.

"None other than Judge Gerald O'Connor, but I'll confirm this recommendation to you in a few weeks. As you know, he is a very fine jurist with excellent credentials."

"That'll be just fine. I'll begin the process and await your call. Give my regards to your employer."

Governor Trevor Hamilton knew that one day he would be called on to provide a significant favor. He had been involved in some rather unsavory activities that would have created massive turmoil within his family, or even destroyed it. His benefactor chose not to expose the mess and instead contributed heavily to his last gubernatorial campaign. He just thanked God that Gerald O'Connor was a sound choice for the judicial vacancy. At least Gerry would be a responsible appointee who would sail through the confirmation process. He sat back for a moment and contemplated the request. He shrugged his shoulders in a "what-the-heck" manner and thought out loud. "That was easy enough. But, damn it, Ned. Next time just call me yourself. You don't need all this cloak-and-dagger crap. Too bad your daughter screwed around with the wrong man and got her tit caught in the wringer." He would call Ned Scott after the trial and invite him to lunch.

●●●●●●

The file relating to the Williams case was at least three inches thick. Joey Kearns decided to review it one more time before going home for the weekend. All in all, there wasn't a whole lot of evidence or testimony that would be offered. The whole matter was relatively simple: the defendant got pissed off and then beat and raped the victim. There was physical evidence to the rape and an eyewitness to the battery. The defendant had even admitted the battery of the victim.

The preparation process had been rather painless except for this KKK stuff, which Judge O'Connor had quashed as an issue. Joey really didn't understand why. He could have excluded any such testimony from the defendant as outside the scope of the trial. In the absence of reports from professionals who had treated the defendant for trauma as a child, the whole issue was just a sad story from long ago. Besides, the A.D. Williams family was known to have been poor in the early 1960's. They had been sharecropper-farmers. It was rather obvious that his parents had no money to get such treatment for their son. Joey even doubted that there was, or could have been, a psychiatrist in Alabama willing to treat a black boy who had allegedly witnessed a KKK lynching in 1964. For that matter, he doubted that any black family would have allowed one of their children to disclose such an incident to a white doctor, for fear of later retribution.

Whatever the reason for Judge O'Connor's decision, at least it made his job easier. After all, this was his big break. He was

Railroaded!

going to show the legal world what he was really made of. Joey Kearns was ready.

In advance of his time in the sun, Joey decided to relax for the whole weekend. He just wanted to take his mind off everything. He called a few friends and made plans to play tennis and swim on both Saturday and Sunday. The temperature was predicted to be in the low 90's, with no rain. Swimming would be very refreshing after a set or two of tennis. On Sunday night, he would conduct a final review of his opening statement.

As he thumbed through the documents, he looked at the lab reports the prosecution had received on the fluids recovered from Ms. Scott's vagina. The report seemed different from what he remembered reviewing earlier. He read it closely. The facts were still the same. Whatever it was that caught his attention, he could not recall. "Oh, well," he thought, "as long as it does the trick." He finished his cursory review of the paperwork. Everything was in its proper place. He closed the file and left his office for a relaxing weekend.

Chapter 18

The weekend before the trial was one of logistical madness for Tony and Shelli. Errol had already returned from New York and was a great help to his friends. Tony's parents, A.D. and Gladys Williams, arrived from Los Angeles early Saturday morning. They had taken a "red-eye" flight through Atlanta on Eastern Airlines. Tony and Errol picked them up at 9:30 from the airport. Errol still hadn't disclosed what he had learned from Harvey Sloan. Now certainly wasn't the time. "Mr. Williams?" Errol asked. "What does the A.D. stand for? After all these years, I don't have a clue."

"Neither does Tony, young man." Errol looked at Tony in a quizzical way and scrunched up his face. "So it's like this." Tony rolled his eyes, wondering what his father was going to say. "I was the sixth boy of ten children. There hadn't been any girls born in our family in three generations. When I was born, Tony's grandmother said in disgust, 'Another damn boy?' Your grandfather standing nearby heard her and said, 'That boy's name will be A.D.' There were no birth certificates made out in those days for black children. So the name A.D. was given to me by my father and that's how I was baptized, as A.D. Williams."

"I guess you could say you're just Another Damn Williams!" Tony blurted out.

"Shame on you, Tony!" retorted his mother. The car was silent for a moment. Then Gladys Williams broke out laughing. "Every word of that story is true." The rest of the ride back to Tony's house was one of continuous laughter from jokes and tales of old.

Later that morning, Shelli and Steven drove to the airport to pick up her parents, who came in on Continental from Oklahoma City. They had to change planes in Chicago, where they suffered through

Railroaded!

an almost hour-long delay on the connecting flight because of mechanical difficulties. Upon arrival in Pittsburgh, James and Verna Anderson were a bit tired, but not so tired that Shelli's mother couldn't start in on her daughter right away. Verna relayed her dreams to her daughter, telling her to prepare for the worst. James, when he could get a word in edgewise, kept telling his wife to leave their daughter alone. They were supposed to be there for support, not antagonism. Nonetheless, Shelli understood and was not put off by her mother. She loved her parents dearly and got along famously with her mother. The fact that she was having bad dreams about the trial was very disquieting. She decided that she wouldn't share these revelations with Tony.

The balance of Saturday was spent like a mini family reunion. There was a lot of food and even more conversation, especially about the childhood exploits of Tony and Adrian. Some of the stories were pretty embarrassing. Listening to these stories made Errol wish that he had never left California. The Forrest family had moved to Detroit, Michigan, and then Denver, where Errol had attended high school. He got to visit his friends only during summer vacations.

At 4:00 P.M., everyone camped around the television set and watched the Denver Broncos make mincemeat of the New Orleans Saints. Adrian had a fantastic first half with six catches, two of which went for touchdowns. Despite the fact that the Pittsburgh game was televised, it was not watched.

After the game, Adrian called and to tell Tony he was going to take a flight directly from New Orleans at 6:30 Sunday morning. There was no need to go back to Denver since he was already on the Gulf Coast. He would arrive in Pittsburgh at 11:10 A.M. on the Delta flight from Atlanta, where he had to stop and change planes. Shelli and Errol would be out to pick him up. Tony wanted to go but decided it would be better to avoid any public contact until Monday morning. Now that everything was set with family and friends, Tony called Raymond and invited him over Sunday afternoon at 2:00. He told him to make sure that the whole defense team came. He wanted everyone to meet his and Shelli's parents. When the socializing was finished, they could retire to the family room and review the entire strategy for the trial. Raymond agreed to make sure that everyone was there: Loren, David, Arnold, and the secretarial support staff. Raymond asked whether he could bring Dot Jensen, who had come up from Washington. Of course, Tony said it was okay.

● ● ● ● ● ●

Sunday morning, the 19th of August was very pleasant. It was clear and cool despite the prediction that the high temperature would be 94 degrees. At 10:00 A.M., the temperature had risen to only 69 degrees, not much higher than the low for the night. Ned Scott had awakened at five, but lay in bed until seven. All the while, he analyzed everything he had heard from Marianne and Tony, as well as his mother's admonitions to "be a Scott." After a quick shower, he dressed casually and went to his study, where he spent an hour before sitting at the breakfast table with his mother and daughter. Ned assured both ladies that the *family* was on track.

Elizabeth Cobb was pleased with her son's display of fortitude. Marianne felt that she had been convincing enough in her performance to make her father believe in her. By 9:00 A.M., Ned Scott was out walking the grounds of his heavily-treed, sprawling estate. At 10:00 A.M., he bid the ladies to have a peaceful afternoon and left for his office. He drove the Ferrari BB so that no one could get in touch with him; it was the only one of his eight cars that did not have a mobile telephone. He arrived at the office in only twenty minutes and then waited. The phone rang.

"Listen, Ned," said his mother on the other end, "I think Marianne and I are going to go out and do some shopping. I need a new dress or two for the trial."

"Fine, Mother. I'll be here for at least a few hours. Take your time, okay?" Ned was totally nonplussed at his own demeanor.

"Well, then, we'll have lunch and see you at home for dinner."

"Fine, Mom," said her son. Ned Scott waited for fifteen minutes and then called the house. The housekeeper answered and confirmed that Marianne and Mrs. Cobb had just left. Ned relayed that it was nothing important and that they should call when they got home if he wasn't yet there.

Railroaded!

Next, Ned made a call and gave the person on the other end some very exacting instructions. "When the job is complete, call me immediately so I can come down and identify the men. I'll be waiting for your call."

"We appreciate your assistance, Mr. Scott."

●●●●●●

Across town, the rather rotund cousin, Frank, three relatives who were also portly in stature, and four active members from the Mississippi Klan, all dressed in jeans and lightweight flannel shirts, were casually lounging in their respective rooms. All eight men typified the timeworn appellation, "rednecks." They had just finished having breakfast at a Waffle House on Imperial Road. Holding out in a hotel room was not their idea of fun, but until the trial started, they were following Aunt Lizzy's instructions to the letter. There were two football games on TV, one starting at 1:00 P.M. and the other at 4:00 P.M. Watching football would round out the day until dinner.

About one half-hour after the first game started, all eight men were in Frank's room. They had five cases of cold Budweiser and plenty of potato chips and Fritos. The first game was exciting from the beginning. Despite the drapes being open, not one of the eight noticed the fifteen unmarked Ford Crown Victorias, each carrying four heavily armed men, that pulled silently into a strip-mall parking lot across the street from the EconoLodge motel on Steubenville Pike. The armed men scattered and took up positions on the roof as well as in front and back of the motel.

At 2:15 P.M., one of the armed men knocked on the door. "Housekeeping. I have the ice that you requested." Carly Pope answered the door and was knocked to the ground immediately. Fifteen men rushed into the room and immediately subdued Frank and his comrades before anyone knew what was happening.

"Frank Cobb, you're under arrest for criminal trespass, crossing state lines with intent to do bodily harm, disturbing the peace, and attempting to incite a riot. Before the day is finished, we will come up with more, much more. Take them all away. No phone calls;

all men are to be confined until we receive further instructions."
Special Agent Jason Moore was pleased with the results.

"Maybe we should light up eight crosses and have us a big
barbecue. There's enough beer here to last a good while and plenty
of pot-bellied porkers to go 'round!" exclaimed one of the other
arresting agents.

Frank Cobb was terrified. Dealing with the local boys was one
thing; getting arrested in Mississippi meant appearing before the
magistrate, payment of a $20 fine, and immediate release. Dealing
with the feds was entirely different. He wasn't in the confines of
his own safe haven near Natchez, Mississippi. He was in Yankee
land, apparently cut off from his benefactor. What he did know
was that he and his boys were in big trouble.

Another thought crossed his mind. He and his boys had to have
been set up. No one knew they were here except Aunt Lizzy, who
had requested their presence and paid for everything. This trip was
more of a vacation than anything else. Why did Aunt Lizzy turn on
him like this? Or maybe the nigger had something to do with it
. . . and if he did, he was a dead man.

● ● ● ● ● ●

During half-time of the Green Bay-Baltimore game, the regular
broadcast was interrupted with a special news bulletin. FBI Special
Agent Moore announced that, with the help of Mr. Ned Scott, the
persons responsible for the cross-burning on the front lawn of Mr.
Anthony Williams had been apprehended. They were in custody
awaiting arraignment on federal charges that could take at least a
week to ten days to process. The bond was set at $5,000,000 for
the eight men, who were not expected to post bail. The issue of the
KKK's reemergence in Pittsburgh had been quashed.

After the FBI agent finished his short speech, Ned Scott came to
the podium and made the following announcement. "Apparently,
some very distant relatives of the Scott family with active Ku Klux
Klan ties in Mississippi came to Pittsburgh after hearing about the
charges leveled against Mr. Anthony Williams by my daughter
Marianne. These men were not invited here by me or anyone I
know. They were not invited here to rain terror upon the Williams

family or the greater Pittsburgh community. They are in custody awaiting arraignment and prosecution for their crimes. Despite their possible connection to my family, I could not let these renegades and their terrible deed tear apart this community or implicate the Scotts of Pennsylvania as perpetrators of such racist deeds. That's all I have to say." Ned stepped away from the podium, shook the FBI agent's hand, and disappeared. The impact of this move was far-reaching. At least his NFL franchise was out of danger.

Tony Williams was stunned. So were his cadre of family, friends, and lawyers. Lew Dobson was flabbergasted at these events. Joey Kearns didn't see the report until the evening news because he was lying next to a swimming pool. The governor was thoroughly annoyed by Ned's self-righteous grandstanding. Guy Markham was somewhat perplexed over this move but shrugged it off because he was being well paid. Judge O'Connor was relieved because his ruling on the subject matter was not going to be scrutinized. Marianne was perplexed because her father seemed to be supporting the Scott family, but had turned his back on another branch and hung them out to dry. Elizabeth Cobb, however, silently declared war.

●●●●●●

Ned arrived at home at precisely 5:45 P.M. He walked into the dining room, where Marianne and Elizabeth were already seated for dinner. He reached into his pants pocket and threw a cassette tape at his mother that landed squarely on her dinner plate.

"Don't you ever pull a stunt like that again, Elizabeth. Your relatives are going to cool their heels in custody for ten or so days and then be released to go home uncharged. The FBI knows you called them in." Marianne was now even more stupefied by the events. "You just remember this and remember it clearly. I am the head of this family. If that's not to your liking, then you can get the hell out of my house and our lives forever." Elizabeth started fuming, but before she could respond, Ned had walked over to Marianne's seat and stood behind her. "If you are telling the truth, young lady, then you've nothing to fear from the trial. I will support you till death." Ned bent over and kissed his daughter on the cheek. "But if, on the outside chance, you have told any piece of a lie, then not only will you be cut off from everything and be faced with life as a working-class stiff, but the beating you got will be chickenshit compared to the one that I'll give you!" Marianne flinched inside as Ned walked to his seat and sat down. "My father was a hard-nosed businessman, as was his father and his father before him. But they were always fair. Don't the two of you think for a moment that you can put any bullshit over on me, especially as it affects the family business, or the family's reputation!" He paused for a moment and then started in on Elizabeth once again. "Your fine fat relatives will be going home without a hassle after the trial is over. There will be no more of your interference, Elizabeth Cobb!"

"You address me as 'Mother,' you ingrate of a man!" the old woman lashed out.

"I'll address you any damned way I please. When you act like a mother, instead of a motherfucker, then I'll treat you with the respect owing to *my* mother!" Elizabeth stood up to leave. "Sit your narrow behind down right this minute, or leave this house forever!" Ned's levy on his mother was intense and sincere; he meant every word. She felt the hostility in his attack, hesitated for a moment, and then looked at Marianne, who was on the verge of tears. Elizabeth Cobb did not want a war with her son. Her position in the family had finally been supplanted. Her shoulders fell while she sighed aloud with resignation.

"I'm sorry, Ned. I shouldn't have interfered in these affairs. I didn't want to see my granddaughter hurt. There was no harm intended. I didn't want that Williams boy . . ." Ned pounded his fist on the table and looked at her harshly. "I didn't want Mr. Williams to think that he could get away with anything at all. This whole incident has everyone on edge."

"Indeed it does. That's why your outside intervention was inappropriate. It's time for everyone to calm down and let the chips fall where they may. Based on the truth," Ned stared at his daughter, "Marianne is the victim, not the perpetrator. Therefore, I expect Mr. Williams to mount a vigorous defense."

"Will you be attending the trial, Daddy?" asked Marianne.

Railroaded!

"Every day with bells on," replied the undisputed head of the
family.

The Trial

August 20, 1979

Chapter 19

Monday, August 20th

Monday morning found Gerald O'Connor in chambers at 7:00 A.M. His arrival was earlier than usual, but then again, this was no regular case. He had to give the appearance of being fair and impartial without being seen as if trying to "railroad" the defendant's case into a conviction. The whole matter was a mess. He uncharacteristically wheeled around twice in his desk chair, came to a stop, and continued to ponder the case while staring out his window.

Someone wanted Anthony Williams put away. The "why" just did not make sense. That same *someone,* had the political strength to all but guarantee his dream of a seat on the Pennsylvania Supreme Court. That same *someone* had the financial strength to deliver a million-dollar credit line -- without the obligation of repayment -- for his cooperation. The naked reality was that Gerald O'Connor wanted the Supreme Court appointment. He was tired of the day-in and day-out garden-variety trials. He sat there in the quiet of his chambers and devised his strategy. The requirements for impartiality and the ethics of fairness were not paramount in his thoughts.

At precisely 9:00 A.M., he entered the courtroom to the usual "all rise" from the bailiff, who announced the case, "People v. Anthony Williams, Case Number CR79-6539, the Honorable Gerald O'Connor presiding." Judge O'Connor sat down as did everyone else in the courtroom. From the elevated position of the judicial bench, the first thing he did was survey the people in the courtroom. His eyes first locked onto Marianne Scott. Despite being smartly dressed in a black suit, her face was still showing evidence of a vicious attack, allegedly committed by the defendant.

Railroaded!

He focused on her with a harsh, but blank, stare. After a moment of having interlocked eyes, Marianne, feeling as if she were being telepathically examined, squirmed uneasily and turned away.

Next, Judge O'Connor turned to Anthony Williams. He noticed that he was wearing a navy blue blazer, white shirt and yellow paisley tie. The defendant, along with his defense team, was calm. He could sense their quiet confidence. Judge O'Connor cracked a hint of a smile, pondering his earlier thoughts in chambers. After this brief hiatal scan of the court, he turned to the documents in front of him.

"Ladies and gentlemen, we are here to see that justice is done. This case, unfortunately, is fodder for the national press, so I must begin with certain basic issues. First, the media will not be allowed to take photographs of the proceedings. Next, I expect order to be maintained as a strict matter of course. If not, the courtroom will be cleared. I hope this is clearly understood." He paused for a brief moment, cleared his throat and continued. "Also, standing room will not be tolerated. If there is not an available seat, you will not be permitted to remain during the proceedings. The bailiff is hereby instructed that the seating capacity of this courtroom will be strictly enforced." The people standing along the back wall on both sides of the entry doors knew their time for attendance was being cut short and they would have to leave momentarily. "Last, this case has heightened racial tensions in this city because of incidents that need not be recounted here." Looking at the attorneys in attendance, he continued. "Any hint of the insertion of such prejudicial issues will land the perpetrator in jail for thirty days on contempt charges." The entire room was silent. "Now that I've gotten these matters out of the way, Mr. Kearns, are you ready to proceed?" Joseph Kearns, dressed in a new black, double-breasted suit, stood and acknowledged his readiness.

"The People are ready, Your Honor."

"Mr. Sutter, are you ready to proceed?"

"The Defense is ready, Judge," responded Raymond Sutter.

"Then let's get on with it. There is an available jury pool of fifty people, from which you are to select twelve members. Since this trial is scheduled for one week, there will be only one alternate selected. My preference is that the selection process should be completed today as well as your opening statements. Any problem with these time frames?" Both lawyers nodded their assent to the judge's suggestions. "Okay, then, Mr. Kearns, this is the moment you've been waiting for. Welcome to the 'Big Leagues.' Begin."

"Thank you, Your Honor." Joey Kearns was ready.

Voir dire -- the process of interviewing citizens for jury participation. Raymond Sutter was used to this maddening procedure; Joey Kearns was a rookie. Albeit a bit shaky, he had decided on two simple questions -- "Are you a Steelers' fan," and "are you acquainted with the defendant in any way?"

Raymond Sutter would take a different approach. He had only one question -- "Are you opposed to interracial marriages or relationships?" The interview of the first jury candidate started the war.

Seated in the jury box, the forty-five-year-old white male stated his name and address for the record. "Mr. Green, is it?" Joey was being a bit coy, as if he were very experienced at this process. The jury candidate nodded, affirming that he was indeed Mr. Green. "I have only two questions for you, sir. The first is, are you a Steelers' fan?" Judge O'Connor was immediately irritated with the prosecutor. Pounding his gavel on the bench to silence the courtroom commotion, he unloaded on Mr. Kearns.

"Listen, young man. I am a Steelers' fan. You'll be hard-pressed to find anyone in Pittsburgh who isn't!" Joey Kearns was prepared and responded.

"Your Honor, I am not a Steelers' fan, nor a fan of professional football at all. Furthermore, if Your Honor is a Steelers' fan, maybe his Honor should disqualify himself and submit the case for review by another judge." O'Connor was livid and desperately wanted to crucify Kearns. Instead, he maintained his decorum and questioned Kearns.

"What is your second question, Mr. Kearns?"

"Your Honor, my second question is very simple -- is the candidate acquainted with the defendant in any way?" Joey Kearns was steadfast and unflinching in his presentation; he wasn't intimidated by the reaction of Judge O'Connor.

Railroaded!

"If these are the only two questions that you will offer, then they will be allowed. But don't you ever question my authority while I'm sitting on this bench, or you'll be sitting on a cold metal bench in the county jail!" The prosecutor received the admonitions and sat down. The seated jury candidate admitted that he had once shaken the hand of the defendant but otherwise was not acquainted with him. Joey Kearns, despite being chastised, was now feeling a little smug. He had won an accommodation from the judge. This boded well for the presentation of his case.

When Raymond Sutter asked his sole question, he was immediately cited for contempt and ordered to spend thirty days in jail. The court was in a total uproar as the bailiff approached to take the defense attorney into custody. Raymond, however, refused to back down, scuffling with the bailiff. His associates immediately came to his aid, with the situation almost resulting in a brawl. At the top of his lungs, above the din in the courtroom, Raymond argued that his case involved the perception of a black man beating and raping a white woman. "If a juror is predisposed against interracial relationships, then consciously or subconsciously, the juror will be predisposed to convict the defendant." After what seemed like incessant pounding of the Judge's gavel on the bench, order was finally restored. Everyone returned to his seat, and as quickly as it all began, cooler heads now seemed to prevail.

"Your Honor, in fairness to my client, you cannot preclude us from making this determination about potential jurors." As much as he wanted to lash out in anger at the defense attorney, Judge O'Connor knew that Raymond was right. He hated to reverse his contempt order but had no choice. Now was not the time to blow this case . . . there would be plenty of opportunities to manipulate the proceedings later. He also knew that it was too early to be loose with his rulings. The media would eat him alive. That would be intolerable.

"Mr. Sutter," Judge O'Connor cleared his throat, "I rescind my ruling ordering you into custody for contempt, but a stern warning to you both. Do not try my patience or my authority. Future orders will not be rescinded. Is that clear, gentlemen?" There was a nod from both counsel.

After the reversal of the contempt order, Judge O'Connor called a ten minute recess to allow all parties to calm down, including himself. He called for counsel in his chambers and reiterated that this trial was not going to turn into a freak show. Counsel from both sides apologized for the initial fireworks and swore that the remainder of the *voir dire* process would run smoothly. And that it did. Despite the fiery start, after the recess and resumption of the proceedings, the *voir dire* process seemed to move at a quickened pace.

By 12:15 P.M., a jury had been selected: Two black elderly women ages sixty-one and sixty-seven; one black man age thirty-eight; three white women all in their late thirties, each of whom acknowledged they were football "widows"; and six white men ranging in age from twenty-seven to sixty-three. Every juror acknowledged being a sports enthusiast, but not a Steelers' fan. The single alternate was a white male, age thirty-six. The mix actually suited Raymond. Joey had no experience in this process and would have preferred more women on the jury for sympathy purposes. Raymond knew this and had focused entirely on selecting male candidates.

Once the jury was seated, Judge O'Connor gave a series of brief instructions and called for a lunch recess. Court would reconvene at 2:30 P.M. for opening statements. Raymond walked over to the prosecution table and said, "Congratulations, Joseph, on an outstanding *voir dire.*" The two combatants shook hands and wished each other good luck. Joey was feeling very good and left to have lunch with his boss. Raymond left with his defense team. Tony and Shelli, their family, Adrian and Errol, and a few other friends left together for a luncheon. Marianne and her father left to lunch at the private club. Elizabeth Cobb was not present and, in fact, had stayed home.

●●●●●●●●●

At precisely 2:30 P.M., Judge O'Connor re-entered the courtroom. "All rise," said the bailiff flatly. The judge surveyed the courtroom and noted that everyone was in place.

Railroaded!

"Well, Mr. Kearns, this is the moment you've been waiting for. Are you ready to proceed?" Joey Kearns nodded his assent. "Then, young man, please proceed." Judge O'Connor made himself comfortable in his high-backed, brown leather chair, expecting a rather long diatribe from the freshman prosecutor.

"Thank you, Your Honor." Joey stood up, and with a legal pad in hand, walked over to stand in front of the jury box. After clearing his throat, he began. "Ladies and gentleman of the jury . . ." Joey paused for a moment and looked at his prepared notes. He flipped through them briefly and decided on a change in strategy. The hesitation was a bit unnerving to Raymond, who knew that something other than what had been planned by the prosecutor was about to unfold. Joey quickly walked over to the prosecution table and handed the yellow legal pad containing his prepared statement to his boss, who looked at him quizzically. Joey winked at Mr. Dobson. Despite his apparent confidence, Lew Dobson was squirming uneasily in his seat and becoming a bit perturbed at not knowing what was about to happen. The district attorney had approved of everything his most junior associate was doing . . . up to this point. But now, the whole matter was out of his hands and in the hands of an upstart. He could see his re-election slipping away.

Joey, however, with a cool demeanor, walked over to the rail in front of the jurors, put both hands squarely on it, leaned forward, and began again. "Ladies and gentleman, this is my first real trial . . . but I believe I am more than up to the task at hand. Unfortunately, the defendant is one of Pittsburgh's favorite sons. Unfortunately, the victim is the daughter of another of Pittsburgh's most noted citizens. What we have here is a clear mess." He paused for a moment as he noticed two jurors squirming uneasily. "Nevertheless, ladies and gentlemen, a crime has been committed, and it is the duty of the prosecution . . . it is my duty to uncover the truth." He paced back and forth in front of the jury as if he had done this many times instead of it being his first. "And that truth must be supported by incontrovertible evidence, or you have a duty to find the defendant not guilty." He paused for only a moment and then continued. "Today, and in the days to follow, I will positively and conclusively prove to you that Anthony Williams committed certain crimes against Marianne Scott and should be found guilty as charged on all counts." He paused for a moment and went back to his seat. "Now, I know that the entire world saw the defendant sustain an illegal block during a professional football game. However, you cannot be predisposed as to his ability or inability to commit the alleged offenses. We shall prove that, despite what you think you saw, Mr. Williams had the physical strength to commit the crimes for which he is charged." Joey Kearns did not see Marianne Scott shifting her body position within the confines of the court seat, but Judge O'Connor did and so did Ned Scott, who was seated behind her. "Ladies and gentlemen, the defense is going to do everything possible to cause a reasonable doubt in your minds about the guilt of the defendant. There is an eyewitness to the assault as well as forensic evidence that the victim was indeed raped. These facts are not disputed. Therefore, I will not detain you any longer except to say that, when we are finished with our presentation, any verdict rendered by you other than guilty will be a travesty of justice." Joey Kearns smiled at the jury and returned to his seat. Judge O'Connor was amazed at the brevity of the prosecutor's opening statement. He motioned with his gavel to Mr. Sutter, who was also caught by surprise. "Because of the short and very succinct opening statement of the prosecutor, we will now have the opening statement of Mr. Raymond Sutter."

"Thank you, Your Honor." Raymond cleared his throat and remained seated. He then asked Tony to stand up and quietly told him to direct his attention to the jury. Tony did so reluctantly. Judge O'Connor gave a quizzical look and held back from lowering the boom on Raymond. Surely this was going to be a grandstand act. "Ladies and gentlemen of the esteemed jury, I want each of you to look at the defendant and study him carefully. Mr. Anthony Williams is a well-respected family man and renowned combatant of our Pittsburgh Steelers. He is accused of committing assault, battery, and the heinous crime of rape on the daughter of the owner. Surely you have heard how there are closet cases of professional men who, in the dark of night, commit outrageous and brutal crimes against our female citizenry. Mr. Williams is not one of those closet cases. In fact, despite what the prosecutor has told you in such brief form, we will prove that the so-called victim, Marianne

Railroaded!

Scott, daughter of the highly esteemed Ned Scott, is nothing more than a party woman with an insatiable sexual appetite for black athletes!" The courtroom exploded in a commotion that took a full two minutes to quell by Judge O'Connor. Mr. Sutter then continued. "We will prove that there are major holes in the Prosecution's case, facts which will put you in a position to render a verdict nothing short of 'not guilty.' We do not dispute that the Defendant assaulted the victim . . . but it was not out of anger or disgust for the victim. Instead we will prove that the defendant struck Ms. Scott only after *she* attempted to sexually assault his person." This comment caused the entire audience to stir again. Judge O'Connor stood up and heavily pounded his gavel five or six times to restore order in the courtroom. After order was restored, he sat and started barking at the audience.

"Any more outbursts and the courtroom will be cleared. I hope this is well understood by all in attendance." The courtroom was again quiet. "Please continue, Mr. Sutter."

"You can sit down now, Anthony." Tony responded and resumed his seated position next to his advocate. "There are many inconsistencies in the story of the victim. Please listen carefully to her testimony and our cross-examination. I promise you that you will find it most enlightening. Also, I must ask that when the prosecutor begins his presentation, you please pay close attention to the time line offered by Mr. Kearns. There are problems . . . serious problems that cannot be made to disappear or evaporate into thin air. These facts are of critical importance to the prosecutor and critical to the acquittal of our client. So rather than bore you with a long, rather meaningless diatribe, we will acknowledge that the prosecutor has set the stage for a fast-track presentation and we are ready to proceed." Raymond returned to his seat and sat calmly.

"Are you finished, Mr. Sutter?" asked an amazed Judge O'Connor. He had expected to spend the entire afternoon listening to a boring recollection of the facts. Instead, both advocates squared off and took a 'let's-get-to-it' approach. It was only 3:20 P.M. After an affirmative nod from Raymond Sutter, Judge O'Connor called a ten-minute recess and told all parties to be back at 3:30 P.M., when the prosecutor would call his first witness.

Chapter 20

"The People call as its first witness, Detective Will Spencer," was the announcement from the prosecutor. A rather nondescript man dressed in dark brown pants and tan sport jacket made his way from the gallery to the witness stand. He was sworn in first and then seated. "Please state your name and occupation for the record," said Joey Kearns. The witness complied in a rather monotonic voice that was completely without any animation whatsoever. "Detective Spencer, you were the officer in charge of this case, correct?"

"Yes, sir."

"And when did you first receive this case?" asked the prosecutor who was a bit nervous, although not apparently so to the outside observer. This was not moot court. His first trial had been an exercise in plea bargaining; this was the real thing and his stomach was feeling as if tied in a million knots. "Get a hold of yourself, Kearns," he thought to himself. With this self-admonition, the nervous feeling passed quickly as he focused on the task at hand.

"I happened to be standing in the lobby of the main precinct when Ms. Scott, the victim, walked through the door. She appeared to have been brutally assaulted. So I helped her sit down and then started asking her what happened. In a sobbing tone, she said she had been raped."

"Objection, Your Honor. Hearsay, and calls for speculation on the part of the witness." Raymond Sutter remained seated.

"Overruled," retorted Judge O'Connor. "Please proceed, Mr. Kearns."

"With this pronouncement on the part of the victim, what did you do next?" asked the prosecutor.

"I got the help of another officer and we immediately took her to Allegheny General Hospital," responded the detective.

"And what about taking her statement, getting information from the victim?"

"That wasn't done until after we started the drive to the hospital."

"And why not?" asked the prosecutor in a flat tone of voice similar to that of the detective.

"Because she told us who she was and we wanted to keep the whole matter quiet. We didn't want it to go out over the air. That's why we took her to the hospital in an unmarked car instead of calling an ambulance."

"I see. So you made a judgment call on how to handle this case. Correct?"

"That's correct, sir."

"And when did the victim reveal the circumstances of her heinous encounter?"

"On the way to the hospital and again after the examination by the attending physician."

"Now, Detective Spencer. When did the victim reveal to you the name of her attacker?"

"Objection, Your Honor," was the statement from the defense counsel.

"Rephrase the question, Mr. Kearns," stated Judge O'Connor.

"Did the victim know who attacked her?" asked Joey Kearns.

"She did," was the detective's flat unemotional reply.

"And whom did she say assaulted and raped her?"

"Mr. Anthony Williams." There was a rush of commotion through the courtroom. Judge O'Connor pounded his gavel three times and order was restored.

"What did you do then, detective?"

"While she was being examined, we tried to get in touch with her father to notify him of the situation, but he wasn't immediately available."

"When did you complete your questioning of the victim?" asked the prosecutor.

"Before her father arrived. It must've been close to 7:00 A.M."
Joey cringed inside at the mention of time. He wanted the detective

to paint a picture using a brush of only broad generalities. He wanted to avoid specifics until later.

"That's all, Detective Spencer." Joey looked at Raymond and said, "Your witness." The prosecutor quickly returned to his seat with the expectation that Detective Spencer would be torn apart by the lead counsel for the defense. Raymond Sutter, however, did not stand. Instead, Arnold Benton stood to conduct the cross-examination. This tactic puzzled even Judge O'Connor.

"Please enter your appearance for the record, young man." Judge O'Connor smirked to himself, thinking that this trial was going to turn into a battle of a rookie prosecutor versus a rookie defense lawyer. He sat back in his chair and waited.

"Mr. Arnold Benton appearing for the defendant, Your Honor." Smartly dressed in a navy blue blazer and grey slacks, Arnold Benton smiled at his former nemesis sitting across the way and walked toward the witness stand.

"Thank you, Mr. Benton. Please proceed," stated the judge.

"Detective Spencer . . . it has come to our attention that you are an avid Steelers' fan. It has also come to our attention that you are a season ticketholder and, in fact, attended the game on July 27th. Is that correct?"

"I attended the game between the Steelers and the Broncos, yes." The detective finally appeared to get a bit antsy.

"And did you witness the injury sustained by the defendant?" asked Mr. Benton.

"Objection, Your Honor." Joey Kearns stood and remained standing for the judge's response.

"Where are you going with this questioning, Mr. Benton?" asked the judge.

"This question goes to foundational issues that relate directly to the detective's interaction with the victim, Your Honor." Judge O'Connor sat back in his chair for a brief moment and then leaned forward to respond.

"I'll overrule the objection for now, but keep it clean, Mr. Benton. Keep it clean!" Arnold Benton shrugged his shoulders and cleared his throat. He looked at Raymond Sutter, who nodded his approval at Benton's handling of the matter. "Answer the question, Mr. Spencer," said the judge.

Railroaded!

"I saw the block that caused the injury to the defendant," responded the detective.

"That took place about 9:00 P.M. Correct?"

"Yes, sir," he responded in a flat tone.

"And at what time did you first encounter the victim?" Joey Kearns was starting to squirm in his seat.

"It was about 4:30 A.M. on the morning of the 28th."

"What time did you report for work, sir?"

"I came in at midnight," responded the detective.

"And the game was over at 11:00 P.M. Right?" asked the defense counselor.

"Actually, it was over at 11:15 P.M."

"How long does it take for someone to travel by car from the main precinct to Allegheny General Hospital?"

"It only takes ten minutes, twenty if there is traffic on one of the river bridges."

"Okay, so when you drove Ms. Scott to the hospital, it took you only ten minutes to get there. Is that correct, Detective?"

"That's correct, sir."

"And, for the record, Detective, which way did you travel to get to the hospital?"

"We took the 9th Street Bridge to Cedar Avenue, which dead-ends at the hospital."

"So you took a route that literally allowed you to pass the site where, according to your report, the victim alleges she was beaten and raped. Is that correct?" asked Arnold in a slightly animated tone.

"That is correct, sir."

"Don't you find it odd that the victim came crawling into the main precinct when she was literally within a short walking distance of Allegheny General Hospital?" There was a rush of commotion in the background as Joey Kearns jumped to his feet to yell an objection. Judge O'Connor stood while pounding his gavel on the bench in an attempt to restore order. After several minutes, the din finally subsided.

"Mr. Benton, your question is indeed irrelevant. So I'll sustain the prosecutor's objection. I told you to keep it clean. Another such stunt and you'll be put away on a contempt order. Is that clear?" Arnold looked at Raymond, who was unmoved. He winked at Arnold.

"Very clear, Your Honor. In fact, sir, the question is very relevant. The defense would like to present a map of the downtown area of Pittsburgh and ask for the detective's expert knowledge to point out certain landmarks. Is that acceptable, Your Honor?"

"Please hurry up, Mr. Benton. You are sorely trying my patience."

"Detective Spencer, will you please point out, so that the members of the jury can see, where the main precinct is located, the route that you took to the hospital, the hospital, and any police substations that may be in the vicinity of your traveled route." Joey Kearns was cringing inside as the detective pointed everything out in clear detail.

"Two final questions, sir. In your estimation, how long would it take to walk from the 9th Street Bridge to the Allegheny General Hospital?"

"Maybe forty minutes."

"So to walk from the site of the alleged attack to the hospital would take a shorter time. Correct?" Arnold Benton was on fire and Joey Kearns was feeling the heat. Arnold Benton didn't allow the detective to answer the question before asking another. "And to walk to the Ohio Street police substation might take ten minutes or less. Right, Detective?" Raymond Sutter was smiling to himself. Judge O'Connor was furious. Again, before the detective could respond, Arnold Benton stated, "No further questions for now. We reserve the right to recall the witness." The junior associate walked back to the defense table and sat next to Raymond Sutter. The court was in an uproar. Judge O'Connor threatened to clear the court if order wasn't instantly restored.

"Any redirect, Mr. Kearns?" asked the judge in a harsh tone.

"Not at this time, Your Honor," responded the prosecutor, who seemed to be preoccupied with other thoughts.

"I want counsel in my chambers at 8:00 A.M. sharp. Understood?" Both tables acknowledged the order. "From now on, we are going to begin one-half hour early. Court is in recess until 8:30 A.M. tomorrow morning." With a pound of his gavel,

Railroaded!

he dismissed the court. Both Raymond Sutter and Loren Johnson congratulated Arnold on a job well done.

Joey Kearns leaned back in his chair and stared at the judge's bench. He felt the pressure of being a prosecutor. He was actually relieved that the cross-examination had not been more devastating. He began to reconsider his strategy. He had to strip the defense of its momentum. But another emotion welled up within Joey Kearns; it was anger. He was not pleased with the victim or her story. Despite all the evidence that linked Anthony Williams as the perpetrator of the crimes, his gut reaction was different. This whole affair was a jumbled mess out of which he had to make sense. He now knew why he was chosen as the fall guy to prosecute this case. It never crossed his mind that Arnold Benton had whipped his butt again, this time in a real courtroom setting. The fact was that he admired the job done by his opponent. Tomorrow, however, would be a different day.

Lew Dobson approached the junior associate ready to launch into him. Instead, Joey took the offensive. "Listen, Lew. I don't have time to talk to you now. I've got to plan for tomorrow. I need to regroup and figure out what our alleged victim is trying to pull."

"What? Are you out of your mind, Kearns?"

"Shut up and leave me alone," retorted Joey in an explosive tone. "My ass is on the line, just like yours. So instead of giving me a ration of shit, why don't you tell me what's really happening here?" Joey gathered his files and put them in his briefcase. The district attorney was shocked at his most junior associate's emotional outburst. He backed off and changed his approach.

"Listen, Joey. Why don't I take you to dinner so we can both relax and hash out a few things? Your opening statement was good, really good. You handled a difficult witness as well as could be expected. The detective didn't cooperate as we wanted." Lew paused for a moment. "You like Chinese?"

"Chinese is just fine. Sorry for my outburst, sir," was the apology from Joey.

"We're all on the edge. Let's go." Lew Dobson extended his hand to shake his young associate's hand. Joey smiled and responded in kind. "Between you and me, Joey, this case is going to get very stinky. I want you to expose the truth whether we, I mean the district attorney's office, takes the fall or not. Just do your best."

"I will, boss . . . I will." They left the courtroom to dine together.

● ● ● ● ● ●

The first day of the trial had come to a close. Raymond Sutter was pleased with the work of his young associate. The lead defense counselor was 100% confident that Tony Williams would be acquitted. He had to be. There were gaping holes in the prosecution's case. There were no holes in Tony's defense. The worst that could happen was that Tony would be found guilty of simple assault. But under the circumstances, the whole matter could be plea-bargained into oblivion. The fact that there was an eyewitness to a knee-jerk reaction didn't bother Raymond at all. What did bother Raymond was that this case was being prosecuted in the first place. Surely Joey Kearns had to know there was a deep chasm that had to be crossed -- the time between the alleged assault and rape, and the time when Marianne strolled into the main precinct station -- a space of more than three hours. And why hadn't she gone to the Ohio Street substation with which she was previously acquainted? These facts also bothered Errol and Adrian. How in the world was the prosecutor going to get around these issues? Would he claim the victim was unconscious for three hours and then walked in the wrong direction, when the hospital at the end of the street was in clear view and the police substation was only a few blocks away? Marianne Scott was not that stupid.

Shelli drove Tony home and led a caravan of three cars carrying other family members and friends. Adrian and Errol accompanied the counselors to their offices for a late afternoon pow-wow. Not present were Dave Robinson and Guy Markham. For all intents and purposes, the investigator's work was finished. Dave Robinson had to meet another client.

Errol Forrest, once a bartender during his college days at Dartmouth, offered to fix drinks for all in attendance. When everyone had a drink in hand, Loren Johnson hoisted his glass for a toast to Arnold Benton's first major courtroom performance.

Railroaded!

After the toast, Errol asked a difficult question. "I understand strategy, I understand laying a foundation for witness examination. I don't understand why you didn't let Arnold rip the detective to shreds when he was ripe for the kill." Loren Johnson gave the first part of the reply.

"You will be graduating from law school next spring. Right?" Errol nodded in the affirmative. "And, in three years of law school, there's one thing no professor can teach you -- and that's instinct."

Raymond walked around the conference table and then sat on the edge. He provided the second part of the answer. "Joey Kearns, despite his lack of experience, is a formidable opponent. He's got a method to his madness that isn't yet clear. And until it is, I just want to be careful, very careful." Raymond took a sip of his scotch and soda and continued. "We could have obliterated the detective today, no doubt. But then what?"

"You want to recall him after the testimony of Marianne, don't you?" asked Adrian.

"I'd be willing to bet he's going to call the detective as a hostile witness during the defense presentation," added Errol.

"You're both right," retorted Raymond. "The almost four hours between the time when Tony was picked up by the limo and when Marianne walked into the police station is going to be the prosecution's undoing."

"Has Guy Markham come up with anything further that we can use?" asked Errol.

"Like what?" asked Raymond. "You really don't trust this guy, do you? Something's been bothering you about him for quite a while. Anything we need to discuss, young man?" Errol picked up a piece of paper and began to write on it. He handed the paper to Raymond. Loren Johnson looked on in a perplexed manner. The note read, *"I will not discuss Guy Markham in this office. Suggest we go to a nearby restaurant."* Raymond took the cue and said, "I guess not. Anyway, I'm hungry and thirsty. How about some light fare and another round of drinks at a nearby happy hour?" Everyone acknowledged this as a good idea, gulped down their drinks, and left the conference room.

In another building in downtown Pittsburgh, the man known as "Viper" listened carefully to the conversation in the conference room at Johnson, Owens, Sutter & Moss. From this secure listening post, he heard the question asked of the Forrest kid. Errol's failure to answer was dismissed as nothing more than unsubstantiated, idle curiosity. But maybe he needed to keep a closer eye on this young man. Errol Forrest was not like Anthony Williams. The man known as "Viper" lit a cigarette, blew a perfect smoke ring, and left the room for the evening.

●●●●●●

Errol, Adrian, Loren, Raymond, and Arnold reconvened their skull session at *Scoglio's,* a quaint Italian restaurant known for its pasta and pizza. The lawyers were regular patrons there since it was only a few blocks from their office. After everyone finished ordering a round of drinks, Raymond asked Errol, "So why didn't you want to discuss our investigator in our offices? What do you know about Guy Markham that has you so edgy?" Just as Errol was about to respond, his facial expression changed abruptly. Raymond noticed the change and asked in a concerned manner, "What's the matter, son? You look like you've seen a ghost!"

Guy Markham, smiling like a Cheshire cat, walked up behind Raymond Sutter and said, "Hi guys! The next round's on me!"

Chapter 21

Tuesday, August 21st

Every attorney associated with the case was present in Judge O'Connor's chambers at 8:00 A.M. sharp. He issued a stern warning to the entire group that the fireworks of the previous day were to be avoided. Raymond, instead of acknowledging his assent to the judge's directive, challenged the judge. "Excuse me for saying so, Judge, but this case is nothing more than a bunch of inflammatory bullshit. And when it's over, we intend to pursue civil charges against the so-called victim for defamation of character and anything else we can add to reflect the damage done to the defendant!"

"You arrogant, self-righteous bastard!" countered the judge. "This is my court and until you are elected to sit on the bench in my stead, I'll be damned if I'll hear any more of your crap. I don't care if you are the high and mighty Raymond Sutter. I don't care if your client is the priceless safety for the Pittsburgh Steelers. I don't care that the victim is the daughter of Ned Scott. I'm telling you right now that I will hold you, Loren Johnson, and you, Lew Dobson, completely responsible for the performance of your lackeys. Is that clear?" Loren was highly disturbed at where the judge was headed but instead also got angry.

"What's the matter with you, Gerald? Why are you going ballistic over nothing? This is a high-profile case. It's no different than the case you handled on the bank matter. In fact, it was even more inflammatory than this because there were real issues that needed adjudication. This case is entirely different, and I certainly resent my professionals being called 'lackeys.' Mr. Kearns is doing an excellent job, and I'm sure that Lew also resents his prosecutor being called a 'lackey'."

"Have you all gone mad?" retorted the judge. "I expect and demand that you all toe the line and very carefully. Is that clear?" Everyone nodded, but Raymond was not very happy. Something had set this man off and the undertone was not good. Compounded by the fact that he had not been able to talk to Errol Forrest the night before, Raymond's intuition was going wild.

"Listen, Mr. Kearns. I hope you are not going to follow the same path with your witnesses as you did yesterday. You must clear up the apparent holes in your case immediately so we can proceed with a smooth adjudication of this case." Loren and Raymond couldn't believe what they were hearing: The judge was telling the prosecutor he was in trouble and to clean up his act, rather than telling him that if the problems weren't resolved, the judge would dismiss the case. Joey Kearns couldn't believe he was hearing such an accommodation. Lew Dobson was, quite frankly, relieved.

Loren instructed his troops to leave the chambers and reconvene in the hallway. They paid no attention to Judge O'Connor, who was barking at them as they left. "What the hell was that all about?" asked Arnold Benton. "What did I do to cause the judge to freak out like that? Didn't I do what I was supposed to? I really could have drop-kicked the detective, but I went easy on him as you instructed, Raymond."

"You did exactly what you were supposed to, Arnold. But something else is happening," responded Raymond. "Maybe we should file motions to have the trial reassigned to another judge. I don't like the way this is going. Dammit, we haven't even gotten started." Loren nodded and said he would do some checking for reassignment during the morning's testimony. Raymond looked at his watch and said, "Let's go, men."

●●●●●●

After the defense lawyers stormed out and the prosecution lawyers left his chambers, Judge O'Connor opened his desk drawer and found a note that must have been left during the night.

Railroaded!

Get a better handle on the case or your nomination and appointment will be withdrawn. You've been paid well to see to it that the defendant does not get off. Do not fail.

Gerald O'Connor was sweating profusely. His anger had boiled over and caused him to act irrationally in front of some of the most renowned lawyers in Pittsburgh, lawyers who were once his friends. He tore the note into little pieces and flushed the evidence down the toilet. He straightened his tie and splashed a bit of water on his face. The coolness allowed him to regain his composure and think about what had just transpired, as well as what he would do next.

●●●●●●

The defense attorneys marched into the courtroom and took their positions with the defendant. Lew Dobson was seated with Joey Kearns at the prosecution table. The judge entered the court to the time worn "all rise."

"First things, first. Mr. Sutter and Mr. Dobson, please approach the bench." They did so and heard the following. "If you so much as even think about having this case reassigned, I'll put you in jail for contempt. Further, I'll block any attempt you make to do so. Don't mess with me, Raymond. You and I go back a long way, and I'd like to think that we have further to go." Raymond remained expressionless. "As for you, Lew, just make sure your associate cleans up the holes or you both will face my wrath. Understood?" Lew nodded. "Now, why don't you both make sure this case is conducted in a professional manner and not like a street fight or no-holds-barred wrestling match?" Both men agreed and returned to their seats. They each recounted what the judge had said to their associates. Raymond sent Dave Robinson to find Loren. He didn't want to make matters any worse.

After conferring with his boss, Joey called his first witness of the morning. "The prosecution calls Mr. Ned Scott." This pronouncement caught Ned by surprise as well as Marianne, who started squirming uneasily in her seat. It also caught the defense by surprise. Raymond Sutter asked for a one-day recess to prepare for cross-examination of the witness. Judge O'Connor denied the motion. Arnold reassured Raymond that he could effectively cross-examine Mr. Scott without the benefit of preparation. He winked at Raymond and pleaded for the opportunity. Raymond agreed and sat back to listen to the prosecutor's questions and the responses of the owner of the Pittsburgh Steelers.

After the swearing-in formalities, Ned Scott, dressed in a medium brown gabardine suit with a pale pink shirt and paisley tie, took the seat at the witness stand. He made the required statement of name and occupation and waited for the prosecutor to begin.

"Mr. Scott, let's get right to the point. NFL players are typically nothing more than massive physical specimens on an ego trip, aren't they?"

"In some cases, that's true."

"How many times have you fielded complaints about your players overpowering women in sexual encounters?" asked the young prosecutor.

"I wouldn't know . . . that's not a statistic that we monitor, young man."

"Well, then, Mr. Scott, is this the first time that one of your players has been charged with sexual assault?" asked Joey.

"No, it isn't. It is the eighteenth time, to be exact."

"Thank you, Mr. Scott." Joey walked to the front of the jury box and stood firm. "Is Mr. Williams capable of committing sexual assault?"

"Objection! Calls for speculation." Arnold beat Raymond to the punch with his objection.

"Sustained! Mr. Kearns, you will kindly remember my admonitions in chambers."

"Yes, sir." Joey turned to Ned Scott on the witness stand and continued. "Mr. Scott, have you conducted your own investigation into the events surrounding the assault and rape of your daughter, Marianne Scott?"

"I have," was Ned's terse reply.

"And, in your opinion, based on your investigation, did the Defendant, Mr. Anthony Williams, physically assault and rape your daughter?" Ned Scott paused before answering. The courtroom was silent. Everyone waited for his response.

Railroaded!

"I want to preface my remarks by saying that my investigation was nothing like the police investigation . . ." Joey Kearns cut him off.

"Yes or no, Mr. Scott. Answer the question, yes or no."

"I won't answer the question because there is no basis for me to answer." This pleased Raymond but angered the prosecutor.

"Your Honor?" said Joey.

"You are directed to answer the question, Mr. Scott." Ned was cornered. Deep down inside he didn't believe Marianne despite the fact that she was family. He knew that Anthony Williams was a well-respected family man. He knew that Anthony had been seriously injured and couldn't have raped his daughter. He knew that Anthony couldn't have assaulted and raped his daughter without doing further serious injury to himself. Yet he had the picture of Anthony and Marianne together in bed in Hawaii. He pulled the picture from his jacket pocket and threw it at the prosecutor like a frisbee. At the same time, he blurted out, "Yes, dammit. Are you satisfied?" Lew Dobson was satisfied. Joey Kearns was satisfied. Ned Scott was furious and glared at his daughter. The objections of the defense were unheard amidst all the commotion.

But then Ned Scott stood up and pointed at Marianne. "You may be my daughter, but you better be telling the whole truth, Marianne Scott. If I find that you are lying about any piece of this matter, I personally will see to it that you are prosecuted to the fullest extent of the law." Next he turned to Anthony. "If you raped my daughter, then my wrath will be worse than anything you can imagine."

The court was in a virtual state of panic. Judge O'Connor called for a recess and ordered the courtroom to be cleared. It would be reconvened at 9:30 A.M. He ordered counsel into his chambers immediately as well as the current witness.

The battle raged on in the recesses of the judge's chambers. The issue was whether the picture of the defendant and the alleged victim would be admitted into evidence. Judge O'Connor saw this as his first opportunity to damage the credibility of the defendant. He ordered the picture admitted. The defense extracted a concession, however, by getting the judge to agree that its admissibility would depend on the testimony of the photographer.

Ned told the attorneys who had taken the picture. Judge O'Connor signed an order to have her brought in as the next witness. Ned agreed to personally oversee her getting to the court as soon as possible. She lived only twenty minutes from downtown. Ned left by a rear entrance with the bailiff and the subpoena for the photographer's immediate appearance.

All agreed that Ned wouldn't return to the stand until after the appearance of the photographer, which was scheduled at 10:30 A.M. Silently, Joey Kearns and Lew Dobson were thanking their lucky stars for such a break. Despite the apparently damaging nature of the photograph, the defense team from Johnson, Owens, Sutter & Moss was unmoved and unimpressed. As a matter of fact, they were glad that Ned Scott had taken an active role in getting to the truth. They were glad that he and an officer of the court were going to show up unannounced on the doorstep of the photographer. They were glad that there would be no communication with Marianne on this matter.

●●●●●●

The unmarked police vehicle pulled up in front of the Seymour residence. The bailiff banged loudly on the door. He was accompanied by another policeman, who had driven, as well as Ned Scott. Alan Seymour answered the door and was shocked at the parties standing at the entrance. "What's going on?" he asked.

"We have a subpoena and order for Leslie Seymour to appear immediately and give testimony in the County Court," said the bailiff. "Is Ms. Seymour here?"

"She's getting dressed upstairs," responded her father. "What's this all about?"

"I believe you know my daughter, Mr. Seymour. My name is Ned Scott. Your daughter accompanied Marianne last January to Hawaii . . ."

Mr. Seymour cut him off. "Aw, shit! I was hoping that Leslie wouldn't have to get involved in that mess. I told her to be careful. I told her not to trust rich people. And now look what's happening." Alan Seymour walked to the stairs and yelled for his daughter. "Leslie, get yourself down here right now." After two

Railroaded!

minutes, Leslie, an attractive woman with a short pageboy haircut, came hopping down the stairs. Upon seeing the three men waiting for her, especially Marianne's father, she figured she was in real trouble. "I told you not to trust that little rich girl. Now look what you've got yourself into." Ned didn't like the tone of his daughter's best friend's father.

"Don't worry, Daddy. I'll be okay. I don't have anything to hide."

"Ms. Seymour, we have a subpoena for your immediate appearance at County Court. The judge is waiting," said the bailiff.

"That's fine. Is my attire acceptable?" She was smartly dressed in a multicolored, below-the-knee, sleeveless sundress. Leslie actually had taken the day off to prepare for a family vacation to Athens, a late college-graduation gift from her parents.

"Quite acceptable, Ms. Seymour," responded the bailiff.

"We'll be leaving now, Mr. Seymour. And by the way, all rich people are not bad. I just want to get to the bottom of this nasty mess. I'm sorry your daughter is involved. We just want to know the truth."

"Then the truth you will get, Mr. Scott. Leslie's never lied a day in her life. And I don't suspect she'll start now." Ned shook Alan Seymour's hand and left with his daughter, followed by the court officials.

During the course of the recess, Marianne had been an absolute wreck wondering where her father had gone and why. She didn't even know that her father had the picture. That nervousness was intensified when court resumed at 10:30 A.M. Judge O'Connor took the bench and admonished everyone in the courtroom to maintain decorum and exhibit a calm demeanor. In the absence of such behavior, he would bar any and all spectators. The response from the gallery was complete silence.

"Bailiff, please bring the jury in." The jury entered from their anteroom and took their seats. "As a result of the events of this morning, there has been a change of witnesses. I have ordered that the photograph that Mr. Scott launched at the prosecutor be admitted into evidence, but only after the photographer has testified as to its authenticity. Bailiff, please bring in the witness." From the judge's chambers, Ned Scott emerged with Leslie Seymour following behind him. Marianne began a state of internal panic. She figured that Leslie might be called but only to corroborate her presence in Hawaii. Marianne hadn't planned on Leslie testifying about the picture she took of Anthony and herself in bed. She hadn't even had time to talk to Leslie about this eventuality.

Ned Scott sat next to his daughter and took her hand. "Why are you shaking so, baby?" She got a hold of herself and responded to her father.

"I just remembered what Tony did to me . . . and the complete feeling of helplessness. It made me shake inside." Another academy award performance. Reality was that Marianne was scared to death about her best friend being on the witness stand.

"Nothing else?" inquired her father.

"Nothing, Daddy. That's all."

After the bailiff administered the oath to Leslie Seymour, the prosecutor went straight to work on the witness. "Ms. Seymour, are you the person who took this picture?" Joey Kearns handed it to her for examination. She looked at it and handed it back to the prosecutor.

"Yes, sir, I am." Arnold Benton, instead of paying attention to the questions, was looking at Marianne Scott. Ned's daughter seemed to be emotionless.

"And where did you take this picture, Ms. Seymour?" inquired the prosecutor.

"I took the picture in Hawaii, earlier this year," responded Leslie.

"And why did you take the picture, Ms. Seymour?" Everyone was on the edge of their seats, especially Marianne Scott.

"I took the picture . . . because I always took pictures of Marianne and her men. I have a scrapbook full of such pictures. We were roommates in college for the entire four years at UCLA." The prosecution was annoyed with her chattiness but continued. Arnold Benton now refocused his attention on the witness and started scribbling notes on his legal pad. Adrian passed a note to the defense table that was read by Raymond Sutter and then passed to Arnold Benton.

Railroaded!

"Were you at the party in Hawaii where it is alleged that the defendant and the victim had a personal confrontation?"

"I was there, yes."

"And was the defendant there also?"

"Yes, he was there with another player from the Denver Broncos."

"You mean he was there with Mr. Adrian Christopher."

"That's his name, yes." Leslie was smiling a bit.

"And was there a boisterous confrontation between the defendant and Marianne Scott?"

"Not that I recall."

"Are you sure, Ms. Seymour?" asked the prosecutor again.

"I'm 100 percent positive."

"No further questions, Your Honor." Joey Kearns returned to his seat after making sure that each jury member had seen the incriminating photograph. The minute Joey sat down, Arnold Benton leaped up and tore right into Leslie Seymour.

"Are you a trophy collector, Ms. Seymour?"

"No, sir, I'm not."

"Then why would you intrude on the privacy of a couple to take pictures of their sexual activities?" Leslie flinched and recognized she might be in a bit of trouble.

"Marianne and I always took lots of pictures of the men we were with. In college, dormitory rooms are not suites. Everything is out in the open."

"So you witnessed your roommate having sex before?" asked the defense counselor.

"More often than I care to admit." Marianne was cringing inside at the response from her long-time friend.

"Why did you smile when the name of Adrian Christopher was mentioned?" Ms. Seymour started to blush again.

"He's a great dancer and a very kind man. He was drunk but wasn't abusive or overbearing like most of the NFL players." Adrian, sitting in the gallery next to Errol Forrest, was embarrassed at these comments. "We took a long walk on the beach and just talked. There was no sex despite the fact that the party turned into an orgy of sorts . . . not that I would've minded one bit." There was a laugh from the gallery. Even the judge was amused.

"So it's possible that you missed the confrontation between Marianne and the defendant, is it not?" asked Arnold Benton.

"No, I remember it clearly."

"You remember what clearly?" Arnold was very pointed with his questions.

"I remember the party clearly. I remember that Anthony had been sitting in a corner talking to another player. He wasn't doing too much except drinking rum and coke. Marianne asked him to dance and he accepted. That's all there was to it."

"And that was sufficient contact for them to wind up in bed together?"

"Well, that's not what I would have done . . ." responded Leslie. Marianne continued her squeamish movements at her seat. "I saw them disappear together, arm-in-arm. Afterwards, that's when I went with Mr. Christopher to walk on the beach."

"So why did you take the picture of Marianne and the defendant? Did Marianne ask you to?" Marianne started sweating bullets. There was a bit of commotion, which stopped immediately on one pound of the judge's gavel.

"I went looking for Marianne after I came back from the walk on the beach. Mr. Christopher and I had another drink, but he sat down and fell asleep on a sofa. Everyone else was pairing off and disappearing. Actually I wanted to go back to our hotel. I opened a bedroom door and there were Marianne and Mr. Williams. I took the picture and left the party."

"So, to sum up your testimony today, Marianne Scott had a one-night stand with the defendant, you just happened upon them in bed together, and took a picture of their encounter. Right?"

"Yes sir, that's right."

"Now, Ms. Seymour, would you characterize yourself as a good photographer?"

"I think so," responded Leslie.

"Okay, then, you know the difference between a posed and a candid shot, do you not?"

"I certainly do," responded the witness.

"I want you to look at the picture very closely and tell me if you see anything out of character for a candid shot."

"I don't understand what you mean," said the witness.

Railroaded!

"Okay, then, when you are involved in a sexual encounter, would your hair remain as pristine as is your friend's in this picture?"

"Objection!" came the interjection from the prosecutor. "That question is preposterous!"

"Sustained!" retorted the judge.

"You admit that you've seen Marianne after many sexual encounters. Isn't that right?" Leslie was now starting to squirm a bit.

"Yes, sir. Unfortunately I have."

"Then, is the appearance of Marianne in this picture normal or not?" Before allowing her to respond, Arnold Benton interjected, "Remember, Ms. Seymour, we can always subpoena your scrapbook and compare notes, so respond very carefully." She looked at Marianne and smiled.

"Marianne is Marianne. She was always a glamour plate. Her hair was always perfect no matter what she did . . . sex, sports, you name it. Look at her now . . . not a hair out of place. My other pictures show the same." Marianne breathed a sigh of relief.

"How long have you known Marianne Scott?" asked Arnold Benton, frustrated at her responses.

"I've known Marianne since second grade . . . for almost fourteen years."

"Have you ever covered for your friend to get her out of trouble?" asked the defense counselor.

"Objection!" exclaimed Joey Kearns.

"Sustained!" retorted the judge. "Watch yourself, Mr. Benton. You're treading on very dangerous ground."

"Thank you, Your Honor. I'll take your comment under advisement," responded Arnold Benton. This was a high-end manner of telling the judge to "bug off." Arnold rephrased the question to make it more palatable. "Has Marianne Scott ever asked you to cover for her in any manner or matter whatsoever?"

"Objection!" again from Joey Kearns. Judge O'Connor was cornered by this question.

"Overruled! The witness will answer the question." Marianne knew the answer. Leslie was not a liar. She knew her fate was sealed.

"I've never had to cover for Marianne Scott. My friend always took care of herself, and me when I got into trouble -- not the other way around." Marianne couldn't believe what she heard. She started to feel good inside . . . she started to feel as though she was in control again.

"Are you certain of this, Ms. Seymour?"

"Entirely certain. Marianne hails from a very wealthy family. I'm just her best friend. Marianne has always been able to take care of herself without my help." Arnold stood right in front of the witness box and looked . . . stared into Leslie's deep green eyes. He knew she was lying. He could see her sweating. Yet, there was nothing he could do about it. She didn't flinch once. Leslie Seymour was good, very good. He broke his stare, returned to the defense table, and sat down. He didn't see Leslie wipe her brow with a tissue.

"One last question, Ms. Seymour. Were you ever in love with a Lucas Johnson?" Leslie thought this was a weird question for him to ask.

"What?" she asked with a snarled look on her face. "Are you kidding me? Better you ask that question of Marianne. She and Lucas Johnson were the last of the red-hot lovers! Whatever gave you the idea I had anything to do with Luke?" Marianne was annoyed at this honest response from her friend, but so what? She hadn't been betrayed.

"No further questions, Your Honor."

"You are excused, Ms. Seymour. Thank you for your prompt appearance. The photograph is admitted into evidence as People's No. 100." Joey Kearns nodded his approval, as did Arnold Benton. "Court is in recess until 2:00 P.M. At that time, Mr. Scott will retake the witness stand." With a pound of the gavel, the morning proceedings were over.

Leslie Seymour walked up to her long-time friend. Marianne hugged her. "Thanks, Leslie. You really are my best friend." Leslie Seymour whispered her response in Marianne's ear.

"I just perjured myself to save your butt. I told you not to drag me into this mess with your black boyfriends. We'll discuss the cost of my allegiance later." They broke the embrace to

Railroaded!

Marianne's offer of lunch and walked out smiling as if nothing had happened.

● ● ● ● ● ●

Ned Scott was furious at what he had just heard from his daughter's best friend. He went to a payphone and made a series of calls, one of which was to his mother to summarize the testimony of the morning session. After ten animated minutes, he hung up. Elizabeth Cobb was pleased with the report from her son. She told him to "keep his chin up" and remember that he was a Scott. She bounced around the house and decided to go to the afternoon session to demonstrate moral support for Ned, who would be returning to the witness stand.

She made a call to an old friend and invited her to lunch. She made another call and barked a series of instructions. She hung up the phone and went to her upstairs suite to get dressed. Since it was going to be a hot afternoon in Pittsburgh, she dressed very casually and donned a floppy sunhat that matched her dress.

Twenty minutes later, the chauffeur pulled up and waited for the elder Scott, who now used her maiden name, to get into her Bentley.

● ● ● ● ● ● ● ● ●

Shelli Williams was completely exasperated that a picture actually existed of her husband in bed with a white woman. She never doubted her husband, yet, if she didn't know about his childhood experience and absolute fear of white women, she might have been tempted to go down the hall and file for divorce proceedings. She looked at Tony and shook her head. He was teary-eyed at the pain that the morning had caused his wife. "I never did anything, baby. I never did anything." Shelli put her arms around her husband and kissed him on the forehead.

"That arrogant bitch is gonna pay dearly for what she's done to you . . . what she's done to us. She's gonna pay." Shelli knew they were playing with fire, very rich fire. But her mind was also on fire with anger. Despite her raging anger, she was thinking very clearly.

Shelli was an accomplished photographer as well. She suggested to Raymond that they subpoena the photo album of Leslie Seymour and examine the rest of her "pictures." A professional photographer would be able to compare the various pictures taken by Leslie Seymour and determine whether she had perjured herself to cover for Marianne. Raymond agreed with this strategy.

Raymond sent Dave Robinson and Arnold Benton back to the office to prepare a *subpoena duces tecum*, an order to produce documents or records, for Leslie Seymour. Raymond could see the frustration on the faces of Tony and Shelli. He took both his client and his beautiful wife to lunch to try and smooth ruffled feathers.

Chapter 22

A large panel truck pulled up to the modest house on Lincoln Avenue not far from the city limits. Two men got out of the service truck marked with decals indicating that the vehicle belonged to the Pittsburgh Gas & Electric Company. Both men, in PG&E uniforms, started polling neighbors about reported gas leaks. Most of the residents were not home. There was also no answer at 8695 Lincoln Avenue.

At each residence, the two men went into the backyard to check the gas meter and left a tag detailing an inspection and the service provided. At 8695 it was necessary to do an inside inspection. The neighbors on either side of the house were not at home. One of the men removed a glasscutter from his vest and carefully cut a small circle in the window of the back door. Both men entered the house and went upstairs to the bedrooms. After only two minutes, one of the men was successful in finding what they had been sent to retrieve. A careful "once over" was enough to extract exactly what was wanted. Afterward, the intruder carefully soaked each page of the album with lighter fluid.

While one finished the work upstairs, the other man descended the stairs and busied himself with the task of cutting and refitting the glass pane in the back door. After not more than seven minutes, the two men were finished. No one would ever know they had been there. Mission accomplished.

They quickly left the house, but not before disconnecting the gas line to the stove and leaving a small plastic device behind it, something that looked like a transistor radio. Outside, the two, acting as if they were working on the gas meter, marked it with a service tag and left the residence. Inside the truck, they radioed that they had been successful in acquiring the appropriate property.

"Excellent," said the voice on the other end of the radio. "I have confirmed that no one will be in the house until after 4:30 P.M. Activate the device and set it for ignition at 3:17 P.M." The man in the passenger seat complied with the instructions as the two men drove away. "Take the truck back to the service garage and follow your normal instructions. By the way, we should have a full-course dinner this evening."

"Understood, sir," was the response of the driver. This invitation pleased them both. It was an acknowledgment for a job well done with payment of at least $25,000 in cash. The two men continued their journey and talked of playing nine holes of golf later that afternoon.

●●●●●●

Everyone was in the courtroom and seated when Judge O'Connor entered. "Mr. Scott is going to take the witness stand and depending on the length of his testimony and cross-examination, court will probably be recessed early this afternoon. Of course, this is entirely up to you, the esteemed counsel." Everyone appreciated the judge's attempt to be light after the heaviness of the morning session. "Mr. Scott, would you please come forward and take the witness stand? Remember that you are still under oath." Ned Scott, seated between his mother and daughter, complied with the instruction. Leslie Seymour was seated next to Marianne.

Joey Kearns enjoyed lunch with his boss, during which time they assessed the events of the morning and how they would approach the balance of the day's testimony. They both had decided that the evening hours would be spent redeveloping their approach to the case. They both realized they were caught in a "no win" situation, but they had to persevere to the end in pursuit of the truth.

Joey stood and began his questioning of the owner of the Pittsburgh Steelers. "Mr. Scott." Joey paused for a second . . . but before he could continue, Ned spoke up.

Railroaded!

"First, Mr. Kearns, I would like to apologize to you and to the court for my abhorrent behavior of this morning. Second, I would like to apologize to Judge O'Connor for turning this trial into a circus. My anger, both as a father and NFL team owner, momentarily overwhelmed my sense of propriety. For that I am sorry." Judge O'Connor was impressed with the apology and thanked Mr. Scott for his sincerity.

"I also thank you and am sure that the defense counsel accepts your apology as do we from the district attorney's office," said Joey Kearns. There was a brief round of applause. Judge O'Connor did not pound his gavel to restore order but instead joined the attendees in the gallery. Lew Dobson was very pleased with the public demeanor of his most junior associate. "Now, Mr. Scott, I don't have very many questions for you this afternoon. We will stick to the facts as you know them and nothing else."

"That's fine, Mr. Kearns," responded Ned. Raymond Sutter sat there and thought that the defense would not be so forgiving or accommodating.

"On the night of the preseason game between the Steelers and the Broncos, where were you, sir?"

"For the first half, I was in the owner's box at Three Rivers Stadium. Moments after the end of the second quarter, I had my chauffeur drive me to my private club in downtown. From there, I watched the rest of the game on closed circuit television."

"And did you witness the play during which the defendant was injured?" asked Joey in a concerned tone of voice.

"I did, like millions of viewers. I saw it very clearly. I had it replayed on my screen several times so I could try to determine the extent to which Anthony Williams had been injured."

"And why is that?" asked the prosecutor, probing for more information.

"I wanted to know if he was seriously injured, would be out for a few games, out for the season, or worst, if his career was over."

"So, what did you do next?"

"I called the stadium and told the trainer to spare no expense for Anthony's medical treatment and rehabilitation."

"Did you do anything else, Mr. Scott?"

"Yes, sir, I did. I called the Broncos's owner, who was a guest at Three Rivers and told him that every single dime that it cost to rehabilitate Anthony was going to be his cost. I told him that, if he didn't cut the son-of-a-bitch who hit Anthony, I was going to file a complaint with the rest of the owners."

"And what happened?"

"He complied, and after the game, the coach of the Broncos cut the rookie running back. I received a call at the club from Blu Stiller stating that he had complied with the owner's request. Quite frankly, he agreed with the decision."

"What did you do then?"

"I told Howard Werner, my chauffeur, that I wanted him to take the limo to the stadium, pick up Anthony, and drive him home. That's a practice that I instituted some eight or nine years ago for injured players. Besides, it was much too late for Shelli Williams to drive back into town to pick up her husband."

"And what time did the limo leave the club?" continued the prosecutor.

"He left at 12:30 A.M. I took a cab home because I was both tired and had been imbibing myself -- a little on the heavy side. After all, it's not every day that you see one of your key stars taken out by an assassin-like hit."

"Thank you, Mr. Scott." Joey paced around in front of the witness stand. "What time did you get a call from the Pittsburgh police about the situation with your daughter?"

"It was about 5:45 A.M. Detective Spencer called me from Allegheny General Hospital. All he said was that my daughter had been involved in very serious foul play. I asked if she was all right, and the detective told me to get over to the hospital right away."

"And did you?"

"Yes, sir. I got up, got dressed, and drove myself to the hospital."

"So, from the time you left the club in a taxicab till the time you received the call, you had no idea of the whereabouts of your daughter or your chauffeur. Is that correct?"

"Yes, that's correct."

"Mr. Scott, the next question is going to be a very difficult one for you to answer. Please do your best." Ned Scott nodded his

Railroaded!

understanding and approval. "When you learned that your daughter had accused Anthony Williams of brutally assaulting and raping her, what did you think?" Ned Scott shrugged his shoulders.

"I thought she was full of crap. I saw the illegal hit that Anthony took, and I had received a telephone report from our team orthopedic doctor. Anthony could hardly walk!" Raymond was smiling at this response.

"So what changed your mind, Mr. Scott?" Ned bowed his head and sighed before responding.

"The picture of the two of them together in bed." There was a subdued level of commotion in the courtroom. Two strikes of the gavel silenced the gallery attendees.

"Thank you very much, Mr. Scott. I've no further questions for now." Mr. Kearns looked at the jurors and felt that he had scored serious credibility points. Joey was feeling pretty good.

"Mr. Sutter, I presume?" stated Judge O'Connor.

"You presume correct, Judge. But I would like to suggest a ten-minute recess before I begin the cross-examination of the witness." Judge O'Connor looked at the prosecutor, who nodded his assent.

"After your cross-examination, Mr. Sutter, we will conclude today's activities. I assume that you will finish your cross today?"

"We will indeed, Judge," stated the lead defense counsel.

"The court hereby stands in recess for ten minutes."

●●●●●●

After the recess, Ned returned to the witness stand. Raymond Sutter approached him and started the cross-examination process. "Mr. Scott? We of the defense team would like you to know that, despite the fact that Anthony Williams is the defendant in this case, he holds no malice against you personally. But, against your daughter, that is another issue." Joey Kearns stood as if he were going to object but instead sat back down.

"When you saw the defendant sustain the illegal crack-back block by the Denver Broncos running back, and you saw the defendant lying on the field motionless, what did you think?"

"I thought perhaps that either his back was broken or he had sustained severe nerve damage that could have resulted in a case much like Darrel Stingley."

"And what happened to Darrel Stingley?"

"He was hit, blind-sided by a defensive player and paralyzed from the neck down."

"And you believed that was what happened to the defendant?"

"Yes, Mr. Sutter. I thought he was finished."

"And how long was it before you got the orthopedic doctor's report?"

"He called me midway during the fourth quarter."

"Okay, then. And what did he report to you?"

"He reported that Anthony had sustained severe spinal trauma resulting from two compressed vertebral discs that were the direct result of the illegal hit."

"And the prognosis for recovery?"

"The report was that he would eventually recover 100 percent use of all of his faculties. However, it was recommended that he retire from the game of football. One hit the wrong way could paralyze him for life." The reaction of the audience was short but noticeable.

"When did you learn who had hit your player?" asked the defense counselor.

"Not until after Marianne left the club. She asked me to call the limo and have it pick her up so that Howard could drive her to an 'after' party."

"And what time was that?"

"It was moments after 1:00 A.M. when I called the limo's mobile phone."

"And so, after Marianne left the club, you went back upstairs to your office?"

"I did, and then I found out that Lucas Johnson was the one who hit Anthony."

"And what did you do then, Mr. Scott?" asked Raymond, who was turning up the heat.

"I screamed aloud and vowed to severely punish my daughter. I knew that somehow she had to be involved." Joey Kearns was starting to feel a little nauseous.

Railroaded!

"Now, Mr. Scott. Would you say that you're in good shape?"

"I would . . . I think I am," responded the owner of the Steelers.

"Have you ever injured your back?"

"Yes, sir, but not the way Anthony did."

"Very well, then. When your back was injured, did you ever have sex with your late wife, or subsequently another woman?"

"Objection, Your Honor. The question is irrelevant and immaterial," stated the prosecutor.

"On the contrary, Your Honor, I'm asking this man a very simple question that is based on his own experience, nothing more."

"Overruled, Mr. Kearns." Joey sat down. He knew he was in big trouble with this line of questioning. "Answer the question, Mr. Scott."

"No, sir, never."

"And why not?" asked Raymond, closing in for the kill.

"Objection! Calls for speculation by the witness," exclaimed the prosecutor.

"Sustained! Mr. Sutter, please clean it up!"

"Mr. Scott, if your back were seriously injured, you wouldn't engage in sexual intercourse because of the fear of aggravating the injury, right?"

"Objection!" The commotion in the court was rising. Judge O'Connor pounded his gavel five times to get the courtroom's attention.

"Mr. Sutter, I find you in contempt of court and hereby order you to pay a $500 fine forthwith." Raymond Sutter walked to the bench, stared straight at the judge, and barked an order.

"Mr. Johnson, would you please come forward and count out five crisp new $100 bills for His Honor, and don't forget the receipt!" Raymond never took his eyes off Gerald O'Connor until Dave Johnson had taken the receipt and returned to his seat. He broke his stare and walked to the witness stand. "Mr. Scott, while you didn't get a chance to answer such a simple question, I think we both know the answer." Mr. Scott nodded his assent without answering. Raymond got what he wanted. The jury saw the reaction. Lew Dobson was furious and called for a side-bar conference.

"Pull another stunt like that, Raymond, and I'll have your butt thrown in jail immediately," stated the judge.

"We need sanctions against the defense counsel, Your Honor," stated the district attorney.

"Not in this life, Lew," retorted Raymond.

"No sanctions for now, gentlemen, but I'm warning you, Raymond. You better toe the line." The side-bar conference broke up and the district attorney returned to his seat next to his junior associate. Raymond resumed his questioning of the witness.

"Mr. Scott, when you heard that Anthony Williams had been accused of raping your daughter, what did you think?"

"As I said earlier, I thought it was impossible," was Ned's response.

"Why?" was the simple question from Raymond.

"Well, for two reasons. The first is that his injury, in my mind, wouldn't have allowed him to commit such an act."

"And the second reason, Mr. Scott?" Ned looked at his mother and knew that his answer was going to infuriate her. Nevertheless, this was a search for truth. And he would tell only the truth, regardless of the cost.

"Anthony wouldn't touch, let alone hurt a white woman." The audience was stirring up in another commotion but was calmed with a few pounds from the gavel of the judge. Elizabeth Cobb was livid at the response from her son. The prosecutor was on his feet in an outrage.

"This violates your pretrial order, Your Honor! Mr. Sutter is flagrantly disregarding the parameters set forth in the pretrial conferences." Joey Kearns left his seat and was standing before the bench. Raymond turned and responded to the young prosecutor in a very harsh and pointed tone.

"Young man, I have done no such thing! Your own witness has unknowingly violated the judge's orders and opened the door for a new line of interrogation by the defense. The judge has no choice but to let us inquire further." Both men turned to Judge O'Connor.

"That's where you're wrong, Mr. Sutter. I previously ordered that there would be no discussion of racial prejudice in this trial. And there will not be." Judge O'Connor turned to the jury and told them to disregard the last statement of the witness. Raymond was

Railroaded!

furious and immediately called for a mistrial. Judge O'Connor denied the motion and told the defense lawyer to settle down and proceed, or else. Raymond asked for a five-minute recess to confer with his associates. Judge O'Connor granted him two minutes only.

During the time the defense lawyers were huddled at their table, no one noticed that a uniformed police officer had come in and handed a note to the bailiff. The bailiff read the note and handed it to Judge O'Connor. Before the two minutes were up, he called court back to order and made the following announcement: "Ladies and gentlemen, there has been a terrible accident. A few minutes ago there was an explosion that leveled two houses near the city line. While there were no injuries, both houses were completely destroyed in the blast and ensuing fire. Unfortunately, the incident has a bearing on this case, especially the destruction of the house at 8695 Lincoln Avenue." Leslie Seymour stood and started screaming hysterically. "Bailiff, take her to her parents." Judge O'Connor paused as he let the bailiff take Ms. Seymour from the courtroom. "Unfortunately, court will have to stand in recess for the balance of the afternoon. Mr. Scott, you are excused."

Judge O'Connor disappeared into his chambers. The commotion in the courtroom was highly charged as people flowed into the hallway.

●●●●●●

In the midst of the hysteria before everyone cleared the courtroom, Raymond Sutter went to Errol Forrest and handed him a business card with a short note written on the back. It said, "Call me at this number at 7:00 P.M. to arrange a meeting."

Chapter 23

Errol shared the note on the business card with Adrian but not with Tony. Since Tony had a house full of family guests, it was easy for both men to use the excuse of going out for a beer to talk about old times at Dartmouth. Tony didn't suspect anything other than that his best friends wanted a break from all of the commotion at the Williams residence. Tony wished them well, and off they went in Errol's Pontiac Firebird.

After driving around for almost a half hour, Errol stopped at a payphone and called the number given him by Raymond. He answered on two rings. Errol, being very cautious, told Raymond to go to a phone booth immediately and call him back. Raymond agreed and left his residence to do so. The wait was short.

"What the hell is going on, Errol?" asked Raymond in a tone that suggested complete confusion and frustration.

"There are heavy-duty players involved in this case. Surely you don't believe that the explosion and fire at the Seymour house were accidents, do you?" Errol continued his allegations. "And don't think for a minute that your offices aren't bugged. Don't you find it surprising that Guy Markham showed up at the restaurant last night after I said there was nothing to discuss?"

"I admit it seemed more than just coincidental. Or at least so it seemed," responded the lawyer.

"Listen, Raymond. We have to talk face-to-face now, while everyone is still preoccupied with the Seymour incident. Where should we meet you? Just tell us a place and we'll find it." Raymond thought for a moment and then made the following suggestion.

"You know how to get to the airport?"

Railroaded!

"Sure do," replied Errol.

"Then meet me at the ticket counter for Eastern Airlines. We can walk and talk there. Be there in forty-five minutes." Both men hung up the phone and left for their destination.

●●●●●●

Elizabeth Cobb was both charming and consoling to Donna Seymour. Conrad Seymour was in a virtual state of shock. Ned Scott was on his car phone barking instructions to insurance agents and bankers.

"Listen, Mrs. Seymour," said Elizabeth with her arm around the woman's shoulders, "this case is terrible. That Anthony Williams will stop at nothing to defend his position. He's a very powerful man in many circles. But don't you worry at all, dearie. My Ned and I have decided that since you got involved in this mess because Leslie went with Marianne to Hawaii, we will pay for the immediate reconstruction of your house. In the meantime, you are more than welcome to come and stay with us." Ned, walking up to his mother and Mrs. Seymour, countered the last offer.

"I think it would be better if we offered a rental home at our expense. That way they can maintain their own privacy."

"That's fine, son. I was just trying to be neighborly in their time of tragedy . . . just trying to be hospitable. Of course a rental is much better for them." Elizabeth smiled at her son and walked away with Mrs. Seymour.

There was a myriad of fire engines, police vehicles and investigative squads crawling over the smoldering wreckage of what was once a beautiful home. PG&E acknowledged that they had received reports of gas leaks in the area, but since these were not reported as serious, they weren't scheduled for service until the following day. Company officials were in a quandary as to how and why someone had "serviced" the homes that day.

The media was having a field day with the events. Speculation was running wild. There were rampant accusations that Ned, or even Marianne, had hired someone to destroy the contents of Leslie Seymour's photo album. While the remnants of the album were found, it was burned beyond recognition. Any evidence that could have been used in the case was now just an afterthought.

Marianne sat on the curb and watched the throng of people pore over what was once the home of her best friend. After a few minutes, Leslie walked over and sat down next to her. "So this is the price of our fourteen-year friendship." She looked at the wreckage and continued. "My mother and father wanted to move out of this neighborhood anyway. I hear your grandmother and father have offered to have the house rebuilt and pay for the cost." She looked at her feet. "That was a fine gesture and my parents will be appreciative. But there's still you and me, kid." Leslie looked at Marianne with a face filled with disgust and continued. "I'm told I'm basically out of the case now. What I want for having my life wrecked is . . . is for you to tell the truth and end this charade right now." Marianne responded immediately.

"I can't do that! Are you out of your mind? Look around you. This has to be played out to the end."

"Until someone winds up dead just because you didn't get another black guy to fuck your brains out? You really are sick, Marianne!" Leslie got up to leave.

"Where are you going?" asked the Scott woman in a terrified voice.

"I'm going to put an end to this right now. There are more than enough media representatives here to take my story."

"Wait a minute, Leslie. Just wait a minute." Marianne directed her to a place where it was less crowded and where they could talk privately. "What . . . or how much do you want?"

"I want the same amount you paid Lucas for covering your narrow behind."

"Are you crazy? I thought you were my best friend!"

"If you give me what I want, I will be. What you didn't know was that after you paid Lucas and dropped him at the airport, he didn't leave town right away. He came by to see me later that night and told me you paid him $350,000 in cash for him to perform that little tap dance on Anthony Williams. He showed it to me . . . nice new $100 bills. By the way, it's not too hard to figure out who did that outrageous make-up job on your face and why the doctors say you were raped. You had that little pussy of yours filled with his orgasmic juices, didn't you?" Leslie paused for a moment and continued. "You say you love the guy, have him commit a textbook foul on another player, pay him to fuck your brains out, then have him tap dance on your face. Sick, sick, sick! All because a decent family man wouldn't succumb to your seductive bullshit? Listen, dear heart. If I don't get $350,000 in cold, hard cash, I'll blow the whistle on you, Marianne."

"Whatever you want, Leslie -- whatever you want." Inside, Marianne was both exasperated and angry, but she decided to pay Leslie what she wanted. After all, Marianne was standing on Lincoln Avenue looking at smoldering rubble where there used to be a home. Even though she didn't understand the reason why, she knew the destruction of the Seymour home was indirectly her fault. She hugged Leslie and remembered that Leslie always covered up her mistakes. "I guess it's time for me to cover you like you did me for all these years. I don't want to lose you as a friend." Compared to Marianne, Leslie was a saint. Despite the fact that she was being blackmailed, she didn't perceive it as such. Marianne Scott knew that Leslie was indeed a true friend, if not the only real friend she had.

As they parted company so Leslie could rejoin her parents, another emotion welled up inside her. It was pure, unadulterated anger. Marianne was furious that Lucas had discussed their affairs with a third party. For this breach of confidence, he would someday pay dearly.

●●●●●●

Raymond was dressed in a jogging suit, a Pittsburgh Pirates baseball cap and dark sunglasses. He was seated in a rather conspicuous place near the Eastern Airlines ticket counter. Errol and Adrian walked up dressed in short-sleeved polo-type shirts and casual pants. They recognized Raymond immediately and left the terminal to go for a drive in Errol's car.

"Okay, Trees, what's the real deal?" asked Adrian from the back seat. Raymond sat in the passenger seat with an inquisitive look on his face.

"Trees?" asked Raymond, smiling.

"Represents the last name. It stuck with me as a kid. Anyway, I have a friend and fellow alumnus from Dartmouth who has given me some very devastating information about your Mr. Guy Markham."

"You mean Harvey?" asked Adrian.

"That's right, A.C." responded Errol.

"And what's the source of his information?" asked Raymond.

"Harvey works in a special unit at INTERPOL. Errol and he were really tight at Dartmouth. I know that Errol keeps in contact with him from time to time. Right, Trees?"

"Right. But first things first. This is to stay between the three of us and can go no further. Not even Tony can know of what I'm about to tell you. I don't want him to freak out. Besides, he's a little more loose with the lips than we are." Adrian and Raymond agreed.

"Guy Markham used to be a Navy Seal before retiring and starting his private investigation company."

"That's fine, but what does that have to do with anything?" asked Raymond.

"Because he still does jobs for the government and very high-end individuals," stated Errol.

"What kind of jobs?" asked Adrian. Errol's heart was beating fast as he thought about what he was going to say.

"Guy Markham is one of the best assassins there is, and he is the lead investigator for Johnson, Owens, Sutter & Moss. I can pretty much tell you that all of your offices are bugged and that the surveillance on this case is extraordinary."

"But why?" asked Raymond. "Why would he tell us about Marianne's run-in with the police at the Ohio Street substation?"

"Because he's a professional and has to make everything look good," countered Errol.

"Please don't take this the wrong way, but for now, aside from his community activities, Tony is a football player with aspirations of starting an architectural design firm," stated Raymond.

"We all want to start that firm," interjected Adrian. "The night that Tony and I found out Marianne was the witch that was terrorizing him and Shelli, we decided to call a press conference the next day and announce our retirement from pro-football at the end of the season. We never got the opportunity because of Marianne Scott's intervention into our lives."

"Yeah, but why is everyone so afraid of Tony Williams?" asked Raymond. "He's one of the nicest guys anybody could ever know."

"Somebody out there is afraid of Tony, or just hates him enough to want him put away. A while back, Guy Markham was asking a lot of questions about Tony's political aspirations. I told him Tony had none. He didn't believe me at all," answered Errol.

"So, you think the destruction of the Seymour home was deliberate?" asked Raymond.

"There's no doubt in my mind. It damned sure wasn't accidental." Errol paused for a moment as if quizzing himself and then continued.

"But Guy Markham wasn't in court today," stated Raymond. "How would he have known about the photo album to destroy it?"

"Why not just break in and snatch it?" asked Errol. "Why destroy the house and risk killing some innocent people?" Errol was full of unanswered questions.

"But if Guy Markham is an assassin, then for whom does he work?" asked Adrian. Errol answered the question.

"That's just it. We don't know, and have no way of finding out. If we confront him, then the whole case is blown. Tony could wind up dead."

"I agree. So we have to pull out all the stops and make sure that we obliterate the prosecution's case. That's the only sure way we'll get Tony cleared."

"What can I do to help?" asked Adrian.

"You can work with me in my offices doing a little research, and, who knows, maybe we can even do a 'bug' hunt." All three men laughed. But then Errol added more information that changed the demeanor of the two men.

"You both should know that Ned Scott's former wife committed suicide. She was having an affair with a Steelers player. Apparently, Ned found out and his wife freaked. But before she killed herself, the player wound up dead. Guy Markham used to be head of security for Ned Scott's land development company. There was never a connection, but the coincidence is too great."

"Aw, shit!" said Raymond. "I went to college with John Clayton. He was a damn good man . . . a damn good man."

"You know the details of the case, Raymond?" asked Errol.

"We can talk about that later." Raymond seemed very sad and subdued at this revelation.

"Then we have to talk about another possibility," added Errol.

"What's that?" added A.C.

"Did you notice anything about Judge O'Connor today, Raymond?" asked Errol.

"What? That he's a world-class asshole looking to bust our chops?"

"No . . . but try 'he's a world-class asshole 'trying' to bust Tony!" responded the third-year law student.

"Are you suggesting that Gerald's on the take? Why would you think that, Mr. Trees?" Errol looked at Adrian and smiled.

"There was one class I took last year that I hated above all others. Evidence is the most confusing thing I've ever dealt with. There's no rhyme or reason to the rules of evidence. However, when Ned Scott brought up the issue of Tony's experience, you should have been able to drive a Mack truck through that open door. Instead, Judge O'Connor shut you down cold. From what I remember of your telling us about your relationship with the judge, he should have flung open the door after Ned cracked it."

"What the hell are you guys talking about?" asked Adrian.

"Maybe you should go to law school and learn this shit. You never know when it's going to be important," stated Raymond. Adrian laughed and responded.

"One lawyer in our ranks is enough, thank you." They all laughed aloud for a moment. Raymond explained how it was that a subject that was prohibited by court order from discussion during examination could be discussed. If, during the course of the examination, the witness were to mention the prohibited subject on his own, then the prohibited subject could be addressed openly. Adrian understood. Adrian also understood that Gerald O'Connor had something to hide . . . that his sense of impartiality and fairness had been tainted. "After this, you still want to be a lawyer?" asked Adrian of Errol.

Railroaded!

"I want the education, but have no desire to practice. You know that, A.C." Errol was adamant about not practicing law even though he would have been a brilliant advocate and litigator.

"If you ever change your mind, let me know. You'd be a valuable addition to the firm, Errol. Besides, I could use the company of another black face there. It's a great firm, but we are few and far between."

"I'll take that under advisement, counselor. But I can tell you that I'd never fit in here in Pittsburgh because I'm a diehard Broncomaniac!" Errol was laughing, along with Raymond and Adrian.

They continued their drive and pulled into a Burger King to get some food. Afterward, they dropped Raymond at his car back at the airport parking lot. They checked it for bugs, or worse, explosive devices, and assured themselves that all was safe. "Remember, Raymond. Don't talk to anyone about this, not even your friend at the FBI. It's not safe."

Chapter 24

Wednesday, August 22nd

Raymond Sutter spent a long, restless night. While he slept, dreams of Guy Markham invaded his mind -- terrible dreams. Tony Williams was in grave danger. He had to be a virtual Superman to save an innocent man. He awoke and knew that this challenge was going to be greater than any he had ever faced. He prepared himself with his usual regimen of daily exercises. He showered and dressed, skipped breakfast, and headed straight for the office. It was only 5:45 A.M. when he arrived and started searching his office for signs of tampering. It wasn't long before he found the first listening device in his office, neatly camouflaged as the screw-bolt to hold the lampshade in place.

As he continued, he found one in Loren's office, one in Arnold Benton's office, and three in the main conference room. He mused to himself that the interlopers wanted to listen "in stereo." He noted the locations and left everything intact except the one in Arnold's office, which he restationed in the main conference room. Arnold's office would potentially be a "safe" room.

Feeling rather proud of his accomplishments, he changed his endeavors and began to review the case materials. He felt that today the prosecution would put Marianne on the stand. He wanted to be ready to destroy this vixen from hell. He also had to figure out how to terminate the firm's contract with Guy Markham's company. That would be a little tricky. He thought of using the ploy of needing to cut costs and having to let the contract out for bidding. The partners would surely agree to this tactic without suspicion, especially since it could mean a potential increase in individual earnings. Additionally, he could play on the conflict of interest that existed by his representing the defendant against a former employer.

Railroaded!

At 7:30 A.M. when Ms. Young arrived, Raymond pulled her aside and told her that absolutely no one was to go into Arnold's office during the course of the day. She was to take note of anyone who tried and let him know. Ms. Young agreed. The door was locked and Raymond put a thin piece of transparent tape on the bottom that was virtually unnoticeable, reminiscent of a trick that he had seen in a James Bond movie. Ms. Young would eat lunch at her desk so as to have a full view of Arnold's office.

Raymond assembled his troops in the conference room. Together they left the office to walk the short distance to the courthouse. Everyone was in a jovial mood as they kidded about the "beast from hell" being on the witness stand.

●●●●●●

The courtroom was completely silent when Judge O'Connor entered. The bailiff said the usual "all rise." Everyone complied and immediately sat after the judge. There was again complete silence. Judge O'Connor noticed that every eye was staring at him. For the first time in all his years as a judge, he felt uncomfortable. The silence was eerie. He felt compelled to make a statement about the destruction of the Seymour home. Instead, he launched into a judicial discussion of the event and its impact on the trial. "I assume that the *subpoena duces tecum* that was ordered by the defense will now be quashed as moot." Raymond nodded his approval. "It has come to my attention that the photo album that was the point of the subpoena was completely destroyed in the explosion and ensuing fire." He paused for a moment. "Therefore, I order that the requested subpoena be quashed and Leslie Seymour be excused as a witness."

"Not so fast, Judge!" Raymond instantly exploded. "The defense has the right to recall the witness and we do not choose to relinquish that right, photo album or not!"

"Mr. Sutter, you are out of order. I've made my ruling." After a night of restlessness and better understanding of the fire with which he was playing, Raymond wasn't about to back down to a potentially crooked judge.

"No, Judge, it is you who are out of order!" shouted Raymond. "You cannot subvert the Rules of Procedure to suit your own folly!" The silence was broken and replaced with utter chaos. Judge O'Connor felt the whole courtroom close in on him. Yet even with this claustrophobic recognition, he retaliated against the defense counselor.

"Mr. Sutter, you are in contempt of court and ordered to pay a fine of $5,000 for your egregious error. I wish to continue this trial so I won't throw you in jail. But one more word on this subject, and I will increase the fine, as well as levy time for incarceration."

"Give it your best shot, Judge. I can take anything you dish out. When this case comes up on appeal, this exchange will surely be at the top of my hit list. A cashier's check will be here in thirty minutes." Raymond sat down, motioned for Dave Johnson to do the honors of getting the check, and crossed his fingers waiting for the judge's next assault. But it didn't materialize. Instead, the silence was instantly restored as everyone waited for the judge's response.

"Mr. Kearns, are you prepared with your next witness?"

"We are, Your Honor."

"Well, then, get on with it."

"Before we do, sir, what is your final ruling with respect to Leslie Seymour? Is she excused or not?" asked the prosecutor, not wanting to create a procedural error that could place the outcome in jeopardy. Judge O'Connor was not amused at this question. He pounded his gavel and screamed to the audience.

"Court is in recess for one hour. Kearns and Sutter, in my chambers, now!" He stormed out like a wild man flinging his arms under his black judicial robe.

"Who do you gentlemen think you are? The Seymour house was destroyed. The evidence was destroyed. This case is under scrutiny from every corner of the country, and I've got to sit here and listen to your stupid allegations of judicial impropriety! How dare you?" The judge uncharacteristically poured himself a morning scotch, turned, and, in a conciliatory gesture, offered each man a drink. Raymond declined, but Joey accepted.

"Listen, Your Honor. I just want to avoid a potential problem later," stated the prosecutor.

Railroaded!

"I understand your concern." Gerald walked around his desk and sat in his chair. "I don't want any problems either." He turned to Raymond and asked, "Do you really expect to call the Seymour girl back to the stand?"

"At this time, no. There's no apparent necessity at this time." Raymond was direct.

"Then, if you find a need, examination will be in chambers. Transcripts of the testimony will be given to the jury afterward. Is this an acceptable arrangement, gentlemen?" Both nodded their assent. Raymond asked a hard question.

"Why the necessity for charades, Gerald? What the hell is going on?" asked Raymond in a tone of familiarity. Judge O'Connor swivelled his chair and looked out.

"After yesterday's events, Raymond, who knows? Both of you leave now, and be back on time!" He sipped his scotch as the two attorneys left his chambers. Gerald O'Connor sat back and turned two complete revolutions in his chair. Coming to a stop, he buried his head in his hands and was soon lost in thought.

●●●●●●

Court resumed punctually at 9:30 A.M. The silence was again powerful, but not overbearing. "Call your first witness, Mr. Kearns," stated the Judge.

"The People call Dr. Phyllis Martin." This was an interesting turn of events which, though surprising, was not totally unexpected by the defense team. They were prepared. Dr. Phyllis Martin represented the calm voice of reason before a storm of idiocy. This tactic was a "let the doctor testify to add credibility to the less than credible Marianne."

Dr. Martin, while not very attractive, was very elegant and powerful in her demeanor. She stood about five feet five inches tall and her weight was in proportion to her height. Her blonde hair was pulled back and rolled so it was impossible to tell its length. She was dressed in a burgundy suit with a camel-colored blouse. Dr. Martin was totally prepared and ready to do her job. After being sworn in, she was seated in the witness stand and waited for the prosecutor's first battery of questions.

"Dr. Martin, tell us a bit about yourself." This was a different approach. The witness would get a chance to ramble on and on.

"I graduated from Barnard College and Stanford Medical School. I completed my internship and residency requirements at Stanford. I specialized in gynecology. I moved to Pittsburgh in 1974 with my husband, who is also a physician. He is engaged in private practice. I am the chief gynecology resident at Allegheny General Hospital. In that capacity, I unfortunately, from time to time, have to examine victims of sexual assault."

"So, on the morning of July 28th, what time did you arrive at the hospital?" asked the prosecutor.

"I checked in at 5:00 A.M.," responded the doctor.

"Were you the attending physician who examined the victim?"

"I was, yes, sir."

"When did you examine the victim, Dr. Martin?" continued the prosecutor.

"Almost immediately after my arrival. The detective told me that the woman had been raped and also who she was."

"So what did you do then?"

"I immediately began an examination of Ms. Scott based on procedures required for victims of alleged sexual assault and rape. I also ordered a series of cranial X-rays."

"Very well, Dr. Martin. And did you follow those procedures?"

"Very explicitly. I didn't want anyone questioning the thoroughness of my examination. I took careful notes and took pictures of the victim. I believe your office and the defense team have been accorded the results of my findings."

"We have, and thank you very much for your cooperation. Now, Dr. Martin, we need to get into the details of your report. During your examination of the victim, what did you find?" This was an open-ended question that the defense didn't appreciate. But rather than object, Raymond thought it better to let this witness talk rather than badger her and the prosecutor with objections. Cross-examination could then be more intense.

"The victim's face was badly bruised, which was the result of having sustained multiple blows. It's almost as if someone was standing over her and hitting her from side to side."

"And what else, Doctor?"

Railroaded!

"I determined from the X-rays that there were no broken bones in the maxilla-facial area. So afterward, I conducted a topical examination and found no other bruises, contusions, lacerations, or abrasions. I then proceeded to conduct a pelvic examination."

"And what did you find, Doctor?"

"While there was no torn or ruptured labial tissue as is typical from forced intercourse, there was an abundance of seminal fluid in her vagina which indicated that she had been penetrated. I took several specimens of the seminal fluid and sent them out for DNA testing."

"So tell us, Dr. Martin. In your professional opinion, was the victim, Marianne Scott, raped?" The physician paused for a minute, then responded.

"Marianne Scott was severely beaten in the region of her head. Marianne Scott claims she was raped and there is evidence of penetration by reason of the abundance of seminal fluid found in her vagina."

"But, was she raped?" asked Joey in a heavy tone of voice. Dr. Martin paused again before her answer.

"In my professional opinion, it is likely that she was."

"Likely, you say? Was she or wasn't she raped, Doctor?" Joey was becoming a bit intimidating. Dr. Martin did not want to answer the question because she had been at the Steelers game and saw the "hit" sustained by the defendant. She decided to turn the tables on the prosecutor.

"Mr. Kearns, the victim was physically, and probably sexually assaulted. I believe that, based on my findings and the statements from the victim, you have made a statutory determination that Marianne Scott was raped. I am here to report my findings. I will not render any other opinions so as to be misleading to this esteemed court." Joey was furious.

"I can have the judge order you to answer my question. You are a highly regarded gynecologist. You have seen hundreds of rape victims. You have testified in court numerous times about the incidence of rape. You are an expert. Now, and for the last time, Dr. Martin, was Marianne Scott raped or not?" She looked at the judge, who ordered her to answer the question.

"Probably." At least this was a modicum of progress.

"Probably?" repeated the prosecutor. "Your Honor, please order the defendant to answer the question 'yes' or 'no'." Judge O'Connor acted on the request and again, ordered the witness to answer in the required format.

"Yes, dammit, yes! Is that what you want, you tyrannical son-of-a-bitch?" Dr. Martin was infuriated and unloaded on Joey Kearns. "She was screwed by a man, yes. Which man? Who knows?!" The audience was in an uproar. This was a huge break for the defense.

"That's enough, Dr. Martin. Your Honor, will you please admonish the witness?" Joey returned to his seat in the midst of a continuing uproar over her unsolicited response. He pulled out a lab report and other papers and returned to the witness stand while the judge gave Dr. Martin a tongue-lashing for her derisive demeanor. She regained her composure and sat back in the uncomfortable chair. "Would you please identify these documents, Dr. Martin?" Joey asked in a more suitable tone.

"I would be happy to do so," replied the doctor, also attempting conciliation. "One is a report which was filed with your office, a copy of the request for a lab test on the vaginal fluid recovered from Ms. Scott, and the third looks like the results of that report from the Tucker Labs. The hospital uses their services to conduct DNA tests, among other things."

"Thank you, Doctor. And have you reviewed the test results?"
"I have."
"And what do they confirm?"
"They only confirm that there was a substantial amount of seminal fluid present in the vagina of Ms. Scott."
"Anything else?"
"Please, Mr. Kearns. Let's not go down that road again," stated Judge O'Connor.

"Is there anything you would like to add, Dr. Martin?" asked the prosecutor, knowing fully that she would not cooperate.

"Nothing at all, Mr. Kearns." He returned to his seat and gave way to the defense. Raymond Sutter stood to conduct the cross-examination. Dr. Martin took a glass of water from the bailiff, took a few sips and sat back to receive the questions of the defense lawyer.

Railroaded!

"Good morning, Dr. Martin. I can assure you that I will be far less pushy than my esteemed counterpart." She smiled in appreciation of this comment. "Now, Doctor. You testified that you examined Marianne Scott literally from head-to-toe, is that correct?"

"Yes, it is."

"Considering that the patient claimed she had been raped, was there anything that troubled you about this case?"

"Yes, sir, there were several things."

"So, let's start from the top. What about her facial injuries? Was there anything that bothered you when you examined the victim's face?" Raymond handed her a picture of the victim, which Dr. Martin acknowledged as one she herself had taken.

"The bruises seemed to be uniform. There was not the random distribution that one would expect."

"Objection, Your Honor. Dr. Martin is a gynecologist, not a pathologist."

"Au contraire, Monsieur Kearns," said Raymond in a perfect French accent. "Dr. Martin has completed a second residency in pathology. Is that not correct?" asked Raymond.

"I completed the rotation here at Allegheny General just days ago. I went through the program since I was handling victims of sexual assault." Where the hell did this piece of news come from? How come Joey didn't have this information in his arsenal? He had been set up to be obliterated by the defense.

"The objection is overruled," stated Judge O'Connor.

"So, Dr. Martin, when you stated that the victim had been beaten with repeated blows in a side-to-side manner, it appeared suspicious to you?"

"Sexual assault is a violent act of irrational passion. There has never been a rapist, to my knowledge, who exacted perfect symmetry in his work. The blows to Marianne Scott's face were not the work of a crazed man in the heat of sexual assault." The audience reacted and Judge O'Connor was quick to pound his gavel.

"Was there anything else you noticed that seemed peculiar, Doctor?"

"In such situations, the victim is usually very combative . . . she is trying to fight off her attacker. In this case, there were no signs of such a struggle. There were no bruises on the wrist that would indicate that the victim was or had been restrained. I also checked her fingernails. There was no evidence of scratching which one would suspect. In fact, it was curious that someone who had experienced such a brutal event seemed to have such perfectly manicured nails!" Some members of the audience laughed, but not so Judge O'Connor. He slammed his gavel one time on the bench to restore order.

"So, in your estimation, Doctor, and as you stated in your report, there is probable cause to believe that the victim was raped, but there is no medical evidence to definitely reach that conclusion, is that correct?"

"Objection, Your Honor."

"Sustained," was Judge O'Connor's reply before Raymond could even get a word in edgewise.

"Was Marianne Scott raped?"

"Objection, we already have the witness's testimony on that question," stated the prosecutor.

"Sustained! The witness is directed not to answer that question. Mr. Sutter, need I remind you of your pledge to keep it clean?" Raymond was getting frustrated with the judge. The likelihood of judicial tampering seemed more evident with this latest interchange.

"Dr. Martin. In your report, you mention the volume of seminal fluid found in the vagina of Ms. Scott. Correct?"

"Yes, I made a notation because I thought it was abnormally high for someone who had been raped. It seemed more like the amount to be found inside someone whose partner had achieved orgasm twice or more in a single setting."

"Objection, Your Honor. The victim is not on trial here. This testimony is all speculation." Dr. Martin tried to interject a statement, but things got out-of-hand.

"Sustained!" barked Judge O'Connor.

"Maybe, but the credibility of the victim is on trial and will be fully tested when she takes the stand!" exclaimed Raymond, staring directly at the standing prosecutor.

"If she takes the stand, Mr. Sutter . . . If!" retorted Joey Kearns, now in an attack mode. Judge O'Connor slammed his gavel on the bench and stood up.

Railroaded!

"The court stands in recess until 2:00 P.M. Gentlemen . . . my chambers, now!" The black robe of the judge was flying as he stormed into the recesses of his chambers with attorneys trailing behind.

Chapter 25

"Dr. Martin?" said Judge O'Connor to get her attention. "You are excused as a witness. The Prosecution will now continue with its case. Mr. Kearns, please call your next witness. And I entreat you to remember our latest discussions in chambers." How could he forget? Judge O'Connor threatened both attorneys with six months in jail and fines starting at $25,000 for any further extracurricular confrontations or departures from the facts. Maybe Raymond Sutter could afford these sanctions, but not Joseph Kearns.

"The Prosecution calls as its next witness, Howard Werner." Always impeccably dressed as required by his employers, Ned Scott and Elizabeth Cobb, the tall, thin fifty-seven-year-old chauffeur took the witness stand and was sworn in.

"Mr. Werner, I will try to be brief. Did you see Marianne Scott make sexual advances toward the defendant as he has alleged?"

"No, sir, I did not." Howard Werner was very cold with his response.

"Did you see the defendant strike Marianne Scott?"

"Yes, sir, I did."

"Did you stop the limousine after picking up Marianne Scott from her father's private club?"

"Yes, sir, I did."

"Why did you stop, Mr. Werner?"

"I stopped at the request of Mr. Williams."

"And where was that?"

"On Cedar Avenue, as requested."

"Again, why did you stop?"

Railroaded!

"It appeared that they were having a sort of lovers' quarrel," stated the chauffeur in a matter-of-fact manner.

"Objection!" shouted the defense counselor. "This is unsubstantiated speculation on the part of the witness. Move to strike, Your Honor."

"Members of the jury will disregard the last answer of the witness. The objection is sustained." But, of course, the jury had already heard the speculative remark. Elizabeth Cobb was pleased that the jury heard the comment despite the fact that it was ordered stricken from the record. "Mr. Kearns, please continue," stated Judge O'Connor.

"Okay, Mr. Werner. What did you see?" asked the junior prosecutor.

"In my rearview mirror, I saw Mr. Williams strike Ms. Scott just after I stopped the car."

"No further questions, Your Honor." Joey Kearns was true to his word. Raymond Sutter, before beginning his cross-examination of the chauffeur, stood and first addressed the court.

"Your Honor, the issue of battery is not in dispute. The defendant has acknowledged that he hit Marianne Scott in an attempt to get her off him. We therefore stipulate that there is no issue of contention relative to this witness's testimony. But I do have just a few questions for him."

"So stipulated. Please proceed, Mr. Sutter," stated Judge O'Connor.

"Mr. Werner, was Mr. Williams awake before Marianne Scott got in the limo?"

"No, he was dozing, sir. He drifted into sleep moments after settling into the back seat when we left Three Rivers Stadium."

"If he was asleep, did he awaken when Ms. Scott got in the car?" inquired the defense lawyer.

"No, he was still asleep."

"I see. So, Ms. Scott would have had to disturb his sleep. Is that correct?"

"I would think so, but I really don't know."

"Do you always pay attention to what goes on in the passengers' compartment of the limo?"

"It's most often impossible not to, sir."

"Okay then, what did you really see, Mr. Werner?" Joey started to object, but restrained himself from the interjection.

"I saw -- I heard Mr. Williams yell to stop the car. He was adamant about wanting to get out. I followed his instruction. Just then I saw him strike Ms. Scott."

"With a balled fist, open-hand slap, or what?"

"I really didn't see how, just that he hit her."

"Okay, Mr. Werner. Then what happened?"

"Mr. Williams literally crawled out of the car and mounted his crutches. There was a phone booth nearby. I assumed he was going to call his wife or a taxi to come get him."

"Why did you assume that?"

"Because Ms. Scott also got out of the car as well. I didn't know what to do so I left them there standing on the corner. I didn't want to be involved."

"So, against your employer's orders, you left a severely injured man standing on a street corner in the middle of the night. Is that right?"

"Yes, sir, that's correct."

"Okay, Mr. Werner. As a professional driver, and in your estimation, how long would it take to drive from Cedar Avenue to Mr. Williams's house at around 1:00 A.M.?"

"Not more than thirty minutes, in my opinion."

"Okay, Mr. Werner, so it is entirely possible that if Mrs. Williams received a call from her injured husband, she could reach him by car in thirty minutes coming from her house to Cedar Avenue, is it not?"

"At that hour, sure, that would be my guess," stated the chauffeur in his cold, flat tone of voice.

"So you figured that he would not be left on the street very long, did you?" asked Raymond in a cutting voice. "Why didn't you call your employer and inform him of the circumstances that had developed in the back seat of your limousine?"

"I tried, but there was no answer on his private line."

"Very well, Mr. Werner. This is my last question. What time was it when you left Marianne Scott and the defendant on Cedar Avenue?"

Railroaded!

"It was exactly 1:20 A.M., sir. I remember looking at my watch and noting the time."

"No further questions." Raymond had accomplished what he wanted. He firmly established that Marianne and Anthony were dumped from the car before 1:30 A.M. From this point on, it should be a simple task to establish it as impossible for his client to have committed the alleged rape, especially with the testimony of Shelli Williams during the defense portion of the presentations.

"Call your next witness, Mr. Kearns," stated the Judge. Joey Kearns stood and turned to face the jury.

"The People call Marianne Scott," stated the junior prosecutor. All eyes in the courtroom turned to Marianne, who was dressed in a black and white sundress. Her hair was styled in many wavy curls. She received a hug from both her father and grandmother and then slowly walked to the witness stand. Raymond Sutter just smirked, thinking to himself about her trying to extract pity from the jury and audience by walking to the witness stand with a bowed head. Tony looked at her with utter disgust. Shelli sat in the audience with unbridled rage building in her heart. Adrian and Errol looked at her with hatred in their eyes. Marianne could feel their rage, so she focused on her grandmother, who was beaming with pride. Ned Scott, while supportive, was still skeptical as to his daughter's truth and veracity in this whole nightmare. The Scott woman took the stand and was duly sworn in to testify.

As Joey Kearns watched the victim take the witness stand, he decided on a new strategy that should, for all intents and purposes, catch the defense by surprise. Joey smiled to himself and looked to his right at his boss. "Do you trust my judgment, Lew?" whispered Joey as he leaned over closer to the district attorney.

"What's going on in that brain of yours, Kearns? What are you planning to do?" asked Lew Dobson with a quizzical look on his face.

"I'm going to smoke out and sink the defense in one fell swoop. This should prove interesting." Joey smiled at his boss and stood at his table to begin the questioning of Marianne Scott. "Ms. Scott?"

"Yes, sir," she replied in a rather quiet voice.

"Were you assaulted and raped on the morning of July 28, 1979?"

"I was."

"Is the perpetrator of the crime in the courtroom today?" asked the junior prosecutor.

"He is, sir."

"Is the perpetrator of the crime the defendant in this action?"

"He is, sir."

"Thank you very much, Ms. Scott. We have no further questions, Your Honor." Joey sat down amidst an uproar. He did not take his eyes off Marianne Scott. Instead, he watched her squirm, not knowing what had just happened. Lew Dobson was shocked at the tactic employed by his junior prosecutor.

"Are you crazy, Kearns?"

"I asked you if you trusted my judgment. Now let's just wait and see what happens." Then it dawned on Lew Dobson what his junior associate had done. Lew patted Joseph on the shoulder and sat back in his chair to await the defense response. After getting the courtroom back under control, Judge O'Connor sat back and also contemplated the prosecutor's impetuous move. This was the break he had been waiting for, and it had been delivered by an inexperienced lawyer who was seeking to make a name for himself. He smiled a devilish grin, shook his head as if in disbelief and turned to the lead defense counsel.

"Your witness, Mr. Sutter." Raymond had not fully recovered from the shock of such a short examination. He recognized the tactical maneuver and decided to ignore it.

"Ms. Scott, did you go to Hawaii earlier this year for the NFL Pro Bowl Game?" asked Raymond.

"Objection -- foundation," shouted the prosecutor.

"Sustained!" retorted the judge.

"Ms. Scott, did you have an encounter with the defendant, Anthony Williams, while in Hawaii?"

"Objection -- foundation," shouted the prosecutor again.

"Sustained!"

"Ms. Scott, did you have a sexual encounter with the defendant while in Hawaii?"

"Objection -- foundation," shouted the prosecutor again.

Railroaded!

"Sustained!"

"Did you write letters to the defendant's wife, Shelli Williams?"

"Objection -- foundation," shouted the prosecutor.

"Sustained!" retorted the judge.

"Have you ever been in trouble with the law? Has your father ever fixed a legal problem for you?" Raymond was shouting over the objections of the prosecutor. Judge O'Connor pounded his gavel to restore a semblance of order. Ned Scott, sitting in the audience, knew that his actions were coming home to roost. He hung his head in shame while the heated exchanges continued.

"At what time did you leave your father's private club?" Joey stood and leveled his next volley of objections.

"Objection, Your Honor. There is still no foundation for this line of questioning."

"Sustained!" barked the judge.

"Ms. Scott, at what time were you assaulted and raped?"

"Objection, Your Honor. There is no foundation for this line of questioning. Besides, it was established that the crime was committed between 1:30 A.M. and 4:30 A.M. All that matters is that the crime was committed between those hours."

"Sustained!" barked the judge again.

"Listen, Judge. I need latitude to question the witness in order to get to the truth and veracity of her credibility, demeanor, and character as it relates to this case."

"I believe, Mr. Sutter, that the Prosecution asked the witness three questions with very succinct answers. Therefore you will confine yourself to cross-examination as it relates to those three questions or risk being in contempt."

"What? Are you out of your mind?" Raymond went on the attack. "This little witch has accused my client of rape. And you're not going to let me question this witness because of the prosecution's legal tactics?"

"That's what the law is all about, Mr. Sutter. You know the rules, so proceed." Joseph Kearns was all smiles inside. He had beaten the defense at their own game. Raymond Sutter was a man possessed and determined to break the judge at all costs.

"Have you ever had sex with Lucas Johnson?" asked the defense counselor.

"Objection!" Kearns remained standing, assuming that he could object to every question asked by the defense attorney.

"Sustained!" was the same response from the judge.

"Have you ever been to the Ohio Street substation?"

"Objection, Your Honor."

"Sustained! Mr. Sutter, you better clean it up really fast. This is getting very old!"

"Clean what up? I can't do my job. Maybe it's you who need to clean up your act, Judge. This is a serious matter and you're treating it too damned lightly."

"That's enough, Mr. Sutter."

"Enough? Enough? I'm just getting warmed up. You're going to let an innocent man get railroaded into a conviction and hung out to dry because the prosecutor has conspired with this witch!" The court was in a state of pandemonium. Joey sat down.

"You're finished, Mr. Sutter. Sit down now, or else!" shouted the judge. Despite the implication, Joey Kearns was ecstatic. Lew Dobson was so impressed with his junior associate that he leaned over and whispered in his ear.

"You've just been promoted to the number three associate. Care to try for number two?" Lew felt a little more at ease with his re-election prospects. But Raymond Sutter was still on the rampage.

"If I didn't know better, I'd swear you've been paid off, Gerald!" Judge O'Connor slammed his gavel on the bench.

"That's it, dammit! Bailiff, clear the court. Sutter, you are fined $15,000 for your insubordination. I want a cashier's check on my desk in one hour!"

"Made out to you, Judge?" shouted Raymond back at the judge while turning his back on the justice. "Go get another cashier's check, David, and bring it back over here for that asshole. Make sure you inform Loren what's happened. I'm going out for some air and a drink. Where is Errol Forrest?" Raymond spotted Errol and Adrian and immediately made his way toward the two men in the midst of the continuing pandemonium.

"Court stands in recess till 8:30 tomorrow morning," stated the judge under his breath on his way into the recesses of his chambers. Things were again out of control.

Railroaded!

As the bailiff executed the judge's orders, Errol Forrest huddled with Adrian. He knew that his suspicions were correct. Despite the fact that the legal ploy of the prosecutor was a brilliant move, the judge had the latitude to enable the defense to get to the truth and veracity of the witness. Errol and Adrian were both convinced that their best friend was in serious trouble. Raymond Sutter joined the two men and left for a local watering hole. Tony, while embracing his wife, saw his two friends leave with Raymond. He knew that his defense was coming apart, and felt helpless to do anything about it. He said a silent prayer for his friends and Raymond -- for God to guide them with clarity and wisdom.

Elizabeth Cobb was thrilled with the results of the afternoon session. She had Howard take Marianne, Ned, and herself to the private club rather than go back to the estate. Marianne, while thrilled that her appearance on the witness stand was abbreviated, didn't have a clue as to what had happened. Ned even breathed a sigh of relief that a bit of dirty laundry did not have to be aired in public.

●●●●●●

When Joey Kearns walked into the main door of the DA's office, everyone was standing and applauded his brilliant efforts. Joey blushed out of embarrassment and thanked everyone for their support. But while Joey had won a great battle, the war was not even close to being over. Raymond Sutter was a tenacious opponent and would not take this assault lying down. He had to prepare himself for the next round. But in the meantime, he would go out for pizza and beer and then head home for an evening swim.

●●●●●●

After an emotionally-charged morning in court, Tony sat quietly in the library of his home and reviewed a summary of his financial affairs. He was concerned that, if anything happened to him, or he was falsely convicted and forced to go to jail, Shelli and the kids would be taken care of. All of the investment assistance from Errol and his friends had paid off handsomely. Tony had cash and securities of $5,267,000. He owned one apartment building for investment purposes (worth $750,000) and his home, valued at $400,000. Earlier in the day, Tony had signed quitclaim deeds conveying his entire interest in the house and apartment building to Shelli. She was not happy with this move but tried to understand. Of the cash and securities, Tony established a trust with granted value of $1,500,000 for each of his two children. The balance was placed in a new account in Shelli's name only. He cleaned out his personal checking account except for $10,000. While drinking a rum-based concoction created by Errol, the bartender, Tony sat down and wrote a will. He first reviewed it with Shelli and then went to sit on the back porch with his friends. Everyone was in a somber mood.

Adrian, wanting to change the dark mood of the evening, started querying Errol about going to law school. Apparently, he had become enthralled with the action of the trial and figured that he could use the additional knowledge. After all, Errol was doing the same thing; he intended to complete law school and use the knowledge gained for business. Adrian now thought this was a good idea; he could be just as dedicated and use the acquired knowledge for contractual negotiations in their soon-to-be-formed architectural design firm. That way, if Errol wasn't around to handle some legal affairs, Adrian could take care of them. After all, Tony was the most talented of the three in architectural design.

Despite being focused on Adrian's conversation and trying to keep things lively, Errol could sense that Tony and Shelli wanted to be alone. So, rather than continue the somewhat contrived conversation, Errol grabbed his friend during a natural break and told him it would be better if they left the Williams residence for the evening. Adrian agreed without hesitation. They collected a few clothes to wear to tomorrow's court session, packed them in overnight bags, and left to stay at a nearby Holiday Inn.

●●●●●●

Sleep for Tony was not peaceful. He tossed and turned during the course of the night. Drenched by a cold sweat, he lay on perspiration-soaked sheets. Shelli had tried to awaken him but was

Railroaded!

unsuccessful. Instead, she prayed for his deliverance from the evil with which he struggled.

After what seemed like hours, the thrashing-about ceased and his body relaxed. Shelli thanked God for this break. She continued to wipe the sweat that was streaming from his brow. She bent over and kissed his forehead. Tony opened his eyes and smiled at Shelli. In a groggy state, he said, "I'm going home, baby." He closed his eyes again and fell into a deep sleep. Shelli continued to wipe the sweat from his body and covered him in a fresh top sheet and blanket. While she didn't understand his statement, she wasn't going to wake him. He lay there so peaceful, so handsome. She couldn't understand why they had to experience this madness. Again, she began to pray.

Chapter 26

Thursday, August 23rd

Thursday morning was stormy and cold. Remnants of an early morning thunderstorm were still passing through the greater Pittsburgh area. The forecast was for rain, rain, and more rain. Raymond Sutter was up as usual, engaging in his morning routine. At six, he called the Williams residence to speak to Errol. Shelli gave Raymond the number where they stayed for the night and inquired if things were all right. He responded that they were and that the trial should be over today. Shelli was thrilled with Raymond's confidence and asked how this was going to be accomplished. Raymond suggested that everyone meet at the Holiday Inn for breakfast, where he would explain. Shelli hung up and got Tony prepared for the day's events. Tony popped out of bed as if he had never been injured. There appeared to be no stiffness, no slowness to his movements. Whatever happened overnight, she thanked God for her husband's relief from the effects of his injuries.

Raymond called Errol and told him of the breakfast meeting. Errol liked frontal assaults and was pleased with Raymond's tenacity. Errol rousted Adrian, who was smiling in his sleep. "Wake up, you turkey! You're dreaming about some woman again! Who is it this time?"

"To tell you the truth, I was thinking about going sailing in the islands." Adrian spoke through a big yawn. "The three of us were chasing women around the deck of a big yacht. Tony was with Shelli, you were with Sharla, and I was with Lisa." Errol laughed aloud and threw a pillow at Adrian.

"Raymond called. He wants to meet with us at seven downstairs in the restaurant. Tony and Shelli will be here . . . so will Loren.

Railroaded!

Apparently, he wants to turn up the heat and wipe out Marianne after yesterday's fiasco." Adrian sat up in bed and shrugged his shoulders.

" 'Fiasco' is the understatement. I never thought a judge would let something like that take place. Like you, I'm starting to believe that the judge has been paid off by someone. I just wish we knew how to find out."

"No time to worry about that now. Just hit the shower, kid. You always take longer than me to get yourself together," stated Errol emphatically.

"That's because I'm prettier than you," retorted Adrian in a feminine-sounding voice.

"What a faggot!" Adrian unleashed a barrage of pillows at Errol, each of which found its mark. Adrian disappeared into the bathroom to shower and shave. He was dressed in fifteen minutes. Errol followed suit and likewise was ready in twelve minutes. At precisely 6:55 A.M., both men were downstairs waiting for the arrival of their friends and associates. After a lively breakfast discussion, everyone braved the driving rain, got in their cars, and headed for court.

● ● ● ● ● ●

Joseph Kearns felt great. The momentum of the case had shifted entirely to his side. Today he would continue his frontal assault on the defense. As the judge entered to the bailiff's announcement of the case, Joey felt strong -- Joey felt confident. Joey was going to be a winner. Marianne Scott took the witness stand as a continuation of the previous day's events. Judge O'Connor first asked Raymond whether he had any further questions of the witness that could be confined to the foundation laid by the prosecution. Raymond did not speak but instead shook his head in the negative. "I take that as a 'no.' Therefore, Ms. Scott you are excused." Marianne made her way to her seat between her grandmother and father. "Mr. Kearns, call your next witness."

"The prosecution calls Dr. Kenneth Tucker." Kenneth Tucker was a medical doctor who had specialized in pathology. He was the president and majority owner of the pre-eminent analytical and pathology laboratory in western Pennsylvania. When Dr. Tucker spoke, it was rumored that, sometimes, even God listened.

"Dr. Tucker, you are the President of Tucker Laboratories. Is that correct?"

"It is, sir, but we are called 'Tucker Labs'." Dr. Tucker was smartly dressed in a light, camel-colored silk jacket, white shirt, yellow paisley tie and navy slacks. Adrian, looking at his dress, wrote a note to Errol betting that he was Ivy League born and bred.

"How long has your company been in existence, sir?" asked the prosecutor.

"Eighteen years in October. Despite its relative young life, Tucker Labs has achieved recognition for being the most comprehensive pathological laboratory save for the university medical centers at Pitt, Penn, and Johns Hopkins for that matter. By the way, Johns Hopkins is my *alma mater*. I was a resident and research fellow in pathology there. After I practiced for eleven years, I retired to start Tucker Labs with my associate, Dr. George Laidlaw."

"Thank you, doctor. And do you routinely conduct DNA tests on semen specimens from rape victims?"

"Unfortunately, we are all too often charged with that responsibility."

"And did your company have the responsibility of examining a specimen taken from the victim in this case?"

"We didn't know who the victim was until much later. The specimens are logged in and the analysis is performed. Afterward, the results are sent back to the hospital and police crime lab."

"So, when you received the specimen, you didn't know that it involved Marianne Scott, did you?"

"No, sir, no one knew until much later."

"Did you give the specimen any special treatment?"

"No, sir, it was handled on a routine basis," responded the doctor. Joey Kearns wanted to eliminate the specter of tampering or special handling so that the jury members could not use it against him later. He took out a copy of the report and attached analysis and handed it to the doctor. The doctor gave a cursory glance at the report and then looked at the prosecutor.

Railroaded!

"Are these the analytical findings and report from your laboratory, sir?" asked the prosecutor.

"They are indeed. They show a high concentration of seminal fluid, which presumably was gathered from the vagina of the victim."

"Please enter these reports into evidence." Joey handed them to the bailiff for insertion into the formal court records. "Now, Dr. Tucker, is there anything else you need to add?"

"Only that the tests were conducted under the highest levels of security and laboratory standards. We have no desire for our internal errors to be translated into wrongful convictions."

"Thank you, Dr. Tucker. I have no further questions." Joey sat down and watched Raymond Sutter intensely. Raymond stood and was ready to deliver what he believed would be the blow that would sink the prosecution's case.

"Dr. Tucker, I would like you to look at the reports from your company that the prosecution has submitted into evidence." The bailiff brought the reports over and handed them to the witness. He examined them again. "Okay, Dr. Tucker, you are an expert pathologist. Correct?"

"I believe I would qualify as an expert witness, yes."

"Then will you look at this report and tell me your opinion?" Raymond opened a sealed manila envelope and pulled out an analytical report. He handed it to the doctor and said, "This is an analysis of a semen specimen that was taken from the defendant and analyzed in the finest crime lab in the United States. In your professional opinion, is there a match between the findings in your report and those reported from the Federal Bureau of Investigation laboratories in Washington, D.C.? Take your time, Doctor."

After a full minute of comparison amid dead silence in the court, Raymond noticed that the doctor was squirming in his seat. "Unfortunately . . ." The doctor was speaking in a low voice. "Unfortunately, these are from the same person." Shelli fainted. The tumultuous uproar was overwhelming. Tony started crying in utter disbelief.

"That's not possible!" Raymond was cursing at the top of his lungs. No one heard the additional remarks of Dr. Tucker. Judge O'Connor pounded on his gavel and ordered the courtroom cleared.

It was categorically and physically impossible for the results to have been the same. But the jury now looked at Tony Williams and began thinking "rapist." Joey Kearns didn't move from his seat. He sat and savored the apparent victory. Errol sprang into quick action and left the court with Adrian close behind. Time was of the essence if they were going to clear the name of their friend.

●●●●●●

Viper smiled at the thought of having earned an easy $2.5 Million. Instead of taking a sample from the police evidence lockers and going through an elaborate process, all Viper did was replace the actual evidence taken from Marianne Scott with the fresh material just taken from Anthony Williams at the FBI labs. Unknowingly, the prosecution had been placed in the driver's seat to put Anthony Williams away. The defense would never be able to explain how it was that the police evidence matched the defendant. What a beautiful scam -- no weapons were used. There were no bodies to dispose of. The jury would convict Williams on both counts. Point - set - match.

Guy Markham would sell his business to the employees and discreetly disappear. Added to the $7.2 million he already had in numbered Swiss accounts, he could leave the country and live in style. The Cayman Islands suited him just fine. Besides, Swiss Bank Corporation had an affiliate office there, which would make for easy access to his money.

He lay back on his bed and lit a cigarette. After blowing several perfect smoke rings, he thought out loud, "Shit, it was never this easy with the Seals." Guy Markham looked at the picture of his target and wondered why his client wanted him put away so badly. He hadn't done anything to anybody. Marianne Scott was a spoiled little bitch who was used to getting her way. She damned sure wasn't worth dying for. The only real question was, who did the make-up job on Marianne's face? According to his research, the running back was in love with her and never would have done anything to hurt her. What was the real story? He looked at the picture again and closed the file. "I'm sorry, Anthony, but money talks and big money screams."

Railroaded!

Guy Markham smashed the cigarette in the ashtray on his night stand, turned off the Tiffany lamp in his windowless room, and drifted off for an afternoon nap.

●●●●●●

Errol ran out of the courthouse to the first available public payphone. He frantically dialed a number in Europe. While waiting for the connection, he barked instructions at Adrian. "Listen, A.C. Go find Raymond and bring him here. He's so distraught he's not thinking, so we have to do his thinking for him. This whole thing sucks. Not only is Tony in trouble, so is Raymond's girlfriend. To make matters worse, she's probably the only person who can clear Tony."

"So what do you expect Harvey to do for us? I assume that's who you're calling, isn't it?" asked Adrian.

"We need all the help we can get. Harvey will figure out what to do and provide us some much-needed support. Just go get Raymond and bring him here." Adrian complied and, in a flash, disappeared back into the courthouse. The telephone connection was completed to his friend, and Errol, in not more than three minutes, explained the entire situation. Upon acknowledging a quick course of action, Errol hung up and waited for Adrian's return.

Moments later, Tony emerged from the courthouse surrounded by a sea of reporters. It was like watching sharks in a feeding frenzy. There was no regard whatsoever for the emotional upheaval he had just experienced or the fact that the events that had unfolded were a frame. Loren Johnson shouldered the media responsibilities for the firm. The throng of reporters that harassed Tony and Shelli afforded Adrian and Errol the opportunity to slip away with Raymond, virtually unnoticed except for one man, who just days before, had been on Lincoln Avenue.

The three men went back to the Mellon Building and retrieved Raymond's car. Errol assumed they were being followed but still had to act according to the instructions given him by Harvey Sloan.

First and foremost was the safety of Dot Jensen. Errol and Adrian got Raymond to shift his focus from anger and rage to the well-being of his girlfriend. During the drive to one of the lookouts on Mt. Washington, they spoke only of irrelevant matters, such as the weather. Once there, Raymond parked the car, and the three men walked to one of the platforms that was free of spectators or tourists. They stood close to each other and leaned on the railing, acting like tourists enjoying the view of the city below.

"Someone at the FBI is feeding information to Guy Markham. There is absolutely no other explanation for the switch in evidence that should have cleared Tony," stated Errol. "That means that, when they figure out that Dorothy's testimony is going to be critical in clearing Tony, her life won't be worth ten cents. You follow me, Raymond?" Raymond calmed himself and listened to the young men who sat in his car.

"They are going to expect you to go to Washington and get Dorothy, Raymond," stated Adrian. "But that's where we come in. The focus of attention is on Errol, not me. So Errol is going to head immediately back to New York and pick up some support. I will drive Errol's car to Washington. Errol and company will meet me in Washington on Saturday." Raymond was a little confused but continued to listen.

"You're going to drop me at the airport in two hours and we're going to be as blatant as possible about punking out on our friend. From there, you'll call Dorothy and tell her what's happening. But she'll have to go out and call you back." Errol was acting like a field general.

"And what if we're followed?" asked Raymond.

"After the scene we'll put on at the airport, the report from whoever is watching should be negative. Let's hope that we can buy some time. That's all we want . . . to buy some time."

"Then what?" asked Raymond.

"During tomorrow's afternoon rush hour, I'm going to take Errol's car and drive to Cleveland. The Broncos have a preseason game there on Saturday, so it's the perfect ploy. Once I arrive and check in with the team, I'll head to Washington in Errol's car. They won't be looking for the car going to Washington from Cleveland. They'll be looking for me to be on the playing field. Someone else will suit up in my stead and play the game."

"Who are you guys?" asked Raymond.

Railroaded!

"We're just a couple of crazy brothers with some heavy connections who are trying to get our best friend cleared as well as keep you and your girlfriend alive," stated Errol.

"You would do this for Tony and Dot?"

"Without a second thought," added Adrian.

"A.C., you need to call Coach Stiller and clue him asap," stated Errol.

"Got it, Trees! Are you ready, Raymond?" asked Adrian. He nodded in the affirmative.

"What did you mean by support, Errol?" asked Raymond, still trying to get a handle on things.

"Better that you don't know right now. The most important thing is that you arrange some stringent security when we get back here from Washington. I don't expect that whoever is behind all this is just going to roll over and die. Suffice it to say that we're going to fight fire with fire."

"I hope that doesn't mean what I think it means . . ." stated Raymond.

"You used to work for the government. You figure it out. You know I'm talking to a guy at INTERPOL. *Res ipsa loquitur.*" Raymond smiled. Errol started on a whole new line of thought. "The other thing you need to do is talk to Arnold. He is on good terms with the prosecutor. He needs to understand what's real and what's not. He needs to know that there is a key witness that can clear-up this whole mess and that he doesn't want to be on the bad side of anyone when the shit hits the fan." Errol's demeanor was very somber.

"Why not let him just take the heat?" asked Raymond.

"Because he was the fall guy in the beginning. Besides, I admire the man. He's good, real good. It takes guts to stand up and try this kind of bullshit case. He shouldn't get caught in the crossfire on one of his first outings."

"I see your point, Errol." Raymond was silent for a moment and then continued. "Who's behind all this?"

"Everything points to Ned Scott. No one else makes sense. If we believe he's the man responsible for this madness, then so be it. But if he's not, then who is?" asked Adrian as he stood up straight and shrugged his shoulders.

"All I know is, we have to be careful to a fault. If a Navy Seal assassin is heading this operation, then life is cheap. I want you two boys to be careful. You'll need some armor. Dot has a cabinet with two 9mm automatics and two hunting rifles. Take your pick," stated Raymond.

"Errol used to be on the rifle team at Dartmouth. He's a crack shot with both rifles and handguns," stated Adrian. "We've been out target shooting and hunting together in Maine. I have to admit, the old boy is impressive." Errol smiled while listening to his friend's accolades.

"Well, I guess we prepare for a short assault, or war as the case may be," stated Raymond.

"We're already in a war, Raymond. This is the final battle. The only thing at issue is the outcome," stated Errol. There was silence at this point as all three men knew that the lives of two totally innocent people were at stake. Raymond looked at the two young men in his car and felt a deep sense of pride . . . pride that two young black men would stand up and fight for the life of their friend . . . that two black men would do what it took to protect the woman he loved . . . that these two black men were intelligent, observant, and even looked out for his best interests. Silently, he prayed for their safety and success.

●●●●●●

Within two hours, Raymond dropped Errol at the airport. As planned, they all created a wild scene. Errol acted the most disgusted and left, taking the evening flight to New York. The man who trailed their moves reported this event to his superior. He even reported the parting conversation Errol had had with Raymond which was heated and boisterous . . . that he was "through with Tony's crap." The New York contact later reported that Errol Forrest had gone home directly from the airport without a detour.

An hour after dropping Errol at the airport, Raymond and Adrian pulled up in front of Tony's. Shelli greeted them warmly and related that Tony had already gone to bed. He had taken a couple of his painkillers. Because the house was still under police

Railroaded!

surveillance after the Klan incident, there were no apparent bugs on the phones at the Williams residence. While Adrian explained the course of events that was to take place over the next few days, Raymond called Dot and told her to call him back on his carphone in thirty minutes. At least it should be a secure call.

Dot, who had been in court for the opening arguments on Monday, had returned to Washington on Tuesday morning before everything had started coming apart for Raymond. She could only imagine what evil forces were driving a train to run down and destroy an innocent and highly respected black man, and all over a woman's failure to get screwed! She hated to think that there was an informant/mole in her office. She hated to think that Raymond's life and her own were in jeopardy. She hated to think that her professional life had been compromised because she wanted to help someone who was being tormented by the senseless and wanton sexual desires of a rich, white bitch. Maybe it was time to leave the Bureau. If she survived this affair, she would submit her resignation.

As she wandered around her condo doing nothing in particular, she thought to herself, "I'm a computer specialist, not a combat commando." She said aloud, "Who's going to look out for me? A football player and a law student? Some cavalry." She paused for a moment and then finished her thought. "Raymond, I hope you know what you're doing." She continued her pacing for fifteen more minutes before going out for drive-through at McDonald's on Georgia Avenue.

Chapter 27

Friday, August 24th

Friday morning in court was again calm. As the attorneys for the case filtered in, Arnold Benton walked up to Joey Kearns and handed him a note that read, "If the Prosecution is supposed to expose the truth, then meet me during the lunch break. We need to talk." Joey didn't respond or show the note to his boss. He tore it into little pieces and put them in his suit-jacket pocket.

"All rise!" Judge O'Connor entered the courtroom and surveyed the audience. The newspapers, television and radio all had crucified the defendant. Anthony Williams was now characterized as the *"crack-back rapist."* Everyone jumped on the bandwagon except one local sports reporter from the "Pittsburgh Evening Gazette." Terrence Feldman liked to believe he was an amateur sleuth. He didn't believe for one moment that Anthony Williams was guilty of rape. He noticed that, at the end of yesterday's testimony, Dr. Tucker had tried to add to his commentary but had been unable to do so. Before settling in to watch the proceedings, the reporter slipped a note to Dave Johnson of the defense pointing out this fact. Dave Johnson shared the note with Raymond Sutter.

"What the hell is going on here?" Raymond thought to himself. He didn't respond, only acted.

"The court is now in session. After yesterday's events, Dr. Tucker has been excused. His testimony stands as reflected in the record."

"Excuse me, Your Honor, but we would like to continue the cross-examination of Dr. Tucker," stated Raymond.

Railroaded!

"I don't think so, Mr. Sutter. After your little grandstand play backfired on you and your client, the witness has been excused. Now sit down." Raymond complied. He wrote a note to Dave Johnson, and after reading it, he left the courtroom. "Mr. Kearns, please call your next witness."

"The Prosecution rests, Your Honor." This move, while anticipated, was not entirely what was expected by the defense.

"Well, then, Mr. Sutter, it seems that the ball is now in your court."

"Your Honor, we would like a recess until Monday. We are bringing a witness who can testify to the veracity of the analytical tests and the conditions under which they were conducted. I hope you will grant us this accommodation."

"And who is it, counselor, that will be testifying, Santa Claus?" Raymond maintained his demeanor despite wanting to rip the judge apart.

"On the contrary, her name is Dorothy Jensen. She is a special agent with the Federal Bureau of Investigation who oversaw the tests that were conducted with the defendant. She has agreed to appear without the necessity of a subpoena. She *will* be here Monday morning. Everything is all arranged." Raymond spoke like a man possessed . . . with fire in his voice, as if daring anyone to mess with his love. He turned and looked at the owner of the Pittsburgh Steelers. "Is that clear, Mr. Scott? She will be here Monday morning!" Ned saw the anger in Raymond's eyes but did not respond.

Judge O'Connor couldn't deny the defense the opportunity for testimony by a material witness. He sighed heavily and responded, "Your request is granted. Court stands in recess until Monday morning at 9:00 A.M."

The gauntlet had been dropped. Viper was now confronted with a serious challenge. He decided to examine every aspect of that which he faced and the job that had to be done. First he checked on Errol Forrest.

● ● ● ● ● ●

Friday morning, Errol went to Hofstra Law School to register for fall classes which were to begin in ten days. After registration, he took a bus to Jones Beach, where he sat for several hours before going home. He talked to no one except an unkempt and disheveled island man trying to hit him up for money.

Viper decided that, despite Errol Forrest's keen powers of observation, there was no need to waste time on a young and inexperienced law student. He recalled the surveillance team to Pittsburgh. There were more important matters that needed attention.

Also on Friday afternoon, it was confirmed that Adrian Christopher was going to play in the preseason game on Saturday in Cleveland. He was followed in Errol's Firebird to the Ohio-Pennsylvania state line and released. Again, Viper decided not to waste resources on a dumb, black jock. All attention would now be focused on Dorothy Jensen. She had to be disposed of in a direct approach. She could not reach Pittsburgh to testify on behalf of the defendant.

●●●●●●

Gerald O'Connor returned from lunch at 2:30 P.M. On his desk was an envelope marked "Personal and Confidential." He opened it to find a note that read --

Your work is done. You performed admirably.
The credit line has been validated.
Enjoy it, Mr. Supreme Court Justice.

He tore the note into little pieces and sat in his chair to reflect on what he had done, and the fact that he wouldn't have to sit in judgment on many more trials.

●●●●●●

Dave Robinson pulled up to the offices of Tucker Labs and burst into the reception area like a man possessed. Dr. Tucker had expected someone from the defense to show up, but not so soon.

Railroaded!

He received the young associate and related the fact that while the reports matched, they were too close a match. That was a statistical impossibility. He spent the whole morning starting a new test regimen on the remainder of the specimen. If his suspicions were correct, someone in the chain of custody had tampered with the evidence. The staff was going to work through the weekend to get the new results. They would be ready Monday evening. Dr. Tucker agreed to testify for the defense, if necessary, and share the results of his new DNA scans. He didn't want his reputation and the good name of his company to be soiled in any way whatsoever. He would call Mr. Loren Johnson with initial results on Monday afternoon.

●●●●●●

Arnold Benton sat with Joey Kearns at the bar in the *Common Plea*, a favorite haunt for attorneys. Arnold told Joey that while Joey had initially been chosen to handle this case because of seniority issues, he had done an outstanding job. He congratulated his opponent. But he also queried as to whether it was more important for an innocent man to go free or for tainted evidence to be allowed to convict that innocent man and ruin his life. "Could you live with that eventuality, Joey? You were one of the most idealistic assholes I knew while in law school. You harped on the truth . . . the truth at all costs."

"Yeah, Arnie, I remember. So what do you want?"

"Do you think a lawyer like Raymond Sutter would intentionally set up his client to be exposed as a fraud when, in fact, he was innocent? Do you think he would go to the trouble of playing a hole card that could sink his client if he knew it was tainted? You'd burn the card, wouldn't you?"

"No shit, man! Burn it, bury it, whatever . . ."

"Then why don't you and I find out what the truth really is? Dorothy Jensen is coming here over the weekend. I suggest we all interview her on Sunday. If there is any truth to what she says, then you decide where we go from that point. But if she's a liar, then hang Tony Williams out to dry. Do I have your agreement?" asked Arnold.

"Shit, Arnie! I just got a promotion. You're asking me to throw in the towel, aren't you?"

"Nothing of the sort, Joey. I'm asking you to give me a chance to have the truth told, outside of the court, outside of the press. Just you, me, Raymond, Ms. Jensen, and a court reporter."

"Okay, Arnie. Call me. I gotta go now." They shook hands as Joey Kearns got up to leave the restaurant. While Arnold was taking care of the bill, he noticed that Joseph was followed. He acted as if he didn't notice the tail and went straight back to the firm's offices. There he reported the results of the meeting to Raymond and the fact that Joey had been followed.

"So, the stage is set. I really hope everyone knows what he's doing." Raymond retreated to the privacy of his office, got down on his knees, and began to pray.

● ● ● ● ● ●

Errol got on a Nassau County bus at Jones Beach and rode into Hempstead. While he didn't notice anyone who seemed to be tailing him, he couldn't be too careful. He was following Harvey's instructions to a tee. When he disembarked from the bus at the Hempstead Bus Terminal, he was greeted by a uniformed taxi driver with a sign that read, "Mr. E. Trees." Errol understood and got in the car. He was presented with a suitcase and a letter. "My instructions are to take you home, and then pick you up at 2100 hours, sir. Mr. Sloan sends his best regards." Errol thanked the driver and told him he would be ready. Moments later, in the quiet of his room, Errol read the letter and surveyed the contents of the bag.

Mr. Trees,

In the valise that accompanies this letter, you will find everything you need to take care of yourself. I have made sure there is one set of 'clothes' for you and one for Adrian. I assume that because of your hunting abilities and skills with weapons from the days on the rifle team, the included item will be of interest and assistance should matters get out-of-hand.

Railroaded!

The driver will collect you at the appointed hour and take you to a secure rendezvous point for the drive to Washington. Good luck. I'll see you on arrival in Pittsburgh Sunday morning.

Wah-hoo-wah,
H.S.

Errol opened the valise and took inventory of everything that was included: two bulletproof helmets, two bulletproof jackets, leather gloves, and .45 caliber ammunition. He opened the box containing the rounds and found another note, "*Hardware available in D.C.*" Errol could only guess what that meant. He assumed it meant one of the new Israeli Uzis that he had heard about. He looked at his watch, but was distracted by someone knocking at the door. Cautiously, he looked out and saw that it was his girlfriend, Sharla Hampton. He yelled, "Just a minute," and quickly stuffed everything back into the valise. He opened the door and let her in to a thousand questions, none of which he wanted to answer.

"Listen, baby, I don't have time to go into all the details right now."

"Since you're home, I figured we could go out for dinner. How about the Dixie Pig? We could order take out and come back here. Anyway, you've been gone a long time and I want to fool around." Errol looked at his watch again and decided that a sexual interlude with Sharla would help calm both their nerves.

"Okay, okay." Errol embraced her and tried to relax.

"What's wrong with you? You're more tense than I've ever seen!" She saw the bag lying on his bed and asked, "Are you leaving again? What's going on, Errol?" Maybe he had made the wrong choice. He didn't want to answer any questions.

"Can we please just go to dinner and talk?" Sharla, not wanting to be put off, sat on the edge of the bed and motioned for Errol to sit beside her.

"I saw the news about Tony. It looks really bad, doesn't it?"

"It's worse than you know. But everything should be all right in the end."

"So where are you going this time, Errol?" He decided to trust Sharla and tell her the truth. But, again, this was probably a bad choice.

"I'm headed to Washington to assist in escorting Dot Jensen to Pittsburgh." Sharla started screaming.

"You can't do this, Errol! It's not your fight!" Errol held her tight and tried to be reassuring.

"My best friend is in trouble. I'm going to do whatever it takes to help him. Besides, Adrian will be there as well, and we've got lots of professional support."

"Like who?" she asked, still sobbing.

"Like, why don't we forget dinner and just make love, baby?" Errol kissed her again and again to calm her fears. Sharla lay across the bed and let Errol have his way with her.

After an impassioned session of lovemaking, they did what came naturally . . . they ordered in a pizza to satisfy their other appetite. Just before leaving, she gave him her St. Christopher medallion and wished him safety and success. After a last impassioned kiss, she left Errol's living quarters and drove home. It was 8:40 P.M. He had twenty minutes to finish getting ready.

At exactly 2100 hours, Errol closed the door to his studio and walked to the front of the house. The uniformed taxi driver was waiting for him. After throwing gear in the trunk, Errol got in the back seat and settled in with his copy of *The Art of War.*

They traversed the southern part of Queens and Brooklyn. They crossed the Verranzano Narrows Bridge into Staten Island and then took the Outerbridge Crossing into Elizabeth, New Jersey. They continued southbound on the New Jersey Turnpike to its termination point at the Delaware Memorial Bridge. In Wilmington, Delaware, they stopped for gas. Immediately after refueling, they again headed south on Interstate 95. Errol noticed that, during the entire trip, they had been followed, but the trailer was far enough back as not to be noticed in the darkness. The driver didn't seem to be concerned. Errol didn't question what was going on. At this point he was along for the ride.

● ● ● ● ● ●

Railroaded!

At 1:00 A.M. Saturday morning, the two men arrived at what would be the stopover point for the night. The taxi pulled into a warehouse building in Beltsville, Maryland. Errol got out of the car and watched as another car pulled in behind. It was a brown Firebird Formula that looked exactly like his! And then another identical car pulled in behind the first. Out of the second car came a familiar body.

"Harvey! What the hell are you doing here?"

"Somebody's got to look after your butt, mate!" The two men hugged each other and went about the task of discussing plans. "You know, I like this Firebird. It's not an Aston Martin, but it sure can kick ass!" Errol just laughed at his old schoolmate.

"Why two identical cars? Who's paying for all this?"

"Actually, there will be three. The third one's en route. Adrian is footing the bill." This news caught Errol by surprise. While standing there with his mouth open, Harvey continued. "This operation is costing about $125,000, including the cars. After it's over, the cars can be sold. Listen, Errol. I'll explain everything in the morning when Adrian arrives. In the meantime, you must get some sleep. I need your body and your mind to be completely fresh and alert."

"When does Adrian arrive?" asked Errol, recovering from the surprise.

"He should be here about 8:00 A.M. He's coming in by private plane from Akron, Ohio. I made sure that we have a stand-in for him. That Coach Stiller was very helpful. During the game, the stand-in will be injured on the first play and stay out for the balance of the game as a precautionary measure. After the game, the stand-in is going to drive a Firebird back to Pittsburgh. That will be expected. Everyone would assume that Adrian would return for the trial." This ploy made perfect sense to Errol. "By the way, Errol, your performance at the airport was rather convincing. Viper terminated his surveillance of you and recalled his two-man crew to Pittsburgh after watching you register for classes and sit on the beach for five hours. But he's brought out the big guns for this assignment. To this point, we've been able to confirm not less than twelve men here in the area to deal with Ms. Jensen. Now, will you please get some sleep? We can discuss all this later on in the morning!" Harvey was adamant with his directives, so Errol complied and retired for the balance of the morning.

A million questions raced through Errol's mind . . . why was Adrian paying for this operation when it could have been taken care of from the donated funds from the NFL Players Association? Why was Adrian now in the loop dealing directly with Harvey? Errol definitely heard Harvey say "a" Firebird was going to be driven to Pittsburgh, not "his" Firebird. Every question became a jumbled mess. Errol was tired and his brain was shutting down.

After Errol had drifted off to sleep, Harvey first checked on the arrival of Adrian. He was on schedule. Instead of arriving by private plane, he was arriving in Errol's car, the third of the identical Firebird Formulas. Next, Harvey called in his most trusted operative. Despite his appearance, the unkempt island man was a brilliant field strategist. Together, they spent the next three hours planning for the safe delivery to Pittsburgh of one female agent from the FBI.

Chapter 28

Saturday, August 25th

At 6:15 A.M., the third brown Firebird Formula with Colorado license plates pulled into the warehouse in Beltsville, Maryland. The doors opened and from the passenger's side, Adrian Christopher emerged. Errol was awakened by the commotion and got up to investigate. He immediately recognized his car and one of his two best friends. "Good morning, Trees! You know, your car handles very well considering you drive it on New York City streets."

Errol answered, still trying to figure out why his car was in the Washington area. "I try to keep the front end aligned and the suspension checked regularly -- but fuck the damn car. What the hell is going on? Harvey told me you're bankrolling this operation. How come the Players Union isn't footing the bill, or Tony for that matter?"

"Because Tony doesn't have a clue about what's about to go down. Tony doesn't need to be worried about what we're doing. Would you want to know about this shit?"

"Know what, Adrian? You haven't told me jack shit!" Errol was flying off the handle. "What the fuck is my car doing in Washington? Care to answer that, Adrian?" Adrian knew Errol was extremely angry because twice he had been called by his first name. So Adrian had to contain Errol's anger by himself becoming enraged.

"Dammit Errol, I didn't want him to worry about us! He's got enough on his mind. Besides, I listened to you very carefully." Adrian got right up in Errol's face and matched his demeanor. "Raymond wasn't thinking very clearly, so we had to do his thinking for him. That's what you said in Pittsburgh. Now, dammit, it's time for me to do the thinking for the three of us."

"What the fuck does that mean? What's happening here?" Errol put a little distance between himself and Adrian and tried to calm down. He realized that continued confrontation would be counterproductive.

"Listen, Errol. After you left for New York on Thursday, I called the alumni office and got Harvey's number. I caught him just before he left to come to the States. He briefed me thoroughly and discussed a plan of action. We both decided that Guy Markham was more concerned about you than me. So we decided to oblige him by making sure that the focus of attention was indeed you. To Markham, I'm still the dumb-ass jock."

"So what's my car doing here?" Errol asked in an incredulous tone of voice.

"It's here because you're going to drive it back to New York when this operation begins tonight." Harvey Sloan's interjection caused Errol to turn and do a double take. "You're going to be a decoy that's going to confuse Guy Markham. In the confusion, we should be able to safely deliver Dot Jensen to Pittsburgh."

"What? What kinda shit is this?" asked Errol, again becoming agitated at being kept in the dark during the planning.

"The kind that says you're going to go back to New York and finish law school," stated Harvey.

"The hell with law school! I'm here to help Tony."

"No shit, Errol. We all are! So why don't you sit your tight ass down and just cool it, man! We don't have time for this confrontational bullshit."

"He's right, mate," interjected Harvey. "I'm here unofficially. I assume that there are going to be a few dead bodies after this affair is over. There have to be. A Seal assassin is being well paid to dispose of Dorothy Jensen. We can't let that happen. Let's just get back to the business at hand."

"This isn't right, man. This isn't fair. Tony is my friend, too. I don't want to let him down now."

"You've already done more than he could have ever asked for, Errol. Listen, if you want to do anything, you can come to the celebration next week when this mess is over. In the meantime, let

Railroaded!

Harvey and me finish what you've started. Go back to New York and rest peacefully in the knowledge that your observations have kept us ahead of a very dangerous man. Remember, your driving back to New York is part of our scheme to create havoc with Guy Markham. The last thing he's going to suspect is you having your car. He thinks it's in Cleveland!" Adrian and Harvey slapped hands.

"In the meantime, gents, we've got some more planning to do. We can use that brain of yours, Mr. Trees, until it's time for you to go," stated Harvey, trying to lighten the intensity. At that moment, a door opened to one of the warehouse offices, and out of the shadows walked the unkempt island man, whom Errol remembered seeing in New York. In a heavy Jamaican accent, he spoke after walking up to Errol Forrest.

"I believe you know who I am." Errol nodded his acknowledgment. The island man, in a swift motion, squarely punched Errol with his right fist, knocking him to the floor. Adrian and Harvey both winced. "That was for taking Carla from me." He then reached down to help Errol regain his footing. "That was for me not having realized she was not the right woman for either of us!"

"No shit!" said Errol, now standing again. "How is Carla anyway? I haven't heard anything about her . . ."

"She and I got divorced a while back. Right now, single is better. I can slip in and out of life without anyone knowing who I am."

"I'm glad you're on our side." Errol attempted to laugh as he adjusted his lower jaw.

"Do you have a name?" asked Adrian.

"Island Man. That's all you need to know, Ivy League boy."

"It's Mr. Ivy League to you, Island Boy," retorted Adrian. All four men laughed at this exchange.

"When you least expect it, I will emerge from shadows, always looking out to cover your ass. Some say I live in the spirit world. You'll never know where I am."

"Well, then, brother, do what you do best," stated Adrian. "You know this guy, Errol?" Still smarting from the punch, Errol just smiled in the affirmative.

"Gentlemen, I think we should go get some breakfast and finish our planning. Dot Jensen is already under surveillance. She's been given a hand-held radio so we can confirm our departure time. She expects us at 2100 hours. That way, we'll arrive in Pittsburgh with the sun."

They all got into a utility van and drove to a nearby diner for breakfast. While Errol was not pleased that he had been cut out of the main action, he knew in his heart that if Dot Jensen was going to make it to Pittsburgh alive, these men would see to it and be successful. For the first time in weeks, he felt confident. Adrian, on the other hand, had started focusing his entire being on the task at hand. Adrian was preparing for war, not on the gridiron, but one that had life and death consequences.

●●●●●●

Viper figured that the disposal of Dorothy Jensen would be made to look like an accident. A car would sideswipe hers on the Interstate and force it into a deep ravine. The crash results, if not fatal, would be sufficient to keep her from testifying. The defense would have no alternative but to proceed without its star witness.

His two most trusted men, the same men who had handled the Lincoln Avenue affair, were positioned along U.S. 40. He believed that the car carrying the FBI agent should stay on the Interstate and take the Pennsylvania Turnpike into Pittsburgh. As a result, he planned for the alternative routing.

The two mercenaries set up surveillance along a stretch of highway near the Cumberland Gap in Maryland. While beautiful, the area was notorious for trucks that would lose their brakes on either side of the mountain pass. In the cab of a huge Mack truck, the two put the finishing touches on their communications network. At 1800 hours, every man under the command of Viper was in position. "The drive from Washington to Pittsburgh is not more than six hours under nightmarish conditions. Today the weather is completely uncooperative. It is raining sporadically from the Cumberland Gap to Pittsburgh. Use this to your advantage. Make sure the hen doesn't get out of the henhouse. Good luck, men, and keep me informed. Upon completion, there will be at least a six-

Railroaded!

course meal available." The two men acknowledged the instructions and smiled at the thought of receiving at least $300,000 for their crew in this disposal effort. After confirming network communications between all of the field operatives, the two lead men settled in for coffee at a truck stop near Berkeley Springs.

Despite the fact that his best men were on the case, Viper was uneasy. Everything was going too well. He sat in his communications command center and decided to turn on the television and check in on the Cleveland-Denver preseason football game. The game was already in the waning minutes of the fourth quarter. Cleveland was ahead 21-17, but the score was not important. He scanned the squad and noticed that Adrian Christopher wasn't playing, despite the fact that the first string offensive unit was in. He called the local network affiliate and inquired as to what had happened. Viper learned that Adrian Christopher had gone out of the game because of injury early in the first quarter. It seemed to be nothing more serious than a sprained ankle. He would be expected to play again next week.

Viper was not pleased at this news. As he surveyed the sidelines during the telecast, he spotted Adrian's number, but the player was helmeted. An injured player who was sitting out the rest of the game would have removed his helmet and probably gotten dressed in street clothes after halftime. This was not good. "So I underestimated you, Mr. Christopher. Where the hell are you if you're not in Cleveland? Did you come back to Pittsburgh?" He sat back and lit a cigarette. After blowing a near-perfect smoke ring, he accessed the computer system of the airlines and determined that there was no Adrian Christopher on a flight from Cleveland to Pittsburgh. Viper picked up the phone and made a call to an old associate in Cleveland. The game would be over in not more than fifteen minutes. "I need you to go to the Stadium and check on Adrian Christopher. Tell me if he gets on the team bus for the airport."

"Done, my friend," responded the person on the other end. "I'll call you as soon as they leave."

"For your trouble, I'll send you a five spot regardless of what you find out." A "five spot" was $500 cash.

The game was over at 7:00 P.M. The Broncos lost 21-20. At 8:10 P.M., Viper received the call he had been waiting for. "Negative on Mr. Christopher. He did not board the team bus."

"Are you sure? This is of grave importance," said Viper, becoming agitated at having misread an adversary.

"Fifty-five players were supposed to get on two buses. Only fifty-four players departed Cleveland Stadium. Adrian Christopher was not with the team when it left for the airport."

"Your five spot is en route. Thanks for the last-minute assistance." Viper hung up the phone and started pacing around the room. "Where are you, Adrian Christopher? Where the fuck are you?" Instead of panicking, Viper did what he did best under fire -- he sat down in his high-backed leather chair and lit another cigarette. Blowing perfect smoke rings allowed him to focus on the task at hand.

As he sat there in the confines of a room lit only by computer and surveillance monitors, his focus sharpened. Dorothy Jensen was going to be escorted to Pittsburgh by Adrian Christopher. But why? Why would Raymond Sutter, a former Justice Department attorney, trust his girlfriend to a professional football player, a man who had no military training? Why would he allow Adrian Christopher to drive her from Washington to Pittsburgh knowing that there was imminent danger? Who was helping them and why? He wondered whether Raymond Sutter even knew.

As he read over the dossier on the football player, it became obvious that this Christopher fellow was a potentially formidable opponent. He was an Olympian, a graduate with honors from Dartmouth College, and had a legitimate IQ of 176. The man was no doubt a genius, and if pressed into a corner, his training on the gridiron would prove to be useful. He obviously wasn't afraid of very much if he could endure blitzing linebackers, as well as speedy cornerbacks and safeties who sought to tear him apart.

He closed the file and continued sharpening his thoughts. Errol Forrest knew who was helping Adrian. But he was safely tucked away in Hempstead, New York, resuming his life as the ever-diligent law student. The revelation of Anthony being a potential rapist had sent Errol over the edge. He had taken himself out of the loop. And now Adrian Christopher had taken his place. Viper checked in with his field operatives and confirmed that all was in readiness. He looked at his watch -- 2045 hours. He calculated that everything would begin within minutes.

●●●●●●

At 7:15 P.M., the utility van stationed itself in Rock Creek Park near Dorothy Jensen's home on Blagden Terrace. With its sophisticated surveillance equipment, it had picked up coded messages indicating three distinct transmission points. But none of them appeared to be within firing distance. Harvey took this information as a sign that the main assault would come somewhere on the road. These three signals would be surveillance and trailers.

At 8:45 P.M., Dot Jensen turned on her two-way radio as instructed. At 9:15 P.M., she received the following simple message: "Time to go, Ms. Jensen. Open the back of the radio and follow the instructions." Dot complied and found a handwritten note which read as follows:

"In exactly ten minutes, three identical cars will back into your driveway. You are to exit the side door of your house and get into the open door of the first car. Do not be alarmed by the driver."

She replaced the back of the radio and received another transmission. "Seven minutes." Dot was a nervous wreck considering what was about to happen. She went to the bathroom for two reasons -- first, she had been drinking coffee like a fiend, and second, she didn't know if there were plans to stop while en route. She put on the bulletproof jacket and helmet as instructed and positioned herself by the door.

One of Viper's surveillance crews was on 16th Street and saw the cars turn onto Blagden Terrace. He panicked at what he saw and reported it to the command listening post. "There are three identical brown Firebirds here. We must assume that two will be decoys. One of them has Colorado plates. The other two have Washington and Maryland plates. The driver of the car with the

Colorado tags looks like that Errol Forrest guy whom we tailed in New York yesterday."

The news was relayed to Viper, who instantly flew into a rage. Both Adrian Christopher and Errol Forrest were in Washington. Who was their damned sponsor? No time to worry. Viper started thinking of alternative plans to accomplish his mission. He would not fail. In the meantime, he instructed his surveillance crew to stay in close proximity to all three cars and advise of any deviations.

"Cars arriving now." Dot Jensen looked out and saw the tail-lights of three identical Firebirds as they backed up along her inclined driveway. All three passenger doors opened and two identically dressed persons got out as if to perform a "Chinese fire-drill." She did as instructed. Appearing to get into the second car, Dot made a quick move and got into the lead car. The three cars pulled away from the house and headed north on 16th Street to Georgia Avenue. They were closely followed by three black Ford sedans that emerged from their surveillance points. Upon reaching the Capital Beltway, they headed south the few miles to pick up Interstate 270. It was as if a caravan was making the trek north to Pittsburgh. Harvey and the island man smiled as the game led the hunters.

The first seventy miles went off without a hitch. At Frederick, Maryland, the three Firebirds stopped. Each driver got out in a light misty rain to commune for just thirty seconds. Then, in a strange move, every person got out and shuffled their places. In only fifteen seconds, the move was complete, all under the watchful eyes of Viper's surveillance crew. The car with the Colorado license plates did not continue on the same course. One of Viper's operatives noticed that the passenger of the lead car got out and slipped into the front seat of the second car. The lead car, now with a single driver, headed east on Interstate 70 in the direction of Baltimore. Errol Forrest was doing as instructed. He was heading back to New York.

This move concerned Viper, but he did not panic. Instead, he told everyone to concentrate on the two remaining cars headed for Pennsylvania, one of which obviously contained the FBI agent. The game was about to get caught in the trap. Errol Forrest was just a

Railroaded!

decoy. "No need to waste good manpower on him," ordered Viper. The caravan now consisted of three black Ford sedans following two identical brown Firebird Formulas.

Adrian and Harvey congratulated each other on their ploy. So far so good. None of Viper's surveillance crews had seen the shadowy figure get out of the second car and stay behind. After the six cars had departed, a black utility van pulled off the exit ramp to the spot where the six cars had just left. The unkempt island man got into the van and followed a well-conceived plan. He thanked the heavens for the misty rain, which had provided a perfect ally.

One hour later, Errol Forrest received a coded message . . . a series of three consecutive beeps that indicated that he had not been followed. He could really relax now and breathed a deep sigh of relief. "Thank you, Jesus," he said quietly. At that moment, a stowaway sat up in the back seat.

"Well done, Mr. Forrest, or should I call you 'Trees'?" The stowaway took off the helmet.

"What are you doing here?" Errol was in shock to see Dot Jensen sitting in the backseat of his Firebird.

"We're headed to New York to meet Raymond, Arnold Benton, and Joseph Kearns. I'm supposed to give you this message. You're supposed to drive at a leisurely pace and stop for ten minutes at the entrance to the New Jersey Turnpike. We're supposedly being shadowed by friendlies."

Dot climbed into the passenger's front seat and settled in. Errol noticed that she was a very attractive and shapely woman of about five feet six inches. She had recently gotten her hair cut in a style that accented her pretty face. Raymond was a lucky man.

"What about Adrian and Harvey?" asked Errol.

"They've gone into the dragon's mouth. I'm praying for them as you should be. My only fear is what the Seal is going to do when he finds out he's been had."

"Whatever he does, I know that we can't underestimate Guy Markham. I know he'll go ballistic and pull out every stop," answered Errol in a somber tone.

"That's what I'm afraid of . . . that's what I'm afraid of."

Errol Forrest was glad he was still involved in the affair to clear Tony of the charges. But, as he drove northbound on Interstate 95, a sense of foreboding came over him. He was terribly concerned for the safety of both Harvey and Adrian, as well as Tony, who was waiting in darkness, for a miracle.

Chapter 29

Sunday, August 26th

Adrian was completely alert as they began the ascent up the eastern slope of Cumberland Gap. As the passenger in the car, his responsibility was to be the lookout. He was not to miss anything. If anything at all seemed suspicious, he was to radio it to Harvey, who was driving the second car. The three black sedans that had been trailing rather closely for the last hour started to fade in the distance. Harvey noticed the transition and reported it to Adrian.

"Look alert, mate. The chase cars are backing off. I believe this is where we will have to run the gauntlet." Halfway up the mountain, Adrian told the driver to stop the car and pull over. He radioed for Harvey to close the gap and stop one hundred yards behind. This maneuver would smoke out the intentions of the black sedans. Harvey agreed with this strategy. Two of the black sedans closed the gap and passed the two Firebirds sitting on the side of the road. They quickly disappeared into the heavy night mist that shrouded the mountain. The third Ford was nowhere to be seen. At least a frontal assault was not their intention. Harvey's curiosity was piqued by this move. But Adrian chose not to be concerned, instead focusing on what was ahead.

He remembered reading *"Spiderman"* comics when he was a kid and how the superhero's "Spider Sense" would become active whenever there was danger. Adrian's "Spider Sense" was running wild. He told the driver to turn off the engine and radioed for Harvey to do the same. He opened the window and listened. The rain clouds that had settled on the Gap provided a perfect sound reflector. Adrian could hear the faint growl of a big truck idling and revving its huge diesel engines. Harvey could barely make it out but agreed with Adrian's assessment.

The road was damp from rain that had stopped about a half hour earlier. Adrian studied the terrain and the detailed map he had of the downhill side of the pass, which began not more than a thousand yards in front of them. "Interesting, very interesting," he said to himself. "Harvey, get up here. I want to show you something on the map." Harvey pulled the second Firebird to within six inches of the lead car, got out, and walked around to the passenger side. As he bent over to look at what Adrian wanted him to see, the ground exploded about one hundred feet behind the second car.

"Go on, get out of here!" yelled Harvey. He raced and got into the second car to pull off behind Adrian. A second projectile landed and exploded about fifteen feet behind Harvey and his passenger. It was as if they were being motivated to continue.

"We're all right, Adrian. Just keep going and keep your eyes open." As they accelerated to reach the crest, Harvey pulled up alongside of Adrian. "Stay tight, they'll think that you're the mark, Adrian."

"They're not going to shoot us. They intend to run us into a deep ravine at the bottom of a long curve. That's why we heard the truck . . ." It was too late.

After passing the summit and starting down the western slope, the first challenge presented itself. The two black Fords formed a roadblock which caused the Firebirds to decelerate to avoid an immediate collision. The Mack truck appeared as if from nowhere and began its short run to ram the cars. Harvey yelled but never engaged the radio. The black sedans, now facing each other, moved in reverse to get out of the way as the truck bore down and made contact with the two Firebirds. The occupants of both cars were violently jolted from the force of the impact. The power of the truck was no match for the quasi-racing cars, but the drivers couldn't risk accelerating because the road conditions and their unfamiliarity with the terrain would spell immediate disaster.

The two Ford sedans circled in behind the truck. The driver of Adrian's car turned the steering wheel in an abrupt move to the left and caused the car to spin out of control as the truck continued to pick up speed, pushing Harvey's car down the hill. When the Firebird came to a stop, the two black sedans moved in to intercept.

Railroaded!

The Firebird's driver instinctively opened his window and sprayed both cars with bullets from an Uzi. The result was swift and effective. Both cars stopped their advance and didn't move.

The driver handed the Uzi to Adrian and gave him a fresh magazine with which to reload. He swung the car around and accelerated down the slope. "Hang on, Harvey. We'll be there in a minute," radioed the driver. Harvey didn't respond. He was too busy focusing on maintaining control of his car while being ram-rodded by the Mack truck. "When I pull alongside, shoot out the front tires of the truck. That's the only way to stop it," yelled the driver. Adrian reloaded the automatic weapon and opened his window.

"Why don't I shoot out the back tires?" he yelled to the driver in the onrushing wind.

"Just concentrate on the front tires. It's the only chance they have." The driver gripped the steering wheel tightly and accelerated even more. Adrian tensed up in preparation. Yellow warning signs were getting closer and closer, indicating a sharp turn to the right and drop-off ahead. Adrian's driver accelerated and passed the Mack truck. "NOW!" Adrian aimed and fired a continuous burst as they passed the truck. The driver continued his acceleration to pass the Firebird that was under the stress of being rammed and then downshifted to brake the speed of the engine.

Several of Adrian's shots found their mark. The truck careened to the left and spun wildly. Harvey jammed down hard on the accelerator to disengage from the truck. Almost immediately, he downshifted and applied hard pressure to the brakes while steering to the right. The truck's occupants were screaming at the top of their voices as they lost control of the vehicle. After a complete 360-degree spin, the damaged wheel dug into the pavement, causing the truck to flip over and explode before sliding into the ravine that had been intended as a deadly graveyard for Dot Jensen and her escorts. Harvey was able to regain control of his vehicle and stop just short of going over the edge. He and his passenger watched as the Mack truck slid over the edge of the embankment, not more than one hundred feet above them. After a quick check to determine that everyone was okay and the cars able to complete the journey, the two brown vehicles left the fiery scene and proceeded to their intended destination.

The third black Ford sedan drove slowly by the other two cars and surveyed the results of a failed mission. Further down the slope, the driver stopped for only a moment, opened his window, and observed the burning truck. He closed his window and drove off, reporting all hands lost. Following a series of animated instructions from his superior, he reversed the direction of his car and stopped at the point where the two black sedans sat lifelessly. He placed a small cache of material on the front seat of each car next to the deceased driver, put each car in neutral and pointed it downhill to roll off the cliff into the ravine. He then got back into his car and headed for Interstate 81 to travel in the direction of Harrisburg. Moments later, both of the black Ford sedans exploded in a sea of flames as they went over the cliff.

The report of the mission failure sent Viper into a rage. He had also just received word that Joseph Kearns and Raymond Sutter were not in Pittsburgh. As usual, he vented his anger by lighting a fresh cigarette and concentrating on blowing perfect smoke rings. What had started as a simple mission of switching evidence had turned into the ultimate chess game, especially since he was playing against an unknown opponent. This was the first time in years that Viper had to operate in the blind. He relished this opportunity to fine tune skills that had gathered a bit of dust in the mundane world of civil investigations. This confrontation with neophytes presented an amusing challenge. "Whoever you are, I will win . . . I will win because our goals are not the same. I will win because you don't know what my mandate is. That's my edge." He continued to blow smoke rings and began rethinking his next series of moves. "At least I saved three hundred large." He smashed the cigarette in the ashtray and smiled at the thought of not having to deplete his bank account.

Viper looked at his watch and estimated that the crew in two cars would arrive in Pittsburgh in about two and a half hours. It was only 1:45 A.M. "Time to set a new trap," he thought out loud. "They'll be going to Anthony's, and I'll be waiting to take care of you myself, Ms. Jensen," stated the assassin as he gathered needed

Railroaded!

equipment for the operation. "Nice ploy, Raymond. Leaving town to throw me off. It almost worked."

●●●●●●

Like clockwork, the two Firebirds pulled into Tony's front yard at 4:20 A.M. The commotion aroused Shelli, who in turn wakened Tony. As the occupants got out of the cars, they removed their helmets and bulletproof jackets and threw them into the back seat of the cars.

A night-vision scope was a perfect companion to the specialized long-range silenced rifle. The first three people got out of the car. The assassin recognized the football player. He did not recognize the two drivers. He formed a mental image of these two men and assumed they were skilled in combat as well as espionage. As the last person got out of the heavily-damaged Firebird, the assassin focused and readied himself to squeeze off a fatal round. "I have you now, Dot Jensen!"

The person turned, and to the surprise of the assassin, it was another man. He wanted to shriek but instead retreated from his blind position into the forest like the snake that he was. Anger was running rampant through his veins . . . anger that he had again been thwarted by unknowns. Quick decisive action was required . . . the kind of action that required clear thought and clean execution. The drive back to his command center would provide the time needed for contemplation. He quickly formulated yet another plan of attack. He would check with his employer in short order to get clearance. Two hours later, he had the clearance he needed. The assassin would make one more third-party attempt to silence Dot Jensen. Regardless of the results, there would be no further mistakes.

Back at his command center, he radioed the driver of the last Ford sedan. He gave a series of instructions, which were followed explicitly. Viper assumed that the operative would fail. The field agent knew that his employer expected him to fail. "Who are we up against?" asked the operative.

"Unknown," responded Viper. "But, should you succeed, you will be invited to the same six-course dinner originally prepared for your associates."

"Understood. There will be no contact until I reach the target area, approximately three hours. Next contact at 0900 hours, sir."

Viper acknowledged and terminated the transmission. Instead of focusing on the assignment of the last surviving operative, who like himself was a well-trained assassin, Viper began preparations for what needed to be done locally on Monday. He recalled the images of the men he had seen earlier. "Whoever you are, you will not win. The mandate has changed. Knowledge is power. It is my edge. Checkmate!"

The group went into the Williams house. Shelli put on coffee and instructed everyone to relax. Adrian and Harvey went into the study to explain what had transpired. Tony was more concerned with Errol's safety. "Call him yourself. He should be home by now," stated Adrian. While Tony was busy dialing Errol, Harvey went over to Adrian and shook his hand. Adrian responded with a hug.

"Thanks for saving my life, Adrian."

"I could do no less. Anyway, you've earned the right to call me A.C., my fellow granite-head." Both men laughed at the fact that they were still alive. But Harvey knew the ordeal was not over. Silently, he prayed for the watchful eye of his shadowy companion.

●●●●●●

At 3:35 A.M., the third Firebird with Colorado tags pulled up in front of the house where Errol rented a small room in the back. "You live here?" asked Dot Jensen. Errol nodded in the affirmative. "Not bad for a third-year law student."

"You might want to hold your opinion," responded Errol as he got out of the car and stretched. He took a deep breath of the night air, that was crisp and clean. The wind was blowing from the southwest off the nearby Atlantic Ocean. One could smell the influence of the salt water on the wind. After a quick walk around the left side of the house to his private entrance, Errol opened the

Railroaded!

door and entered. Dorothy Jensen followed. "Welcome to my humble abode."

"Humble is right. Maybe spiritual is a better word. How long have you lived here?"

"Almost two years. It's convenient to the law school and the price is right." Errol's living quarters were indeed small. He lived in an eight-foot by twelve-foot room that was furnished with a twin bed, one dresser, a small table and chair, and a bookshelf. Despite the size and character, the room was spotless. Everything was very clean and in perfect order. It showed the mark of an intelligent and well-organized man. The only thing that was out of character for the Spartan quarters was a rack that held almost sixty bottles of some rather expensive wines. "I started collecting these a little over a year ago. There are some of the best French and California vintages on that rack. I even have two bottles of a new Chilean cabernet." Errol was trying to be hospitable in rather inhospitable surroundings. "I have few visitors. No space. Most of my social interaction is at the law school just a mile away. Only my girlfriend comes by and spends any time here."

"I see." Dot looked at the dark surroundings and wondered what kind of man Errol Forrest truly was. She knew that he was very loyal and dedicated to his friends. She knew that if not for his keen sense of observation, Tony Williams, Raymond or even she herself could be dead. "Do you plan to practice law when you graduate?" she asked, changing the subject.

"Nope, I have no desire to get involved in litigation, even though I've been told that I would be a damned good trial attorney."

"Then what do you want to do when you graduate?"

"If we all survive this mess, Tony, Adrian, and I plan to open an architectural design firm. Tony is the best architect I've ever seen. Adrian's damned good also. I've got a background in ancient architecture and am pretty good at commercial office design, but I'm more the businessman of the group. I'll let them design and build. I'll get the projects financed and keep them out of trouble." Dot looked at her watch and started to worry. She worried that there had been no news of Adrian and Harvey since they had stopped at the New Jersey border.

"Hopefully, everyone should be here by 7:30 A.M. In the meantime, you should get some sleep, Errol."

"Listen, you can go ahead and sleep in here. I'm going to drive around the block to make sure everything is okay. Then I'm going to park the car down the street and just watch. If you need me, beep me on the radio. No verbal messages, okay?"

"Okay with me. Where's the bathroom?" Errol pointed to the brown and white door that Dot thought was a closet. It could have doubled as a closet, as small as the room was.

After she emerged, she looked at Errol, who was busy securing the small room. In the dim light, she could see that he was an extremely handsome man. He was risking his life to protect hers. After he finished, she approached him tentatively. She embraced her protector and kissed him. "Thanks for looking out for me and Raymond." Errol rubbed her shoulders.

"Get some sleep, Dot. The rest of the day is going to be very long. I'll wake you when Raymond gets here."

"But what if he doesn't get here?" Just then the phone rang. Errol answered and listened to a barrage from Tony. Errol gave Dot a "thumbs up" to indicate the safe arrival of four men in Pittsburgh. Errol had remembered six people leaving Washington. He acknowledged that everything was okay and put Dot on the phone to talk to Shelli. Errol quietly left the room and locked the door behind him. As he walked to his car, he took a deep breath, and, at the same time focused his powers of observation. In the calm of that moment, he could sense that he was being watched, but by whom?

Chapter 30

At 7:45 A.M., a dark gray Chevrolet Impala pulled up to the house on MacDonald Street where Errol lived. He immediately recognized the occupants, even from a distance. He started his Firebird and drove up to the house as the three men got out of the car. Errol's sense that someone was watching was even more acute. He got out of his car to greet the men. "To whom does this belong to?" Errol asked, pointing to the car.

"It was donated, courtesy of the Pittsburgh police," responded Arnold, who maintained ties to the department. Errol smiled but quickly ushered the men into his small living quarters.

Inside, Raymond and Dot embraced and kissed. Errol was formally introduced to Joey Kearns. "Boy, this looks familiar," stated the prosecutor. "Brings back memories of days of Spartan living while I was in law school. It's my pleasure to meet you, Mr. Forrest. I understand that most of this mess is your responsibility."

"I would say that this mess is the responsibility of one sex-crazed Marianne Scott," retorted Errol, trying not to be sarcastic as they shook hands.

"Touché, and please accept my apologies. Arnold and Raymond both have spoken very highly of you and your skills. I want you to know that, while I am here unofficially, most important is the search for the truth. I have no desire, on my first real case, to have an innocent man convicted for crimes not committed. I'm here because I want to know the truth so that I can properly evaluate the matter before us."

"Then the truth you will get, Joey," stated Raymond. After the ten-hour drive from Pittsburgh, all three men had become acquainted enough with each other to now be on a first-name basis.

"In the meantime, I'd like you to meet Dorothy Jensen. She is a special agent with the Federal Bureau of Investigation." Joey extended his hand.

"I wish I could say it's a pleasure to meet you, Ms. Jensen. I must admit that Raymond and I were worried sick that you might not be here when we arrived. Apparently all went well. I'm glad you're safe." Joey paused for a moment and then continued. "I hope you won't mind, but I would like to see your identification."

"Certainly, Mr. Kearns." Dot reached into her back pocket and pulled out a small, black leather case which contained the requested ID. Joey perused the ID and smiled while returning it to the agent.

"Now that we've got that out of the way, please call me Joey. As I stated, this is an unofficial interview, but it will help me with some very difficult decisions."

"So where do we start?" asked Errol.

"How about some breakfast?" asked Arnold.

"Not a bad idea," added Joey. "What do you suggest, Errol? This is your town."

"There's a diner just four or five blocks from here that has very good breakfasts on Sunday morning. We can get in and out of there quickly at this hour. We don't need too much public exposure. I've also arranged to have the actual interview videotaped at the law school. One of my classmates will meet us there at 9:00 A.M."

"Then breakfast it is," stated Raymond. He noticed how uneasy Errol was at the thought of cruising around. As everyone left, Errol asked Raymond to ride to the diner with him. Dot could ride with the Prosecutor and effectively be in his custody. "What's up, Errol?"

"I know we're being watched."

"Come on, man. Don't overreact. Dot is safe! She's alive and you're responsible. I can't thank you enough."

"That doesn't detract from the fact that we're still being watched. Adrian told me just a while ago that at least four men, maybe more, died on the Cumberland Gap last night. They were all hired by Guy Markham to make sure that Dot was liquidated . . . to make sure that she didn't make it to Pittsburgh to testify. So, if that many men are expendable, then how many are here now?" asked Errol.

Railroaded!

"I see your point." Raymond became a little less animated and more concerned. "Listen, I want to thank you and your friends for exposing yourselves to risks that you didn't have to take. I'm proud of what you've done, and I want you to know that Dot and I will always be grateful for your help." Errol smiled as they pulled up in the parking lot of the diner. "You go ahead and get out. I'll join you in a moment. I want to cruise the streets and make sure everything at the law school is ready." Raymond understood the order and did as instructed. Errol was gone twenty minutes and then rejoined the group enjoying breakfast.

At 8:55 A.M., they left the diner to make the short drive to the law school. They pulled into the back parking lot and went into a downstairs room that had been set up for the occasion. Once in the room, Joey began.

"Ms. Jensen, as an agent of the FBI, your testimony is critical. Additionally, as a federal government employee, you recognize that there are severe sanctions for perjury. Correct?"

"Yes, sir, I do."

"Okay, then, we're going to keep this as simple as possible. Did you arrange to have a semen specimen taken from Anthony Williams and analyzed at the FBI Crime Lab in Washington?"

"I arranged the test to be conducted on a Friday afternoon a few weeks ago."

"Why did you do this?"

"I did it because Raymond, Mr. Sutter, asked me to. He wanted to have a clean test analysis to use to refute the evidence that had been taken from the victim. In a comparative test, it would prove that the defendant was not the perpetrator of the crime because it would have been impossible for the semen of the defendant to magically appear inside the victim's vagina."

"And did you witness or supervise the entire procedure?"

"To the mild embarrassment of Mr. Williams, I did."

"So you can testify that the chain of custody of the evidence has been clean and unbroken?"

"That I can," responded Dot.

"Do you have a copy of the test analysis?"

"No, but Mr. Sutter has a certified original." Raymond pulled it out of his briefcase and handed it to Dot. "This is it. It has the FBI seal over my signature."

"There is no question in your mind that this is the original, true, and accurate report?"

"None at all. There are even two places on the report that contain my initials. I'll point them out. I did this to further verify the report as authentic. Any copy should have these initials on it." Dot pointed out the two locations where she had inscribed "DLJ." All of the parties present acknowledged seeing the faint initials of Dorothy Jensen.

Joey Kearns pulled the report of Tucker Labs from his briefcase. He perused it carefully, but did not find any initials on the report. Everyone acknowledged that this was the case. Dot Jensen looked at the two reports and did a simple comparison.

"Did Mr. Williams provide a fresh semen sample to Tucker Labs?"

"Why do you ask?"

"Because these were taken from the same sample. That is, the results from Tucker Labs should be skewed to allow for vaginal secretions. There should even be traces of urine present. But there are none. The Tucker Labs report is exactly the same as ours. That means it was taken from a clean, uncontaminated specimen. Listen, I'm not a pathologist, but I've seen a few of these in my day. I can tell you positively that the report from Tucker Labs was written from tests conducted on pure male semen. The specimen did not come from a woman who had been raped or had sexual intercourse." This announcement unnerved Joey, but he was still not convinced that there was a real problem. Dot could see that Joey was fidgeting and continued with her own analysis.

"Listen, Mr. Kearns. Forget the sample for a minute. Why are you here?"

"To get at the truth, of course."

"No, no, no. Why are you here in New York? Why aren't we in Pittsburgh discussing this?"

"Because of safety issues, I suppose."

"Whose safety?"

"Yours, I presume."

Railroaded!

"Okay, then. Let's assume that the report is valid. My testimony is irrelevant and Tony Williams gets convicted. Correct?"

"Yes, that's correct, Ms. Jensen," stated the prosecutor.

"Then why are people trying to kill me . . . to prevent me from testifying?" she asked.

"Are they, Ms. Jensen?"

"You better fill him in, Errol," stated Raymond. "Tell him why we're here in New York."

"Eight hours ago, two of my classmates were caught in an ambush on Cumberland Gap. They were able to survive because they were assisted by agents from INTERPOL. The perpetrators were not so fortunate. We know that there were at least four casualties." Errol continued with a detailed report. Joey, wanting to hear it for himself, took a break and called back to Pittsburgh. He spoke to both Harvey Sloan and Adrian Christopher. Little did he know that the conversation was being monitored on the Pennsylvania side. When he returned to the room after the ten-minute discussion, Joey was visibly shaken but continued with a new line of questions.

"What happened to the semen specimen after the analysis was completed?"

"Already in a test tube, it was labeled and placed in secured and refrigerated storage."

"And who has access to that storage?"

"Lots of people do. Why do you ask?"

"Because someone saw what you were doing and reported it to your 'Viper' -- is that possible, Ms. Jensen?"

"The Navy Seals have complete access to our files. They may be military, but we definitely work together."

"That's what I'm afraid of." Joey was angered that his first case was replete with tampered evidence and non-credible witnesses; an explosion and fire that destroyed the Seymour house, the possibility of tainted evidence from Tucker Labs, and the possibility of a compromised judge! All of these thoughts went through his head. "What's the motive here, Raymond? Why is Marianne Scott so bent on destroying Anthony Williams? Why are there so many big guns operating behind the scenes? What is it that we don't know?

Why me?" he asked. "I wonder how many people have been compromised? How in the hell will we ever get to the truth?"

"We can start by recalling the witnesses and both of us tearing them apart. We can question anything and everything. If you don't object and allow the questions, then the judge can't intervene and stop us. In this manner, we can expose the truth in a formal setting." Raymond was relentless in his desire to get back into the arena with a strong ally.

"I don't think so, Raymond. I think I'd rather dismiss the case and let the chips fall where they may." Joey hung his head for a moment and then made the following pronouncement: "You have my word that no one in my department will seek to further prosecute Anthony Williams. I looked at the tapes of his injury and should have known better. My hatred for football players got in the way. Even Marianne slipped up one day in my office. I should have pursued it further and ordered her to take a polygraph. I guess that in my zeal to do a damned good job, to make a name for myself, I forgot about seeking the truth. Arnold reminded me of that. That's why I'm here now."

"You're a better man than I ever was, Joey," stated Arnold.

"Listen. We need to get back to Pittsburgh. I need to discuss this whole matter with Lew. I suggest that we call a news conference and announce my findings as well as the fact that we're dropping the charges against the defendant. I'll call you Monday morning and let you know the time." Raymond went over and hugged Joey.

"I'm proud of you, Joseph Kearns. You are a gilt-edged credit to the legal profession. You have my utmost admiration and respect. Let's get out of here. We've got a long drive back to Pittsburgh. I assume that you're going to stay here, Errol?" asked Raymond.

"Yeah, I'll come over later in the week. In the meantime, I have a woman who needs some of my attention. Tell Tony congratulations for me, and I'll drive over on Wednesday or Thursday."

The meeting broke and the videotape was secured in its case. Errol thanked his associate for his videotaping assistance, and the whole group left the room and climbed the stairwell to the first-

Railroaded!

floor rear exit. Errol walked out first with Arnold Benton. Raymond followed with Dorothy, arm-in-arm. Errol stopped dead in his tracks as he saw a black Ford sedan sitting at the end of the parking lot. He strained to see whether there was a driver but there was none. Where was he?

Errol started making quick moves with his head, looking for Viper's operative, but he was nowhere to be found. "What's wrong, Errol?" asked Raymond.

"Get back inside, now!" yelled Errol. Just then, a single shot rang out. Errol's natural reaction was to duck, to take cover. But there was none. Dot Jensen screamed wildly as the bullet did its damage. But it had found the wrong target. Raymond's shoulder exploded in pain as the .270 caliber bullet entered his flesh. In shock and pain, he collapsed to the ground.

The assassin surveyed the scene from the roof of the elementary school that was adjacent to the law school parking lot. He immediately calmed himself and readied another shot. Dot Jensen was in clear view, huddled over her fallen lover. He aimed and . . . felt his back explode in pain as a knife gouged and twisted his insides. He dropped the rifle and looked around into the face of a black devil. The unkempt island man had appeared from nowhere and disappeared into thin air.

Moments later, the utility van that Errol had seen in Washington appeared and picked up the entire group. Raymond was still conscious but fading rapidly. Arnold applied pressure to the wound to prevent further loss of blood. Raymond was taken to the Nassau County Hospital, which was only minutes away. The van dropped the men and woman at the hospital and disappeared. Despite how it looked, Raymond would fully recover; the actual wound was not serious.

Joseph Kearns was furious at being exposed to such madness. He was angry that he had allowed himself to be duped by a member of the rich Scott family. Once he determined that Raymond was going to be okay but would be required to remain in the hospital for a few days, Joey went into action. First, he called the FBI office and explained what had happened. Dot Jensen was taken into protective custody. Errol was instructed to stay in New York and not return to Pittsburgh for his own safety. There was no mention of the former Seal. Joey figured that he would be handled when back in Pittsburgh, but only after consultation with Harvey Sloan.

●●●●●●

"I must apologize about Mr. Sutter. He should fully recover. The mark was using plain rounds. In the meantime, the location has been swept clean."

"Good work, my friend," said Harvey to his shadowy associate. "You need not come to Pittsburgh just yet. I will signal you when I need you."

When the FBI went to the roof of the elementary school to look for evidence of an assassin, they found nothing -- no shell casing, no blood . . . nothing. Unnoticed, the unkempt island man left Hempstead and headed for New Jersey. In an old shipyard, he watched as the van was hoisted onto and placed into the hold of an old rusted freighter that was to be taken out to sea and retired into oblivion. There, in the depths of the ocean, the van and the body of one of Viper's operatives would be erased from existence.

●●●●●●

After leaving the hospital, Errol drove Arnold Benton and Joey Kearns to LaGuardia Airport and dropped them for an afternoon flight home. "Thanks for all your help, Errol. I hope your friend doesn't hold a grudge."

"Tony doesn't have a bad bone in his whole body." Errol hugged the men and bid Arnold and Joey goodbye. He would see them again later in the week.

Before boarding the Piedmont flight to Pittsburgh, Joey made two calls. The first call was to his boss, Lew Dobson. Lew agreed to meet them at the airport. He would advise Loren Johnson of what had happened and bring him along to the airport for a full briefing. The second call was to the Williams residence to speak to Mr. Sloan. Harvey instructed Joey to forget about Guy Markham and his previous affiliation. That matter was far too dangerous. The Seal would be dealt with in due course.

"Just concentrate on clearing Tony, Mr. Kearns."

Railroaded!

"Thank you for all your help, Mr. Sloan. Consider Anthony Williams cleared of all charges. As a matter of fact, if he is there, I would like to tell him myself." Harvey said goodbye and handed the phone to Tony. After a moment of listening to Joey Kearns, he thanked the novice prosecutor and agreed to receive them after they arrived. Tony hung up the phone and fell down on his knees in silent prayer. For all intents and purposes, the nightmare was finally over. Shelli was relieved, but Adrian and Harvey had just lived through a hellish experience and knew that the snake was still in the weeds, recoiling for another strike.

●●●●●●

Viper listened intently to the report given to the district attorney. When the conversation was finished, he picked up a phone and dialed his employer. "My suspicions have been confirmed. I will proceed on the previous mandate. The associated fee will be doubled. At such time as I have a confirmation of funds in my account tomorrow morning, I will complete the assignment."

"You will be able to confirm as of 6:00 A.M. Is that sufficient time?"

"More than acceptable. You will not be disappointed." Viper hung up the phone and lit a cigarette. He knew that in light of what he had heard, his field operative had failed. He still didn't know who was providing cover. Now, however, it didn't matter. "Knowledge is power . . . and I know what you don't. You have no way to defend against me!" He blew three perfect smoke rings and smiled to himself, thinking of the islands and developing a new strategy for the evening.

Ex Post Facto

(After the Fact)

Chapter 31

The flight arrived on time at Pittsburgh International Airport. Joey Kearns and Arnold Benton walked down the jetway into a throng of reporters. Apparently, news had leaked out that Raymond Sutter had been shot in New York. This was an unexpected turn of events that caught Joey by surprise. Lew Dobson had deferred the responsibility for all comments to Joey. "Ladies and gentlemen, I can only tell you that while I was with Mr. Raymond Sutter, he was shot by an unknown assailant. I have no further information, except to tell you that there will be a news conference tomorrow at the courthouse."

"What time?" yelled one of the reporters. Joey looked at Lew who again deferred.

"Two o'clock," stated Joey. Lew was amazed at his young associate. He was proud of the way Joey handled the matter. He was proud that Joey had kept an open mind. Lew was pleased at Joey's tenacity to get to the truth. Right then and there, Lew Dobson decided he was sick and tired of political office and would not seek reelection.

●●●●●●

The news came as a Special Report that pre-empted regular programming. It announced that Raymond Sutter had been shot and was recovering in the Nassau County Hospital in East Meadow, New York. It also reported that Joseph Kearns had been at the scene, but the details were sketchy. Tomorrow there would be a news conference.

Railroaded!

Marianne Scott tried to keep her cool, but was panic-stricken inside. "So what now, Grandma? What do we do now?"

"You cool those jets of yours. You'll just have to live with the consequences, Marianne. I told you about hanging around with those nigras, but you wouldn't listen. And now it appears that one of those boys is going to have his way with you. This justice system of ours is all screwed up. White women are never to be taken advantage of by such animals." Elizabeth Cobb stormed out of the room to the sanctuary of her bedroom.

●●●●●●

Again, an unexpected opportunity presented itself to Viper. The news report would give him the ability to conduct a frontal assault on the district attorney, as well as on Mr. Harvey Sloan from the special investigation's unit of INTERPOL. He left the confines of his communications center and went to dress in his best summer gabardine suit. He looked at his watch and estimated the confrontation would begin in about one hour, just shortly after 7:00 P.M.

Guy Markham pulled up and parked behind several cars that were already in the driveway of the Williams residence. He walked up and rang the doorbell. Inside, there was a party spirit. It ceased for a moment when it was announced who was at the door. In walked Guy Markham carrying roses for Shelli. "What are you doing here?" asked Adrian.

"I came to offer my congratulations on the findings. I talked to Dorothy Jensen at the FBI office in New York. I understand that Raymond is going to be okay."

"That still doesn't explain why you're here," stated Adrian.

"I want to commend you all on a job well done. I also want you to know that, as the investigator for the law firm, my responsibility is surveillance and information-gathering. I want you all to know that indeed, I used to be a Navy Seal, and a rather good one. I was responsible for carrying out many missions that called for the liquidation of many men. But I want you to know that I had nothing whatsoever to do with what you've experienced. Yes, I know about everything. That's my job, just like yours is to get at the truth, Mr.

Dobson. Your Mr. Kearns did a marvelous job of handling a difficult case. I would like to applaud him. In the end, didn't we all get what we wanted and what Mr. Williams deserved? Aren't you a free man now?"

"Yes, he is a free man, Mr. Markham," stated Joey Kearns. "The trial is over and the charges will be dismissed by our order tomorrow."

"Well, then, I brought along a case of champagne. It's in the back seat of my car. Shall I go get it?" asked the smiling snake.

"Why not? Go right ahead. As a matter of fact, I'll help you bring it in," said Harvey Sloan. "I'll take over from here, everyone." Harvey walked up to Guy Markham and shook his hand before the two walked outside. "Boldest stroke I ever saw, bloke. You're talented, cold, and mean-spirited, which makes you even more dangerous, Mr. Markham, or should I say 'Viper'?"

"Likewise, Mr. Sloan," stated the assassin.

"Me? A snake? I don't think so. Don't delude yourself, you arrogant bastard," stated Harvey coldly. Viper remained calm.

"I'm amazed at how you took people with no formal training and turned them into a force that not only thwarted my plans but caused the untimely demise of my men!"

"Because we had nothing to lose and were not paid, we could think clearly."

"I'm paid to think . . . to always think and execute."

"Execute? Destroy lives? Shit, man. You have no soul. Have you no feeling for the lives that have been needlessly wasted? And for what? So a stupid little rich bitch could get a woody stuck in her?" For a brief moment Viper felt pained at the reality of the situation . . . the loss of his men, over sex. But then again, he thought, all major wars were fought over women and loss of sexual privilege. He maintained his cold demeanor while starting to churn inside.

"They were casualties of war. You are the victor to whom go the spoils of war, which is continued life."

"Then why don't you execute this move? You've made your point. You know who I am and who my employer is. Why don't you leave these good people alone and call it a day? They've suffered enough. As for you and me, our business is finished unless you choose to keep the file open." Viper smiled and lit a cigarette. He blew a smoke ring that quickly dissipated in the night air.

"The case is closed, Mr. Sloan. Tell Mr. Johnson that I will submit my resignation as his firm's investigator in the morning. I'll expect payment in full of my account. You've been a worthy opponent, Mr. Sloan." Viper retrieved the case of champagne from his car and set it on the driveway in front of Harvey. He got into his Ford Bronco, started the engine, and said, "Good evening." Harvey stood there and watched him drive away. He knew that the man called Viper was lying. A snake had come out of the bushes to test Harvey's resolve. Now was the time to be even more watchful. Harvey Sloan knew the case was not yet closed.

●●●●●●

Thirty minutes after everyone left the house, Tony and Shelli took a walk through the neighborhood. For the first time since they had moved in, the wooded area seemed to be an enchanted forest filled with wildflowers. The play of moonlight among the leaves of the trees wove a spell of magic that embraced them both. Several times they stopped to admire the beauty of their surroundings. Several times they stopped to embrace and kiss. Several times they stopped only to hold each other close. Shelli shed tears of joy as they walked silently.

After an hour spent strolling up and back the tree-lined streets, the two walked silently, arms around each other, back to their home. There, they retired to the privacy of their bedroom. The couple did not speak, but instead removed their clothes and stepped into the shower. After softly washing each other, Tony reset the faucet to fill the tub. There, they sat for quite a while drinking a bottle of chardonnay from California that Shelli had brought in from the kitchen. Shelli recalled when they had met at the University of Colorado and how shy Tony had been. She confessed that, when she first saw him, she knew that he was the man whom she was going to marry. Tony was amused at this revelation. Almost embarrassed, he admitted that he had never been with another woman except Shelli. She smiled in admiration and splashed her husband with water. "You just make sure it stays that way, young man!"

They explored the crevices and curves of each other's bodies. They gently massaged each other and refamiliarized themselves with each other's points of pleasure and excitement. The tender touches of Tony excited Shelli till she couldn't contain her passion any longer. The warmth of the bath water and the softness of Shelli's body rubbing against his own increased Tony's desire to make love to his wife for the first time since the injury and arrest.

Suddenly, Shelli stood and got out of the tub. She didn't speak, but extended her hand to her husband. Both now out of the tub, she began gently stroking every inch of Tony's muscular frame. She led her man to the bed and lay down first. Still wet, Tony straddled her legs and began to stroke her breasts with his tongue. Shelli reached up and pulled Tony's head to hers and kissed him with renewed passion. Tony responded in kind and lay fully on top of Shelli. He raised his legs to allow her to adjust her body to receive him. Slowly and gently, Tony descended on his wife and penetrated her to the full depth of her desire. After a few moments of slow, deliberate thrusts, Tony withdrew and began the process of stroking and massaging every inch of Shelli's beautiful body. Tony treated her in a way that heightened her desire to have more of him inside her. Each merging lasted longer and longer. Each time, Shelli's passion intensified. Tony continued this process until she wouldn't let him go. She made Tony roll over onto his back so she could mount her virile husband and not aggravate his injury.

Shelli grabbed her husband's hands, intertwining her fingers with his. She held on tight and continued to suck him into her as deeply as possible. She threw her head back and sat up, continuing to hold his hands. Tony began stroking her breasts as her intensity increased. In a moment of unbridled passion, she exploded in ecstasy, as did Tony. He pulled her body close to his as the power of their combined orgasm took complete control.

As it began to subside, Shelli kissed Tony continuously. He felt the titillating spasms of the muscles that surrounded him inside her. His body tingled all over. He held his wife close and continued to kiss her in the steam of their passion. After all this time of silence,

Railroaded!

words came from his lips. "Thank you for loving me. I will always love you, Shelli. No matter what happens to me, I will always love you."

Chapter 32

Monday, August 27th

Frank Cobb and his associates had been the guests of the federal government for almost ten days. At 8:00 A.M., Special Agent Jason Moore received a call from a superior to release the prisoners. Processing the release would take a few hours. He figured they would be free to go about lunchtime. He was also instructed to return their weapons, which consisted of a .30/06 caliber Remington hunting rifle equipped with a twelve power scope, a Weatherby 7mm Magnum equipped with a 15 power scope, and one 9mm automatic pistol. The weapons would be returned to the men after lunch about 1:00 P.M.

After sitting in a jail cell for the last eight days, the anger inside Frank was raging. He wanted to know why he was sitting in jail and a nigra man was walking the streets, having raped his cousin. He wanted to know why he and his boys had been put in jail and by whom, especially after he had been requested to come up from Mississippi by his Aunt Liz. She was a powerful woman who should have intervened on their behalf. Frank was not a happy man. After he retrieved his weapons, he was going to get some answers to some very hard questions.

● ● ● ● ● ●

"Thanks for letting me try this out! I'm thinking about heading to Montana to do some deer and elk hunting this fall. I need to get a new rifle," stated Viper.

"Anytime at all," was the reply from the rifle range attendant. Viper handed the man an oversized manila envelope that contained $10,000 in cash.

Railroaded!

"You better hurry and get these back. I hear the owners are being released from custody in a few hours. I'm sure you understand."

"Completely, sir!" The man stood back and saluted his former commanding officer. "And, thank you, sir, for the opportunity to be of service." The assassin left the rifle range and made some final arrangements. He had already confirmed that $5 Million had been transferred into his numbered account at Swiss Bank Corporation, as requested. He confirmed that the news conference was indeed going to be at 2:00 P.M. Viper would enjoy the rest of the morning before going into action for the last time, before retiring.

●●●●●●

Anthony and Shelli awoke feeling at peace and refreshed. His injuries seemed to be healing rapidly. Tony felt he could complete his contract. He figured he would miss the first eight regular-season games, complete the season, and retire. As she gently massaged his back, Shelli reminded him that his back was not something to be taken lightly. "The Scotts have caused us enough trouble, Tony. Why don't you just march over there and demand an early retirement with full pay? There's no need to risk re-injuring your back. Besides the doctor's already told you that one hit the wrong way could be even more devastating than the first." She jabbed him lightly in the region of his injury and he winced, getting the message.

"Okay, okay, darling. I just don't want people thinking I'm a quitter."

"You never have been before. But these circumstances are different. There's still someone crazy out there who's been trying to have you done in! We don't need the aggravation. We can live comfortably for the rest of our lives. The kids are taken care of, and certainly your architectural firm will do well. We just don't need this. You don't need the NFL anymore!" Shelli was lecturing her husband. He turned over and kissed her to stop her in her tracks. Tony agreed and would speak to Ned Scott, but only after the dust had settled.

After showering together with Tony, Shelli fixed breakfast for Adrian, Harvey and Tony. The kids had stayed with her parents at the hotel. "Too bad Errol is not here now to enjoy our victory," stated Tony.

"He's better off in New York," responded Harvey. Adrian was sitting there staring at Tony with the strangest look on his face.

"What's the matter, A.C.? You look like you've seen a ghost!" Adrian immediately snapped out of it and came back to the world of the living.

"Nothing . . . nothing at all. I just had a premonition of something. But whatever it was is gone." Adrian was lying. His vision was awful. Excusing himself from the breakfast table, he went to the confines of the bedroom and called Errol.

"Listen, Trees. Tony's in serious trouble. Don't ask me how I know or why. If we don't do something quick, he'll be dead soon!"

"You've got to calm down, A.C. Everything's gonna be all right. But you've got to calm yourself so you can think." Adrian took a series of deep breaths and did relax. "Now, what did you see?"

"I saw an angel standing behind Tony when we were having breakfast. What does that mean, Errol?" Errol was troubled by his friend's revelation. He sat down on his bed and pondered. After a moment, he sighed and responded.

"I guess it means his life is in God's hands, and there's probably nothing we can do about it."

●●●●●●

"I suppose you're here to request a continuance of the trial," stated Judge O'Connor. "I heard about Raymond Sutter." Joey dismissed the comment about his adversary-turned-ally and went straight to the point.

"On the contrary, Judge. I'm here to tell you that the formal position of the district attorney's office is that the charges are to be dropped immediately. It will be announced at the news conference in a few hours." Gerald O'Connor turned away from his gaze out the window of his chambers and looked directly at Joseph Kearns.

Railroaded!

"Are you out of your mind, young man? You've won this case. Look what it does for your future!" Joey Kearns was completely nonplussed at the judge's remarks. So was Lew Dobson, who had just entered, running a couple of minutes late for the meeting.

"Additionally, Judge, there will be no further prosecution of Anthony Williams," stated Lew Dobson. I want to make it very clear that no one anywhere is going to prosecute Anthony Williams over bullshit. And I want you to be the first to know that I am not seeking reelection."

"Great! The whole world is coming unglued behind this damned trial. Rumors are running rampant. Everyone's suspecting everyone else of wrongdoing. Sooner or later, I suppose they'll even suspect me of doing something wrong."

"Is there cause for concern, Judge?" asked Joey. Gerald O'Connor saw red after that remark.

"Get out of my chambers now, you insolent asshole! You too, Lew. Take your lackey and get the hell out!" In the hallway, Lew inquired about his young associate's remark.

"Are you out of your mind, Kearns? What the hell did you do that for?"

"Because I believe that the judge didn't conduct this trial with fairness and impartiality, as required. If he had, there wouldn't be dead bodies lying all around us. Have you ever seen a judge give the benefit of the doubt to a rape victim as he did? Shit, Lew, he rolled with my punches and never gave the defense an even chance. It's as if he had been paid off or set up to 'railroad' the defendant into a guilty verdict. While my tactic of laying no foundation was a good legal move, any reasonable judge in the country would have allowed the defense to thoroughly cross-examine the victim. Doesn't this whole thing smell shitty enough?"

"What are you suggesting?" asked Lew.

"I'm suggesting that maybe we should investigate Marianne Scott and Gerald O'Connor. Maybe there is complicity somewhere between the two of them that can be proven. I believe that's where you'll find the real case."

"You really like playing with fire, don't you, Joey?"

"Only if I'm wearing an asbestos suit, Lew!" Joey started laughing aloud. His boss followed in the levity of the moment.

Lew put his arm around the young associate as they walked down the hallway.

"Well, I think you'll need that suit this afternoon. You're really going to piss off someone who wants Anthony Williams to take a fall," stated Lew in a less than serious manner. But Joey responded with a contemplative demeanor.

"I only wish I knew who it was . . . I only wish I knew."

●●●●●●

There must have been twenty-five hundred people milling around the courthouse steps, waiting for the 2:00 P.M. news conference. There were news reporters from every quadrant of the United States. The major networks were standing by to put on "Special Reports." Everyone was speculating as to the announcements that would be made by the junior prosecutor.

When Frank Cobb and Carly Pope, another of the portly relatives, and their assortment of associates were released from custody, they split up into two groups. Frank and Carly decided to stay behind and see what all the commotion was about. Besides, they had to attend to some unfinished business. "Y'all get the hell out of here now and don't look back. There be too many snakes in the grass. Now go'won home. We'll be along." Frank was adamant with his instructions. Uncharacteristically, their compatriots didn't resist and left Pittsburgh immediately, heading straight for Mississippi. Carly loaded their personal belongings into the back of their 1976 Chevy pick-up truck. Frank placed the 30/06 rifle and the Weatherby on the gun rack in the back window of the cab. When Carly got into the truck, he sniffed at the rifles once but dismissed the smell as nothing. Like themselves, the weapons had been in the custody of the FBI -- under lock and key. After the news conference, they would head out to the Scott estate and confront Aunt Liz.

"Ya know, Carly, I still can't figure this shit out. Why the hell did we sit in a jail cell for damn near ten days when Aunt Liz could've got us out?" asked a distraught Frank Cobb. He rubbed his forehead and put on his favorite ballpark-style cap with a "John Deere" emblem on the front.

Railroaded!

"I bet that nigger got to go home every night while we had to rot in jail," stated Carly Pope in an angry tone.

"This shit ain't right! Dammit, it ain't right!" Frank was furious. Now he could show his real anger instead of the restraint he had exercised while in custody. He still couldn't believe that he and his friends had been incarcerated for such a long time for doing something that in Mississippi, wouldn't have even rated a slap on the wrist.

After getting settled in, the two men pulled their truck to the edge of the crowd and got out to stand on the bed of their vehicle. That way, they could see the podium better and actually hear what was being said.

Gerald O'Connor looked out from his chambers' window at the crowd that was getting larger the closer it got to the scheduled event. He felt uneasy about being caught in the middle of something this egregious. But, according to the last communication, he had done his job and was off the hook. He would wait a few months before using the credit card with the extraordinary line of credit. He would wait to see if he actually did get the Supreme Court appointment. If not, then he would destroy the card.

●●●●●●

Joey Kearns sat in his office and pondered what he was about to do. He leaned back in his new office chair and contemplated how far he had come in such a short time. He contemplated whether he wanted to prosecute "bad guys" for a career. Maybe Lew Dobson was taking the right approach by *"constructively"* resigning. Maybe Joey needed to stay on and make sure that the district attorney's office became a model for seeking truth rather than an institution for making people miserable based on allegation and circumstantial evidence. Joey Kearns knew that his idealistic view of the law was being tested. This case had brought him back to reality from the edge of the abyss of cynicism and mediocrity.

The phone rang and snapped him out of the deep thought. He picked it up to hear the voice of Arnold Benton.

"Listen, Joey. I don't have much time, but someone here wants to speak with you."

"Who is it?" Joey looked at his watch. It was 1:40 P.M. Only twenty minutes to go.

"Mr. Kearns, this is the friend of Messrs. Williams, Forest and Christopher," stated Harvey Sloan.

"I recognize your voice," stated the prosecutor.

"Is it possible for me to convince you to postpone this news conference until later?" Joey knew that several thousand had already assembled.

"I don't think so. I want to hurry up and get this finished. I have to consider my next moves against Marianne et al."

"Then listen to me very carefully. When you step up to the podium, I want you to scan the buildings around you. If you see anything unusual, get down immediately."

"I appreciate the warning and advice. It is taken under advisement. By the way, I never got to thank you for all your help."

"Don't thank me; thank Mr. Benton. Despite the fact that he is an adversary, he really is your friend. Goodbye, Mr. Joseph Kearns." Arnold took the phone and continued.

"Listen, Joey. Just be careful out there today. Despite what Guy Markham did last night, I still don't trust the guy."

"Are you really my friend?" asked Joey, with a tear coming to his eye.

"I always admired you, Joey. I will always be your friend." Joey was momentarily overcome with emotion and was able to get out a weak "thank you" before hanging up.

● ● ● ● ● ●

Arnold Benton hung up the phone and looked at Harvey Sloan. Across the table, Tony was putting on a bulletproof vest under his suit jacket, much to the chagrin of Shelli. Adrian helped his friend. Loren Johnson was seated at the head of the table. "I wish Raymond were here to see this announcement. As I understand it, Tony, you're going to stand with Joseph Kearns at the podium. By the way, I read your comments: they are excellent and very

Railroaded!

compassionate. The community should place you back on the pedestal where you belong."

"Thanks, Loren. But, to tell you the truth, I'm not interested in anything except starting an architectural design firm with my two best friends. I'm finished with the NFL. I'm tired of being the *'speed demon'* of the gridiron. I just want to be Anthony Williams -- architect, father, and husband. Nothing more, nothing less." Shelli hugged her husband and stepped back. There was no warmth at all. In fact, he was ice-cold.

"Are you okay, baby?" she asked. Tony smiled at everyone and answered.

"It's time for us to go."

Just as they were all filing out of the conference room, Guy Markham walked up. He had just cleared his outstanding receivable with the accounting department. Harvey Sloan saw him coming and hung back out of view. "Listen, Loren, I wanted to thank you for everything, and also tell you, Anthony, that there are no hard feelings." He shook hands with Tony and noticed the extra bulk under his jacket. "Besides, I thought I'd walk over with you all."

"You've done your job; now leave us alone," stated Shelli.

"No, it's okay, Shelli. It's better to have him in clear view," stated Tony.

"Loren, why don't you serve as the escort for the esteemed Mr. Markham?" asked Arnold. Shelli didn't want the assassin near her. She got very bad vibes from this man.

"I'll go with Arnold and Adrian, if that's okay."

"Where is your Mr. Sloan? Will he be attending?" asked the investigator. Loren recognized that Harvey had faded into the woodwork. He responded to Mr. Markham's inquiry.

"Mr. Sloan will be leaving shortly and has to complete his travel arrangements. He won't be walking over with us."

"Fair enough. Before I go, I need to make one quick phone call . . . only take a few seconds." The former detective for the firm dashed into a small, empty conference room and made a call that indeed only lasted a few seconds. When he emerged, the group left the building and headed for the courthouse.

Moments later, as they approached the podium set up on the steps of the Allegheny County Courthouse, Tony was met with mixed signals from the crowd. He heard everything from, "We Love you, Tony!" to "Rapist" to "Can I have your autograph?" Tony was distant. His eyes were glazed over in the paradox that comes from experiencing peace and fear at the same time.

Joey Kearns had already taken his place. Next to Joey sat Lew Dobson. He was going to be the third speaker and announce his decision not to seek reelection. As Tony approached the podium, Carly Pope yelled out, "There's the nigger!" Lew Dobson hadn't expected any heckling, so he didn't have a substantial police force on hand. In fact, there were only ten officers assigned for this duty.

"This kind of anti-black dogma is why this country continues to be in trouble! Whoever said that is truly an ignorant man." His words boomed across and silenced the crowd. "We are here today because a terrible injustice has been done. This office is going to correct that injustice. Mr. Kearns will give you the details." It was 2:00 P.M.

"Who the fuck is he calling 'ignorant'? I'll show him who's ignorant, that Yankee sonuvabitch!" Carly jumped over the side of the truck and got in the cab. He grabbed the .30/06 and cocked the bolt making sure there was a shell in the chamber. He sniffed at the gun again, but his anger did not allow him to make the connection. He was going to have himself a little fun and scare the shit out of a couple of uppity white boys and one nigger whom he couldn't touch. He placed the gun at his side and climbed into the back of the truck with Frank.

"What are you gonna do with that?"

"I ain't gonna do nothin' 'cept scare them ole boys," stated the portly man.

"You want us to get thrown back in jail again?"

"Hell, no, Frank. But the Constitution says we have a right to bear arms. So, I'm bearing my arms according to my constitutional right!" Frank laughed and patted Carly on the back.

"You always were the brains of our little group." Carly placed the .30/06 on the roof of the cab and watched the goings on. From that vantage point, the rifle could not be seen by anyone in the crowd.

Railroaded!

As all three men stood at the podium, Joseph Kearns began: "Ladies and gentlemen, the district attorney's office is charged with the responsibility of adjudicating those situations whereby scurrilous individuals have caused you harm. Unfortunately, I have to report to you that the integrity of the people of Pittsburgh has been compromised. Someone, as yet unknown, tampered with evidence and created a nightmare for an innocent man. But perhaps even more egregious is the fact that this case was even brought to trial in the first place. Why so? It is a disaster to even consider that a person can use the court system to carry out his own personal grudges. It is disastrous to think that a man's life can be turned upside down and his family exposed to ridicule and innuendo because of spurned sexual advances. It is disastrous to think that the victim in this case was not the victim but the perpe . . ."

Ned Scott got up to turn off the television set in his office, but instead froze as he watched what unfolded in front of him. He heard two sharp cracks of a rifle. Everyone started ducking for cover. Ned instantly recalled watching the John F. Kennedy assassination on television. But this time it was personal. He watched as the young deputy district attorney crumpled and fell into the arms of his boss. He sustained a shot that pierced his heart. Blood spewed forth from the wound and from his mouth. Ned was paralyzed in shock.

Lew Dobson shrieked to the sky, only to see the second bullet find its mark on the right temple of Anthony Williams. The impact of the large caliber bullet shattered the side of Tony's head. The force knocked him backward onto the three seats that had been reserved for the three men. Death was instant.

Shelli screamed wildly and passed out. Adrian ran to the podium, but it was too late. He cradled his friend in his arms paying no attention to the fact that Tony's blood was drenching his clothing. "It's all right now, Flash. It's all right. You're safe. You can run forever now and not worry." Adrian understood what he had seen earlier.

"Hold on, Joey! Hold on!" Arnold Benton raced to the podium and hovered over Lew and Joey.

"If you are my friend, Arnie, please don't let them get away with this . . ." The young prosecutor tightly grasped Lew's hand, stiffened, and then relaxed. He closed his eyes for the last time.

Errol, watching with Raymond at the hospital in New York, collapsed in the arms of his girlfriend. Raymond and Dot Jensen erupted in screams of terror. Gerald O'Connor watched from his chambers and knew that he had better conform with whatever was requested of him. He had no intention of ending up like the two men on the steps below.

Guy Markham stood and watched the events without emotion. He never even flinched when the shots were fired. Loren Johnson knew he was responsible, but there was nothing that could be done. He had the perfect alibi. Loren looked at the man and saw a smirk on his face. "You will get yours . . . you will, dammit, I promise you."

"I already have, thank you very much," stated the assassin in a cold flat voice.

Harvey Sloan scanned the rooftops but the afternoon sun precluded any detection. Viper knew this. The mere fact that he was standing with Tony's lawyers set him above suspicion. But, as Harvey forced his way through the stunned crowd toward the assassin, Markham turned and yelled, "There they are!" Markham pointed to the two men from Mississippi who were in their pickup truck. Harvey stopped momentarily and looked in the direction where the assassin had pointed, stunned by the pronouncement. Viper, in the frenzy, disappeared like the snake that he was.

Railroaded!

Chapter 33

"I didn't fire. I didn't fire!" yelled Carly. "What the hell is goin' on, Frank?"

"We gotta get outta here now! We've been set up! That bitch is gonna die!" yelled Frank. The two men, in a fluid movement, were out of the back and into the cab. Frank was driving. He headed down Grant Street and turned wildly onto Fort Pitt Boulevard. Speeding alongside the Monongahela River, in a few blocks he could take the exit ramp to the Fort Pitt Bridge and Tunnel that would take him out of Pittsburgh and back home to his beloved Mississippi. But he changed his mind at the last minute when he saw the sign for Three Rivers Stadium. Maybe there he could get some protection until this mess was sorted out. From there, he and Carly could get in touch with Aunt Liz or her son, Ned.

Frank didn't notice the truck that was gaining on him from behind. In the middle of Point State Park, before he could cross the Fort Duquesne Bridge, Frank and Carly were violently jolted as the black Ford Bronco rammed them from behind.

"Am in pursuit of assassination suspects. Need help!" Viper had no intention of needing help at all. Instead, he jammed the accelerator pedal to the floor and intentionally hit the left rear quadrant of the Chevy pick-up. This move caused Frank to lose control of the truck and send the truck into a spin. Viper accelerated again and hit the truck broadside, sending it into a roll. He stopped and watched as the truck came to a stop on its cab. The two men were not conscious. But the violent action had caused the intended purpose. Gasoline leaked from broken fuel lines, and within seconds the truck exploded. If the occupants had been alive, they were not now. Mission accomplished, "Point -- set -- match!" thought Viper.

The police arrived on the scene of the accident as did two pumper trucks from the fire department. Guy Markham explained that he had been standing with Loren Johnson and that, after hearing the shots, he had scanned the crowd and saw a man standing in a pickup truck with rifle hoisted. He ran to his truck, which was parked nearby, and gave pursuit. Upon overtaking the truck carrying the assassins, he rammed the truck to try to get it to stop, but the driver refused. The last impact caused the truck to spin and roll.

"Thanks for your statement, Mr. Markham. If we have any questions, we'll get back to you," stated a policeman. After the fire department had put out the flames, the charred bodies of Frank Cobb and Carly Pope were taken to the morgue. Recovered from the wreckage were a .30/06 Rifle and a Weatherby 7mm Magnum rifle. A ballistics test would be run to determine whether the bullets that killed the prosecutor and star defensive end of the Pittsburgh Steelers had indeed been fired by the weapons owned by Carly Pope, himself killed in the process of trying to escape.

●●●●●●

The people of Pittsburgh were living with an emotional disaster. The media, however, was having a field day. Two men had been killed by an assassin. The apparent suspects had tried to get away, only to be run down by an observer who was attending the news conference. "Those boys were out of control, Marianne. Serves them right. They were instructed to leave town immediately and go home. They should have followed my instructions."

"But they were your cousins. Aren't you even a little upset?" asked Marianne of her grandmother.

"I don't see you shedding any tears over that Williams boy. Look there!" Elizabeth Cobb pointed to the television screen that was showing Anthony Williams being placed on a stretcher and shrouded with a clean white sheet. "Where are your tears, Marianne?" Her eyes and face remained dry because her soul was empty. She left the estate and drove to her townhouse.

Railroaded!

Adrian watched as the body of his friend was placed in the ambulance. He watched as Shelli was comforted and led away to another ambulance for the ride to Allegheny General Hospital. He watched as the body of Joseph Kearns was placed in a third ambulance. The rage built in Adrian till he became a man possessed. Harvey saw the explosion, but before he could get to his friend, Adrian dashed up the steps of the courthouse. Harvey followed behind.

Adrian bolted through the door to Judge O'Connor's chambers and flew past the secretary. He hit the door to the judge's chambers with such force that it swung on its hinges and broke the coat rack that stood behind. Adrian lunged across the desk and tackled Gerald O'Connor. He grabbed him by the throat and started choking the judge. "One of my best friends is dead and you played a part in it!" Harvey entered the chambers and pulled Adrian off the judge.

"Not like this, Adrian, not like this! This won't help Tony!" stated the man from INTERPOL.

"You fucking asshole of a judge! I know you had a part in this. I don't know how or why, but I know you are responsible. One day, I'll be back for your ass. I'm going to turn into your worst nightmare. You'll never know when or where or how. But when I do return, you're going down. Do you hear me?!" Adrian lunged forward one last time and punched the judge. Tony's blood had now stained the judge's clothes as well. Harvey again pulled Adrian away from the judge and grabbed him to control his rage.

As Harvey started to drag Adrian from the judge's chambers, the bailiff charged in, but the judge motioned for him to back off and let them exit. Harvey Sloan was himself now enraged and turned to the judge. "Anthony Williams wasn't a dumb football player. He was one of the best men in this whole damned world. You had best be prepared for the return of my friend here. I can guarantee that we will not take the loss of our friend lightly." Harvey helped Adrian out of the room. Judge O'Connor sat on the floor of his chambers and wiped the blood from the lip that had been torn by the punch from the wide-receiver. He sat there and tried to decide whether he should take the two men seriously.

During the five o'clock news broadcast, Lew Dobson, along with the chief of police, held a news conference. The police chief announced that ballistics tests had positively identified the origin of the shots that had killed Joseph Kearns and Anthony Williams. He stated that they had indeed been fired by one of the weapons owned by Carly Pope, who had been killed in the process of trying to escape.

Lew Dobson, still in his blood-soaked suit, announced that the matter would now be put to rest along with the two fallen men. The case was closed. There was no need to investigate further. Lew lamented over how low people had sunk but praised his late associate for his tenacity in doing what all prosecutors should do . . . get at the truth. "Joey Kearns died before he could finish his remarks. So, to you, Ms. Marianne Scott, the true victims are dead. Wherever you are, I hope you are pleased with the results of your actions."

Marianne panicked, knowing full well that everyone would be pursuing her. She called Leslie Seymour and entreated her to come away with her. Leslie refused. She was too busy gloating over the $350,000 cash she had received the Friday before. "You've got money and power, Marianne. Get yourself out of this mess. I'm not your friend anymore. Just leave me out!"

Marianne called to talk with her grandmother, but Elizabeth Cobb was not in. She had left the estate with Howard Werner in her Bentley. Marianne hurriedly threw a few clothes into a suitcase, grabbed a few cosmetics, stuffed them in the same bag, and left the house. She ran down the steps to her waiting car. She threw the bag onto the front passenger's seat and was about to leave the city headed for Detroit when a white van pulled up behind her car, blocking her exit.

Marianne was descended upon by what seemed like a thousand reporters as carload after carload of the news hounds arrived at her townhouse. In terror and frustration, she rolled up the car window to avoid being questioned about the killings. In a desperate move, she mashed down on the accelerator. The car smashed through the cedar fence and careened wildly onto the next property. She gained control of the car and after a series of evasive maneuvers, drove across a lawn, jumped the curb and onto the street, where she immediately sped off and disappeared.

●●●●●●

Ned Scott walked through the front door of Allegheny General Hospital and inquired about Shelli Williams. He had just braved a host of reporters. He found Shelli in one of the first floor treatment rooms lying on a bed and somewhat dazed from being sedated. She looked at Ned Scott as he entered the room and approached the bed. "My husband is dead," she said in a cold, shaky voice. "He knew he was going to die. I heard him, but I just didn't listen."

"I should've listened, but I was blinded by a father's rage. I didn't hear either."

"But you didn't lose your life or your mate. You still have everything you own. Your family is intact." She took a deep breath and continued. "Get out, Mr. Scott. Just get out of here and leave me alone." Shelli turned her head and stared blankly out of the window. The owner of the Pittsburgh Steelers complied and left the room. "And don't you dare show your face at his funeral."

This last comment cut Ned to the quick. He stormed out of the hospital and drove straight to Marianne's townhouse. When he arrived there, he found that she had disappeared into thin air, as had all of the reporters except one. Terrence Feldman was sitting on the front steps seeming to take in the sunshine. "You know, Ned, this whole mess doesn't make sense. It just doesn't make any sense."

"I assume you're waiting for Marianne?" asked Ned.

"Your daughter's gone, Ned. Vanished. She was descended upon by my colleagues and she panicked. That was her exit route." Terrence pointed to the gaping hole in the fence. "How about you? Care to make a statement in these calm surroundings? You know I'm not given to bullshit reporting like most of the news hounds." Ned Scott actually smiled and thanked Terrence for his calm demeanor.

"This whole world has gone crazy, hasn't it, Terry?" Ned sat down on the steps next to the reporter and gave a statement that indicated his sadness and sense of deep personal loss. The reporter thanked him for the comments, and, sensing that enough was enough, didn't push further. He shook hands with the football magnate and left him to his own contemplative thoughts.

After sitting on his daughter's front porch for almost an hour, Ned left Marianne's deserted residence and drove slowly back to his private club. He was not surprised to find his mother waiting for him. "Where's Marianne?" he inquired in a flat unemotional tone.

"I thought she was with you," replied the elder Scott.

"I guess she's gone. She probably packed a few things and just left -- disappeared."

"Don't worry, son. She'll surface soon, and when she does, we need to be there for her. She's being lambasted as the cause of the death of those two men."

"In an indirect way, isn't she, Mother?"

"What about my losing two cousins, you ingrate of a son?" asked Elizabeth, changing the subject to try to elicit some sense of grief from her son. Ned was neither amused nor grief-stricken about the loss of two men from the seamier side of his family.

"They probably deserved whatever happened to them. They were Mississippi poor white trash. If you hadn't invited them up here to cause trouble, maybe two good men would still be alive today and we'd find out what really happened."

"Well, Ned, my cousins came because I wanted to jostle things a bit. But now that they're dead, I'll guess we'll never know the truth, will we?" Ned looked at his mother and saw a glint of triumph in her eyes rather than sadness as one would expect.

"You're pleased with the results, aren't you, Mother? Where the hell is Marianne? I'm sure you know."

"I really don't know, Ned. But, when she does turn up, I'm sure you'll treat her with the care deserving of a victim of assault and rape -- not like a murderer." Elizabeth Cobb had avoided comment on the first part of Ned's question. Instead, she feigned tears and continued. "Are you going to help with the arrangements for the boys?"

"That remains to be seen." He paused for a moment and then countered, "Fuck no -- just do it yourself!" Ned looked at his mother with disgust and retreated to the confines of the club's library. He closed the pocket doors behind him and locked them to ensure privacy. He poured himself a whiskey neat, took the glass

Railroaded!

and full bottle and placed it on the desk in front of him. As he sat back in his soft leather chair, he pondered his life and the emptiness that he had felt since the death of his wife. Then, too, he had lost his wife and a man whom he thought was a friend. Drinking the whiskey in large gulps, he now felt Shelli's pain. He relived the shootings over and over in his mind. He continued to drink until his mind became a jumbled, swirling series of intense horrible pictures with gnarled faces screaming at him from every angle. He closed his eyes and dropped the almost-empty glass, having succumbed to a drunken stupor.

● ● ● ● ● ●

Guy Markham returned to the sanctuary of his residence. He opened a vault and started counting out cash for placement in a top-opening black briefcase. He went into another room and picked up a small leather bag. He held the leather bag securely and carefully dumped the contents into the case. He closed it quickly and left his home. He drove to a small diner on the south end of town. En route, he received a call on his mobile phone. "Well done. Very well done. I trust you are satisfied with the compensation."

"Very!" stated the assassin.

"Your services are no longer required. Should they be, I will contact you by transmitting a $100,000 'request fee' to your account. Only then will you know I am summoning your services."

"It was my pleasure to be of service. I hope the results are acceptable to you."

"Perfectly. Remember, I did give you clearance to dispose of the Southern trash."

"Viper out." He hung up the receiver and pulled up to the Country Diner. Inside, he walked to a lone man, casually dressed, who sat by himself in a somewhat dimly lit corner. Viper put his briefcase under the table and exchanged it with one already situated there. "That was a fine piece of work, especially the head shot to Mr. Williams."

"Thanks for the tip about the bulletproof vest. Without it, your man would still be alive."

"Three hundred thousand in small bills, as agreed. I knew I could count on you."

"T'was a pleasure to show you my skills," responded the actual assassin. "Call me any time. But, for now, I'm headed for Hawaii and points beyond."

"Your payment is in the case. I would recommend waiting until you are in the safe confines of your car before inspecting the contents. Exposure of these matters to the public is not suggested." The triggerman looked at Viper quizzically but shrugged off his comment as nothing but idle chat.

Viper was finished with his business so he stood and shook hands with the man who had assisted his efforts. He placed a $5 bill on the table, which was a more than adequate tip and payment for the single glass of Pepsi-Cola® the triggerman had ordered. As he drove away, Viper opened the case and examined its contents. There lay a broken-down .30/06 rifle with a super-long range scope. The six pieces would be easily disposable. He lit a cigarette and started to blow a series of smoke rings as he continued driving south to Baltimore, where he would catch a flight to Miami, and on to the Caymans.

Two miles away from the diner, under a grove of trees, the triggerman stopped to check on his earnings. Three hundred thousand in cash was a substantial increase in his pay. As a former SWAT-team marksman for the Harrisburg Police Department, he was just barely making a living as a security guard on a graveyard shift. With the earnings from this job, he could disappear into oblivion in Indonesia. As he opened the case, he thought of the flight he was going to catch to Hawaii from Cleveland in the morning. After a few days there on the beach, he would fly on to Djakarta.

When he opened the second flap of the black case, he was immediately attacked by two angry water moccasins that sprang out at his face. One bit him on the throat near the jugular vein, the other on his arm. The man screamed but could not get away from their incessant attacks. He opened the car door, but it was too late. In a matter of minutes, the fight was over. The assassin, in a series of muscle spasms, died as the venom that ran through his veins shut

Railroaded!

down his nervous and respiratory systems. He lay there amidst the Monopoly money he had received from his employer, while his two killers silently slithered away into the nearby underbrush.

Chapter 34

Trying to Escape the Madness

Driving south on Interstate 79, Marianne decided that it would be better to go to Cincinnati, where the Detroit Lions were playing a preseason game on Friday night. She could hide out in Ohio away from the throngs of reporters who were searching for her, totally away from the eyes of the world. Driving south and then east, she could avoid anyone looking for her. It was longer, but safer. She would call home later in the evening and report that she was safe. Now, however, was not the time.

After she crossed the Pennsylvania--West Virginia state line, she stopped for gas. While she filled the tank, she checked the front end of the car. While there was some damage from plowing through the fence, there was no damage to the retractable headlights on her Corvette. She turned them on and they worked perfectly. The body damage to the fiberglass fender could be fixed later after the heat was off. Maybe she could get it done in Cincinnati before the game on Saturday.

As she drove south on the Interstate, which from time to time turned back into the old U.S. highway, she thought of all that had happened. She didn't know that Anthony Williams was going to be assassinated. She didn't know that an associate attorney for the Allegheny County District Attorney's Office was going to be assassinated. She didn't know that her own distant relatives would wind up dead. But instead of remorse, she felt anger. Marianne Scott didn't recognize that all of the events were her fault. She began shrieking, "Everyone in the whole fucking world is after me and I didn't do shit! Where's the justice in this fucked-up world? I can't help it if someone else wanted those men dead!"

Railroaded!

She drove faster and faster until she recognized that the last thing she wanted was a speeding ticket in another state where she had no influence. Anyway, it was dark now and the Interstate was switching back to two-lane highway for twelve miles. Along the way she would pass through a town called Big Otter. There she would stop and get something to eat.

Six men sat huddled around a table in the Trapper John Café. They too had stopped for food and gas in the sleepy little West Virginia town. When they heard the news on the television in the bar, they froze, both in fear and pain at the loss of their dearest friends. From late afternoon through the early evening, the men sat there sipping on Budweisers, virtually immobilized. A slow burn permeated their bodies. They distracted themselves from their confusion and anger by recounting memories of better times.

About 8:30 P.M., they were about to leave and continue the drive home to Mississippi, when a young blonde woman walked into the café and ordered dinner. One of the men, returning from the restroom, looked at the girl and did a double take. He didn't say anything, but instead went back to the table where his buddies were sitting. "Hey, y'all. I'd bet a million bucks that over yonder is sitting that Marianne Scott bitch." Almost simultaneously, they all looked at her. Marianne felt the stares and turned her head to look in their direction. Despite her heavy makeup, some of the bruises were still visible when she turned to look at the voyeurs.

"Hey, bitch! You're the one who kilt our friends, ain't ya?" asked one of the men as he stood up. The room was completely silent for a moment. Then Marianne bolted out of the restaurant and got into her car. Despite the heavy intake of beers during the last several hours, the men responded as if completely sober. The six men ran to their trucks and followed in hot pursuit.

Knowing nothing of where she was, she misread a sign and wound up driving down a country road. She had no alternative but to continue. If she stopped, the crazed men from Mississippi would overtake her. As she accelerated into a turn, she immediately wheeled sharply to the left in horror. A slow-moving freight train was blocking the road. She tried evasive maneuvers on the loose dirt of the road but to no avail. Her car sideswiped the wheel assembly of a boxcar on the passenger side and, bouncing off, careened into a tree. Marianne was thrown from the car into another tree. Her body hit the ground and immediately went limp. She slipped into unconsciousness, seeing only her life pass before her slowly closing eyes.

The Mississippi men pulled up to the wreckage and surveyed the situation. Rather then help the victim, they returned to their trucks and drove off saying, "Serves the bitch right!"

Railroaded!

Chapter 35

Thursday, August 30th

True to his word, Errol Forrest returned to Pennsylvania on Thursday. But it was not for the celebration that had been desired and foreseen. Despite offers from his girlfriend Sharla to accompany him, Errol decided he needed to make this trip alone. As he drove the distance from Hempstead to Pittsburgh, he thought of Tony *"the Flash"* Williams and all the fun they had in their short lives. He thought of all they could have accomplished together. He continued to see a drawing of a building design they had worked on together during their high school years. He remembered Tony turning down attendance at Dartmouth and opting for the University of Colorado. He remembered the Olympics and Tony's success there. Errol remembered his friend's wedding uniting him with his beloved Shelli. He remembered his excitement at being drafted into the NFL. Errol remembered that he, Adrian and Tony had vowed to be friends till death. And now one of the three was gone, murdered in cold blood. For all intents and purposes, Tony died as had his cousin -- not for putting his arm around a white woman in pre-civil rights Alabama, but for rejecting sex with an arrogant white woman.

●●●●●●

Raymond had recovered to the point of being able to travel. With his arm in a sling, he and Dot Jensen flew to Pittsburgh, turning down Errol Forrest's offer to share the ride. Loren met them both at the Piedmont terminal, along with Lew Dobson. "It's my pleasure to meet you, Ms. Jensen," stated Lew as the two emerged from the jetway. "I wish the circumstances were different." Both men shook hands with Raymond. Loren gave Dot a sustained hug.

The police had formed a line across which the reporters could not cross. Nevertheless, they strained and yelled their questions from afar. Raymond and Dot ignored them all. "We can go downstairs through this door and avoid this madness. There is a car waiting below to take you both to a hotel. The same car will pick you up to take you to the funeral tomorrow," stated the district attorney. All four people left the area hurriedly, opting for the quick exit. As they drove off, Raymond started asking questions.

"Where's the funeral going to be held?"

"At Three Rivers Stadium," Loren responded to his fellow partner. This news surprised Raymond. "A huge crowd is expected. People are pouring in from all over, especially football players. Tony's graveside services have not been publicized and are closed except to family members. We have been asked to attend."

"And what about Joey Kearns?"

"The same as for Tony. His graveside services are closed as well and will be one hour after Tony's. Again, you are invited to attend," stated Lew.

"How's Shelli Williams?" asked Dot.

"She's a basket case. Her mother is there at the house trying to help. Tony's mother had a mild coronary and is in the hospital. She's going to be okay though," stated Loren.

"Maybe we should go to the Williams home and see if there's anything we can do to help." Dot was sincere, so Raymond didn't question her motivation. "If anything, I'm the who should be dead, not Tony or Mr. Kearns."

"Lew? Why don't you instruct the driver to head over to the Williams house? If necessary, we can always cancel the hotel reservations," stated Loren Johnson flatly. Lew tried to smile but it wouldn't come. Instead he complied with the suggestion.

"What happened to Guy Markham?" asked Raymond.

"He was standing with me when the incident occurred. Whoever the shooter was got away clean without a trace. Even Harvey Sloan, despite all of his efforts, couldn't trace him," stated Loren.

Railroaded!

"To make matters worse, Guy Markham supposedly saw the shooters and wound up running them down with his own truck as they tried to get away from the scene," added Lew Dobson.

"We saw that on the news," said Dot Jensen.

"He's covered his tracks like I've never seen. One of the rifles that was recovered from the wreckage was apparently used in the killing. There was an apparent ballistics match. So the case has been closed by the police department," continued the district attorney.

"So, what do you think, gentlemen? Do we have a clue as to who ordered this action? Was it Ned Scott?" asked Raymond.

"We don't have any idea. While all fingers seem to point to Ned, there's no logical justification for him to have one of his star players assassinated as well as an associate district attorney." Loren Johnson's frustration was showing at the thought of a killer and conspirator walking the streets with impunity. "To make matters worse, we received a new report from Tucker Labs that proclaimed Tony's innocence. It showed that, in the specimen tested, there was no presence of female vaginal fluids as would normally be expected. The specimen did not come from a rape victim. Someone changed it before it got to the lab for testing."

"So, for now, unless something drops out of the sky, or someone slips up and makes a mistake, the deaths of Anthony Williams and Joseph Kearns will remain a mystery." Lew Dobson was frustrated and angry. He had vowed that until the Williams case was solved, he would continue to run for reelection as the District Attorney for Allegheny County, with the purpose of instilling and maintaining the idealism of his fallen associate. Lew owed Joey a major debt of gratitude. Joseph Kearns had reawakened Lew's own sense of idealism about legal prosecution, a sense that had long been buried under the cynicism that came from dealing with the negative side of human existence. "But one day, someone will make a mistake, and when they do, I will be there to tear them apart. The truth is what's important, not winning or losing a case, but to get to the truth at all costs. That is Joey's legacy to the D.A.'s office. I will never let that legacy die!"

Everyone listened to Lew Dobson intently. Afterward, Loren guided them in a short prayer for peace for the two departed souls whose lives had been cut short by an unknown assassin. After it was finished, Loren continued on to other business. "On the lighter side, Raymond, if there is one under the circumstances, Adrian Christopher has asked for our help to get into law school. It seems he wants to be well versed in the law so he can go after a particular person."

"Who is it that he's after?" inquired Raymond of Loren.

"He believes Judge O'Connor had something to do with Tony's death. He burst into the judge's chambers and punched the old man's lights out!"

"Shit! I wish I could have been there to see that!" exclaimed Lew. "The curious thing is that the judge didn't have the man arrested. Nor was he charged with assault and battery."

"Well, after what I saw in the courtroom, I'd have to say that Adrian's hunch is correct. So, in the meantime, Loren, what are you going to do about his request?"

"I've already called the president of Columbia University. He and I are old friends. I told him to pave the way for Adrian's entry. I told him that our firm would stand behind his admission and attendance there at the law school."

"I see. So when is he going to start?" asked Raymond.

"Next fall. He's going to finish this season with the Broncos and take a few months off. He and Errol are going to do a little traveling together next summer after Errol graduates from Hofstra."

"Why don't we make Errol an offer to work with us?" asked Raymond.

"I did just that this morning. He patently refused. He and Adrian have already made up their minds. Those two are going to be a formidable pair when Adrian finishes law school. Heaven help anyone in the future who should get in their way or piss them off."

"They were a bold threesome," interjected Dot. Raymond smiled and put his arm around his lady. As sad as he was at Tony's and Joey's deaths, he was equally happy that Dot was alive and well. The intense look on his face evaporated as he stared into the beautiful eyes of his companion. In the presence of his associates, Raymond asked her a simple question.

"Will you marry me, Dot?"

Railroaded!

"Well, it's about time! To think you had to get shot to come to your senses!" Everyone laughed aloud.

"I guess I did. I guess I did."

●●●●●●

Fifteen minutes later, the limo pulled into the driveway at the Williams house. Shelli, dressed in a long terry cloth robe, answered the door and acknowledged Dot's offer of assistance by asking her to stay the night. She could use the company of someone other than family, someone who could understand what had happened. As the driver retrieved Dot's belongings from the trunk of the limo, she kissed Raymond good night and said, "Yes, darling, I'll marry you. But for now, we've got to help a friend. We'll talk about us later." A smiling Raymond, Lew, and Loren left the Woodfield Hills area and continued on to Loren's home, where the three men would spend the night.

Chapter 36

Friday, August 31st

The funeral service for both men at Three Rivers Stadium was attended by more than fifty thousand people from all over the United States and several countries abroad. It was the largest funeral service in the history of Pennsylvania. Despite the fact that he could have been invisible in the mass of people, Ned Scott remained true to Shelli's request. He did not attend but instead let the families mourn the loss of their loved ones in their own way.

Ned observed the event in solitude on the closed-circuit television system at his private club. He sat back and stared blankly at the screen, and thought of his father and his lost love. He thought of his departed wife and the affair she had with John Clayton. He thought of his own daughter and her affair with Lucas Johnson. He thought of his mother's deep-rooted hatred of black people. He thought of the abject ignorance of her prejudice. He thought of her attempts to rid her family of any 'black' influence. He thought of her bigoted existence and, at times, wished she were dead. Too many good people had died because of her racism.

Yet was he not just as racist as she? Each time, he had turned a blind eye to his mother's actions. Each time, he had silently supported her racism by not acting -- by not making affirmative decisions that could have turned things around. He remembered his father's unhappiness with his mother and hated the fact that he was reliving that experience. This time, his actions were not enough. He had failed again.

Ned fought tears as he watched a minister lead the multitude in a prayer for the two fallen men. He watched until the grief was too much to bear. In an outpouring of emotion that had long been dammed up after the death of his wife, the cold and calculating

Railroaded!

owner of the Pittsburgh Steelers, the unemotional and stoic Ned Scott, fell to his knees and cried as a father who had just lost a son.

●●●●●●

After attending the services at Three Rivers Stadium and at graveside, Adrian and Errol went to the Williams residence and spent the balance of the day recounting childhood stories and the good things that they had experienced during the sixteen years they had been associated with Tony. All of this was designed to make Shelli laugh. At times, they were actually rolling on the floor in raucous laughter . . . laughter that was the perfect prescription to treat heavy sorrow. Shelli was inundated with family and the closest of her friends. Everyone participated in trying to cook for a feast. Errol reminded everyone that, in New Orleans, a funeral meant "party time." So, the music played on . . . music from the late sixties and early seventies . . . music that Tony loved and had tried to sing with his scratchy tenor voice.

At 8:30 P.M. Shelli, was about to collapse from exhaustion, so Dot Jensen helped her get to bed. Dot and Shelli's mother also made sure the kids were put to bed. Adrian told them bedtime stories and sat with them until they were fast asleep. Errol was on kitchen detail as were Tony's sisters, Martha and Winifred.

About 11:00 P.M., Errol and Adrian, despite offers to the contrary, left the Williams home to drive back to the Holiday Inn near the airport, where they would spend the night. During the drive to the hotel, they did not speak much. Instead, for a long while, they focused on each other's silent thoughts. Adrian broke the silence first. "You know something, Errol? Tony knew he was going to die."

"How's that?" was Errol's short response.

"Shelli told me he made a comment after a dream, that he was going home. Monday morning I told you I saw a vision of an angel behind him. Tony knew, and there was nothing we could do."

"No, A.C. Tony resolved himself to his fate and didn't resist. He opted for the peace of being with God instead of living through hell." When they arrived at the hotel, they chose not to have a nightcap but to rest their tired bones. Once inside the room, their conversation continued.

"You know we'll find out who's responsible for Tony's death, don't you, Trees?"

"Of course, I do. One day, Marianne Scott's going to screw up. And when she does, it will be time for us to go into action again to really clear Tony's name. By the way, Harvey told me you did some rather fine shooting in Maryland. Seems that it saved his butt!" Adrian just laughed as his friend pulled back the covers to get into the second full-sized bed. After Errol had turned out the lights, he continued, inquiring about something he had heard. "Rumor has it you're going to law school."

"That's right . . . Columbia, as a matter of fact! Loren Johnson at Raymond's firm is helping to arrange my admission." Adrian paused for a minute, then made a similar comment to Errol. "Rumor has it you rejected their offer for employment after graduation next spring."

"Yep, I figured we could go to the islands and chase women for the summer. You'll need the break before starting law school. I'll need the break after finishing."

"And what about you? What are you going to do when you graduate?"

"I'm going to get a job and mark time until you finish, you asshole! So, will you please just get on with it? I'm not thrilled about putting my life on hold for three years," stated Errol rather emphatically.

"You're serious, aren't you?" asked Adrian.

"We were supposed to be opening an architectural design firm. Now you're going to be a lawyer, so I guess we'll have to open a law firm when you graduate. First you chased Tony's butt all over the football field. I'll be damned if you're gonna chase my ass all over the legal battlefield! Shit, I thought we were friends." Adrian laughed aloud at his friend. Errol even laughed for a moment, but then became very serious. "But I need to know one thing, A.C."

"What's that?" asked Adrian, straining to deal with Errol's change from frivolity to a very serious demeanor.

Railroaded!

"Why'd you have to pick such a shitty law school?" Adrian picked up a pillow and launched it at his best friend. Even in the dark, it found its intended target.

Epilogue

May 25, 1980 - Hempstead, New York

"Ladies and gentlemen, and graduates. This is indeed a special occasion. Today's ceremony is an acknowledgment that you have completed the requirements to become lawyers. After you pass the bar exam, you will be entitled to practice law. Law is a profession that has recently become much maligned. There are those who equate us with used car salesmen. There are a plethora of lawyer jokes that depict us as bloodthirsty sharks looking only for the next kill. I am here today because I want to tell you simply that the practice of law has fallen on hard times. We have a responsibility to clean up our reputations. It is important that the process begin with you, the new graduates . . . the new graduates who can pump new life into our ranks.

"Last summer, I lost an associate, who was the newest member in the prosecutor's office. He was given a case that no one else wanted to handle. Despite the fact that he had little with which to work, he set out on a task that seemed insurmountable . . . to convict a man of alleged crimes.

"Yet in the middle of his investigation and trial presentation, and despite strong momentum in his favor, it came to his attention that serious problems had developed, problems that would sink the case. Rather than discounting the new information and covering for mistakes, which we are too often wont to do, he did what all prosecutors are supposed to do . . . to get at and expose the truth, no matter what the cost. It was that tenacity that cost him his life.

"So, I am here today to tell you that the practice of law is not just the ability to write briefs and spout statutory language. The practice of law also measures the character and courage of the man or woman who takes that solemn oath to preserve the rights of others while upholding the law that is both sacred and necessary for civilization to thrive and continue. My fallen associate believed this. His death served to resurrect the same feelings within me. And, until the truth is exposed in the case that caused his death, I will continue to run for the position of District Attorney for Allegheny County, to maintain the idealism within that office that was fostered by my fallen associate." The audience applauded at the fervor of the prosecutor's statements.

"There is one among you whose keen powers of observation and analysis assisted my former associate in getting at the truth in the case that cost him his life. While I know that Mr. Errol Forrest, Jr. has no interest in being a prosecutor and has even expressed a disdain for the practice of law, the District Attorney's Office of Allegheny County, Pennsylvania would like to present a memento of our appreciation for his assistance. Mr. Forrest and Mr. Adrian Christopher lost a very dear friend at the same time we lost our most junior associate, Mr. Joseph Kearns."

The Dean asked Errol Forrest to come forward. Errol was really embarrassed because he wasn't properly dressed. Also, two beers had made him a bit light-headed in the heat. Nevertheless, he carefully made his way to the steps and up onto the platform. There, he received a plaque from Lewis Dobson that read, "Your highest duty in all things is to seek out and expose the truth." He shook hands with the prosecutor from Pennsylvania after receiving the plaque. He shook hands with Raymond Sutter, embraced him, and received a scroll tied with a leather strip. He shook hands with Arnold Benton and Loren Johnson, who were on the platform with Raymond. He shook hands with the Dean and then hoisted the degree and plaque high over his head. He walked up to the microphone and made the following statement:

"I guess I earned the degree. But, as for the plaque, this is for the best free safety the NFL ever saw, the best architect, and best friend I ever had." Errol was momentarily overcome with emotion. "Like Mr. Dobson, Adrian Christopher and I won't rest until we know the real reason behind the death of Tony Williams. We three swore an allegiance to each other till death. Well, Tony, wherever you are, you may be gone to us here, but Adrian and I will never break that oath. You will never be forgotten!" Errol again was overcome with emotion and slowly left the platform.

As he descended the stairs to a standing ovation, Adrian walked up and embraced Errol. Both men did not think of the heat of the sun. Errol stared at the inscription on the plaque and thought of the reason why he had received it. He looked at Adrian and smiled. "This is for Tony, but it won't be fully earned until we find out who killed him and why." The two men turned to the crowd and waved. As they continued to walk alongside the now- seated audience, Errol turned to Adrian and commented, "You know what, asshole? That suit looks pretty damned good on you."

"Then why don't you go put on your gray gabardine so we can show these people what they've got to expect in the future?" As they walked toward the main entrance of the law school so Errol could go in and change clothes, they were stopped in their tracks by a proclamation from a familiar voice seated on a nearby bench.

"You know, this is unusually great weather. I think we should head to the beach. I'm already dressed for sand and surf." The two men turned to see Harvey Sloan dressed in short pants and a tanktop, sporting a magnum of champagne and four glasses. "Congratulations on a job well done, Errol. And a Wah-hoo-wah to you both, my fellow granite-heads." Errol and Adrian both embraced their fellow Dartmouth alumnus. They hadn't seen Harvey since the funeral. "Can you hurry and get a move on, mate? This 'bubbly' is well iced, but it's not going to last very long in this heat."

"The pictures can wait. Besides, it'll be at least another hour before the ceremony is finished. Go ahead and pop the cork," stated Errol.

"Are you sure, Trees?" asked Adrian.

"I've never been more sure in my whole life," retorted his best friend. "By the time the ceremony's over, we should be good and plastered!"

"There may be hope for you, after all!" stated Harvey as he popped the cork on the magnum of champagne.

"When? In his next life?" asked Adrian.

"Shit, man! If you weren't such an ass, you wouldn't be my best friend. So here's to best friends!" Adrian and Harvey both

Railroaded!

laughed at Errol's comment and joined in on the first toast. "By the way, Harv. Did you ever learn how to wash clothes? Maybe we should teach you how to dress!" Harvey broke out laughing and almost choked on his first gulp of champagne. After recovering from the laughter, Errol asked another question. "I noticed you brought four glasses. Who's the other one for?"

"Always the observant one, as usual. It's for me. Did you think that I wouldn't show up for this less-than-solemn occasion?" Errol and Adrian both were surprised to see Shelli Williams. She was looking absolutely radiant in a white sundress. "Harvey's right, you know. This is perfect beach weather." She hugged Adrian first and then Errol. As they held onto each other, Errol shed an emotional tear of joy. He was glad to see Shelli Williams. He was glad that she had come to his graduation. "I wouldn't have missed this for the world. I know you guys miss Tony, and so do I. The last nine months have been tough, but I've got to get on with my life now. You are, and always will be, part of my life. So, don't be a stranger to me, okay?"

"I won't, Shelli. We won't. Whenever you need us, we'll be there for you just as we were for Tony. That you can count on, forever." Errol gave her a kiss and smiled.

"Well, are you going to fill my glass, Harvey, or do I have to drink straight from the bottle?"

As the rest of the graduation ceremony went on, the foursome filled their glasses and raised them in a series of toasts acknowledging the strength of their friendship and the spirit of Anthony Williams that would live within each of them forever.

When the picture-taking sessions and fraternizing with visitors were over, the four remained true to their word. They descended on Errol's small abode, changed into appropriate attire, and left to spend the rest of the day in the hot sun and to frolic in the mild surf at Jones Beach.

About the Author

Whitfield Grant is the pseudonym of the author. He is a college and law school graduate.

Mr. Grant is a multi-dimensional writer. He is currently in the midst of writing the sequel to **"Railroaded!"** entitled **"Derailed!"** Recently, Mr. Grant completed **"Guilty of Innocence,"** which is a fictional account of the Louise Woodward, "Nanny Trial." In addition, he has written a book of romantic poetry entitled **"For the Love of Her**."

Formerly an independent consultant to business and industry, Mr. Grant has traveled throughout the United States and extensively worldwide. His experiences have provided a wealth of knowledge and stories for future publications. He is currently an executive in the natural resource industry.

Whitfield Grant lives in metropolitan Denver, Colorado.

Errol, Adrian and Harvey

will be back in

Guilty of Innocence

And

Derailed!